DICKIE

Sheelagh Kelly was born in York in 1948. She attended Knavesmire Secondary School for Girls, left at the age of fifteen and went to work as a book-keeper. She has written for pleasure since she was a small child, but not until 1980 were the seeds for her first novel, *A Long Way from Heaven*, sown when she developed an interest in genealogy and local history and decided to trace her ancestors' story, thereby acquiring an abiding fascination with the quirks of human nature. *A Long Way from Heaven* was followed by *For My Brother's Sins, Erin's Child, My Father, My Son, Dickie, Shoddy Prince* and *A Complicated Woman*.

D1369194

ALSO BY SHEELAGH KELLY

The Feeney Family Saga

A Long Way from Heaven
For My Brother's Sins
Erin's Child

My Father, My Son
Jorvik
Shoddy Prince
A Complicated Woman

SHEELAGH KELLY

Dickie

HarperCollinsPublishers

This novel is entirely a work of fiction. The names,
characters and incidents portrayed in it are the work of the
author's imagination. Any resemblance to actual persons,
living or dead, events or localities is entirely coincidental.

HarperCollins*Publishers*
77–85 Fulham Palace Road,
Hammersmith, London W6 8JB

The HarperCollins website address is:
www.**fire**and**water**.com

This paperback edition 1999
1

First published in Great Britain by
Century Hutchinson Limited 1989

Copyright © Sheelagh Kelly 1989

Sheelagh Kelly asserts the moral right to
be identified as the author of this work

Typeset in Ehrhardt by Palimpsest Book Production Limited,
Polmont, Stirlingshire

Printed in Great Britain by Clays Ltd, St Ives plc

ISBN 978-0-00-787977-9

All rights reserved. No part of this publication may be
reproduced, stored in a retrieval system, or transmitted,
in any form or by any means, electronic, mechanical,
photocopying, recording or otherwise, without the prior
permission of the publishers.

This book is sold subject to the condition that it shall not,
by way of trade or otherwise, be lent, re-sold, hired out or
otherwise circulated without the publisher's prior consent
in any form of binding or cover other than that in which it
is published and without a similar condition including this
condition being imposed on the subsequent purchaser.

For my friend
Linda Steel

1

Why were they all so nervous of his coming? He should be the one to wring his hands and quell the butterflies, not them. Perhaps it was not so much the thought of meeting him which induced these tremors, but the thought that he was going to kill the old man upstairs; the one so dear to all of them.

There were three people in the room: an elderly woman, her middle-aged stepdaughter and son. The conversation between them was sparse. What could one say when, in the bedchamber above, one's husband, one's father lay near to death? Each tried to avoid this fearful image by steering their minds elsewhere. Thomasin Feeney trained hers on the contents of the room in which she was sitting. A spacious room with elaborate architraving and cornicework, it formed part of a mansion on Peasholme Green in the centre of York. Its furnishings spoke wealth. From its ceiling dripped a huge crystal chandelier. Ironic, that such elegance could be found only ten minutes' walk from the slums where her children had been born ... but that was long, long ago. The Feeneys had lived here for over twenty-five years. During that time the décor had seen many changes. Apart from the chandelier, only the multi-hued Persian carpet had been present at the beginning; those parts of it that had started life as cream were now discoloured to beige by the shoes of four generations of Feeneys; those tottering their first steps of life . . . and those stumbling their last.

Thomasin's grey eyes roamed the potted palms and aspidistras, the overmantel mirror, the gilt-framed miniatures and the portrait of Queen Victoria, trying to keep her mind off the room upstairs. One hand toyed constantly with the pair of spectacles that rested on her silken lap. Those meeting her for the first time would see a benign, aged gentlewoman, short of stature, plump of build, clad in the lace cap and shawl befitting a great-grandmother, snowy hair drawn back from a face lined with every experience of her seventy-four years; an extremely kind face, with gentle creases around the eyes and mouth, less prone to the impulsive glowers of youth. But let those who tried to cheat her beware, for they would soon discover that the peachy bloom of dotage was a smoke-screen. Age may have mellowed her appearance, but the tongue was just as tart and the shrewd, businesslike brain was still very much intact . . . though at this moment it was less decisive, hovering twixt her dying husband and the son she had not seen for twenty-six years; the one who was coming home.

Inwardly berating herself, she tried to concentrate on the pink brocade sofa by the window. Parts of the wadding could be seen in several places. Its threadbare state mirrored the feelings of the inhabitants: their emotions ready to burst through the thin veneer of stoicism when the thread to which Patrick clung so desperately, finally snapped. I really must get it re-covered, thought Thomasin, eyes roving on to the heavy, flower-embossed window drapes. I wonder if it would look right in that stuff or would it be just too much pattern?

Her gaze wavered from the tasselled curtains to a row of photographs on the piano, showing each of her granddaughters in their white veils and dresses at their first Communion, her great-grandson, herself and Patrick at the child's Christening . . .

She wrenched her eyes away to the garden, which this room overlooked. In summer the french windows would be kept ajar to receive the scent of lavender. From early morning soft fingers of sunlight would creep over the threshold, stroking first one wall, then, as the day progressed, the entire room would be painted in its warmth until late evening, when the fingers would slide reluctantly down the eastern wall and into the night. Patrick had loved to sit here . . .

There were no beams to fade the carpet this wintry Monday morning. At ten-thirty the sun had failed to penetrate a sky that threatened rain. Everything looked dingy and desolate, both in here and in the garden, where the frost-bitten stalks of chrysanthemums drooped over the edge of the lawn, awaiting the gardener's attention.

Compelling her own attention to the worn sofa, Thomasin decided that perhaps it might look better if re-covered in a plain maroon velvet like the modern Chesterfield and its partnering easy chairs that formed a square to the hearth. These were a recent acquisition, but still the seating in here was inadequate when all the clan was gathered together . . . as they would be very soon to bid goodbye to their oldest and dearest member. *Oh, Patrick, I can't believe this.* The year 1900 had brought such excitement – a motor car, electricity, a new generation – now it came limping to its end amid all kind of upheaval. She winced, hoisted one aching buttock then glanced at Erin who sat nearby, receiving a tremulous smile in return before looking away to her son.

John Feeney was blind to his mother's scrutiny, his eyes glued to the white marble fireplace which, like the rest of the room, was bedecked for Yuletide – with a swag of red ribbons, pine cones, holly and other greenery. But the heat of the log fire had dried the sap, the holly leaves were folding in on themselves as if contorting with pain, the ivy lay shrivelled and brown. In a far corner, the Christmas tree looked as if it, too, was in mourning, listing heavily to one side, the carpet beneath thick with fallen needles, though its perfume still prevailed. Many of the greetings cards which stood about the room had blown over from the opening and shutting of the door when the maid delivered endless trays of tea. No one had bothered to pick them up – indeed, some were still in their envelopes, tucked behind the ebonised mantel clock whose tick intruded on the silence. News of Patrick's illness had put an abrupt end to festivities.

'I'll have to get Vinnie to take this lot down,' muttered Thomasin, following her son's eyes to the decaying garland, hung only moments before the revelation. 'I can't stick it till Twelfth Night.' Her speech was broadly-accented, but not harsh.

It broke John's trance and he nodded the fine head of auburn hair inherited from his mother; though very much paler these days and streaked with white, it had hardly begun to recede. He had also, his mother's grey eyes and wide mouth, but whereas Thomasin's curled up at the edges, even at this sad time, her son's projected solemnity. This was not a true indication of his character at all, for John – or Sonny as he was still known by his family, even at the age of forty-six – enjoyed a joke as much as anyone. His build, too, decried the sort of man he was. Dress him in rags, shove a pick in his navvy-like hands and people would cross the street to avoid the risk of a brawl. Only his eyes showed the reality; Sonny was a deeply sensitive, artistic man – though this was not to say he had never used his fists in defence of his family; he was after all born of fighting stock.

Erin Teale covered the hand of the woman she had known as mother since the age of five. 'I'll make a start on it.' She stood, rubbed the small of her back, then wandered in dolorous fashion to the mantel and began to collect the cards. 'I need something to do or I'll go crazy.'

'Why don't you finish your knitting?' suggested her mother. Erin replied that she hadn't the inclination. 'You promised it to Cicely for her birthday – that's next week. The rate you're going I can see her walking round in a one-armed cardigan.'

The response was impatient. 'There's too much pattern to concentrate on. I'm pulling out more than I'm knitting. If I don't finish it then I'll buy the child one.'

The intonation was faintly Irish. Erin was York-born but had been raised in an Irish ghetto and had kept the accent. At fifty-three she had long since bidden farewell to the slenderness of her youth and donned a good four inches in circumference. However, being quite tall she could carry it and there were no unattractive bulges to spoil the line of her figure-hugging gown. The colour was mauve – always a favourite with Erin for it complemented her blue eyes – and as she moved, its train dragged the carpet. Her features were piquant and with age could have become severe, but a fringe of soft curls helped to prevent this; she was still a very attractive woman, even if at this moment her beauty was masked by anxiety. The remainder of her hair was swept up and held with a jet comb. It had turned grey quite early in her life – a common failing of black hair of course, but poor Erin had more reason for this premature ageing than most. When she was two years old, her mother Mary died from cholera in the first in a series of tragedies that were to dog her whole life, not the least of these being widowed at thirty with a crippled child to care for. But Erin had survived. Her latter years, spent in the house at Peasholme Green, had brought stability and contentment . . . until her dear father's illness.

Erin paused. Her thumb stroked the plush robin on the card in her hand, but her eyes stared past it. Everyone knew their parents would die some day, so why was it such a shock when it came? Maybe because Erin had expected that one morning her mother and father wouldn't come down for breakfast and the family would find they had just drifted peacefully away in their sleep. She hadn't envisaged such a painful ending . . . it wasn't fair that it should happen to her father, he was such a nice man. Even in his cups he had never been malicious, just . . . daft. *It wasn't bloody fair!* She began to snatch the cards ferociously, slapping them into a pile. The others watched, saying nothing. There was only the tick of the clock, the whine of the log fire, the sound of Christmas cards being shuffled together and the whisper of Erin's skirts as she moved from table to table. The whole house seemed full of whispers.

The door opened, bringing all eyes round sharply, but it was only Vinnie the maid come to ask if she could get them more tea. Normally a bright flibbertigibbet of a girl, she was today very subdued. Whilst collecting the tray, she noticed the fresh fall of pine needles and used a brass companion set from the hearth to sweep them up before leaving. Some minutes later, refreshment was served.

Erin left the pile of cards on top of a black and gold lacquered cabinet and came back to the fire.

'Thank God for tea,' sighed Thomasin, pouring the brew herself and handing out cups to her son and daughter. 'All this waiting . . .'

They were in the process of lifting their cups when someone else entered. Thomasin's eyes rose again quickly to see a manservant admit the physician who had been attending her husband. Loth to voice the question on her mind, she gestured instead to the sofa. 'Come and sit down and have some tea, Doctor.'

The tweed-clad fellow with the ruddy complexion approached the fire. He was in his fifties, and had been the family's physician for half his lifetime. Even so he could not have been here more than a handful of occasions, the Feeneys

6

being generally robust in health. To one less observant their obvious wealth might be unnerving; but amongst the sumptuous trimmings was the odd cheap little ornament – a jug bearing the inscription *A present for Grandmother*, a chalk pussycat won at the fairground – showing that underneath they were just like any other family. With the same ease that he entered the slum hovels, he came to join them. Sinking into voluptuous cushions, he accepted the offer of tea, his expression bland.

Sonny, who had risen out of politeness at the doctor's entry, now tugged at the knees of his charcoal trousers and reseated himself. 'How is . . . ?' It emerged huskily and he coughed behind a fist. 'How is he, Doctor?'

The blandness gave way to the doctor's true feelings. Taking possession of the cup with its pink and red roses he lifted it from its saucer, saying gravely before it met his lips, 'It can't be much longer, I'm afraid,' and drank swiftly as all three mouths showed their concern. Clinking the two pieces of china together, he added, 'I've given him an injection. He's quite peaceful at the moment.' Privately, he found it amazing that the old man was still here; he had seemed to be *in extremis* for days.

A worried crease to her brow, his hostess nodded and said quietly, 'We'll go back up in a moment.' Until the doctor's visit she had been sitting upstairs with Patrick, her husband. Most of the time since his homecoming had been spent thus, especially through the night. She could not bear the thought of going to bed then finding him gone in the morning. A cape of indescribable weariness settled on her shoulders; she fought it off and asked, 'Sonny, what time did you say Nick's coming?' Her grandson had not shown his face since the brief visit to his grandfather four days ago. She knew better than to expect emotion from this cool young man, but he might at least have hidden his eagerness to get away.

Sonny exerted leaden eyes to the clock. His voice was well-spoken, but still retained the flat Yorkshire vowel sounds. 'He should be here any time. He said he was just going to check that things were all right at the store then he'd be coming straight here.' Normally, they would all be at their work, even Mother, but none of them had put in a full day since learning of Father's illness. Sonny himself had been here all the time since Patrick's return from Ireland several days ago. His only contact with the wife he had left in Leeds had been by telephone.

'And what about the other one?' Thomasin did not put a name to the man for whom all were waiting.

Sonny shrugged. The starched white collar bit into his neck, leaving a mark as he lowered his shoulders. 'Who knows?' His brother's letter had said the ship docked on the thirtieth of December; it was the thirty-first today and still no sign, no word. Today was also his own son Paddy's fourth birthday. They'd be having a little party for him at home; Sonny would miss it. He wouldn't be going home until after . . .

'But did he say he was coming here or to your house?' persisted Thomasin anxiously.

Her son's reply was mildly exasperated, as to a trouble-some child. 'Mother, I must've told you a dozen times he didn't say!'

'Oh, please forgive your mother for causing you the effort of having to repeat yourself, Sonny!'

The doctor hid his embarrassment in the teacup. Sonny's face crumpled and he rubbed hard at a ginger eyebrow. 'I'm sorry, Mam . . .'

Thomasin's expression melted too. 'I know, you're just worried . . . like the rest of us.' She ground her blue-veined hands into the cup, as though modelling it. 'I just wish he'd get here and end your Father's waiting. That's all he's

8

hanging on for: to see Dickie. It's not right he should suffer like this.' Experiencing Patrick's agony in her own gut, her hands clamped the china even more fiercely.

'He knows where we both live,' Sonny told her. 'If he turns up at Leeds then Josie'll telephone. He must be here soon.' *For God's sake hurry*, he urged his brother.

Both irritated and worried at the same time, Erin snatched the teapot and poured her third cupful. 'I'm still not convinced we've done right by Belle.' Her daughter, Belle, unaware of the impending death of her grandfather, had gone to South Africa to investigate the reported ill-treatment of prisoners from the Boer War. Belle was forever involved in one campaign or another. That this one was more dangerous did not appear to alarm her, but Erin would not settle until she was safely home. 'I know there's small chance of her getting back in time . . . but if we don't send any word at all . . . well, it'll be me she'll vent her anger on!'

It had been deemed futile to send a cablegram as it would take nearly a month for Belle to journey from South Africa – far too late to see her grandfather alive, or even to attend his funeral. Thomasin had persuaded Erin to let Belle's work take its course, to which she had agreed. All the same, she dreaded the explanation that would have to be made on her daughter's return. After two decades of turbulence, their relationship had for the last five years settled into something more friendly . . . and now this. She could already hear Belle's angry words. The hands cradling the cup appeared as an extension of the fine bone china, fingers delicately tapered, but anguish cracked her facial beauty. 'I mean, it'll look as if we don't care . . .'

At that same instant, the doorbell sounded. Mother, daughter and son froze, then looked at each other. The doctor put down his cup; having been informed of the family reunion, he had no wish to trespass. 'I'll take my leave of you, Mrs

9

Feeney, and will call again this afternoon.' His hands sank three inches into the cushions as he levered himself from the sofa and picked up his bag.

Whilst Thomasin and Erin thanked the doctor, Sonny edged over to the door and peeped round it. However, when his face turned back into the room its anxiety was less pronounced. 'It's all right, it's only Nick.' He followed the doctor out to the hall where the manservant was taking the younger Mr Feeney's hat and coat.

At the sight of the physician's bag and the drawn faces, Nick stopped dead, the shoulders of the coat yoked around his upper arms. Sonny interpreted the look and was quick to reassure him. 'The doctor's been giving your grandfather something for the pain. He's asleep just now.'

Nick was only partly relieved. He had half-hoped his grandfather would be dead by the time he got here. The thought was not a sadistic one, he just didn't relish sitting around waiting for Grandad to die; the poor old devil was in such agony. Seeing him the other day in that state . . .

Hurling the memory aside, the young man allowed his coat to slip into waiting hands. Underneath, he wore a navy-blue lounge suit; like the rest of his apparel, this was immaculate. There was no clue as to the peasantry of his ancestors in Nick's bearing – the clean features and hint of arrogance could have been those of gentry. For this he was indebted to his grandfather who had sported none of the Irish traits beloved by cartoonists – heavy brow, brutish eye, pugnacious jowl – but whose Celtic good looks had inspired much admiration. The merest tilt to the tip of the nose, the expressive eyebrows, the long Irish upper lip, all were Patrick's; the only difference being that Nick was as fair as Patrick had been dark. At twenty-eight he was Sonny's eldest child, but there was nothing of his father in him. He was taller and not so heavily-built. Even allowing for the gap

10

in their ages he held himself more erect, more confidently, than his father had ever done. His eyes were blue not grey, and his fairness came from his mother who had perished in a fire when he was but an infant. For all this he was still very much a Feeney.

With the unwinding of his scarf and the departure of the physician, Nick told the manservant to stable his horse, then he and his father left the chilly hall and went to join the womenfolk.

'Hello, love.' His grandmother's greeting was quiet but fond as Nick stepped across the margin of highly polished floorboards and onto the carpet. 'Come by the fire, you look frozen.' His cheeks were bright pink and he was blowing on his hands. She asked how he had got here – he lived in Leeds – and he replied that he had driven himself in the brougham, hence the bloodless fingertips. 'You shouldn't've bothered coming over in this weather.'

Nick took this as reproval. There was an edge of guilt to his reply. 'I'm sorry I haven't been for a few days, Nan. It's just . . .'

'I know, you've an awful lot to see to.' Thomasin nodded forgiveness, yet to Nick it still seemed like a rebuke. He wanted to tell her that wasn't the reason at all, but before he could speak she was asking, 'How's Win and little John?' She hadn't seen them lately.

His accent was refined but his words were not. 'Johnny's fine, Win's sick as a pig.' Still working at his numb fingers to restore the circulation, Nick perched at an angle on the sofa beside her. 'She's just found out she's in a certain condition again.' He rolled his eyes in disgust – young Johnny was barely six months old. It was actually quite funny that the method of contraception he had used for years before his marriage should let him down now. His father congratulated him laughingly, his aunt and grandmother also.

'Aw, that's lovely.' Thomasin's tone lacked the normal verve but she was genuinely pleased and reached for his icy hand to squeeze it.

Nick laughed, 'Oh, I'm sure,' and pulled out a handkerchief to swab a dew-drop from his nose. His cheeks, which a moment ago had been frozen, now felt a-blaze from the heat that sprang from the hearth.

'Of course it is. Your grandad'll think so too. I'm going to sit with him agian, is anybody else coming?' Thomasin started to prise herself from the comfortable sofa, failed, and toppled back. Nick jumped up to help her. 'Thanks, love.' She rocked her body and hauled on his arm. 'Oh, by gum ... I must be getting old. What I need is a special seat that'll catapult me upwards when I press a button. Now, what have I done with me glasses?' Her grandson retrieved them from the carpet. 'Put 'em safe on that table – oh, sorry Nick, I never thought to ask.' She craned her neck to look up into his face. 'Do you want something to warm you?' Nick eyed the tray and said he would have a cup of tea if there was one in the pot. 'Get Vinnie to make some fresh, Erin,' ordered her mother, moving to the door. 'That'll be stewed by now.'

Nick forestalled his aunt. 'This'll do me. You three go up if you like, I'll just have a quick swig.' It's no good putting it off, he chided himself, watching them retreat, you'll have to face him sometime.

When the women left the room, Sonny did not follow immediately but hung back to ask the younger man, 'Have you seen anything of your mother?'

Warmer now, his son unbuttoned the navy jacket, displaying a gold watch chain. 'Yes, I nipped round before I came here, to take Paddy's birthday present and tell her about the baby. She sends her love.' There were no clean cups. Nick's sophisticated air did not extend to table manners;

12

he tipped the slops of one into another, clashing the china about the tray.

His father watched the tea spurt from the pot, some of it missing its target and dappling the silver tray. 'Any word about . . . ?'

Nick shook his head and made a face as the lukewarm brew met his taste buds. 'Christ, that's terrible. I think I'll have a drop of Grandad's medicine.' Dashing the cup onto the tray he set his long legs in the direction of the whiskey decanter. 'D'you want one?'

Sonny declined sternly. 'No, and you shouldn't either. Not at this time of morning.'

The hand raising Nick's glass paused uncertainly and the blue eyes assumed a look of guilt. 'Sorry . . .' His father had acquired a sudden aversion to whiskey; everyone knew why. 'I don't really want it, it's Dutch courage.' He splashed the liquor at his quivering insides then sucked in his cheeks, looking afraid.

Unlike the young man's grandmother, Sonny guessed Nick's reason for staying away. 'Just so long as you don't use it as a regular crutch like your grandfather did,' he warned. 'We're all scared, son . . .' He moved his head at the door. 'Come on.'

Nick swallowed the remainder of the whiskey, felt it burn its way down his gullet, then tugged his navy waistcoat into place and steeled himself for the ordeal to come.

Patrick was sleeping. The doctor had not been wholly honest in saying he was peaceful, for occasionally the old head rolled from side to side as if its owner were trying to escape some nightmare. Age and illness are always cruel bedfellows and they had shown no mercy here. Patrick's once-tanned cheeks were jaundiced, his eyes sunken by pain; his hair which had been jet-black in youth was now white and barely covered

13

his skull. The handsomeness that had stayed with him long after middle-age had now been completely devastated. He was just a sick old man.

Thomasin smiled at the nurse who, at the entry of the family, had risen from one of the chairs surrounding the bedside. 'Go get yourself a cup of tea, Nurse.' The woman whispered thanks. As discreetly as possible, she collected some soiled pieces of linen and to the accompanying rustle of starched apron, left them. Thomasin scooped her dress under her buttocks, seated herself on the still-warm chair and took hold of Patrick's hand, stroking it. The others joined her to watch in concern.

It seemed unbelievable that a fortnight ago none of them, not even his wife, had known of his condition. When his pain had sneaked up unawares and made him double over he had told them it was indigestion. Indigestion! And none of them had suspected for one moment, had attributed his growing gauntness to his eighty years. How alone he must have felt. So alone that he had made secret plans to fulfil his wish, the wish of every Irishman, to die in Ireland. But to his family's great fortune, he had deposited last instructions with a friend who had divulged his secret, and Thomasin had gone to fetch him home.

She relived the journey, saw Patrick muffled in a blanket to his silver-bristled chin against the buffeting attack of wind and wave, looking so small, so vulnerable. Her husband had always relied on physical power to lift him over the hurdles of life, for in spirit he had been a very weak man. Frail and wasted as he had become, how could he have survived that journey home? And yet, through those hours of swelling torment, his eyes had burned bright with a strength that Thomasin had never seen before.

But the torturous sea crossing, the shock of learning that his long-dead son Dickie was in fact alive and was coming

14

home, each had abetted the cancer in its purpose. Since his emotional return, he had never left his bed. This was the first year that there had been no Christmas party at one Feeney residence or another. Christmas had passed quietly – Thomasin had fully expected her husband to pass quietly with it . . . but here he still was, clinging on, waiting for Dickie.

From time to time, Patrick emerged from his drug-induced sleep to catch the strains of Erin's harp, and listen contentedly to their soft laughter over some old family joke – 'Eh, d'you remember when you and our Dickie smacked old Raper round the chops with that wet fish?' . . . and more than once his husky voice would interrupt, 'Am I late for work?' And Thomasin would pull the covers further round his chin, with soft dissuasion, 'No, love, we'll let you have a sleep-in this morning.'

The hours dragged by. A lamp was ignited, spraying gentle light upon the bed whilst leaving the edges of the room in shadow. The people around his bed came and went, came back again. Floating as he was on a wave of morphia, he could not be sure who they all were, at one poignant stage mistaking Erin for his mother. Only Tommy came through clearly, gripping his hand, lifting his weak head to sip fruit juice from a spout. Sometimes, when the others weren't there, she would stroke his brow and murmur intimate little phrases they had used to each other in their youth. *How could he ever have thought this woman did not care?* How could he have even contemplated dying among a bunch of strangers because he mistakenly thought of that place as home? Home was where she was.

A stab of fear made him tighten his hold on her hand: not fear of dying – death would be a release from this dreadful agony – but fear of leaving her. However, it was not merely this which made him cling; he was waiting for someone to get home. Not Belle, oh no, he didn't want her to see him like this. No ... he was waiting for his son, Tommy's firstborn.

Thomasin returned his grip with both hands. 'You're looking more perky now,' she mouthed cheerfully into his face. 'D'you want something to eat?' The old man shook his head and smiled. Now that he was awake she took a moist cloth and dabbed gently at his blood-encrusted nostril, helped him take his pills, then settled him back down. 'Did you hear what I told you before?' Her question was met with bafflement. 'No, I thought you weren't with us. You're going to have another great-grandchild.'

'Nick?' At his wife's bright nod, he dragged his head from right to left, seeking his grandson. 'Ah ... congrats, son.' He spoke haltingly. 'That's great. Is Win here?'

Nick bent over the old man, defining his words. Grandad had been having trouble hearing lately; all his faculties seemed to be caving in at once. 'No, she's had to stay at home, Grandad. She's not feeling too good. She sends her love though.'

Pat blinked. 'Johnny?'

Again Nick's reply was negative. 'I can fetch him over tomorrow if you ...'

'No, no ... I'd love to see him, but I don't want him coming and being frightened.' For a similar reason he had begged that Paddy and the girls be kept away.

There was kind argument from his wife. 'He wouldn't be frightened, surely. He's only a baby. It'd do you good to see him.'

Pat was thoughtful. 'Aye ... maybe. See what tomorrow brings.' He looked again at Nick. 'What're you doing here anyway? Shouldn't ye be at the store?'

The young man's reply was light. 'Aren't I entitled to a day off, then?'

'Day off? Begod, now I do feel bad. You never take days

off . . . you're like her.' Pat flicked a trembling finger at his wife.

'You don't imagine I came specially to see you, d'you?' kidded Nick. 'I had some business in York and I thought I might as well call in and see if you're still driving everybody mad.'

'Ah, ye young bugger, that's more like it.' Pat smiled lovingly and with great effort touched the other's arm. ''Tis nice to see ye though . . . but don't leave Win too long on her own.'

'She's not on her own. Jim and Nora are there.' These were Nick's parents-in-law. 'I thought I might spend the night here.' He turned to his grandmother. 'If that's all right with you, Nan? We could fix some wheels to Grandad's feet and have a night on the town.'

'I'm all for the night out,' said Thomasin, 'but you don't think I'm carting that old saucepot round with me, do you? He'll ruin my reputation.'

A period of calm reflection followed the banter. Pat's heavy-lidded eyes crept from one perturbed face to the next. How terrible this must be for them. 'I'm sorry . . . I'm taking a long time to die, aren't I?'

'Eh, now you can stop that, you bad lad.' Thomasin directed a finger.

'I feel so guilty, keeping y'all waiting.'

HIs wife's face was stern. 'Patrick, if you aren't careful I shall have you out of that bed and pointing the brickwork up on the front of the house.' She threw a look of warning to Erin who had turned away in tears; there was time enough for that when Pat departed. Right now he needed to be kept cheerful.

He gave a deep-throated whicker, then lowered his eyelids. The strain of speaking had made him weary. 'If ye don't mind, I'll just have a wee nap before I mix me cement.'

'You do whatever you like, love, I'll be here.' Thomasin continued to hold his hand while he dozed.

At his next awakening, he said he had heard a harp playing. Erin told him it had been her. 'Thank God,' he smiled. 'I thought I'd gone . . . My old dad . . . he wouldn't part with that bloody thing even when we were starving . . . used to tell me such great tales about how it came to be in the family . . . I swear to God it was stolen.'

Thomasin asked if there was anything he fancied. He murmured for Erin to read a few pages from a favourite book, which gave them all something more to think about than their own misery. So involved did Erin become with the lives of Dickens' characters that she continued to narrate long after her father had drifted back to sleep. Sonny and Nick listened, unaware that the thought in which they were submerged was one and the same: each remembering this tale from Patrick's lips, watching his calloused, soil-engrained finger trace the sentences . . .

Towards nine in the evening, the rumble of carriage wheels brought Sonny's anxious face to the window, but it was only the doctor on his third visit of the day. With his arrival the nurse checked that Patrick was at ease, then obeyed Thomasin's entreaties to go home. She had stayed longer than normal tonight, expecting the end to come any second and wanting to be here when it did because she had grown very fond of her patient. But still the stubborn old soul clung on. With such tenacity he would probably be here to greet her in the morning.

Whilst the physician attended the dying man, the group at Patrick's bedside drifted downstairs. It was well past the time for dinner but no one felt inclined to eat. Old Mrs Howgego, the cook, had been instructed to send a plate of sandwiches to the drawing room, yet even these were barely touched and in the heat of the room looked ready to take flight.

The door opened and a rough-looking man in his early twenties peered around it. Thomasin glanced up, then formed a soft smile of welcome. 'Hello, Lol. Come in.'

Lol Kearney stayed where he was, half in, half out of the room; a stance which portrayed his status in the household. Neither family nor servant, Lol had never been totally at home here, had felt more like a charity case . . . which, in truth, was what he was. Oh, he was immensely grateful; who wouldn't be in a situation like his? Saved from a life of poverty when he was fourteen, clothed, housed, fed, educated and given employment at Mrs Feeney's factory . . . but gratitude did not buy membership of a family and Lol could barely wait to have his own home and his own people round him – as he would be doing in the summer when he married the sweetheart whom he had met at work. This said, the concern on his face was genuine as he enquired after Patrick.

'He's not too grand, Lol, but thank you for asking.' Thomasin smiled.

Lol returned a grave nod, and hovered awkwardly for a second, before saying, 'Right . . . I'll go get me supper then,' and extracted his head from the room.

'Did you know Lol's getting wed next year?' Thomasin had turned to look at her grandson seated nearby.

'No.' Nick appeared to be more interested in his boots which were tapping relentlessly at the carpet.

'Aye, she's a pretty lass too . . . I'd've liked to give them a nice send off, but her parents see it as their job.' The vision materialised of herself and Patrick at their own wedding, dancing, laughing . . . A soft chuckle brought all eyes to her. 'I was just remembering,' she explained to them, eyes distant. 'I hope Lol's wedding isn't as spectacular as ours was. Talk about the Battle of the Boyne . . . people throwing food at each other . . .'

'What!' She had Nick's full attention now. His father and

his aunt, who had heard the tale before, merely exchanged smiles.

'It's true,' vouched Thomasin. 'And not just throwing food, but damn good punches. A right fiasco . . .'

'Grandad always was keen on the bunching stakes.' Nick smiled and stretched his aching body.

'I beg your pardon, Nicholas.' The old lady feigned a regal expression. 'Your grandfather was quite innocent.' She laughed, then, at her grandson's expression of regret. 'It was probably the only time he didn't start it. No, it was Molly Flaherty, one of your grandfather's Irish pals. Ah dear, poor old Molly . . .'

Upstairs, the physician was about to slip the hypodermic needle into Pat's crêpey skin, when a weak, but clearly bad-tempered objection stopped him. '*Fág an áit!*' A quirk of his condition had been the restoration of his native tongue. Often he addressed them in Irish, sometimes gently, other times more harshly. The doctor, used to these displays, tried once more to insert the needle. Again Patrick recoiled, speaking English this time. 'Don't . . . not yet. The pain's not too bad . . . don't want to sleep . . . want to see my son.'

The doctor hesitated, listening to the laboured breathing. The doses were gradually having to be larger and larger; the next would probably see him off. He laid the hypodermic in a bowl and patted the liver-spotted hand, watchful of his patient's face.

'Is he here yet?'

'Not yet,' came the quiet reply.

'He won't be long,' wheezed the old man, still holding the other's hand. 'I can feel him. Will ye wait . . . just for a bit?'

The doctor nodded kindly and tucked the emaciated arm under the covers. 'Do you want your family with you again?' At the Irishman's feeble nod, he went downstairs to tell them.

Patrick's gaze followed the man to the door. Once alone, his pain-bright eyes began to tour the room. This was not his room, nor his bed. He had refused to deprive his wife of the one they had shared together for so many years. When she lay there on a night he wanted her to remember it as a place where they had loved and chuckled, not as his sepulchre. Besides, this four-poster was not without its happy memories for Pat. It was here that his grand-daughter, Belle, had been born twenty-five years ago. Cocooned in its sage-green bedcurtains with their pattern of vines and leaves, he could lie here and reminisce over all the joy she had brought him. The pillars of yew shone gold in the light of the fire, making death seem a much cosier process than he had feared . . . or was it just the warmth of his memories that made it so?

His tired mind attempted yet again to picture his son as he would be now, but saw only the image that Dickie had left behind. Dickie could be suave and charming, he could be boorish, crude and vulgar – it all depended on the person to whom he was talking and what he wanted from them. Had that side of him changed? *Come on, Dickie, let's be having ye . . .*

'He doesn't want me to give him the morphine,' the doctor was informing Pat's family. Thomasin touched her cheek in concern, but was assured by the physician that he would not be allowed to suffer unnecessary pain. 'He's relatively comfortable at the moment. He just wants to keep his senses about him.'

'Ye know whose benefit that's for,' said Erin darkly and her mother moved her head in sad agreement. 'God! If he has to come at all I wish he'd damn-well hurry.' A worrier at the best of times, this constant tension had driven Erin close to mania. In her mind's eye she struck out at her brother's smug, handsome face.

21

Thomasin apologised for her daughter's outburst, then asked the doctor if he was leaving now, to which he replied that he would wait a while lest Patrick should need him. He stole a look at his watch. Thomasin excused him. 'We don't want to keep you from your supper.'

He told her he had already eaten. 'And I've no one waiting for me at home. I'll come up and sit with you – if that wouldn't be an intrusion?'

'Of course it won't. You've been very kind.' Thomasin moved towards the door which he held open.

'Mam.' Erin's voice halted her exit. A statement had been poised on her tongue for days. Until now this had been subdued by the childish hope that if it went unsaid then all would be well; but withholding the words did not reduce their validity and besides, she didn't want to prolong her father's life only for him to suffer. She had to let him go. The words emerged more calmly than she had anticipated. 'We really should send for the priest.'

'Father Gilchrist?' Thomasin projected alarm. 'Your dad won't thank you for that.' Despite accompanying her husband to church she did not share his religion, but one thing they did have in common was an intense dislike of this particular priest. 'Anyway, can Pat go through all that rigmarole? I thought he was excommunicated years ago.' She drew nearer the door, but was stopped yet again by her daughter's persistence.

'He hasn't been excommunicated,' scoffed Erin. 'That was just a joke to get Father Gilchrist's back up. Besides anything else, he'll have things to get off his chest.' Erin was a devout Catholic. 'Ye shouldn't deny him the chance.'

Thomasin sighed. The doctor was still holding the door open for her; as she turned to answer Erin, he closed it to ward off the cold swell from the hall. 'You know he hasn't been to Confession in years.'

22

'This is different, Mam,' pressed Erin. 'You're not a Catholic, ye don't understand.'

'I wouldn't say your father's much of a Catholic these days either.' Her husband's religion involved the minimum of devotion: he went to Mass on Sundays, prayed, gave generously to the collection and that was his limit. Since the death of his friend Father Kelly, there had been no priest calling at the house.

'But he's still a Catholic! Ye can't dismiss eighty years of teaching as easily as that. It never goes away. I know he'll want the priest here. Ye mustn't rob him of that, Mam.'

Thomasin looked doubtfully across the room and asked the others' opinion. Sonny was rather slipshod in his worship and detested Father Gilchrist, yet he replied, 'Maybe we should go for him,' and conferred with Nick who nodded.

Thomasin bowed to their feelings. 'All right, but if there's any nonsense he'll get thrown out, priest or no. Go tell one of the servants to fetch him, Nick.'

All went back up to sit with Patrick. Nick rejoined them after giving the manservant instructions. The latter returned to the house unaccompanied, saying that the priest was not at home; a message had been left asking him to call as soon as possible.

The old man's face showed that the discomfort had begun again, but still he refused the injection, asking to be helped into a semi-sitting position. When this was painfully accomplished, he made a request of his daughter. 'Will ye fetch me a drink, honey, please?'

'I will not,' replied Erin stoutly, with a glance at the doctor.

'Refuse your father a sup o' water, eh?' His voice was forlorn.

'You know very well you never call water a drink,' she censured.

23

Pat chuckled. 'Ah, they all know me too well. Oh go on, Erin . . . please.'

His daughter objected again and the physician looked none too favourable, but Thomasin muttered, 'It can't do him much more harm now. Go fetch the decanter – and tell Vinnie to put some coal on this fire.' She leaned forward to wrap Patrick's shoulders more snugly in his shawl. Like a baby, thought Pat, smiling into her eyes. A babe when you enter this world and a babe when you leave it. As if to endorse this, his wife chucked him tenderly under the chin.

'Will you fetch me a glass please, Aunt?' Nick called after Erin, then offered an apologetic shrug to his father.

The whiskey was fetched. Erin poured one for Nick then picked up the other. As afterthought, she put this aside and began to tip the decanter at the invalid cup. Her father had the sudden urge to retain some dignity. 'I want it in a proper glass . . . not that bloody spouty whatnot . . . there's some things I can still do like a man.'

Lips pursed in reproof, Erin folded Patrick's dithering hand round the glass of whiskey and helped it to his mouth, feeling like his murderer. A short time later Father Gilchrist arrived bearing the accoutrements of death. Everyone stood, their respect being for the cloth and not the man. Godliness personified, came Thomasin's rancorous thought as Gilchrist insinuated himself among them like a fawning dog, teeth bared in a smile, but equally prepared to nip at the first sign of opposition. Everything about the man vouched austerity: his garb was worn and of poor quality, his face narrow to the point of malnutrition, his nostrils pinched with cold. Gilchrist had bequeathed himself totally to God.

But Thomasin knew what lay beneath this humble countenance; Gilchrist basked in the power which he exerted over his parishioners, used the confessional to exercise his repulsion for women. The closely-set green eyes would always lack the warmth that had made his predecessor so beloved. Choosing not to waste pleasantries on him, she lifted herself from the chair and bent over Pat, murmuring, 'The priest's here, love.'

'Aye, he's been here a while, haven't ye, Liam?' said Pat and smiled at his old friend Father Kelly who stood at the end of the bed.

Thomasin and Sonny exchanged pitying looks. 'No, dear, it's Father Gilchrist.' His wife smoothed his brow. 'We'll wait outside till you've finished.'

'No!' The yellow face turned anxious. 'Don't go.'

She comforted him at once. 'All right, all right, love, we'll stay in the room if you want us to. I just thought you might want to talk in private.' She stopped and, under pretext of kissing his cheek, whispered in the language she had used before her rise in status, 'If the bugger gets too uppity just give me the wink and I'll boot his arse.'

Consoled by her old blunt manner, he released her. She and the others withdrew into peripheral shadows while Father Gilchrist draped a stole round his neck and took a chair by the dying man. Spotting a rosary on the beside table, he picked it up and handed it to Patrick. There was a look of disdain as he noticed that the hands were already occupied by a whiskey glass. Transferring this to a table, he put the beads into Pat's hands and then sat fingering his own rosary.

A lot of murmuring transpired. Thomasin could not decipher its content, but watched Pat's face closely for the first sign of distress. However, her husband appeared to be calm enough at present. She stood by, deeply aware of the rattle in his chest. Erin and Sonny offered their support, one on either side of her, but to the doctor they resembled small children, clustering round their mother for comfort.

The priest stayed for an age. Thomasin grew restless – he was stealing the time that should have been hers. She was

25

set to intervene, when there came the sound of an engine approaching the house.

At his mother's look of alertness, Sonny left her and strode quickly to the window. Hoisting the curtain aside, he pressed his brow to the cold, dark glass to see the outline of a motorcar. He caught a whiff of honeysuckle as his sister moved up close beside him, felt her hand on his shoulder. Both squinted as the figure of a man climbed from the vehicle. The drive was illuminated, but as yet they could not see his face, for his back was to them whilst he spoke to the woman who was emerging from the passenger seat. He was very tall and much broader across the shoulders than the brother they had known twenty-six years ago.

'Is it him?' came Erin's whisper.

There was a strained pause . . . then the man turned to look up at the slit of light, and there was no further need to ask.

26

2

Sonny turned abruptly from the window, leaving Erin still robed in the quivering drapes. He gave what he thought to be an imperceptible nod at his mother, but sick as Pat was, he detected the change in his wife's expression – sensed the thrill that overtook her whole body, leaving her breathless and uncertain. He forgot about the priest and found the strength to raise his head an inch.

'Is it Dickie?'

Immediately, Sonny went to hold his hand. 'Yes, Dad.'

A sigh escaped the old lips and Pat let his head fall back to the pillow, closing his eyes in gratitude. 'Fetch him straight up . . . then the doctor can go home.'

Father Gilchrist showed annoyance at this interruption and made no attempt to vacate his seat. Thomasin was already on her way to the door, saying as politely as she felt able, 'I'm afraid I'm going to have to ask you to leave, Father,' but giving no explanation for this. The priest begged another few minutes, which she granted, albeit reluctantly. 'Very well . . . Sonny.' The last word was said with a summoning gesture. Mother and son left the gathering and went down to meet their visitor.

They had taken to the stairs at the same time as Vinnie responded to the doorbell. When the big man stepped out of the night, both Thomasin and Sonny faltered. The latter felt his mother's grip tighten on his arm. Her other hand squeezed the polished balustrade.

Despite those missing twenty-six years it was impossible for Thomasin not to recognise her son – he looked just as Patrick had done at forty-eight. Only the artful twist to his smile distinguished him from his father; the once black hair turned to gunmetal but still as crisp and abundant, the height, the strong jaw, the thick and quizzical eyebrows, those exquisite blue eyes . . . for a second everything in that sickroom was just a nightmare, and here stood Patrick as he really was.

The moment passed. Once more it was her son who stood here, exuding a brew of innocent charm and danger: eyes that twinkled 'love me' but at the same time warned 'beware'. Her impulses were mixed; which one would she follow? The first – oh, so strong! – was to hurtle down the stairs and clutch him in gladness and kiss his lovely face and welcome him home . . . but the scars he had inflicted on this family, the personal torment he had caused her, told her to march up and slap him. She did neither. Indeed, no one seemed sure what course to take.

Dickie was the first to break the suspense. He came further into the oak-lined hall, put down his valise and gave his homburg, overcoat and gloves to the maid – as did the shadowy figure behind him, whom neither Thomasin nor Sonny appeared to have noticed yet. By now, the red-haired man and his mother had resumed their descent. As they reached the bottom step, Dickie came to meet them, rubbing his palms.

'Well . . .' He spread his big hands, brought them together in a clap that echoed off the black-and-white tiled floor and gave a cautious laugh. 'Hello!'

Thomasin noticed straight away that a piece of his smile was missing: a tiny chip from the corner of a front tooth. But her mind had other things on which to dwell. With this meeting, she had expected the pain of loss to vanish – her

28

son was alive – but it was obviously not so easy to rid oneself of an ache that had been present every day for twenty-six years. Her breast still bore the ulcer that might never heal. Her glance flashed over the L-shaped scar on his forehead, the light-grey, expensive-looking suit, the flamboyant tie of crimson silk with its diamond pin. She felt the coldness of his cheeks against her own though they stood apart. Above the pounding of blood in her head, she heard her own voice. 'Your father wants to see you right away.'

The long Irish upper lip curled into a grin, directed ruefully at his brother. 'Ah well, best get the rough stuff out o' the way.' Dickie raked his fingers through his hair. 'Where is the old sod, then?' The voice came as a surprise – he was saying the same words, but with a different twang.

Thomasin stared at him, seeing a little boy aged five years with his arm hugging her thigh and his head pressed into her flank, blue eyes turned up beseechingly. Then, grim-faced, she spun back to the staircase and began to climb. 'He's upstairs. Come on, he hasn't got time to waste on you.'

Much bemused, Dickie turned to his brother – brother? Stranger would have been more descriptive. No hug, no welcome. Where now was the intimacy of their letters?

'He's dying,' was Sonny's quiet explanation. With this, he escorted his mother back upstairs.

So swift was the blow that Dickie had no time to dispose of his grin; the lines of laughter still fanned his eyes even as his lips parted in horror. Sonny felt that expression brand his back as he ascended. *You rotten hound, you shouldn't've said it like that.*

The message finally reached Dickie's brain. He wheeled to fling a panicked look at his wife. Then, both shocked into silence, they followed mechanically.

The stench of the sickroom met him long before the door was opened. It clung to his mother's skirts, drifted behind her on a slip-stream to flare his nostrils. On the landing it worsened. With the opening of the door it overwhelmed him in a warm and nauseating rush of decay. Somehow, the smell of women's perfume mingled with that of death made it all the more repugnant.

At the click of the door-handle, Erin spared one glance for her long-lost brother. He looked good for his age, the creases on his face etched by sunshine and laughter. Almost vomiting on her own bitterness, she returned her eyes to the deathbed. This was not the time for recriminations . . . but they would come.

Nick studied the newcomer more closely. He had good motive: this man was his natural father, the one he had never really met save as a very young child; the one who had committed the most unpardonable act of treason against his own brother, by impregnating the woman Sonny loved and then running away, leaving his brother to marry soiled goods and legitimise a bastard child. But the most amazing thing about this legend was that even after all this, he had managed to inveigle his brother into forgiving him! So . . . this was the one with all the magic. Nick examined the middle-aged man whose eyes were too preoccupied with the old fellow to notice this inspection. True, he wasn't in bad shape for someone of his years – very good-looking in fact – but Nick was damned if he could detect the power that bewitched others. Right now he just seemed very ordinary . . . and afraid like the rest of them.

Disenchanted, Nick abandoned his review and came to whisper to his grandmother before she reached the bed. 'I'd better warn you, the priest's been touting for money.' When confusion rippled the old brow, he elaborated. 'I heard the word "will" mentioned several times, and not in the context of *Thy will be done* either.'

'The . . . Sonny, get him out of here!' Thomasin was so

furious she could not trust herself to speak directly to the priest. But greater affront was to come. Father Gilchrist approached her with his sickly, pious smile. 'Have comfort, Mrs Feeney. I have prayed that your husband be delivered from his sins . . .'

'Oh, I'm so glad,' Thomasin interjected tersely. 'Did it cost much?' Before the astonished priest could respond, she hissed into his face, 'You despicable, grasping – I call you in here thinking to give my husband the last comfort of his faith and all you're concerned about is milking money from him! Well, you won't get one more penny from this family and you can count on something else too: after he's gone I'll never set foot in your wretched church again. Now get out!' For emphasis she jerked her head at the door then turned her back on him.

Gilchrist's darker side came to the fore. 'Mrs Feeney, your husband was destined for the eternal flame of Hell and so are you if you desert your church . . .'

Thomasin rounded on him. 'Don't try to frighten me with that tripe! It's never been my church. I'm not one of your cringing little flock, I only ever went to church to keep Pat company. If there is a God He certainly doesn't belong to your crowd.'

Gilchrist was astounded. 'You mean . . . you mean to tell me you are a Protestant?'

In spite of her anger Thomasin was half-amused. 'Don't tell me you've only just twigged after all these years.'

The priest reared. 'Then your marriage is invalid and your children are bastards,' came the cold denouncement.

At the sight of his mother's facial collapse, Dickie grabbed the priest's elbow and steered him firmly to the door. 'There's only one bastard around here an' if he's not down those stairs in ten seconds I'm gonna give him a helpful shove – an' don't tell me I'll go to Hell 'cause I'm probably going there anyway. Goodnight!' He shut the door, took a second in which to compose himself as best he could, then turned to face the bed.

Erin found voice to chastise her mother. 'How could you?' she hissed in Thomasin's ear.

'Enough,' snapped Thomasin, then forced a smile for her husband as she approached the bed and told him, 'Look who's here, Pat.'

Patrick, seemingly unmoved by his wife's altercation with the priest, made a weak gesture for his elder son to come nearer. Still pallid from the shock, Dickie had to be physically drawn to the bedside by his mother. Even when he was close to and looking down at his father, he still could not credit what was happening.

The old man smiled and held up a trembling finger. 'Dickie . . .'

His son, mouth agape, accepted the withered hand between his own big ones. 'Hello, Dad,' he managed to stutter cheerfully.

Pat gazed on him for a while, feeling a sense of completion, then spoke in a pain-filled drawl to his wife. 'Ye look tired, muirnin . . . go to bed now . . . an' the rest of yese. I'm buggered if I want to watch y'all fallin' asleep.'

Thomasin, guessing that he wished to talk to their elder son alone, began to comply, telling him she would come back soon, but her other son replied, 'I'm not tired, Dad. I'll stay while Mother gets some rest.'

Thomasin saw the look on Patrick's face; he didn't want to hurt his youngest by telling him to leave. 'You can come back in a while, Sonny. I think your dad just needs a word with your brother in private.'

Sonny gave a comprehending, 'Oh . . .' and, along with the others, made to retire. Erin shared his disinclination, but finally wrenched herself from her father's side, taking

32

her leave with a kiss. The past few days had been rich with kisses. Each time she left the room she pressed her lips to his cheek, fearing it would be the last.

Thomasin bent to kiss him, too. 'Don't be nattering all night. I'm sure the doctor'd like to get to his own bed, he's been here for ages.'

Seeing that the physician was about to exit with the rest, Patrick stopped him. 'Wait, Doc . . . I'll just have a word with me son then I'll take the medicine like a good lad an' let ye get home.'

Thomasin hovered in the doorway, watching the scene for a second or two, then closed the door. On the landing, she looked at her son's wife and smoothed a hand over her brow as if in confusion. 'I'm sorry, Dusty . . . I haven't even said hello to you.' She was still tense over the priest's deplorable act.

'Oh my, don't apologise!' Dusty's slanting green eyes displayed compassion. Thomasin stared into them. Even as a girl her daughter-in-law had never been pretty or stylish, with a snub nose, a hot temper and an overwide mouth that was given to issuing orders, but these eyes had compensated for all her faults. This still held true, though after all these years there would be even more faults to hide, thought Thomasin, consciously seeking them. Strange, how they eluded her critical gaze. Thomasin decided that the expertly-cut outfit was probably a lot to do with it. Anyone could look good with that amount of money on their back. She can't really be that slim, not at her age . . . or maybe it's the hair. Thomasin's eyes rose. The tangled locks had been coiffed by some professional hand into a style which she considered too youthful for one so silver. *You liked her once*, said a voice in her head. *Yes . . . I did*. Thomasin's eyes became less subjective, and she was forced to concede that the attractiveness was not all camouflage. Still deep in examination, she started on realising that the petite woman was speaking.

33

'I feel as if we shouldn't be here at all . . .' Dusty looked ill at ease. Her voice, remarkably, was still quite English. Only with certain words did one catch a trace of American. 'We had no idea about Mr Feeney.'

Thomasin did not enlarge on Patrick's illness, just wrapped her shawl around her and said forlornly to the gathering, 'We'd better wait where it's warmer,' and headed the procession downstairs.

Dickie was still gaping down at his father. 'God . . . I didn't know.' He sank onto a chair, holding Patrick's hand. 'Sonny never said anything in his letters . . .'

'Don't blame your brother,' murmured Pat. 'He didn't know either . . . none of them did till a short while ago.'

Dickie seemed hypnotised by the condition of his father's hand. One of his thumbs stroked constantly at a bone which jutted through the transparent skin. Many a time he had felt this hand round his backside – how it had stung! – now it barely had the strength to return his grip. He shook his head in disbelief for the third time and opened his mouth to speak, but was pre-empted by his father.

'Excuse me, son . . . I need a bottle.'

Dickie's hand reached out to hover uncertainly over the decanter on the bedside table. When he looked to his father for instruction, the old face was contorted.

'Oh, God!' Pat's body shook with painful laughter. 'I ask for a bottle an' everyone automatically thinks I mean whiskey!' Tears in his eyes, he turned helplessly to the doctor who came over and inserted the correct bottle under the bed-clothes. They had wanted to catheterise him but he would not let them. 'Thanks, Doc . . .' The man retreated into the background and Pat looked upon his somewhat embarrassed son. 'Oh, Dickie . . . 'tis great to have a laugh with ye again . . .' He shook his smiling face, closed his eyes and was silent for a moment.

34

Dickie looked down at his own hands. One of his fingers wore a gold ring set with a diamond. His thumbnail scratched at it, played it this way and that to catch the light.

'Can ye take it out for me now, son?'

'Sure.' Dickie came to life, lifted the bedclothes and removed the bottle. Never in a million years could he have imagined himself doing this for his father! He sat there for a second, felt the warmth of the urine through the glass, then slipped the receptacle under the bed.

Patrick's expression changed. 'Now listen . . . before anything else is said, I have to get this off me chest, son. 'Tis about Rosie's killer – don't interrupt, 'tis important. I can't tell your mother or Sonny . . . not now when they've got this . . . bloody ould nuisance to worry about . . . but they have to know some time. If I tell it to you, then maybe in a month or so . . .' In stilted fashion, he told his son about his unexpected meeting in Ireland with his grand-daughter's murderer. Each sentence became increasingly difficult to form. At the end of his statement he was nearing exhaustion. The crackling in his throat became even more pronounced. Dickie begged him to take it easy and promised to relay the confession to his mother and brother when the time was right.

'Oh, God,' slurred Pat, closing his eyes. 'That's a relief.' For a time he remained thus, chest rising and falling noisily. Then, opening his eyes, he said with a faintly mischievous gleam in them, 'Will ye have a drink with me, son?'

Dickie gave a sideways glance at the doctor who stood some distance away and was pretending not to have heard. Loosing his father's hand, he rose and took up the glass that had been Nick's. Placing it alongside the one his father had been using, he filled both with whiskey. A wry smile distorted his mouth. 'I might've expected a smack in the gob, I might even have expected a kick up the arse but I never once expected ye'd be plyin' me with drink – is it that ye have to get me plastered before ye dole out the come-uppance?'

'Ye wee scallywag,' growled Patrick. 'I could still whip you with both arms tied behind me back.'

'Ah, go way with ye.' Dickie pressed one of the glasses into his father's hand which stayed resting on the bedcovers, and raised his own in salute. 'Sláinte.'

'May the road rise up to meet ye.' Patrick forced his trembling hand to lift the glass but it did not rise two inches before the old face grimaced with agony. '*Ah, Jesus . . .*' and the contents splashed over the bedspread.

The doctor came hurrying over and snatched up the hypodermic. Dickie winced as the needle pierced his father's flesh and looked away swiftly. Something was thrust at him; it was the empty glass. Still averting his eyes, he fumbled over it and put it on the table along with his own untouched drink. 'Is he gonna be all right?' He chanced a squeamish look.

The doctor endowed a sardonic glance whilst removing the needle, but otherwise ignored him, confining his efforts to easing Patrick's trauma. Dickie looked on helplessly. His father's face was still deformed with suffering.

The large dose of morphine began to take effect. As Pat's eyelids drooped, the physician started to pack his instruments away. At a loss, Dickie sat down again and took his father's hand.

'Ye know,' croaked Patrick drowsily, 'I'll never understand . . . how ye could do it to your mother. To me, yes, I was a hard man with ye sometimes . . . but not to Tommy. Ye get your selfishness from me. Tried all my life to lose it . . . thought I was being . . . considerate when I slunk off to Ireland. Didn't realise it was just another form of self-indulgence . . . that I was robbing Tommy of last precious moments. Promise me, Richard,' came the strained plea. 'Swear to me . . . ye won't give your mother any more pain.'

Dickie kneaded his father's fingers. 'I promise.'

Pat's head lolled. 'Ah, the old glib tongue . . .'

'I mean it,' swore the other man urgently. 'I never meant to hurt her, or you. It was just . . .' He shrugged and looked down at the prominent veins in his father's hand.

'Just youth.' Patrick smiled, eyes flickering. 'That Dusty tamed ye, has she?' At his son's sheepish nod, he added, 'Ah, I'd like to have a bit o' crack with her . . . she's a good lass, good for you . . . but I can't keep these bloody eyes open. Maybe tomorrow . . . Just sit there an' tell me all about your life in America . . . all the years I've missed.'

'I never intended to cause ye so much heartache, ye know,' said his son and gestured helplessly. 'Christ . . .'

'Ssh, ssh, enough . . . just tell me about America. Is it a good life ye have there?'

In spite of the moment, Dickie conjured a smile and stroked his father's claw-like hand. 'Ah, 'tis a hell of a place. Ye'd never believe the size of it, Dad.' He launched into a rambling monologue about all the wonders he had found in the United States, telling his father how happy he had been with Dusty, about his house in New York . . . when the eyes that had been riveted lovingly on his face, closed.

Dickie stopped in mid-sentence and leaned forward.

Pat's eyelids lifted, drawing a breath of relief from his son. The wizened lips stretched wide and muttered, '*Ná bíodh eagla ort* – don't be afraid,' and motioned for Dickie to carry on speaking, which he did, until he realised that his father was no longer conscious. Abandoning his contrived geniality, he presented a frown to the doctor who was ready to leave.

'He'll sleep for a good while now.' The physician swung his bag from the table top.

Dickie relaxed his taut features and moved his gaze back to his father. 'Ah, well . . . I'm not doing much good here.

I suppose I might as well go down . . .' He pushed back his chair, but a succession of thoughts still anchored him to the bedside.

The doctor was making for the door when he caught the alteration in Patrick's breathing and came back at once to check on his patient. 'You'd better fetch your mother.' His hand lay on Pat's temple. When there was no movement from Dickie he spun and said sharply, 'Right now, please!'

Overburdened with all that had happened in the last ten minutes, Dickie was slow in responding to the command. His father gave a long sigh.

The doctor sighed too, and dropped his chin to his chest, losing all urgency. Finally, he straightened and faced Dickie. 'I'm sorry . . . he'd waited a long time to see you. Are you going to tell your family or would you like me to?'

The dark eyebrows fused in bewilderment. 'He's . . . ?'

When the doctor nodded, Dickie took a quick step backwards and ground a hand over his mouth. His stunned blue eyes watched a tear trickle down the side of his father's nose before he said jerkily, 'No . . . no, I'll tell them,' and backed away to the stairs. The first door he opened produced an empty room; not having visited this house before he was unsure where to find them. However, he was spared long investigation by Sonny who, hearing movements from the hall, came out of the drawing room and summoned his brother inside. At the appearance of her elder son, Thomasin put her hands on the chair arms and heaved herself upwards. 'Right, if he's finished with you I'll go . . .'

'He's gone, Mam,' said her son.

She sat back and trained questioning eyes on him. The look was mirrored by Erin, Nick and Sonny.

Dickie repeated his statement as if disbelieving it himself. 'Dad's gone.'

* * *

Even in the expectation of his death, the shock was no less. After a spontaneous burst of grief, the family congregated for one last time in Patrick's room. Thomasin stared down at her husband on his deathbed, and yet was seized by a strong desire to look, instead, at the ceiling. No longer was Patrick in that tortured husk; she felt his spirit soaring about the room. On impulse, she crossed to the window and pushed up the sash, murmuring tenderly, 'There you go, lad.'

Catching her children's observation, she smiled through her misery. 'Daft, isn't it? But living so long with his soft Irish ways . . . well, as Molly Flaherty would say, "An' how would his soul be escapin' if we don't open the windows for him?"'

Erin began to sob again, comforted by her younger brother. Nick offered a handkerchief, not yet able to accept the reality. Dickie watched them all supporting each other and felt a wider gulf than that which even the Atlantic had put between them. Out of respect, Dusty had stayed downstairs; he felt very much alone.

The doctor had been scribbling on a piece of paper which he now tore off the pad and handed to Thomasin, telling her it bore the details of Patrick's death. Kindness had steered his pen. There was no mention of the dreaded word – only, *Progressive disease of the liver*. He enquired about Patrick's laying out. 'If you like I could . . .'

'No, we've detained you long enough, Doctor.' Unconsciously, Thomasin folded and refolded the piece of paper until it would bend no more. 'And your job's to tend the living.'

The man looked somewhat shamed. 'Actually, I was going to say I could fetch Nurse back.'

'No, no, we won't drag her from her bed.' Thomasin did not want anyone else doing this for Patrick. 'I'll see to it. It's the least I can do for him . . .' The doctor gave what he hoped was a comforting smile. Thomasin shook his hand. 'Thank you for all your kindness. You've been a great help to all of us.'

The man nodded a goodnight to the others. Thomasin asked Erin to see him out and then send Vinnie up with water and other essentials. Erin tarried, passing the back of her hand over a bloodshot eye. 'I'll come and help ye, Mam. He might be a bit heavy.'

Her mother looked pityingly at the body. 'There's hardly any flesh left on the poor lad . . . eh dear, when I think . . .' She shook her head briskly, as much to drive away her pain as to negate Erin's offer. 'No, love, he's my husband, I'll do it. If I need help I'll shout. Go on now, all of you and leave me with your father.' *Go, please go*, she urged silently. When they did, she added a soft goodnight. 'I won't come down again. One of you see to things downstairs for me, will you?'

When alone, she stood there for some time looking about her, then squeezed her eyes shut against her bereavement and chuckled wetly. 'You haven't gone, have you, you old varmint? You're waiting to see how I perform with this . . . think you'll have a good laugh at me.' She broke off as Vinnie crept in with her requirements. Telling the maid to put the bowl on the far bedside table, she watched her tiptoe about the room. 'I'd appreciate it if that Christmas greenery was disposed of before I come down tomorrow, Vinnie,' she requested in soft tone.

Vinnie looked slightly shocked. 'Oh but, ma'am, it's bad luck to take it down before Twelfth Night.'

Thomasin raised a cynical smile and looked upon her dead husband. 'You're joking aren't you, Vinnie?'

A guilty flush prefixed the words. 'Oh . . . yes, ma'am, I'm sorry. Me and John'll get rid of it, of course.' Vinnie bustled over to the dressing table and flung a cloth over its mirror. Thomasin said she could take the decanter and glasses down with her, too. 'Yes'm.' She displayed great care in handling the glasses, not in fear of damaging the expensive crystal, but the greater fear of contamination. Ever since Cook had told her the nature of Mr Feeney's disease, each trip to the sickroom had posed this terrifying threat. When she closed the door now she would rush down to the kitchen and throw the glasses in the dustbin, as had been the fate of all other crockery upon which the master's lips had rested. Then she would plunge her hands into near red-hot water and scrub and scrub until her skin was almost raw. Thank God the mistress had not asked her to assist in his laying out. With Thomasin's thanks she crept from the room.

Thomasin hesitated, then began to roll up her sleeves. 'Well . . .' it came as a shuddering sigh, 'if you're not going yet we might as well shut the window else I'll be freezing to de-ath.' The sash was hauled down and the curtains closed, each movement performed in a state of automation. She turned back to the bed, twisting her wedding ring round and round; for almost fifty years it had encircled her finger. She looked at the gold band, each scratch upon it suddenly acquiring new significance. Her eyes came up to review the backdrop, the sight of the abandoned rosary beads provoking anger. Snatching them from the bedspread she flung them aimlessly aside. They landed with a clatter against a wooden chair, then slid off. With the anger still thudding in her breast, she peeled the whiskey-stained covers right back over the foot of the bed.

Removing Pat's nightshirt was more of a struggle than she had anticipated. 'You old sod, all your life you refuse to wear one of these things and now you won't part . . .' Breathless after the fight, she leaned on the bed column, looking at his skeletal body with its swollen abdomen, remembering how it used to be, thinking too of her own body's decline, then said, 'Away then . . . let's get started.'

41

All the while she talked to him, even braving a joke when it came to the more intimate moment of stopping his bodily passages. 'You know, Pat, there were times when I felt like doing this years ago.' Then, imagining his twinkling, laughing face, she fell across his body and rent her heartbreak.

She cried long and passionately, bathing his corpse in her tears. When her spasm of pain had eased, she straightened, blew her nose and wiped her eyes, then used the towel to dab the smears of brine from his ribs. After a long, long stare she once again bent her head over his body, pressing her cheek to his cool skin, eyelids drawn tightly together. Then with a huge sniff she unbent her spine and grasped the clean nightshirt which Vinnie had brought. 'We'd best put you something decent on – I know you, you'll go mad if folk see you in this.' Discarding it, she went to fetch a shirt and his best suit from the wardrobe. Getting them on was extremely difficult, but Thomasin had never been one to balk at a challenge.

'There,' she puffed proudly when she had triumphed, sloughing the sheen from her brow. 'I hope you're satisfied. You and your vanity – it's nearly given me a blasted apoplexy . . .' She traced a tender thumb across his cheek. It was finished, but she could not bear to leave him.

With a final, somewhat angry tug of the sheets, she picked up the bowl of water and the towel and took them out to the landing. Then, overwhelmed by loneliness, she went back in, stooped to pick up the nightshirt that Patrick had been wearing and pressed it over her face. It was strong with his scent. Leaving the room, she carried the garment with her, took it to her bed, where it might comfort her through the darkness.

Downstairs, little was said between brothers and sister, and not merely because of the crushing grief. Whilst the rest clustered in familiarity, Erin had selected a chair which put the widest possible gap between herself and Dickie. From time to time he would feel her gaze, but when he looked up to meet it she was always evasive.

A disgusted laugh escaped his lips. 'The priests never change, do they? Still pumping that rubbish about hellfire . . .'

Erin stood abruptly, muttering, 'I'd better tell the servants they can go to bed, it's nearly midnight.' She looked at Dusty, eyes settling contemptuously on the ruby necklace round her throat. 'I take it you two will be staying?' The other, after glancing at her husband, said yes, if that was no trouble. 'It's no trouble to me.' Erin was curt. 'Come on, I'll get you some sheets. You'll have to make your own bed up, it's not fair to keep Vinnie from her sleep.'

Dusty offered no retort, accepting Erin's bitchiness as a product of grief. Untypically passive, she followed in her sister-in-law's wake.

The women had barely shut the door when the boom of Great Peter invaded the quiet. For a moment, the Minster bell went unheeded. Then, a clamour of noise from churches all over the city caused Nick to remember, 'Oh . . . it's 1901,' and from outside came the sound of merrymakers spilling out of The Black Swan, bawling their Happy New Years!

'The new century proper,' observed Sonny. He and the family had made more of the 1900 celebrations, decreeing this as the start of the twentieth century, though others had argued that they were technically wrong. He was glad now that they had courted ridicule; there would be no celebrating this year.

'Oh Christ, I hope they don't come first-footing in here,' sighed Nick, who wished fervently that he was at home seeing in the New Year with his wife.

'They won't,' replied his father solemnly. 'At least not the neighbours; they know about your grandad being ill.'

'I notice that hasn't stopped them from doing their luckybirding,' said Nick in sour voice, listening to the rat-tatting of doorknockers and gay laughter.

'Aye, well . . .' His father looked weary. 'We can't expect everybody to feel our loss. They're alive, let 'em enjoy it.'

'Suppose so,' muttered Nick dully. 'I think I'll turn in now if no one minds.' He received a shake of head from his father, at which he rose to his feet. 'I'll have to be up early and get back to Leeds to tell Win. D'you want me to break it to Mother or are you going to telephone?'

Sonny shook his head. 'I'll go myself tomorrow.'

'I don't mind telling her . . .'

'No, I'd rather tell her and the girls personally, son. Besides, I'll have to bring them all over for the funeral.'

'Right . . .' Nick hoped his relief wasn't too blatant. After a respectable pause, he delivered a goodnight to both men.

His father, seeing his eyes linger on Dickie, realised all at once that there had been no formal introduction and emerged from his slouched posture of grief. 'God, I'm sorry! What with all the drama I forgot you two haven't been properly introduced.'

Nick waved the apology aside. 'It's all right, Dad. I think we both know each other's identity, don't we?' At his uncle's grave nod, the young man left.

Sonny's shoulders returned to their miserable hunch, arms resting on thighs. There was a long intermission before anything else was said. Finally, after lighting a cigar, Dickie asked, 'What is it, Son?'

Sonny turned blank eyes on him. 'Our father's just died, or hadn't you noticed?'

'Ye know that's not what I meant,' replied his brother sombrely, flicking the match into the fire. 'Ye've hardly said two words to me. I expected it from the others, but . . .'

Sonny jumped from his seat. 'All right, you want me to

say something? I'll bloody well say it! You've been gone for twenty-six years under pretext of death, you walk calmly in here and snatch the last precious minutes of my father's life – you always were a selfish bastard!'

Dickie was perplexed. 'I don't get y . . .'

'If anybody should've been with him at the end it should have been me!' raged Sonny. 'Or Mother, or Erin – but not you, who's never given a toss about either him or Mam. D'you realise he should have died days ago, but he's been hanging on and hanging on, waiting for you. *You!*' He rammed both hands at the mantelpiece and leaned on them, neck bent.

Dickie bounced to his feet. 'Son, ye don't understand . . .'

The bilious retort was flung over Sonny's shoulder. 'Too frigging true, I don't!'

'He had things to say that he couldn't say to any of you . . .'

'Oh great!' The red-haired man whirled from the fireplace to glare at him. 'From Spring-heeled Jack to Father Confessor, that's an impressive transformation!'

Dickie pressed his hands to his head, the cigar protruding like a horn. 'Look, he didn't want me to tell you yet, but . . .'

'Oh, don't go breaking any confidences, Richard!' Sonny strode up and down the room. 'I'm sure I don't want to . . .'

'Just shut your bloody gob an' let me tell ye!' yelled his brother. 'It was about Rosie!'

'You *what?*' Sonny spun round in disbelief.

The cigar hand was held palm upwards as Dickie tried to explain. 'When he went to Ireland he saw the man who killed Rosie and he just wanted . . .'

'And he told *you?*' Sonny looked like an old bear, ready to lash out. '*You*, of all people?' The grey eyes were lost beneath furrows of confusion.

'Son,' moaned his elder brother in despair. 'Don't ye see?

45

It wasn't 'cause he cared for me that he told me this, but 'cause he couldn't bear to hurt you. He wanted somebody to know, but not anyone who was close to Rosie . . .' Dickie looked away as if insulted. 'He thought I didn't care about her, that I was cold enough to be able to hang onto the information until you and Mam were ready to tackle it . . . he didn't want to add to your burden, to hurt ye. It was pure freak that he died while I was with him . . .' The neglected cigar had gone out; he threw it on a table, looking sick.

For a moment, Sonny's resentment threatened to overcome all else he felt for his brother. He took a menacing step forwards. Apprehension glued Dickie's eyes to the other's temple where a suffusion of wrath had swelled a vein to twice its normal size – always the precursor to a fight when they were boys. An arm was raised . . .

And then the other arm came up and both were used to grab him into a fraternal embrace, chest to chest, ribs squashed, heads clashing. The dark-haired man responded with gusto, hugging his younger brother tightly, whilst from the grey eyes were squeezed tears of rage and bereavement.

After a while, Sonny gave his brother's back a rough series of pats and the two unlocked, but stayed close together, sharing a soft laugh of embarrassment. Then, 'For God's sake, Son, what happened here?' appealed Dickie. 'Ye never mentioned he was sick – an' what's all this about him going to Ireland anyway?'

Sonny was about to tell him, when Dusty entered. Realising she had disturbed an intimate moment, she drew back, 'Sorry . . . I just came to tell you the bed's made up.'

'Just give me a minute or two, chick,' begged Dickie. His wife nodded and told him their room was the second on the right on the first landing, then closed the door. Dickie turned back to his brother's harrowed countenance. 'Well?'

A deep breath expanded the other's ribcage. Maintaining their closeness, he spoke into Dickie's face. 'A short while before Christmas, Dad tells us he's off to Ireland. Course, we all think he's bloody mad going for a holiday at this time of year ... till Francis tells us the real issue – Francis is Mother's business partner, by the way, I think I mentioned him in my letters.' Dickie nodded for his brother to continue. 'It turns out that Dad knew for weeks he was dying, but didn't want any of us to find out. The only reason he told Francis was so he could prepare Mam ...'

'But why did he go to Ireland if he knew he was dying?' enquired Dickie.

'Well, apart from not wanting us to see his deterioration, he wanted to die where he was born.' Sonny hugged himself and looked at the floor. 'I suppose it's just instinct ... Of course, when you wrote, you bugger, and said you were coming home, I had to tell Mam and then Francis felt it was his duty to let us in on Dad's secret. Thank God he did ... Mother went to Ireland – she insisted on going alone. I don't know how she was expecting to find him. Anyway, the luck of the Irish must have been working for once; Dad was already in Dublin when she docked ... waiting for the ferry to come home. He was almost done for when she got him back here. God knows what went on over there ...' He looked up. 'But maybe you can tell me that now.'

Dickie grimaced and looked away. 'I wasn't supposed to tell ye until ye were over this upset. But seeing as I've gone an' opened me big trap ...' He pulled at his earlobe, then began. 'Dad said he met this Timothy Rabb ...'

'The man who killed Rosie,' interrupted his brother.

Dickie shook his head. 'It was all a bit garbled but he did say that Rabb wasn't the one who killed her. It was this other fella. Seems Rabb thought she was still alive ... anyway, Dad

47

just said, tell Sonny that Rosie's killer is dead now, no loose ends. That's all.'

Sonny nodded thoughtfully. 'It might seem daft to some, but I'm glad that Rabb wasn't the one who killed her. It seemed such a dreadful betrayal . . . anyway, that's that.' His voice petered out.

Dickie searched for the abandoned cigar and relit it. 'God, if I'd known about this I would've come straight up here instead of spending the day sightseeing.'

Sonny removed himself from the vicinity of the smoke, fingering the guardchain on his waistcoat. 'It's a good job you did come here and not to my house or you might've been too late. I wasn't sure on whose doorstep you'd be arriving.'

'I expected you'd've told Mam an' Dad so I thought I'd come straight here,' answered Dickie.

'Aye, expected me to do your dirty work as usual,' replied his brother grimly.

Dickie pulled on the cigar, then rubbed self-consciously at his nose. 'What did Nick have to say when ye told him I was still alive?'

'He was the only one I didn't have to tell. Apparently he's known for years . . . been reading your bloody letters.'

'And he never said a word?'

'If you knew him you wouldn't be so surprised.'

Dickie gave a bitter laugh. 'Huh, probably couldn't give a damn if I was alive or dead, eh? Ah well, that's the way it goes . . . Ye say Dad's been hanging on for me. How long?'

'Mam brought him back from Ireland on Boxing Day. Your birthday.' Sonny gave a humourless smile at the coincidence. 'We didn't expect him to survive the night. Christ knows where he got the strength to last five more days.' He looked at his brother's face. 'When did you dock?'

'Last night. We booked into a hotel in London, thought

we'd do a bit of sightseeing before driving up here. I was just going to hire an auto but Dusty said we might as well buy it then sell it again when we leave. Six hundred pounds it cost. I'm still trying to work out what that is in bucks.'

Sonny nodded without interest. Still the same old Dickie, his talk always got around to money or women. He looked at the clock. 'You must be tired anyway. Come on, we'd best get to bed. We can have a long talk tomorrow.'

Dickie clamped the cigar between his teeth and used both hands to grip his brother's arms. 'What about the funeral arrangements?'

'I'll see to it all in the morning before I go to collect Josie.'

'Well, don't be a bloody martyr. If you want any help, ask.'

'I will. Goodnight, Dick.' Sonny watched his brother's naturally arrogant stroll to the door. 'Eh, and Dick.' The latter spun, fixing him with an enquiring blue gaze. 'It's great to see you.'

The blue eyes crinkled at the edges. For one brief, heartwarming moment the old Dickie grin vanquished all sorrow. But when the door closed, Sonny felt a shiver of isolation and, after making the fire safe and turning the lights out, wandered dolefully up to his own room.

Dickie leaned his back against the door he had just closed and stared at his wife who was already in bed. He didn't have to tell her how he felt. Reading his misery, she simply held out her nightgowned arms. He tossed the dead cigar aside and, shouldering himself from the wood, went to bury his face in the fresh-smelling silk of her bosom.

And still he could not believe that his father was dead.

3

Breakfast was like a gathering of rooks. Hemmed in by grief, Nick had declined to eat and gone straight home to Leeds. After Erin's return from church, the rest of the family moved into the dining room. Denuded of their festive chains, the walls in here appeared vast and echoing. It was always this way after Christmas, but this year the emptiness was tenfold.

'Have ye ever felt out o' place?' muttered Dickie to his brother, whose wife had slipped a black suit into his case in readiness. Dickie himself rarely wore sober dress; the only item of black in his possession was a Tuxedo and he could hardly don that to breakfast – though a dinner jacket might have been less conspicuous than the pale-grey one he was wearing. Not even the loan of a black armband could make him look funereal. 'I'll have to go see if I can get fixed up with a black suit in time for the whatsit.'

Sonny told him not to waste his money. 'I'll fetch you one of mine when I come back tonight. It won't be a perfect fit but it'll do.'

Dickie thanked him and both sat at the table. Naturally, little was eaten. Had the loss not blunted their appetites, then one look at their mother would have done. Thomasin's eyes stared into space. One of her hands rested by a teacup, the other stroked unconsciously at a strip of fur on her black crape gown. Though some considered it bad luck to store crape in the house after mourning was over, Thomasin had never been one to waste clothes that still had wear in them; its last airing had been at Rosie's death, eight years ago. My God, eight years, thought Sonny, raising his teacup. Rosie would have been . . . twenty-nine by now, with children of her own. His eyes locked momentarily with Erin's before his sister looked away and picked up the teapot to refill her mother's cup. Still Thomasin's fingers caressed the fur, but when the teapot's motion ceased, she lifted the cup and drank.

At the pathetic little movement, Erin's eyes blurred. She reached into her black beaded skirt for an already drenched handkerchief and wept quietly. No one commented upon it, just stared into their own visions of the past.

When the subdued meal was over, Sonny took his temporary leave, saying that before he went home to Leeds he would go to the Register Office to file his father's death and then to the undertaker's. His mother thanked him with a hug and he left.

At the time of his spontaneous offer, Sonny had forgotten how traumatic a funeral arrangement could be. Faced with a catalogue of coffins from pine to oak, he despaired of which to select. If he chose the best, as was his first impulse, he could imagine what his father would have said – 'Don't waste your money, it's only going to be shoved under the soil. I'd rather have it spent on my grandchildren than in the undertaker's pocket.' On the other hand, if Sonny picked the cheapest or even one from the middle range, it would look to outsiders as though he hadn't thought much of his father.

Finding it hard to speak without betraying emotion, he said gruffly that he would have the very best, and waited to shed his tears until he was at home in the loving company of his wife and children.

When his brother had left the breakfast table, Dickie expected the inevitable showdown with Thomasin over his twenty-six years' deception; but she scarcely spoke to him and when she did it was only chat designed to break the awkward silence. It all grew too much, like being in a foreign hotel, not amongst family. Beneath the Regency table, Dickie pressed his foot against the daintier one of his wife, urging her to provide the excuse that might remove him from this mausoleum.

Dusty tried to prevent her eyes from ogling the abandoned plates of bacon and eggs, saliva flooding her mouth. She was famished, but dared not unleash her appetite for fear of being labelled unfeeling. With no meal being offered last night – which was understandable in the circumstances – the few mouthfuls she had permitted herself had made little impact on her grumbling innards. She struggled for words, shunting a cruet around the white cloth. After being so skilfully coiffeured yesterday in London, her silver hair was now back to its untidy style with pins protruding everywhere; she was not very adept at this task herself. 'I wonder,' she began, 'would it be in order to ask one of your maids to brush my hair up for me? It won't take long, just . . .'

Erin cut in waspishly. 'Why didn't you bring your own maid with you?'

'Well, you're right I should have done, but I knew there'd be someone on the ship who I could hire for the voyage and I thought when I got here . . .'

'I'm sorry,' said Erin, quite blatantly not sorry at all, 'but we don't have a lady's maid. Mother and I do our own hair. There's only Vinnie and I'm sure she's got quite enough to do.'

'Yes, yes of course,' came Dusty's quick reply. 'I'm sorry, I didn't realise you only had the one girl . . .'

Thomasin spoke softly. 'If it's just a matter of sticking a few hairpins in, I'm sure Vinnie can manage that.'

'No, Erin's quite right,' said her daughter-in-law hastily.

'And I can imagine that it might be a bit of an imposition, having us staying here at all what with everything happening.' Her fingers toyed with the silver. 'You'll have enough with Sonny's family coming over to stay. Dickie and I can go find a hotel.'

'I wouldn't hear of it, Dusty.' Thomasin seemed transfixed by the woman's fidgeting hand. 'We've always managed to put our family up, we'll manage again.'

Dusty forced her hands to settle into her lap and said beseechingly, 'Isn't there anything we can do? Anything at all?'

'No, thank you, dear.' Thomasin's voice was hollow. 'It's all being taken care of.' She noticed then how uncomfortable her son and his wife looked. 'And there's no reason for you to stay in moping either; you're on holiday. Go for a drive or something. Erin'll keep me company.'

Dusty looked enquiringly at her sister-in-law, who said in airy manner, 'Oh, don't spoil your holiday, go out and enjoy yourselves.'

'Well . . . if you're sure.' Dusty felt the nudge of her husband's foot again and retaliated by stamping on it. 'We might go for a ride round town, just to reacquaint ourselves. We nearly got lost last night, with it being dark.'

Erin gave no response, and Thomasin had become distrait once more. 'As you like, dear. We usually have lunch about one . . .'

Dickie rose. 'Oh, don't put the cook to any . . .'

'Trouble on our account,' finished Dusty, rising with him. Thomasin had noticed this trait earlier; her daughter-in-law had a habit of completing Dickie's sentences. 'We'll find a restaurant.'

'I don't feel much like eating anyway,' added Dick.

'I suppose Father should be flattered.' It was Erin again. 'I've never known anything put you off your food before.'

Recognizing that all this sarcasm was Erin's way of limbering up for a big row, Dickie planned to accelerate proceedings. But his intended attack was foiled by Dusty who steered him out. Once in the hall, she scolded, 'You're not going to make yourself any more popular by arguing with her!'

Chastened, he slipped an arm round her waist, fingers stroking. 'I know . . . I can understand the way she feels, I just don't think I want to put up with it for much longer.' His eyes drifted up the stairs to where his father's body lay. 'I still can't believe it, Dust. I expected him to be the one to deal out the pezzling . . .'

Dusty put her hand over his. He had kept her awake most of last night talking about his father. She glanced across the panelled hall where the door to the kitchen had opened, enframing the maid. Vinnie, too, was in mourning dress, but unlike her mistress she had put on weight since its last wearing; the fastenings on the black paramatta fought to constrain two very round breasts. She bobbed in deference as she passed on her way to the bedrooms.

Dickie's eyes remained on the staircase, but instinct told Dusty that his thoughts were not solely confined to Patrick's body now. She felt a whiff of disgust and tugged his arm, bringing his surprised face down to hers. My God, he doesn't even realise when he's doing it, despaired his wife. She broke free and, with a futile shove at her hairpins, snapped, 'Come on, get your coat!'

After some ponderance at the car, they decided to go on foot; they were tired, but the cold damp wind might help to revive them and besides, with the streets full of traffic it would be difficult to negotiate the car if they were unsure of their bearings. The greasy pavements were strewn with bits of paper, wet leaves and strands of pine dropped from someone's Christmas tree on their way home. A dainty-fingered urchin picked horse dung from the cobbles as if it were precious treasure. Folk rushed past, heads down against the wind, lifting them only to shout a 'Happy New Year!' to an acquaintance. Carts and carriages vied for leeway, their occupants shouting, swearing, singing, unaware of the Feeneys' loss. Uncanny, how the streets on which both had grown up now seemed unfamiliar. Blank spaces marked the demolition of church and public house alike. Only the odd landmark caused them to exclaim, 'Oh, I know where we are now!' and laugh fondly at each other.

At the top of Coppergate, however, they became lost. Dickie frowned and looked first to his right then his left as carriages and the odd motor car whizzed by, their wheels blurred by muddy spray. 'I don't remember this, d'you?'

His wife was equally mystified. 'No . . . they're all modern-looking buildings down there.' She huddled into the velvet collar of her grey threequarter-length coat, feeling on a par with the weather, then glanced at the nameplate of another street which branched off to her left. 'Oh, that's Castlegate, look. What they've done is knock all those Water Lanes down – well, the best part of them, anyway – and cut a new road through. D'you remember? They used to lead down to the river.'

At first Dickie chewed on a gloved knuckle, unable to visualize the slums as they had been . . . then a smile began to spread over his face.

Dusty knew that look well and observed cryptically, 'I see you do remember.'

His features became saturnine and he announced with great drama, 'It was down one o' those very lanes that a woman robbed me of my virtue.' He threw back his head and laughed at the face she made, then pulled her into his side. 'No need for jealousy, my wee Primrose.' This was his wife's real name. 'It was over thirty years ago. Ah, what a sweet innocent I was then. I can recall it as if it were yesterday . . . ah dear, what it was to be fourteen. I really thought I was it.'

'Some things never change,' observed his wife dryly.

Dickie was still reminiscing with a dreamy grin, his thumb unconsciously stretching the black band that restricted his arm. 'Ye know, I remember just about everything about that house . . .' Coming back to the present he clicked his tongue. 'Sad to say it looks like it's been swept away on the tide of progress.'

The slanting green eyes were mocking. 'What a shame, we could've erected a brass plaque saying, *Here began Richard William Feeney's life of debauchery.*'

'Aw, now now, Primmy.' He used this diminutive when he wanted to tease. A gloved finger harpooned his stomach, drawing a gasp, and she uttered the hope that she was not to be regaled with all his old conquests at every turn of the way. 'Christ no, I can't even remember the second time.' He jerked his head to avoid a cuff and added charmingly, 'Unlike the romantic trysts I spent with my precious wife, of which I can recall every moment.'

'Louse,' said his wife under her breath, but it was good to see Dick laughing after the sorrow of last night. He had begun to move in his habitual jaunty gait, face creased in smiles. Erin, of course, would take this as a sign of indifference to his father's death – in fact everyone viewed him as a bluff sort who hadn't a care in the world – but Dusty knew him better than anyone and did not need to see blood as evidence of his hurting.

After travelling another fifty yards along the unfamiliar Clifford Street, Dusty paused by the imposing gritstone wall of York Castle and remarked. 'Well, that's still here.'

'Mm.' Dickie nodded half-interestedly and tilted the brim of his hat against the drizzle.

'You don't even know what I'm talking about, do you?'

56

For some reason she sounded angry, bringing his face down to say that of course he did. 'Then why were you looking at the Castle? I was referring to the café where we used to meet.'

'I know you were.' A practised liar, his blue eyes never flickered. 'I was just remembering when Dad was locked up in there, that's all.' He nodded at the towering, soot-engrained buttresses.

It had the effect of diverting her annoyance. 'Your father was in prison? I never knew that.'

'It's not the sort o' thing a prosperous fella likes to remember.' While he told her about it, Dickie pretended to be deep in the past, but in truth his eyes were searching for the café which he was supposed to remember. Dammit, there were two of them – which one was it? 'Course, us kids didn't know at the time, we just thought he'd gone away . . .' Whilst still talking, he cast his mind back twenty-six years to the weeks before he and Dusty had set sail for America. He could remember very well what had happened between them, but he was damned if he could recall a common or garden tea house – but she was expecting him to. Oh bloody hell . . . he would just have to take pot luck. 'Anyway,' he concluded, 'it's hardly the time to be talking about the old fella's shortcomings with him barely cold, is it? You were saying about our café – would ye like to go an' have a cup o' coffee?'

Dusty studied him shrewdly. 'That'd be nice. I'd prefer tea though – and something to eat; I'm starving.'

Make it the right one, prayed Dickie as he and his wife waited for a horse tram to rumble past, then picked their way across the dung-spattered cobbles to the café. Much to his relief, there was no angry report as he opened the door for her and followed her inside.

While he flirted with the waitress and passed on their

57

order, Dusty gazed from the window. Don't be stupid, she told herself, it's only a damned café. How could he be expected to remember when the street's been altered so much? *He remembered the other place though, didn't he?* Again, she derided herself – how can you possibly be jealous of something that happened years before he met you? *Because I am!* I bloody well am and I could kill her whoever she was.

The waitress had finally wrenched herself away to fetch their tea. Dickie reached across the tablecloth for his wife's hand. 'The very last time we sat here I asked you to marry me.' He sat to attention and looked pained. 'Well, what are you looking so surprised about? I said I remembered, didn't I?' She had to smile at his posturing. 'Dusty,' his eyes and voice were reproachful, 'how could you ever think I'd forget a thing like that? I seem to recall that I also told you how much I loved ye.' He kissed her hand warmly. 'An' I still do.'

What does it matter if he doesn't remember the place, Dusty asked herself, returning his fond smile and patting his hand. 'And I still love you,' she told him.

Then the tea came.

Sonny telephoned his mother on his arrival in Leeds to relay the undertaker's plans. He himself returned in the afternoon with his wife, daughters and four year old son, Paddy. As promised he carried a black suit for his brother, into which Dickie was now changing. He brought, also, the news that they probably wouldn't see Nick before the funeral on Friday, or Thursday afternoon at the earliest. 'I don't think Win's feeling too good really, and anyhow Nick's got the store to look after.'

'That bloody store, your father would have said,' smiled Thomasin, who had not visited nor even mentioned any one of her chain of shops since coming back from Ireland; not purely out of concern for Pat, but also because for once in her life she bore no inclination to drown her grief in work. She was seventy-four years old; until last week this had had no bearing on her ability, but with Pat's death she suddenly felt her age. Before going to Ireland to find him she had upgraded one of the long-serving assistants to manager of the York store; Francis had informed her that the man was coping well.

She looked round expectantly. 'Where's Josie and Carrot-top then?' Only Sonny and the girls had entered the drawing room where a moment ago they had undergone a wet reception from their grandmother and Aunt Erin, before being introduced to their aunt from America.

Her son smiled. 'She's just smartening Paddy up, they want to make a grand entrance. You'll see what I mean in a minute.'

'What have you told him about his grandad?' asked Thomasin, prodding her eye corners with a handkerchief. She knew the girls were greatly upset by Patrick's death, but with their ages ranging from eleven to twenty they were all able to cope with their grief. Paddy was only four – could barely understand.

Sonny cleared his throat and made a little sound. The onlookers could not tell if it was meant to convey sorrow or amusement. 'How do you tell a four year old about death? I said that Grandad wouldn't be here this time because Jesus had taken him to live in Heaven. He asked where Heaven was and I said it was a long way away. He said, "Is it near Scarborough?"' There was a soft collective chuckle; Paddy had never stopped talking about Scarborough since being taken there for a day last September. 'I said it was a bit further than that. He said, "Is there a seaside at Heaven?" Well, what can you say to that? I told him there probably was.' Sonny inhaled deeply. 'He then asked, when is Grandad coming back? I said, "Grandad won't be coming back because he has to stay with Jesus." Well, you know what a terror he is. He kept asking if he could go and see Grandad in Heaven.'

'Has it really sunk in then, d'ye think?' asked Erin softly.

'Oh, I think so.' Her brother grinned though his eyes brimmed with moisture. 'He said, "When I see that blinkin' Jesus I'm going to smack him for taking my grandad."'

There was tearful laughter. At this point the door opened to admit Dickie, Josie and a tiny red-haired boy. Thomasin shoved her handkerchief away quickly and opened her arms. 'Aw, he's been breeched!' True enough, the little boy's dresses had been discarded; the legs that ran towards her were encased in white woollen trousers. Thomasin hooked her hands under her grandson's armpits to lift him onto her lap and kissed him heartily. 'Let's have a good look at you – by, a proper lad! What did you get for your birthday?'

'A wugby ball,' beamed Paddy. His father often took him to rugby matches.

His grandmother laughed. 'A wugby ball, eh? I bet that wasn't your mother's idea – hello, Jos. I see you've already bumped into our black sheep. Has he changed much?'

Josie was cast from the homely mould. Once, her spouse's description of her as Rubenesque might have been permissible, but now with two decades of marital contentment pumping her girth it could only be classed as loyalty. Her one saving grace was that the eighteen stones were evenly distributed, from her frog-like chin and great bosoms to the little blebs of fat that pouched from either side of her wedding ring. But if Josie's attributes were not to be seen in any mirror, they were constantly on display: generosity, patience and motherliness – none of them exciting to a man like Dickie, nevertheless he twined his arm round her corseted waist and squeezed, beating her to an answer. 'This glorious piece o' womanhood looks even better than I remember. I could take a bite out of her right now if it wasn't nearly teatime.'

Josie pushed him off with a blush and a recriminating laugh. They had barely known each other before he had gone to America and here he was taking liberties! 'He hasn't changed at all,' she told her mother-in-law in mock severity.

Dickie fell away as if wounded and turned his attention to his nieces, dealing each a slice of his special kind of flattery. The two elder girls, Elizabeth and Sophia, were twenty and nineteen but could have been taken for twins. They were of a similar build to their mother, though matronly rather than obese, their whaleboned breasts protruding like corbels. Both had wavy, pale auburn hair, white skin that had a tendency to freckle in summer, round faces – Elizabeth's slightly jollier – and grey eyes. On being asked if they were ladies of leisure, they told their uncle that, being modern girls, they worked at their father's mill.

'God love us,' scoffed Dickie. 'All that brass an' he's got his own daughters picking wool.'

Elizabeth laughed along with her father. 'Not quite. I work in the design office and Sophia's in accounts.'

'How come ye've such posh voices?' asked Dickie.

'Oh, that's to be credited to their governess,' Josie replied with a significant glance at her daughters. 'They're always pulling me up over words.'

Elizabeth and Sophia looked suitably abashed. Their mother had been something of a hindrance to them, especially when friends came to the house. Aside from her accent, the content of her speech could also be very obtuse. Sophia in particular felt crippled at having her for a parent and was sure that only by reason of their father's celebrity as an artist were they saved from total ridicule.

'And is either of ye spoken for?' Dickie was asking. When both shook their frizzy heads – again, silently attributing the lack of partners to some fault of their mother – he looked

61

aggrieved. 'Ah dear, the men round Leeds must be very backward. I shall have to give them a few lessons on how to court a lady.' Sonny was much amused at the chat – his brother was never happier than when surrounded by women. Dickie turned to the next daughter. 'Has your father got you slaving for him an' all – what's your name, by the way?'

'Josephine.' The girl in the black stockings and pinafore, her long hair topped with a black bow, rocked her shoulders self-consciously and looked down at the carpet. 'No, I don't work at Father's mill. I still have to do boring lessons at home.' None of Sonny's girls had been sent away to college, due to their father's unhappy memories of his own education. Josephine would have liked to go.

Dickie put his head to one side. At fourteen the girl whom he spoke to had not yet reached her elder sisters' proportions. 'Josephine Feeney, eh? Sure, that's a bit of a gobful if ever I heard one.'

The girl coloured and said that the observation had been made long ago, that was why she was always known as Feen. She was the only one of Sonny's children not to have inherited the auburn tint; in this she considered herself fortunate, for she deemed it most unattractive. In fact, Josephine was particularly lucky, for she had the best of both worlds: her mother's dark brown hair and freckle-free skin with the Feeney good looks. Dickie was quick to remark on this after greeting the youngest, Amelia. 'Well now, you're all very . . .'

'Stunning young ladies,' echoed Dusty, reading his mind. '. . . but I think Feen's the pick of the bunch.'

The girl almost burst under her uncle's admiration and fell instantly in love with him. While Josie, seeing the frayed smiles of her other daughters, gave an inward sigh for her brother-in-law's tactless selection.

Dickie patted the sofa. 'Come an' sit by me, Jos, I'm in a bit of a draught here.'

'You cheeky monkey,' chided Thomasin, and told her daughter-in-law, 'Just give him a belt round the ear, that'll warm him up.'

Josie returned a bashful laugh, but then her eyes turned sad and she touched Thomasin's arm before sitting down. 'I'm sorry, Mother.'

'Aye, love, I know . . .' Thomasin cognized softly. 'But he's rid of his suffering now.'

'I'll pop in and see him later. I didn't like to go with . . .' Josie inclined her head at her son, to whom Thomasin returned her attention.

'No, that's right, love.' She recharged her voice with cheer. 'Eh, we'll have to see if we can find some pennies for this grand chap! Erin, pass us me bag.' When this was handed to her, she rummaged about amongst the female paraphernalia and came up with a shilling. 'There! Tuck that in your pocket, Paddy. Oh look, your Aunt Erin's got one for you as well.' She set the little boy on his feet and Paddy, wearing a pleased smile, marched up to his aunt to receive another coin.

Erin laughed as he proceeded confidently to Dusty's chair. She turned to catch her father's reaction . . . but Patrick wasn't there. Sonny reproved the child for his manners, but Dusty stroked her nephew's auburn head, asked if she could have a kiss and rewarded him with a couple of shilling pieces.

Isn't that typical, thought Erin. She has to go one better.

'Let's see if there's any money in this suit your Dad loaned me.' Dickie sprang to his feet and thrust a hand into the pocket of the black trousers. 'Well, would ye look at that!' Paddy looked up in apprehension at the giant who towered over him, but was reassured by the warm grin. 'Fancy your dad having one o' these in his breeches!' Dickie bent over, pointing his first and second fingers like the barrel of a gun, a large coin nipped between them. 'There y'are, Paddy, that's a real silver dollar. Ye'll be able to spend it when ye come an' visit me in New York.'

'You stay away from New York, Paddy,' advised his Aunt Erin as he trotted back to his mother. 'That's where all the bad boys live.'

'I think it's time for tea,' said Thomasin firmly.

On the way to the dining room, Dickie laid an arm round Feen's shoulders. It was an avuncular gesture, one which he might make to anyone, but for his gauche niece it brought feelings never experienced before. She did not know how to respond. The arm burnt into her. She felt embarrassed and joyful at the same time. When they reached their seats and the arm was removed she felt almost bereft. She wanted to look at him across the table, but daren't for fear that the others would read what was in her eyes, and worse still that he would know.

But Dickie moved blindly through the meal, unaware of what his earlier compliment had begat. Only the girl's mother caught scent of the infatuation. Startled, she glanced at her husband, but Sonny was too busy wondering whether there had been any set-to's between Dick and his mother since he had left them this morning. Not until the meal was over and they were back in the drawing room did he satisfy his curiosity, dragging his brother over to the window and out of earshot. 'Have you had your bazzacking from Mother yet?'

Dickie ran a finger round the crease of his ear. 'No . . . it's makin' me nervous, this waiting.' He stared at the old lady in the black weeds, whose mind seemed to be far from this room. 'Ye know,' he sounded mystified, 'I was prepared to see the change in her, but well, she doesn't seem like our mam at all.' His brother asked what he had expected. Dickie moved his head in acknowledgement. 'Aye, I suppose she's too flattened to get round to bollocking me yet . . . It's worrying, though.' He made a gesture as though offering something on his palm.

'I mean, our lass wasn't too upset to resist a dig at me, was she? She had a go this mornin' an' all.'

Sonny's mouth twitched. Consciously or not, his brother had adopted the old vernacular; it sounded so comical. 'Sorry, I'm not laughing at our Erin having a go at you, it just sounded funny hearing you say "our lass" in that weird accent.'

'Here's me trying my best not to act the foreigner – don't you start tearing me to shreds an' all.'

Sonny apologised and asked what Erin had said this morning. After relating the incident, Dickie snorted, 'I feel as if I should have a goolie chit to venture into the same room as her, and she hasn't even started to let fly with the real stuff yet. I wonder if her and Mam're waiting till after the funeral before they slice 'em off.' He looked across the room to where Erin sat deep in thought. 'I'd never've recognised her on the street. She's grown into a right old crow, hasn't she?'

Sonny defended their sister. 'I think she looks very well for her age. You're not exactly seeing any of us in our best light today.'

Dickie stuck to his opinion, raising his voice for Erin to hear. 'And she's got fat.' This comment naturally led his eyes on to Josie who was trying to keep her son occupied. He gave a soft laugh of delight. 'That's a grand wee fella o' yours; looks just like you with that ginger nut – at least, like you used to before ye got all these white bits.' He ruffled his brother's hair. 'Pity ye didn't have another little lad with black hair, then the pair of them would just be like you an' me when we were that age.'

'God forbid that I should have a bugger like you.' Sonny smiled as he raked his hair back into place, but soon his expression became serious again. 'I do have another son, though.'

'Ah, yes . . . Nick.' Dickie nodded pensively. 'I hardly had a chance to speak to him last night. I'd like to.'

Sonny's grey eyes swept the collection of mourning gowns. 'I'm sure you can put that right when he comes back for the funeral. He'd like a chat with you, too.'

'Mm . . .' Lost in reverie, Dickie was just about to ask his brother if Nick felt much bitterness towards him, when he caught sight of Erin surreptitiously examining her reflection in a glass-fronted cabinet. He nudged his brother, then called, 'It's mostly at the back, Sis.'

Erin shot him a frown. 'What're you talking about?'

'You were looking for the fat, weren't ye?' His expression changed as his mother gestured tersely for him to follow her. 'Looks like my time's come, Son. If ye see two round things come flying at ye then get ready with the needle an' thread.' He left the room and strode across the tiled hall towards the open doorway through which his mother had just passed.

He found himself in a smallish room, somewhat dark, but cosy rather than oppressive, with a radiant fire in the grate. Russet and gold paper clothed those parts of the walls that were visible; most of them were obscured by shelves full of books, some new, some well-thumbed. The carpet, too, had a background of russet with a deep-blue pattern. The only furniture, apart from a few chairs and a wine table, was a solid leather-topped desk positioned beneath the window. Yet despite its hint of industry, it was obvious that no serious work was intended to be done here, for its occupant would be constantly distracted by the view of the garden. There was no view at the moment for it was growing dark, though the light from the fire dismissed the need for a lamp.

'Close the door and sit down, Richard.' Thomasin was already seated in a well-worn armchair close to the fire.

Richard – she only used his Sunday name when about to rampage. Dickie's eyes sought out a chair. The only ones vacant were of a plain wooden variety; he was forced to take one of these, pulling it round to face the fire and his mother.

Thomasin surveyed his position: stiff spine, palms on knees, elbows stuck out like wings . . . as if he were posing for a photograph, waiting for the flash powder to ignite. Well you're not going to be put out of your misery just yet, lad. 'Give that fire a poke if you're cold,' she instructed. He said he was fine. After another gap, she said, 'So . . . you like America, do you?' On edge and swaying slightly, Dickie replied that he did. 'Bit of a silly question that,' said his mother. 'You'd hardly have stayed there twenty-six years if you hadn't liked it.'

'Mam . . .' His pose collapsed and he leaned forward appealingly, but Thomasin launched straight into another sentence.

'This was your father's room, where he came for a quiet read. These are all his books.' She indicated the well-stocked shelves. 'This,' she patted the faded green arm of the chair in which she was sitting, 'is his favourite chair. Shabby bloody thing. I always threatened to throw it out. Your father used to say, "The minute I get a chair acclimatized to the shape of me bum you want to throw it out – leave it be!"' Nostalgia tinted her smile. She rubbed the chair arm as if caressing the hand of its owner. 'He waited for you.' Her eyes probed deep into those of her son now. 'I hope you appreciate that, hope you realise how much he thought of you.' He said he did, and lowered his contemplation to the patch of carpet at his mother's feet; small areas of hessian were showing through the russet, worn by the feet of the man who had sat there reading. After a pause, Thomasin murmured, 'Good . . . good,' then was silent for a very long time.

At last, Dickie was forced to beg, 'Come on, Mam, get it over with.' Her old face was guileless as she asked get what over with. 'My rollicking – that's what ye brought me in here for, isn't it?'

67

The downy chin tilted as if in defiance. 'Think you deserve one, d'you?'

Dickie sighed and spread his hands. 'Yeah . . . I'm sorry, Mam, for all I put ye through.'

You have no idea what you put me through, Richard, thought his mother: how I'd wake in a hot sweat, unable to breathe, how my head felt as if it were stuffed with cottonwool for months afterwards, and the all-enveloping pain of loss . . . A sad smile played over her lips. 'Do you suppose I'd've allowed you into your father's room if I didn't think you were sorry? Besides, I reckon you've been the loser in all this; you've missed out on twenty-six years of family events. Oh, I know,' she nodded. 'Sonny kept you up to date with his letters, but it's not quite the same, is it?'

Dickie shook his head. The night was almost upon them. In the glow of the fire, his brooding face looked demonic. 'That really hit me when Rosie was killed . . . not that I ever really knew her, but . . . well, she was part of me. Ye don't know how badly I wanted to be with ye then . . . it cut Dad up a hell of a lot, didn't it?'

'Oh, yes.' Thomasin's eyes glazed over as her mind regressed. God, she looks so tiny, thought her son, fiddling with a button on his jacket cuff, so tiny and old. For a while he stared at her mouth with its old woman's downy moustache, urging it to say something. Then, hating long silences, he was compelled to fill the gap. 'Sonny said . . . well, he hit the bottle pretty hard, didn't he?' His mother nodded. 'Was that . . . ?'

'What killed him? Partly, I suppose.' Thomasin hoisted one side of her mouth, ironing the folds. 'That, and the same as gets all of us in the end – old age. It seems criminal, doesn't it? You get to eighty and you'd think you'd die in peace . . . you don't expect . . .'

'Don't upset yourself.'

'No, I don't mind talking about it, it's better than bottling it up, and I think you should know what he went through. I'm not laying any blame, Dickie, just telling you how it was . . .'

Her son moved his head in affirmation. 'Sonny told me that none of ye knew he was sick till a week ago.'

'No . . . he didn't go to our own doctor, otherwise I'd have probably known sooner. On our way back from Ireland he told me everything. It had started off as cirrhosis of the liver . . . well, you know your dad, he was always fond of a bevvy. It just got a bit out of hand after Rosie was killed. I don't know whether it was that particular spell of boozing or just an accumulation over the years. Apparently, he could have had it for ages without feeling too much discomfort . . . Anyway, by the time he was really suffering and decided to go and have it seen to it had grown into something even worse. He must've been in agony and none of us noticed a damned thing. Oh, looking back there were signs, but we were all too busy moaning about him to notice. He tried to spare us.' Her grey eyes became less abstracted and she fixed him with her gaze. 'That's one of the reasons I'm not going to give you the rollicking you deserve – your father was so glad you were coming home . . .' She paused to swallow the clot of emotion in her throat. 'He wouldn't've wanted there to be friction.' An ironic eyebrow was raised at his expression. 'Now that's a relief, isn't it?'

He chuckled softly and stroked an imaginary speck from the black trousers. 'It sure is.'

She smiled too, then. 'By, Dickie, I don't know what your father would have to say to your twang. You sound real American.'

He laughed again, thinking of what his brother had said. 'Not to the Yanks.'

'No, well . . . I'm glad to say I can still detect a bit of

Yorkshire-Irish.' She pondered then over her other children's accents, considering how very different they were. Dickie seemed to be a mixture of all the people with whom he had ever come into contact. For all its mongrel quality, his was a very pleasant brogue. She settled back, asking him to switch on a lamp and ring for a tray of tea. 'We might as well make ourselves comfy while you tell me what you've been doing with yourself while you've been away.'

'You're certain ye want to know about that?' He donated a lopsided grin and looked round for the light switch. Thomasin pointed it out and he went towards it. 'I must say, I found this a surprise, Mam – electricity.'

'Aye, we're nobbut posh. I had it put in about a month ago. Your father was tickled pink with it.'

Dickie flicked the switch, though the effect was only slightly better than the light from the fire. After pressing the bell, he sat down again and smiled through the dull yellow glow. Such a lovely smile, thought Thomasin. But she who knew him had learned to be wary of it. There were times when he had worn that smile to wield such infamy upon his kin . . . 'It'll be a long while in the telling. I could do with a more comfy chair.'

'Sit here.' She began to push herself up but he motioned her to sit back.

'Don't be daft! I was only kidding.'

Thomasin insisted. 'I prefer a hard back, this thing's much too saggy for me. Go on, do as you're blasted-well told!' She pushed him into Pat's chair.

Once they had swapped places, she studied him. It had been an experiment. She had wanted to see how Dickie, who was so much like his father, would look in that chair; to pretend for this moment that he *was* Patrick. But it didn't work. However alike they had been in looks, the character, the spirit, was different.

Dickie saw her eyes glisten and pretended to be checking on the contents of the bookshelves. 'Well . . . d'ye want it from the beginning?'

'You're joking,' said his mother, pulling out a handkerchief to dash against her eye. 'I haven't that much time. Anyway, Sonny's told me a lot of it – though I would be intrigued to hear how you managed to get out of that burning house with nary a mark on you.'

He rubbed the back of his neck in memory. 'I did get a bit scorched, but nothing that shows. I got out the coal chute just before the house caved in.'

'Aye, your brother said.' The face adopted more wrinkles with her frown. 'But how on earth did you manage to climb up it? Just in case I ever need to escape that way meself.'

'Long legs.' Dickie shook a limb in the air. 'I did the splits, and got a grip on the brickwork on either side o' the chute.'

Thomasin looked down at her own legs. 'Huh, I'd probably burn to death if it's long legs that're needed.' Her half-jovial visage regressed into one of concern. 'When you went back into that house, you said it was for Peggy . . .'

'I did try to get her out,' replied Dick sincerely. 'But the fire had spread. I had to leave her, Mam . . . otherwise we both would've had it.'

Wanting very much to believe him, she did not dwell on the subject. A slap of her knee marked a return to more contemporary matters. 'So, what now? Your brother tells me that you're in business yourself.'

'Yes, but not the sort o' business you'd recognise.'

She groaned, then looked at the door as Vinnie came in. 'Bring some tea up, dear, just for two, and pull those curtains before you go.' The maid did so, watched by Dickie, then left.

'Nothing nefarious, o' course,' continued Dickie.

71

'Oh no, it wouldn't be,' agreed his mother.

'You could even call it a charitable concern.'

'You could if you were talking to Soft Mick and not your mother.'

Dickie folded his arms. 'Well, it all depends on your definition of charity. I see it as giving money to people who need it.'

'Giving?'

He wrinkled his nose. 'Well . . . lending.'

'I see.' Thomasin nodded curtly. 'A loan shark.'

'Mother, please!' he cried in bruised voice and smote his breast melodramatically. 'Look at my pretty little teeth. Are these the fangs of a shark?'

Thomasin narrowed her eyes at his flashing smile.

'I promise,' he crossed his heart, 'I've never eaten anybody. I don't know why folk have such a bad impression of our business. I mean, you shopkeepers have your Christmas clubs, don't yese?' His mother laughed and asked what else he did, apart from running his 'Christmas Club'. He re-crossed his arms and leaned back as if thinking, 'Oh, I buy houses, give them a lick o' paint an' sell them again . . .'

'You, soiling your hands with paint?' Her face was held at a dubious angle.

'Well, not me personally.' He grinned. 'My time's spent on more important matters.' At her enquiry as to what these might be, he mused. 'Oh, this, that an' the other.'

'Now *that* I can believe,' said his mother. 'How does poor Dusty cope with you?'

'Very heavy-handedly,' replied Dickie, lacing his hands round the back of his neck and stretching his long body. 'She's a tyrant.' He banged a fist several times against his yawn. 'Sorry! I didn't get much sleep last night.'

'None of us did. Sonny tells me you've no children. That

72

must've been a great disappointment for her. Especially . . . well, you know.'

Dickie knew what his mother meant by especially – especially as he had sired at least two illegitimate children and couldn't even give Dusty one. 'Yes . . . it's gotten worse with her lately as well, what with the adoption societies being uncooperative. She's very low. That's partly why I brought her over for a vacation.'

'What's the other part?'

'I wanted to see my family, of course,' he said brightly. 'Can ye put us up for a few months?'

'Oh, I was going to ask how long you intended to grace us with your presence. I don't know why, but I had the feeling you might want to stay on a bit longer . . . maybe permanently.'

Dickie hesitated before answering; did he anticipate a plea in her lightly-delivered statement? 'Well . . . I don't know about that, Mam. The house an' everything . . .'

'You had a house and everything twenty-six years ago, but that didn't stop you uprooting yourself.'

'Ah, that was a bit different. The law was after me then.'

'Well, that makes me feel a bit easier having you under my roof.' At her son's questioning eye she enlarged, 'Knowing the law isn't after you this time.' After waiting for a response but not receiving one, she added, 'I won't ask why they were after you.'

'Best not,' cautioned Dickie and was saved from explanations as Vinnie brought the tea in – though feeling his mother's stare all the time that the maid was in the room he fully expected her to press the topic when Vinnie had gone.

Instead, she proceeded upon desultory chat which contained no hair-raising questions. 'I'll bet you and Dusty found a difference in the old city after being away so long.' She was told that he hardly recognised the place. 'No, well

73

that doesn't surprise me,' her voice was tart, 'with the bloody Council knocking bits of history down right, left and centre.' For many years Thomasin had been involved with the Yorkshire Architectural Society, whose aim was to save historic buildings from demolition. 'Still . . . I suppose they've got rid of a lot of eyesores as well. Did you happen to see my shop while you were out?' He told her they had passed one of its entrances but hadn't gone in. 'Ah well, you'll have plenty of chance while you're here.' She looked momentarily annoyed. 'I suppose some people'll think I'm a mercenary devil for not closing it today, but never mind what they think . . . Have you any immediate plans?'

His spoon tinkled round and round the cup. 'I did have till Dad died. I was going to take you both all over the place, have a real good time. That's what I bought the car for.'

'You bought it in England?'

'Yes.' He tapped the spoon and laid it in the saucer. 'I'll probably sell it before we go home.'

Home, thought Thomasin, that was a bad sign. 'We've got a car, you know. Aye, our Sonny bought it for us . . .' She took a sip of the tea, which tasted bitter for some reason; possibly because her palate was soured by grief. 'Dickie, about what I said before – don't you think you and Dusty could settle here?'

'Mam, ye don't realise what you're askin' . . . it's not just the house an' business, all our friends are there.'

'But your family's here. At least consider it, Dickie,' begged his mother. 'I've got all of you together again, I'd like to keep it that way.' Once more, the grey eyes misted. 'You know, I remember the day you were born as if it were yesterday. And every year, on your birthday and on the day we thought you'd died, I'd see this little black-haired baby . . .' She regarded him intently. Then, putting her cup aside, she rose and took a step towards him. He looked up at her,

74

askance, but did not move. 'You never did have very good manners – on your feet, lad!' Dickie put his own cup and saucer on the wine table and rose swiftly, but uncertain of face. 'Come here, I want to welcome you back properly.' When he moved forth, she slipped her arms around his body as if he were still a little boy, though her head only came up to his chest. She pressed it there, closed her eyes and prayed – make him stay, Pat. Help me keep him here.

Dickie enfolded his mother's small frame and kissed the top of her white head tenderly . . . just as his father used to do. Thomasin delivered a last maternal pat, then broke free and, averting her face, said briskly, 'Now hop it and send your wife in. I've barely shared two words with the poor lass yet.'

4

'Oh, it's my turn now, is it?' muttered an unenthusiastic Dusty when her husband relayed the summons. 'I wonder what my punishment will be.'

'She's gonna ask you to talk me into staying,' replied Dickie.

Her eyebrows rose. 'And here's me thinking she'd be glad to get rid. No cuts or bruises?' She examined him.

He shook his head. 'Completely unscathed – hey, Dusty!' He pulled her back as she was about to detach herself from the gathering. 'Be careful what ye say, huh? We don't want to get her hopes up.'

Her frivolity evaporated. 'So, you were being serious about her wanting you to stay?' At his nod, she once again used her eyebrows to express surprise before continuing her passage. Dickie watched his wife's exit. Feen was watching her too and thinking, why on earth did he marry her? She's so plain and dowdy, not good enough for him at all. He could have had anybody, I'm sure she must have tricked him into marriage, he would never have chosen her voluntarily. Oh, I wish . . . The door closed and Dickie turned to catch Feen's mooning inspection. At his grin she blushed and looked away quickly.

When her daughter-in-law was seated, Thomasin began. 'So, Dusty, what have you been doing with yourself in America?'

With the points of her elbows resting on her abdomen, Dusty laced her fingers and tucked her thumbs under her chin, meditating. 'Oh, trying to keep your son's accounts legal, scouring the financial papers, a little charity work, celebrating a Silver Wedding ... waiting for a baby to happen.'

Thomasin's face showed sympathy. 'Yes, I'm really sorry about that, Dusty, you would've made a good mother. But still, there's time. Dickie tells me you want to adopt.'

Dusty hesitated and the green lynx eyes fell away from Thomasin. It was apparent how much it hurt to say, 'I doubt there'll be much likelihood of that now; the adoption societies consider I'm too old and my husband's too decadent.'

'I can understand the latter part,' said Thomasin. 'But you, too old?'

'I am fifty-three.' Dusty's lashes were still lowered as though the admittance were shameful.

'You'd never think so to look at you,' said Thomasin truthfully, then tutted. 'Why should the adoption societies think that you have to be in your twenties to be a good mother? I mean, at that age you've barely finished your own childhood. Even thirty seems young to me nowadays. I see these bits of lasses making all the same mistakes with their children that I made with mine ... you don't realise how precious they are till their childhood's gone overnight. If I had it to do now I'd make a much better job of it.' There followed a self-mocking laugh. 'Chance'd be a fine thing.' Then a tear bulged over her lower lid. 'Eh dear, I am missing Pat ...' She flicked the moisture away and braced herself. 'Anyway, I'm getting off the track. Did your husband say anything of our chat?'

Dusty's lips twitched. 'I think he was too surprised to find himself still intact.'

'Ah well, I must admit if he'd come three or four weeks ago he might not have been treated so leniently.' Thomasin's face grew wistful. 'But he's part of Patrick. I'd be a fool to drive him away again, and Pat certainly wouldn't want that to happen. That's why I wanted to talk to you, Dusty, to see how you feel about staying in York, or at least in England.'

At first, Dusty looked speculative, plucking at a fold of black gown. 'Well, it's different to how I remembered it . . .' Then she smiled broadly. 'But it still feels like home. I could settle back here quite happily.'

'And Dickie?' Her mother-in-law's question was tinged with anxiety.

Dusty's shrug was not heartening. 'He's been really looking forward to seeing you all, but I don't know if he'd want to stay for good.'

Thomasin pinned her with a grey eye. 'You could persuade him.'

'Huh! And you could plait quicksilver?'

'You must have some influence over him, Dusty. You've managed to keep him for twenty-six years.' Thomasin caught the sardonic response. 'Oh, don't tell me he's still . . . ?'

Dusty inhaled the musty smell of books, then let out a sigh that told all. 'I'm afraid he'll never alter where the ladies are concerned.'

Thomasin rolled her eyes and nodded ironically. 'But you've obviously learnt to accept his shortcomings.'

Dusty bridled, 'Accept nothing!' then had to apologise for having shouted. Thomasin said it didn't matter and observed that her son had retained his knack of getting folk's hackles up; Dusty was to be admired for putting up with him. Dusty rubbed at her knee. 'Well . . . he overlooks my failings so I guess I have to overlook his.'

'Failings? You mean not being able to have a baby? But that's not of your making, Dusty.'

'No, but it doesn't make me any less of a failure.' How could she explain to this matriarch what it felt like, describe the feelings of longing and frustration that made her want to scream at her misfortune and tear out her sterile womb. She endured again the torment of those menopausal years, when one month stretched into two, bringing fresh hope that at last she might be pregnant. Only to have that hope snatched away time after time and finally dry up altogether, along with the last trickle of her womanhood.

Thomasin stared into the green eyes. Up until now she had assumed the sadness in them to be for Patrick. Now she saw that it went much deeper than yesterday. It had taken years of emptiness to form that look.

Dusty returned to the subject of her husband's mistresses. 'I did leave him once, but it was hopeless. Oh, I had no intention of going back to him.' She assumed a self-deprecating air. 'But he came after me and ... well, you know what it's like when he turns those eyes on.' Thomasin nodded wearily. One look from those eyes and you were ready to forgive murder. 'The thing is with Dickie, they genuinely mean nothing to him. I know it's awful and I know that it seems I'm condoning his behaviour in a way, but if I didn't think he meant it when he says he loves me I'd never stay with him and I can't help despising the silly bitches. But if I ever caught him in the act ...' She shook her head ominously.

'At least he doesn't do it openly, then?'

'Apart from the flirting which I can just about stand, no, he wouldn't dare. But I know when he is doing it. He just gets that look on his face ... Anyway, there's nothing I can do to change him,' she said hurriedly, 'and I only get annoyed when I dwell on it so can we please change the subject?'

'Certainly,' obliged Thomasin. 'Do you mind talking about your adoption plans? I don't want to pry but I may be able to help you.' The listener became alert. 'I know of some children ... the trouble is, you'd have to take three of them.'

Dusty burst out laughing, then remembering Dickie's

father, put a guilty hand over her mouth. 'Lord, I'll take half a dozen if I can get them!'

'Sorry, there's only three.' Thomasin smiled at the other's enthusiasm. 'It may be wrong of me to raise your hopes, but Belle did mention it herself before she went off to Africa – Belle is Erin's daughter.'

'Yes, yes I know all about her from Sonny's letters,' said Dusty, who knew that Belle had abdicated a brilliant career in mathematics to devote her life to waifs and strays. Her cat-like eyes were animated now. 'She runs a sort of children's home, doesn't she?'

'Mm, yes, but that makes it sound like an institution and it's definitely not that. In fact, that's partly the reason she intends to have these three adopted, so it'll allow her more time for the others. The main reason being, of course, that she wants them to have a mother and father.' She watched the flush spread across her daughter-in-law's cheeks and condemned herself for using Dusty's barrenness as a weapon for keeping her son here. 'There's just a small point,' she concluded. 'I don't think Belle would be keen on them leaving the country. She'd want to keep an eye on them.'

Dusty became stern. 'You don't have to use those tactics, Mrs Feeney.'

Exposed, Thomasin laughed guiltily. 'Eh, Dusty, I'd forgotten how shrewd you are ... I'm sorry, it was a dirty trick. It shows you just how low I'd stoop to keep my son here. But that's not to say I don't want to help you in your own problem, lass. As I said, you'd make an ideal mother. Could you coax him to stay till Belle gets back?' Dusty nodded and said she would do her damnedest. Thomasin continued, 'It could be weeks, it could be months. Once she gets a bee up her bottom about something there's no telling. Does Dickie – eh, it seems daft asking you questions about my own son, but he's still a bit of a stranger at present

– how does he feel about adoption? I don't quite picture him as the doting father.'

Dickie's wife defended him. 'For all his faults he does have an awful lot of love in him, Mrs Feeney.'

Thomasin found the loyalty endearing, but clicked her tongue at the 'Mrs Feeney'. 'You'll have to stop calling me that, Dusty. If you can't manage Mother then Thomasin will do.' The younger woman replied that, feeling partly responsible for Dickie's extended absence, she had not liked to be too familiar. 'I *was* damned mad at you when Sonny first told me,' confessed Thomasin. 'But if I can forgive Dickie then I'm sure I can forgive you, and I'm really happy that it turned out as it did. He couldn't have a better wife. I've always thought so.'

The green eyes embraced her. 'Thanks, Mother.'

The warmth was returned in Thomasin's smile. 'It's only the truth – and yes, I know he is capable of love. I can tell he still thinks the world of you, despite his nasty little habits, I know he'd've treasured your children if you could've had them, but this is a different matter: can he be a father to somebody else's?'

'Like Sonny, you mean?' Dusty shook her head in despair. 'I just can't say. I wish you could've seen him when he got the news about Rosie. He was heartbroken. I know he foisted his responsibilities onto Sonny, but I also know how much he regretted that as he grew older. He loved to hear all the news about her and Nick. I've never seen him so upset as he was by her death.'

Thomasin put her head a-slant. 'I hope there's going to be no trouble in that quarter? Over Nick, I mean.' She received hasty assurance that her son had no wish to claim paternity at this late stage. 'Good. It's unsettling enough what with Erin showing her resentment, I'd hate to have Sonny at it as well.' For her next comment she fell back on her old businesslike manner. 'Now then, about these children. Belle isn't going to hand them over just like that, you know. You and Dickie'll have to convince her that you'll make responsible parents.'

'Well,' Dusty arched her spine and gave a bitter laugh, 'if it all hangs on Dickie's sense of responsibility, we have as much chance of adopting those children as King Herod.'

The businesswoman vanished. Only a mother's longing was employed as bargaining power. 'I'll give you all the support I can, Dusty,' swore Thomasin earnestly. 'Just help me keep him here.'

When their parley ended, Thomasin remained in Patrick's study, wanting to be alone with him. The solitude was brief; her friend and business partner, Francis Farthingale called to pay his respects. A servant had been sent earlier in the day to inform him of Patrick's death, but on finding him not at home had been forced to leave a note.

'Thomasin, I'm so very sorry I wasn't able to come before now. I've been visiting family and just got home half an hour ago. I've come straight round . . .' The old man's grey face brimmed with condolence. During all the years she had known Francis he had been extremely thin, but age had emphasised the cavernous hollows of his face, and this evening his aura of sympathy made him look more skeletal than ever. Thomasin conveyed forgiveness into the sherry-coloured eyes, telling him he could not have done anything. 'But I could have been here. My dear, I *am* sorry.' Taking a creaking step nearer, he reached out for her.

After a long tearful hug, Thomasin breathed deeply and moved away. 'At least he's out of his pain, Fran.' She sat down. Francis unbuttoned his frockcoat and sat down too. 'But d'you know,' she looked bewildered, 'I still can't believe he's gone. It hasn't really hit me yet. Every time I open a door I expect to see him sitting there . . .' She remembered her news then and the wrinkles of anguish dispersed. 'By the way, Dickie's home.'

The cadaverous face became alert. 'Did he arrive in time?' On receiving a smiling nod, he relaxed. 'Oh good, I'm so glad. Oh dear . . . what a business. I can't quite believe it either. I *shall* miss him.'

Thomasin's breast rose and she changed the subject to prevent another display of tears. 'Ah well . . . I suppose it won't be that long to dinner – you're staying? We'd better go and join the others then. I'll introduce you to my son.' Before she could even rise, however, the maid came in looking most agitated. 'Ah, Vinnie, I hope Mrs Howgego hasn't gone to a lot of trouble over the meal. I just don't feel like ploughing through . . .'

'I'm sorry, ma'am,' interrupted Vinnie. 'But dinner isn't quite ready yet.' Before her mistress could say that it didn't matter, a round-eyed Vinnie blurted out, 'Mrs Howgego, she's passed on, ma'am!' and ferreted in her apron pocket for a handkerchief. 'She just opened her eyes an' said, "Ooh, Vinnie, I feel sorta funny . . ." an' went just like that.' She blew her nose and wiped her eyes. 'I am sorry for tellin' yer like this, ma'am, what with the master an' all . . .'

Thomasin flopped back into her chair and played absently with the braiding on her mourning gown. 'No . . . that's all right, Vinnie, calm down.' She fought to clear her mind, then said, 'Er, send John for the doctor, he'll have to certify that Mrs Howgego's dead.'

'Yes'm – but what about dinner?'

Thomasin wanted to laugh at the maid's priorities, but restrained herself to grant an impromptu promotion, telling Vinnie to hire herself a girl, as she herself did not feel up to interviews. Upset as she was over the cook's demise, Vinnie was enormously compensated by this rise in status and said for her mistress not to give it another thought.

83

When the new cook had left, Thomasin looked morbidly at Francis. 'Well, that's two gone. I wonder who'll be the third. There's only me an' thee the right age to qualify, which of us is it going to be?' She shivered. Francis hobbled to her chair and helped her to rise, saying with a pat of her hand, that she was far too young. 'I might have agreed with you last week,' came her apathetic sigh. 'Now I don't really care. He's only been gone a matter of hours, Fran, and if I miss him this much already what am I going to be like in the years to come?'

'It will pass, my dear,' he comforted. 'Believe me – and do stop all this talk about popping off. I wager five shillings that I'll beat you to it.'

Thomasin forced a weak smile and matched her pace with his. 'The trouble is, if you're right you won't be around to collect your winnings, will you?'

Rejoining the others, she told them of the latest catastrophe. Sonny promised that he would attend to Mrs Howgego's funeral. 'Right, thanks, love. But don't make it the same morning as your father's, else it'll be a bit of a farce, us hopping from one church to t'other . . . Now, Francis, I want you to meet my son, Dickie.'

The two shook hands and Francis offered his sympathies to all present. Dickie mistook the urbane manners for effeminacy and, once the link was broken, he paid scant regard to the visitor, dismissing him as an old pouf. He wasted neither charm nor energy on the male sex unless they were going to be useful to him. Francis, however, spent a good deal of time weighing up the handsome man who was now lighting a cigarette at the fireplace. Patrick's last request to Francis had been for him to look after Thomasin. Her son had hurt her many times in the past . . . Francis wanted to make certain that he didn't do so again.

The manservant, still flushed from his dash to the physician's house, announced that dinner was served, such as it was. Thomasin summoned everyone to the dining room where they gathered round the large table, fully laid out with china, crystal and gleaming cutlery, though there was little enthusiasm for its use.

By way of escaping from the miserable group, Dusty reminded her husband that they had left a trunk in the car. At which, both excused themselves to go and unpack it, declining Thomasin's offer that Vinnie could do it later. After telling the manservant to put the trunk on the bed and waiting for him to leave, Dickie asked his wife, 'D'ye think it's tactless to give them the presents we've brought?'

'The presents *you've* brought,' corrected Dusty and paused before a mirror to examine her black-clad reflection. How fortunate that she had included this dress in her packing – she hardly ever wore black; Dickie preferred to see her in bright colours. 'And it wasn't exactly diplomatic to bring your father a bottle of bourbon, was it?' She pulled off her elbow-length gloves and laid them on the dressing table.

'He would've appreciated it,' argued Dickie, who unlocked the trunk an threw the lid back. 'He always liked his whisky.'

'Yes, well, I wouldn't mention that to your mother if I were you,' Dusty advised, then wandered over to the cast-iron fireplace and stared into the flames. 'Still, I don't suppose it'll hurt to give the rest of them their presents. I hope the girls like theirs . . . it doesn't seem much to bring them somehow.'

'Aye, ye may be right. Those brooches're a bit dainty for a big stag of a lass like Liz.'

'I didn't mean it that way!'

'That chest o' hers needs something more impressive to adorn it. Tell ye what, I'll slip the spare tyre off the car, that's more her size.'

'Don't be so derogatory! I think I'll ask Josie if I can take them out and buy them a little treat. They're very upset over their grandfather.'

Dickie laughed at the mention of his sister-in-law. 'Good old Josie. I don't know about jewellery – we shoulda brought her a couple o' beefsteaks. I'm sure she really thinks I mean it when I snuggle up to her. Christ, the size of her – if she fell on ye she'd kill ye.' His wife said he shouldn't tease so. He noticed her brushing some mud off the hem of a skirt and demanded to know what she was doing. She told him she dared not give it to the maid for fear of upsetting Erin. 'Gimme that here!' He dumped it on the landing with his muddy boots. 'I'm not having my wife doing that.' On slamming the door, he asked, 'Will ye be taking Paddy on this outing, then? If y'are, I'll come with yese.'

Dusty smiled and came away from the fire to link his arm. 'You like him, don't you?'

The grin spread to his eyes. 'Aye, he's a fine wee fella. I could quite easily slip him into this trunk an' take him home with me.'

Face thoughtful, Dusty began to lift items out of the trunk, draping them over the foot of the bed. 'Might there be room in it for any more?' He asked what she meant. 'Your mother was saying . . . well, we were talking about children and . . . well, you know Erin's daughter has a houseful of them . . .' She turned to him hesitantly.

He guessed. 'She has one she wants to get rid of.'

'Aw, don't say it like that, Dickie!' She punched him and started to remove things from the trunk more rapidly. 'Anyway, it's not one . . . it's three.'

'Christ!' He had recovered his balance after her hefty push but now looked ready to collapse from shock.

'We did agree!'

'On one, yes, but three's a bit . . .' He clamped a hand to his dazed brow.

'Dickie, you promised!'

'You always say that. It's funny I can never remember makin' these promises.'

'Only because you choose not to!' She grabbed two fistfuls of silk gowns and marched to the wardrobe to hang them up.

Dickie flopped onto the bed beside the trunk and watched her pounding angrily backwards and forwards for a moment. Then he gave a sigh of surrender. 'Oh, come on then! Tell me all about 'em.'

She grinned in triumph and clutched a gown to her small bosom, speaking elatedly. 'I hardly know anything. Your mother just said that Belle thought they needed proper parents.'

His own smile was sceptical. 'An' my mother thought I'd make a proper parent, did she?'

'You know full well she didn't!' Dusty grew angry again and rammed a hanger into the shoulders of the gown. 'What reason have you ever given her or any of your family to make them regard you as a responsible adult?' The hanger was hooked noisily over the rail and the door closed. 'But you *are* going to be one, *aren't* you, Dickie.' Her eyes drilled him.

He tried to defy her glare, looking instead around the modernly furnished room with its bird of paradise wallpaper and chintz curtains, but was soon compelled to face her. She wanted these kids so much . . . After the briefest resistance he gave a snorting laugh at his own weakness, and nodded.

With that one gesture all anger was dispelled. She hoisted her shoulders in gladness and went to hug his head to her chest. 'I thought I might ask your mother if we can go and meet them as soon as possible.'

He linked his hands in the small of her back, pulling her between his legs and nuzzling her enthusiastically. 'Ye mean before Belle gets back?' He spoke into her breast.

She picked thoughtfully at a strand of his hair. 'I'm not proposing anything underhand, but Belle won't let them go to just anybody, she's got to be sure they're in good hands. If we can get to know them before she comes back and she sees how well we get on with them . . .' She gave his face a gentle shove with her chest. 'Will you stop that, you're making my dress all damp.'

He lifted his face, but continued to rest his chin on her breastbone. 'An' what happens if they're right little . . . scallywags? I'm not putting up with any truck, ye know. Anyway,' his mouth acquired a sulk, 'they might not like me.'

'Tut! How could anybody not like you?' She squashed his cheeks between playful hands and kissed him, dancing away before he got too responsive. 'Can I ask your mother, then?'

He sighed at being thwarted in his desires, then thought for a while, looking into her eager face. This visit had been intended as a holiday; his father's death was a big enough bombshell, but to be told he was about to be made a father – and to three at once! It took some digesting. Nevertheless he nodded, kissed her, then lay back on the thick lace bedspread, pulling her on top of him. 'You ask an' I'll obey . . . if you pay me the same honour.' His face cracked in a puckish grin.

'We're meant to be unpacking the trunk,' she scolded, but now that she had what she wanted, no longer tried to escape.

'Stuff the trunk.' He tucked a hand under the lid and flipped it shut, then dragged her into a more comfortable position, whence a long passionate kiss ensued. When he drew breath he began to undo the buttons that ran all the way down her spine. 'Ye know,' he tasted her again, speaking into her mouth, 'these dressmakers must be right frigid biddies. All these buttons, they're a sod to undo when you're rarin' to go. Oh God, stand up!' His wife chuckled as he pushed

88

her to her feet and spun her around to manage the buttons. 'I hate to see ye in black, anyways. All them lovely clothes ye brought . . .'

'I can hardly wear them now, can I?' When he had finished undoing her she moved away to peel off the gown.

Dickie shed his boots and stockings, then his borrowed jacket, tossing it anywhere. His wife was down to her underskirts which she delayed removing to say guiltily, 'We shouldn't really be doing this. Your father . . .'

Dickie unfastened one gold cufflink and laid it on the table, his gaze never leaving her. He did not answer, no you're right we shouldn't, but stroked her body with his eyes and murmured sensuously, 'Just get your hair down, lady.'

Dusty's fingers sought between the curls for her hairpins and one by one unpicked them. Her hair was not the kind which performed a romantic cascade to her shoulders, but rather descended in an untidy clump and had to be manually shaken into order. But from the look in Dickie's eyes that was no deterrent.

He had loosened his black tie and collar stud. Dusty felt overwhelmed by her passion for him. A passion which had remained constant throughout the twenty-six years of marriage. Approaching middle-age, she had expected it to cool; but her summer years had turned to autumn and still it ran as fiercely as ever through her veins. Stepping from her petticoats, she pulled at the ribbons on her camisole and took it off. There were no corsets to struggle over; Dusty's slim figure needed no restraint. Her husband savoured the body that was almost the same as when he had first looked upon it, unblemished by childbirth. He had seen bodies half that age which could not stand comparison . . . But then maybe that was because he loved her so very much. At this moment his love was suffocating.

With a flourish his shirt was off and he stood to embrace

89

her, pressing her belly to his and burying his face in her silver hair so that his words were muffled. 'Dusty, I don't know what I'd ever do if I lost you.' The embrace was so tight she could hardly breathe. She knew that half of his intensity stemmed from fear, fear of his own mortal span. But it didn't matter. When the last obstacle to their union had been removed, they fell on the bed and all thoughts of death were obliterated.

The tread of people on the stairs roused them into dressing. A shared look at Dickie's watch told them it was past the younger children's bedtime and so, bearing the gifts, they went down to rejoin the family.

Being adults, Elizabeth and Sophia had not yet gone to bed. Their aunt prefaced the distribution of gifts with an apology. 'It's not much . . . just a little token. If it's all right with your mother I'd like to take you out for a shopping trip tomorrow and buy you something more substantial. It's so nice to be here with you all.' She looked at Josie who in turn looked uneasily at her mother-in-law.

Thomasin sensed what was wrong. 'I don't expect you all to sit moping, you know. You go out and have a good spend. I might even come with you – if I should get invited, that is. Away, Dickie!' She injected her voice with liveliness for the other's sake. 'Are we going to see what you've brought us?'

Her son began to hand out the gifts, which provided a light moment as each pondered over the shape of the wrapping and tried to anticipate what on earth it could be. The unveiling complete, Thomasin held a statuette of 'Uncle Sam', Sonny an alabaster eagle and Josie a turquoise necklace. 'Is there meant to be some significance in this?' asked Erin tartly, studying the automaton they had brought her – a grizzly bear which, when activated, bared its teeth and swiped the air with its paws.

'Dickie, you've given her the wrong one!' Dusty snickered behind her hand.

'Have I?' His face was a mask of innocence. 'Oh sorry, that was for Paddy. Ah, this must be yours, Erin.' He swapped the automaton for an inlaid box.

'You did that on purpose,' scolded Dusty in a private aside.

'I decided it was rather more apt than the box,' chuckled Dickie. 'Grizzly old bugger that she is.'

Composing her face, Dusty tried to repair the damage. 'We've brought something for Belle too,' she told Erin. 'A turquoise brooch. I hope she likes it.'

'Belle rarely wears jewellery,' replied her sister-in-law. 'But I dare say she'll appreciate the thought.'

Dusty looked unhappily at her husband and said, 'Oh dear . . . maybe we could buy her something more suitable while we're in York.'

'I hardly see the point in that,' retorted Dickie. 'I bought these things 'cause they'd been made in America.'

'I might've known you'd bought them.' Erin eyed the collection of gifts which were rather tasteless in style.

Dickie took offence. 'Hey! I spent a load o' money on those.'

Thomasin intervened. 'And they're very much appreciated, dear,' she said firmly, then went around the room seeking a suitable niche for Uncle Sam. At last she seized a fine porcelain vase, shoved it into a cupboard and put the statuette in its place. 'There! It was made for that corner.'

Sonny agreed and thanked his brother once again for the eagle. He wrapped it up. 'I'll put it somewhere Paddy can't get his mitts on it.'

Erin sniffed. Later, she was brought to book for her disparaging reception of the gifts. Thomasin, on her way from the bathroom, encountered her on the landing and took hold of her daughter's arm. 'Ah, I want you! Come in here a minute.' She led her into a bedroom and closed the door, expression stern. 'Now then, I won't mince words . . .'

'As if you ever do,' muttered Erin, finishing off an acid drop given to her by one of the girls.

'You're to stop all these constant digs and pokes. If you want a fight with our Dickie than go out and have one, but for God's sake get it over and done with. I know how you feel about him coming back . . .'

Erin gulped down the sliver of acid drop and said angrily, 'It's not just him coming back! It's everything he did before he went, what he did to you an' Dad.'

'Never mind me and your father! If I've got any punishment to dole out I'm quite capable of doing it myself. And if you're that concerned about my feelings you'll stop treating him like you are doing; it doesn't help me, you know.'

Erin was unrepentant and gave a mirthless laugh. 'Marvellous, isn't it? Twenty-six years he's been away yet he gets welcomed back with open arms while I get the tongue-lashing for being nasty to the poor little mite!'

Thomasin reached out. 'Erin, I understand your . . .'

'No ye don't!' Erin's lips tightened over her outburst. It was no use putting voice to all the things she felt about Dickie; Mother would still find an explanation in his favour.

'No . . . you're right, I don't.' Thomasin shook her head in defeat, the white plait slipping off her shoulder to dangle between her shoulderblades. 'You've probably got good reason for your anger, but I wish you'd go about it more honestly.'

Her daughter's mouth fell right open. The acid drop had left a yellow patch on her tongue. Thomasin's eyes became glued to it as the acid was transferred to Erin's speech. 'Honest?! That's a good one when we're talking about the most dishonest, the most treacherous . . .'

'Oh give over!' Thomasin cut her off with a tired sigh. 'I'm not getting into an argument at bedtime, it's bad enough trying to sleep with your father lying dead next door.'

Erin showed instant and total remorse and collapsed against her mother. 'Oh, Mam, I'm sorry . . . you're the last person I wanted to suffer.'

'Then just get your grievances sorted out,' commanded the old lady. 'I've got my son back, Erin. After twenty-six years of thinking he was dead I've got him back and I don't want him to grow as sick as I am of all these bitchy remarks of yours and clear off back to America. By all means give him a good thumping if you must, I'd be the first to agree he deserves it, but then let it lie. All right? Now I'm off to bed.' Her severity evaporated, but she was still firm as she kissed her daughter and pressed her from the room. 'Goodnight.'

Erin turned and walked to her own bedchamber, tears streaming down her face.

5

On Wednesday morning, at her first opportunity, Dusty asked Thomasin if it would be in order to go and visit the children.

Her mother-in-law could see no harm in this. 'But you'd better take a note from me, otherwise the girl who's looking after them won't let you past the front door. I think they once had some trouble from a parent and they have to be careful who they let in.' She looked for her spectacles, then scribbled the note and handed it to Dusty. 'I'd be grateful if you didn't say anything about Pat in front of the children; Erin doesn't want Belle to hear the news that way. If you get the chance, tell Sally in private and make sure she keeps it a secret.' Her eyes scoured Dusty's gown. 'You'd better wear something else or it'll be obvious to the older children. Go on! It won't harm for one morning and I'm sure you've got plenty of nice outfits you'd rather wear. And tell Dickie to take that armband off too.'

'Will ye ever look at those two!' exclaimed an outraged Erin after Dickie and his wife had visited the drawing room before taking their leave. 'Dressed up like a brace of pheasant and Dad not even buried! That must be the shortest period of mourning in history – he's not even wearing an armband!'

Amelia and Feen exchanged smirks, but receiving a sharp nudge from their mother, bent low over the handkerchiefs on which they were embroidering a black border.

94

'That's because I asked him not to,' said Thomasin. 'They're going to Belle's house. I told them what a fine job she's done with the children and they said they'd like to see for themselves.' No need to tell Erin about the adoptions just yet, she decided. 'I thought it better if they weren't both encased in black from head to toe; the children might ask questions. You said yourself you don't want Belle to find out from someone else.'

Erin was making no concessions. 'I'll bet he didn't need much encouragement, nor her!'

'Liz, would you and the girls take Paddy out for a little walk,' instructed Josie, before any more uncivil comment could be made. In dutiful order, the four girls collected up their embroidery silks and, with Paddy in tow, left the room. Once the door sectioned them off from the others, Elizabeth told Amelia to take Paddy up to get his coat. The youngest girl demanded to know what the others were going to do and was told not to argue. Amelia retorted that if they didn't let her listen she would tell. Elizabeth gave a heavy sigh, then said to Paddy, 'See how fast you can run and get your coat, Pad,' and watched him scamper up the staircase before turning on her youngest sister. 'You spiteful cat!'

'No, I'm not!' Amelia was more like a disgruntled beaver, her teeth far too big for her mouth. 'You're always leaving me out. Why were you three allowed to go and see Grandad and not me? It's not fair, I've never seen a dead body.'

'Stupid child, it was certainly nothing to enjoy! Anyway, shove a sock in it or we're going to miss everything.'

Bad temper turned to giggles as the girls pressed their ears to the woodwork; Aunt Erin could be relied upon to provide some entertainment for the next five minutes or so.

'Erin, we all know your feelings, so would you please try not to be so free with them in front of the girls.' Sonny's reproof was backed by his wife.

'Don't ye think it's as well that they're educated against such rogues?' snapped Erin defensively. 'Apart from any moral aspect, he's corrupting both their manners and their speech, coming in here with his American talk and his cursing!'

'I've heard you chuck a few buggers and bloodies about in your time, Erin Teale,' scoffed her brother.

'Eh, just modify your language now,' Josie tapped his arm. 'Those daughters of yours might be listening in the hall.'

Sonny raised his voice. 'Not if they don't want a hiding, they won't.'

The young women scattered and missed the conclusion of the argument.

'Well,' said Erin tritely, 'he might not know how to conduct polite conversation but he's lost none of his old wiles, has he? He can still twist you daft eejits round his finger – but!' She staved off her mother's complaint. 'I shall bite my tongue and not upset any of ye . . . only you just see who's right.'

'I reckon somebody's put a curse on this blessed thing,' grunted Dickie, on his eighth attempt to jerk the Daimler into life. 'The engine must be frozen solid.'

'It doesn't take much guessing who's responsible,' muttered his wife, hopping from one patent leather boot to the other and clapping her gloved hands. Under Erin's cold scowl she had felt like a criminal in her blue fitted coat and feathered hat – and in no way could it be considered disrespectful; it was a very dark blue and she had chosen black accessories.

'Balls to it.' Dickie ignored his wife's objection to the vulgarity, straightened and tossed the starting handle down with a clatter. 'We'll have to walk. Unless ye want me to ask if I can borrow Dad's car?' He buttoned his Chesterfield and picked up the walking cane that had been propped against the car.

'Don't bother.' Dusty set off ahead of him, eager to see the children. 'It's cold enough without having to face the Ice Queen again. Come on, it isn't that far, and we've wasted enough time already.'

Peeping around the curtain that had been drawn in respect for her grandfather, Feen leaned on her elbows and thought dreamily to herself, gosh, he's so handsome. I can't understand why Aunt Erin doesn't like him. Aunt Dusty's so lucky . . . So intently did she watch him, that her eyes blurred out of focus. But even when he'd gone, his image remained.

As Thomasin had predicted, they did need the note to gain entry to the terraced property in Lawrence Street, but on being informed of their identity Sally, the young woman in charge, became less hostile and led them down a passage into the back parlour.

'We're on holiday from America,' Dusty told her, surveying the interior which was shabby in comparison with the one they had just left, though an attempt had been made to brighten it with a pretty floral wallcovering. 'Mrs Feeney said we should come and visit Miss Teale's children as she might not be back from Africa before we have to go home ourselves.'

'I'm sure you're very welcome, Mrs Feeney.' Sally, a fair-haired, fresh-complexioned girl, lifted a pile of ironing from a leather sofa. 'They're having their lessons at the moment. All except two of them who've been a bit off-colour lately. They're in the kitchen, *helping* me.' She pulled a face, making Dusty smile. 'Oh, let me take your coats.' She hung these in the passage, calling, 'Do please sit down! I'd better just go and see what they're up to else they'll be eating too many currants.'

Dusty stopped her hastily and seated herself on the old-fashioned sofa. 'Er, before you do . . . we have some bad news.' She glanced at Dickie, but it was obvious by his preoccupation with Sally's figure that he wasn't going to volunteer the information. 'My mother-in-law would like it keeping from the children if possible. It's Miss Teale's grandfather . . . I'm afraid he died on Monday evening.' While the other expressed her sorrow, Dusty repositioned a tapestry cushion and leaned back on it, adding, 'Miss Teale's mother would like to break the news herself, so we'd appreciate it if . . .'

'Oh, I won't say a word,' vouched Sally. 'Has it been in the paper?' Dusty told her it would be appearing tonight. 'I only hope no one else blabs it out before Belle gets home, then. Oh dear, it's terrible . . .' She returned to her senses. 'Anyway, I'd better just see what those little 'uns are up to. Excuse me.' She rushed off.

Dusty chafed her husband. 'By rights that should've been your job.'

'What? Oh . . . yeah, thanks for doing it for me darlin'.' Dick sighed. 'How can I tell folk he's dead when I don't even believe it myself?' He began to view his surroundings with a critical eye. Dusty followed his example.

'It's not what I expected, is it you?' she whispered to her husband. 'A bit cramped for so many children. And did you hear the maid refer to Belle by her first name? I thought that was a bit chee . . .' The comment was lopped as Sally reappeared.

Dusty greeted the woman's companions, one a boy, the other a girl, wondering if either of these could be 'hers'. The little girl, though not exactly pretty, was quite attractive with alert brown eyes and similar coloured hair. The boy, though, had a pasty face and features that not even the kindest heart could call attractive – still, he had been poorly, the maid had said.

Sally introduced the two as Julia and Frederick. She

noticed that Dickie was studying the boy's chin which was a mass of yellow pustules and scabs. 'Don't let him come too close, he's got impetigo.' Dickie made a distasteful move backwards on the sofa. The information did not seem to deter his wife who bent nearer and asked if they were good, to which Sally replied, 'When they feel like it.'

Upon her last word, there came the high burble of more children from along the passage and in seconds they spilled into the room gawping at the visitors whom Sally introduced as relations of Aunt Belle. Another woman entered, a rather mousey sort, too mousey for Dickie to spare her more than a glance as she apologised for intruding. This, it turned out, was the person whom Belle had hired as tutor for the children in her absence. When she had gone, Sally asked if the couple were staying for lunch. They refused, but said they would accept a cup of tea and, while she went off to make it, began to chat to the children.

There was a girl on the verge of womanhood who appeared to be the eldest. Dusty asked her name. Anna told her, adding that she was thirteen. The American woman asked how many children there were altogether. Anna replied, 'Nine . . . I think. I lose count, some aren't with us very long. These,' she prodded two of the others, 'are my sisters. My brother Eddie's still busy with his work. He's hoping to go to university.'

Obviously these were not the children up for adoption; Thomasin had told Dusty about the four older children whom Belle intended to keep. She directed her attention to the ones who might be eligible.

'Are we coming to live with you?' It was the little boy, Frederick.

'No,' said Dickie immediately. Dusty scolded him with her eyes for the abruptness of his tone and he tried to make amends with a forced smile. 'We're just visiting,' he explained to the unattractive child.

'Oh.' Frederick looked him over from head to toe, then spoke to the curly-headed lady with the funny face. He had once seen a picture of an Egyptian cat-god with great green slanting eyes; this was what the visitor resembled, but Frederick decided that he liked her all the same. 'Aunt Belle said we might be going to live with somebody else; a real mother and father.'

So this was one of them. Dusty regarded him with new eyes. 'Oh, and would you like that?' When he said yes, she looked pleased and was even more so when Julia said she was of the same mind. 'So . . . you must be Frederick's sister?' She was surprised to receive a nod from this highly-strung little creature who never seemed to be still.

'And her.' Frederick jabbed a thumb.

'Does *her* have a name?' asked Dusty lightly.

'He means Faith,' provided Anna, attempting to press forward the small girl who had been using her as a shield.

Dusty smiled encouragement and Faith, thumb in mouth, came a little way out from her cover, her free hand clutching nervously at Anna's skirt like an animal which has been parted from its mother too early. She was as different again from her siblings, having blue eyes and very wispy blonde hair through which her scalp could be seen. Dusty asked, 'And how old are you, love?' Faith mouthed something behind her thumb and Dusty laughed softly. 'I can't hear you. Come stand by me and take your thumb out, I won't hurt you.'

'She never lets go of my dress,' explained Anna. Dusty laughed again and said she must let go of it sometime. 'No, never. Except when I change into my nightie, then she holds onto that instead. She's frightened of being left on her own.'

'Oh.' Dusty lost her amused expression and held out her hand to the girl. 'Won't you come and hold onto my skirt instead? Come on, it's nice and soft. Feel.' With a little more

100

coaxing the child dropped Anna's skirt and made a grab for Dusty's. 'There, now take your thumb out and tell me again how old you are.'

'Four.' Faith's hands screwed the material of Dusty's gown.

'I'm eight,' announced Frederick, stepping closer in an obvious attempt to displace his sister who squeaked her alarm. When the woman lifted Faith onto her knee he turned his attention to Dickie who virtually ignored him, centring his charm on Julia and asking how old she was. He received the answer seven. The child held up a doll which had a bandage around its head. 'Look, she's got a poorly head.'

Dick assumed concern. 'Gee, that looks serious – what's wrong with it?'

Julia beheld him as if he were stupid. 'I've just *told* you, it's *poorly*.'

'Oh, my apologies,' Dickie looked at his wife and pulled a face, Julia then told him that Father Christmas had brought it for her. 'I'd've thought he coulda brought ye one that wasn't so sick,' replied the man. 'What did the rest of ye get?'

The other children gave details of their gifts. Dusty, looking at the meagre decorations, felt pity for them; they probably wouldn't have had much of a Christmas at the best of times and even less when Belle had gone off on her do-gooding expedition. What sort of woman set up an orphanage then deserted the children at the most crucial time?

But Anna offered unsolicited evidence to the contrary. 'We've had a lovely Christmas. Usually we're invited to Nan and Grandad Feeney's for a party, but this year we went to tea with the Lord Mayor! It was spiffing. We made hundreds of friends and we all got new clothes.'

Dickie remarked that if nothing else Belle kept them all nicely dressed. His wife was not concerned with their clothes – these children could soon be hers! She returned to the

101

most important issue. 'And even though you've had such a lovely time here, you're still keen to have a new mother and father?'

At this juncture, Sally served tea. 'Oh, they aren't bending your ear about their new mother and father, are they, Mrs Feeney?' She sighed. 'I don't know, I wish Belle had never broached the question, they've been on and on about it all the time she's been away.' Dusty took the cup of tea from her and said they weren't being a nuisance. 'They're always a nuisance,' said Sally, at which there was a baby's wail from an upstairs room. 'And there's another. Excuse me, I'll have to go see to him.'

'Oh, will you bring him down!' Dusty called after her, then sipped her tea and spoke to Julia. 'So, you have a baby living with you?'

As Julia's mouth was occupied in ripping shreds from her fingernails – which were already bitten to the quick – Anna answered for the child. 'Yes, someone brought him yesterday, his mother's died. I forgot about him – that's ten of us. Aunt Belle will have a surprise when she comes home from Africa.'

'I'm sure she will,' smiled Dusty. 'I expect he'll be wanting a new mother and father too.'

'You dare,' warned her husband under his breath.

'Oh, Aunt Belle won't have any difficulty in finding someone to take him,' said Anna sagely. 'We've had lots of babies here; they go quite quickly.' She spoke as if referring to some commodity. 'Though I don't know if it'll be so easy to get rid of Freddie and the girls.'

'Oh, I'm sure there'll be someone who'd love to be their mother and father,' contradicted Dusty, rocking the child on her lap.

Anna remained pessimistic. 'Nobody wanted the four of us. Aunt Belle wouldn't split us up.' The woman said that surely this was a good thing, but Anna added, 'I don't think I'd've minded if it meant having a proper mother and father.'

'Are you going to take us?' asked Frederick, with a thoughtful finger up his nostril.

'I've told you,' said Dickie in firm tone. 'We've just come to inspect . . .' He caught his wife's disapproval. 'I mean, visit you.'

The maid reappeared with the mewling baby, saying he was always hungry. Dusty put aside her cup and said eagerly, 'I'll feed him while you attend to your jobs.' She kissed the small girl on her lap, relinquished her to Anna's care, then held out her arms as a grateful maid handed over her burden and also a feeding bottle. Dusty cradled the tiny head to her breast and inserted the rubber teat in his mouth, laughing in soft delight as the baby ceased crying to suck greedily. 'Oh, look at him, Dickie, isn't he lovely?'

Dickie looked. Parts of the baby's head were bald where the first hair had been rubbed away. 'He looks like a monk.'

His wife laughed and contradicted him, crooning to the baby all the time he drank. When the bottle was drained, she laid him over her shoulder and oh, the ecstasy of feeling that tiny lolling head against her cheek, his breath in her ear, elating in the scent and feel of him . . . she never wanted to let him go, never.

Oh, Dusty, why did ye have to do it? Dick bemoaned silently, feeling her rapture. Why do ye always have to torture yourself like this? She was the same at home, grasping any chance to hold an infant, always being plunged into depression when she had to let it go.

'It's puked down your back,' he observed dully.

Sally heard, raced in with apologies and a cloth, then removed the baby upstairs.

There ye go, what did I say? Dickie, seeing his wife's forlornness, started to rise. 'Anyway, we'd better be on

103

our way. Ye said ye wanted to take Sonny's mob out, didn't ye?'

'There's ample time for that.' Dusty took solace in the little girl, lifting her back onto her lap and much to his displeasure, leaned back in a pose that told him they were going to be here for some time. With an annoyed tug at his trousers he sat down again, wishing that the boy would stop goggling at him. He was one of the most unappealing children Dickie had ever seen. Somehow, he managed to entrap a sigh as the youngster leaned on the arm of the sofa to study his gold guard chain.

'Are you very rich?'

This was answered with disdain. 'What sorta question is that to be askin' a gentleman?'

Dusty's eyes flashed, but she said with a sweet smile for the boy, 'I'm sure Frederick can be excused for not realising he was addressing a gentleman.'

Dickie felt that perhaps he ought to show some willingness and so began to interrogate little Julia, though he was not very proficient at conversing with children. This was rather an anomaly, for they seemed to be drawn towards him. Perhaps it was his good looks which lured them. Whatever it was, Frederick had apparently been hooked too, though Dick tried his best to repulse the adoration. Whenever Frederick butted in with an answer of his own, he would say, falsely polite, 'Is that a fact?' or 'Ye don't say?' then ignore him to ask Julia another question.

His ordeal lasted over an hour. He hoped it was about to be terminated when the children were herded to the lunch table, but even with his back to the man, Frederick somehow managed never to take his eyes off him. When, on the way home, Dickie showed no signs of volunteering an opinion, Dusty was forced to ask eagerly, 'Well, what did you think?'

His eyes wandered across the wide muddy road to where two horses bent their heads over an iron trough. 'I think you make me mad the way ye act over babies when ye know ye can't keep them. Why do ye do it to yourself, Dusty? Ye know it always gets ye down.'

'Do I look down?' she asked.

On turning to her, he was forced to admit that she didn't. 'No, and that worries me too. You're thinking it's all cut and dried an' it isn't.'

'At least they like us,' argued his wife. 'That'd be Belle's main consideration, I would have thought. How d'you feel?'

'The girls're all right,' he muttered, swinging his cane as he ambled deep in thought. Catching her stunned look he added more gently, 'Aw come on, Dusty, what d'ye expect me to say – he's an ugly little sod.'

Dusty pulled up and snatched a furious look around her, but saw that there were too many folk to witness an assault on him. Instead she flensed him with her eyes. 'What a despicable thing to say!'

Seeing she was not about to move, he leaned against the wall of The Rose and Crown, inhaling beer fumes. 'Well, ye're surely not going to tell me ye'd want that looking at ye over the breakfast table every morning, sat there covered in scabs, pickin' his nose.' At her further fury he said, 'Look, Dusty, when ye have children of your own you're stuck with them no matter what they're like, but when you adopt ye've got a choice. Ye wouldn't go into a shop an' pick all the bruised apples, would ye?'

'Knowing my judgement, yes! I probably would. In fact I've already done it, haven't I? Picked the rottenest damned apple of the lot!' She grabbed the end of her black fur boa and gave it a vicious swing round her neck.

'Aw, Dust . . .' He used a thumb and forefinger to pull indecisively at his nose.

'Don't "Aw, Dust" me! And stop picking your nose!'

His hand fell away swiftly. 'I was only scratching!'

'Huh!' the boa slipped from her shoulder and, with great irritation, she flung it back into place.

A man staggered out of the public house, suspending debate. Dick threw an irritated look at the sky, then resumed his mitigation. 'Dusty, I'm only saying he's not exactly the sort I'd choose for my son an' heir – eh, where're you off to? Dusty, come back here!'

He pursued her as far as the limestone fortification that marked the entrance to Walmgate, but she hissed at him to go to hell, glistening rage in her eyes, and took the route along Foss Islands. With a low curse, he ceased his harassment and whacked at the stone Barbican, watching her jogging figure get smaller and smaller.

In the wake of his wife's scorn, he didn't quite know which direction to take. He had no wish to follow her back to Peasholme, for there he would get another earful, if not from Dusty then from his sister. With a philosophical shrug and a swing of his cane he decided to go and investigate the old haunts which he had neglected the other day when in his wife's company. So deciding, he passed under the arch of the Bar.

Progress had barely touched Walmgate. If anything, it was even more rundown than when he had lived here, with derelict buildings and mean-looking people. Little attention was paid to the courtyard where he had been born. He didn't really know what had brought him down here in the first place; he hardly wanted to be reminded of his lowly upbringing.

He was debating whether to go into one of the many pubs in the thoroughfare, had just made up his mind to do so, when he pictured Dusty's tearful outrage. She'd been so full of enthusiasm when they had set out – more so than he had seen her for along time – and what had he done? Opened his big mouth and spoilt it for her. And there had been no need for it; all he'd had to say was, 'The girls are beautiful, we'll take them', and she would have been happy with that. He'd had no call to say what he did about the boy. It was just disappointment made me act like that, he told himself. After getting used to the idea, he had been quite looking forward to being a father.

It was no good, he would have to go and make peace with her. Slewing abruptly from the pub door, he crashed into somebody. Had the old man been less stoutly-built he would have toppled. As it was, he grabbed hold of Dickie's coat to steady himself.

'Do excuse me, sir!' He attempted to smooth Dickie's grey vicuna coat where his hands had rumpled it.

Dickie doffed his homburg, smiled charmingly and said it was entirely his fault, before marching briskly on – until the dreadful thought struck him that he could have been the victim of a pickpocket and he stopped to make frantic examination of his wallet. Finding it still in place, he sighed with relief and strode on, puzzling over the old man with whom he had just collided; he was sure he knew him.

The thought harried him for a good while longer until he passed a row of bloody carcases hanging outside a butcher's shop and the realisation came – Edwin Raper! The man whom he and Sonny had terrorised as children and vice versa. How his brother would laugh when Dickie told him about the way old Bacon Neck had offered profuse apologies and smoothed his coat. Had he known Dickie's identity there would doubtless have been a few choice insults. My, my, Edwin Raper! He must be positively ancient – had seemed ancient forty years ago. The coincidence caused Dickie to take more careful stock of his surroundings; he should be somewhere near Violet Nesbitt's house now. It might be fun to call on her. But though he looked for her windowbox which in many summers past had provided him with bouquets of violets for his concubines, he was disappointed. As Walmgate finally came to an end he took one last glance over his shoulder for anything that might bring back memories, before striding on . . . then stopped and wheeled slowly to glare at the small figure who stood ten yards behind him. With a menacing scowl, Dickie crooked a finger and Frederick approached warily. 'Would you be followin' me by any chance?' Frederick hung his head at the aggressive tone and scuffed his boot around a paving flag. He wore neither hat nor coat and his face was pinched with cold.

Dickie cupped a hand to his ear. 'I think I must be going deaf, I never heard a thing then. I said, are ye following me?'

Frederick mumbled a yes into his brown jersey, and was asked why. 'I wanted to see where you lived.' The man enquired of his reason. 'I wondered if it was a nice house.'

'An' so it is, it's a very nice house, but I can't see why that would be of concern to you.'

There was a pause, then Frederick cocked his pudgy, scab-encrusted face at the tall man. 'So you're not my new father, then?'

Dickie was exasperated. 'Hang me! Didn't I make that clear back there?'

'Are you going to have them two to live with you?'

'The girls?' Dickie shrugged uncaringly. 'May do.'

'They can't go without me,' the voice was priggish. 'Aunt Belle says so.'

'Does she now?' Dickie bent down and thrust a satanic face at the child. 'Well, they'll have a bloody long wait, won't they? Now turn around an' get back to where you're supposed to be, else ye'll have Sally fetching the police to look for ye.'

'I don't know my way back,' said the boy. His mawkish face was even more repugnant in its forlorn state – if that were at all possible, thought Dickie, who salvoed, 'Ye'll find it well enough with my boot up your arse. Now vamoose!' He straightened and watched the boy slouch away, then called him back. 'Oy! What was that you said?'

'Bother,' replied Frederick innocently.

'No, it wasn't! You called me a bugger – get back here!' Dickie jabbed at the ground. But Frederick had more sense. Despite the man's repeated order he continued to widen the distance between them. 'I'll have you next time!' Dickie speared a finger at him, then spun on his heel and marched over Foss Bridge, muttering, 'Little bastard.'

The stop he made at a jeweller's to buy a trinket for his wife turned out to be wasted; when he arrived back at Peasholme Green he found he had missed Dusty by seconds. She had gone out for the afternoon with Mr Sonny's family, Vinnie told him on his entrance. 'She said she'd take lunch out, sir.'

He extracted his gold watch. 'What about everybody else – have they eaten?' All of a sudden he was famished.

'Yes, sir. Mrs Feeney wanted to be finished for the undertaker coming.' When Dickie nodded his understanding, Vinnie added, 'The mistress an' Mrs Teale have gone out as well. I'm to stay here and look after Mr Feeney.'

'So I'm on me own?' He looked piqued.

'Yes, sir, just you an' me.' Vinnie blushed on realising that had sounded a bit familiar and hoped he didn't take it as an invitation. Though she had not known Mr Richard in his youth his reputation had preceded him. Mindst . . . he was lovely. 'I meant that John's accompanied the mistress, sir, so I'm on me own as well.' That sounded just as bad.

He draped his long frame over the end of the balustrade and gazed upon her, filling the hall with his personality. 'So, what're we going to do with ourselves, Vinnie?'

Her cheeks glowed more pink under this ocular rape. 'I've plenty of work to keep me busy, sir.'

Dickie's voice caressed. 'Is there anything I can do for ye?' What simple enjoyment was to be had from making a woman blush.

'Oh no, sir!' Vinnie's intention had been to go upstairs and collect something, but the way he was looking at her . . . he might see this as an inducement. Instead she headed rapidly for the kitchen.

Dickie grinned at her retreating back. In the taut dress little bulges of fat hung over the top of her stays. 'Er, Vinnie, would ye mind doin' something for me?'

She hardly dared turn. 'What might that be, sir?'

'Would ye fetch me a bite to eat? I've a terrible hunger on me.'

'Oh, yes – yes of course, sir! Right away!'

Dickie laughed inwardly at the sound of relief. The poor girl, she really thought he was going to ravish her, and with his father lying dead upstairs.

'Is there anything special you'd like, sir?' called Vinnie, poised to slam the kitchen door should his answer not be decent.

He couldn't help his natural inclination and treated her to a lascivious smile as he pushed himself from the balustrade. 'Oh, any of your special bits and pieces that ye think I might be partial to, Vinnie.' His eyes roamed wantonly over her as he made for the drawing room. 'I'll be in here when ye want me.'

The maid vanished, leaving him to chuckle deep in his chest. Later, however, his humour was to desert him when Vinnie announced that the undertaker had arrived with the coffins, making him realise that he was the one who would have to deal with the man. After directing the lugubrious gentleman and his helpers to the correct place, he retired to the drawing room to puff morosely at a cigarette. What a homecoming.

6

Paddy, having been bought his present, began showing signs of boredom as the girls um-ed and ah-ed over what to choose and so the family had split into two groups. In the event, it was Dusty and the girls who were the first ones to return. After a cursory greeting Dickie's wife ignored him, devoting her time to her nieces who had obviously enjoyed their afternoon with her – even Feen, who had sufficiently overcome her dislike of her aunt to allow the purchase of the blue dress which she now displayed. Her uncle said how splendidly it suited her. 'But sure, you'd look good in anything, Feen.' Her coquettish response spawned amusement amongst her sisters and she bumped the nearest giggler with a hip. His addition that his wife had very good taste was, however, met by a different air.

'Oh no, I chose it myself,' replied Feen, somewhat officiously.

Dusty overlooked the implication in her niece's tone and said it was an excellent choice. Unaccountably, this seemed to annoy Feen and she stalked off to her room, leaving her sisters to parade their gifts before their uncle. Dickie paid all the correct compliments, but in secret watched his wife's expression at the girls' preening. When eleven year old Amelia came up to accept his flattery he said with a less than gentle tug of one of her red-gold curls, 'Ah I hope our daughters are as fine as you when they grow up.'

'I didn't know you had children, Uncle Dickie,' said Liz.

111

'Not yet, we haven't,' replied Dickie. 'But we're going to.'

Dusty pinned him with a curious eye, then, at his smile of encouragement, said without thinking to her nieces, 'Why don't you go upstairs and put your new dresses on as a surprise for your grandmother when she comes in?' and could barely wait for the door to close before saying to her husband, 'Was that just a flippant remark or had you anything definite in mind?'

He got up and strolled across to her, luring her onto a sofa. 'I have someone definite in mind – if ye still want them.' He traced gentle fingers over her cheek, and purred, 'I'm sorry, Dust. D'ye forgive me?'

She breathed a sigh and put her own hand over his, pressing it to her face. 'Oh, Dick ... d'you mean it? I couldn't bear to build my hopes up.'

'Course I mean it.' He pressed his lips to hers in confirmation. 'They're lovely kids, an' I could tell they like the idea of havin' you as a mother. We'll maybe call again tomorrow an' ask if we can take them for a drive, if that goddamned car'll go.' Dusty was suffused with excitement which showed in the way she gripped his hand and asked where they would take them. He grinned fondly at her eagerness and flapped his arms. 'Oh, I dunno ... you know better than me what girls like to do.'

'Yes, but Freddie might not ...' She broke off as he appeared to get something in his eye and rose from the sofa, his back to her. 'What's the matter?'

With his face still averted, Dickie made to light a cigarette. 'I was thinking we might just take the girls.' There was only hush. A furtive peep over his shoulder gauged her response; she was dumbstruck. He closed his eyes, took a bolstering drag, then employed gentle reasoning. 'Three's a bit too many for beginners like us, Dusty. We should give ourselves time

112

to cope with a family, maybe get a lad in a few years' time.'
He dropped the match into an ashtray and blew the lungful
of smoke at the chandelier.

His wife beheld him speechlessly for a moment, then put a
finger to her chin and began to muse. 'Mm, yes, you're right
... maybe then we'll find one who fits our requirements, one
who's not so ugly as poor Fred.'

There was another exasperated rush of cigarette smoke.
'Aw, Dusty, it isn't because . . .'

'Yes, it is!' She leapt to her feet.

'Not just because he's ugly!' Still he avoided her eye.

'Why then?' she demanded, arms folded.

'I don't like him!' Again, he sucked deeply on his cigarette.

'You've only met him once!'

He did not tell her about the boy following him. 'Once
was enough. I always know if I'm gonna like a person in the
first few seconds.' He faced her now and spread his hands.
'Dusty, I know how much ye want these kids an' I'm more
than willing to take the girls. Won't that suffice?'

'It would do, yes, if we'd be allowed to just take the girls,
but we're not! Your mother says Belle wouldn't hear of them
going to separate homes, that's why she took them in the
first place, because they were going to split up.' Dusty felt
like crying.

'She's being stupid! Ye can see for yourself Fred doesn't
give a damn for them.'

'How can you tell?' She was told he just could. 'It takes
one to know one, eh? Just because you don't care about your
sister doesn't mean everyone else is the same.'

'Okay, forget sisters and let's stick with Fred! I ask ye,
Dusty, who'd want to take him? Be honest, ye didn't think
much of him yourself, did ye?'

'Yes, I did!' She tried to ignore his sceptical eyes but failed.

113

'Oh . . . all right! He hasn't much to recommend him, I'll admit – but for pity's sake! If everyone thought as you did the poor child would never find a home. Nobody expects us to love him straightaway, but I'm positive once we get to know him . . .' She shook her head emphatically. 'I'm sorry, Dick, but even if we were allowed just to take the girls I couldn't do it, couldn't bear to see the rejection on that child's face. You're viewing this from a very selfish attitude.'

'All right, so I'm selfish!' he acknowledged insolently and flicked the cigarette ash at the hearth. 'But in this case I think it's the right thing to be. If we take these kids it should be because we want them for what they are, not from some sense of benevolence. What sort o' people would we be if we took them 'cause we felt sorry for them, then didn't spend any time with the little sods 'cause we didn't really like them?'

'What sort of logic is that?' Dusty hollered at him . . . but then she recognised that there was a certain kind of sense to his words, and after a moment she came to stand with him, face desperate. 'Couldn't we just take Fred out with us once or twice?' she implored. 'Give him a chance to show us his graces?'

Much as he detested the idea, Dickie had only to look at that tormented face to know he couldn't refuse. It would be tedious, yes, but it did not have to mean further commitment and it would serve to keep Dusty quiet until Belle came back. At which point, Dickie could manipulate his niece – because he was adamant that when he returned to America, Frederick would not be sailing with him. 'Oh . . . all right, we'll take old grog-blossom too.'

'Aw, don't call him that, Dick!' But she was happier now. Along with the compromise, he gave her the present he had bought on his way home. 'Oh, my birthstone! Aren't you clever. It's lovely.' Dusty tried to slip the ring of beryl stones on a finger but it jammed at the knuckle.

'It's supposed to go on the little one,' he corrected her fondly. 'Apparently it's a Christening ring but I didn't know that when I pointed it out to the jeweller, it just caught me eye. He said it was for a man to give his wife on the birth of their first child and, well . . . it seemed a good idea. I know it's kinda premature, but I thought it might bring us a bit o' luck.'

She gripped her finger, caressing the ring with blissful eyes. 'I'm sure Erin'll be the first to notice.'

'Hey, now don't you take any more sass from her,' warned Dickie; his wife had brought with her some very expensive jewellery which she had not yet worn, partly because of her father-in-law, but mainly because of Erin. 'If she says anything . . .'

'Oh, she doesn't say anything,' responded his wife. 'She just has this very eloquent sniff.' She laughed and was thanking him with a kiss when his mother and the rest of the family returned, their cheeks and noses pink from the cold. The couple broke away at the jocular comments from Sonny and, with a laugh, Dick swung his small nephew into the air. Now why couldn't I have one like this? he asked himself at Paddy's squeal of laughter as a bit of rough and tumble ensued. Dusty watched them and, reading her husband's mind, felt the old familiar pang. Then she noticed Erin's eyes on the ring and instinctively covered it with a hand.

'Guess who I saw this afternoon,' Dickie told his brother. 'Old Bacon Neck.' He spent several minutes laughing over the episode, until his mother broke in to enquire if the undertaker had been. Dickie stopped laughing and said that he had.

'I suppose I should have been here to deal with him,' said Thomasin, 'but I just couldn't face it.' Dickie told her that he had not been sure if she would allow Mrs Whatsername in the same room as his father, so had asked them to shove her in the front room across the hall and leave Patrick upstairs.

'You make it sound like you're discussing an old bit of furniture, shove her in the front room indeed. I don't mind them being together. Your dad liked Mrs Howgego. Anyway, you can bring him down later. I'll just go and see what they've done to him.' Her daughter asked if she wanted company but Thomasin made soft refusal. 'Not just now, love. I'd like to be on my own for a while. Go up and see him later if you like.'

Why it should make a difference, seeing Patrick in that box after he had been dead for two days, Thomasin could not say, but it did. The horror showed on her face when she slipped back into the drawing room. There was further upset when Sonny's girls made a dramatic twirling entrance in their new outfits. Whilst their mother condemned their insensitive actions, Dusty sagged in recognition of her own thoughtlessness and apologised on the girls' behalf. Her mother-in-law was quietly dismissive. 'Don't be daft. Pat loved a bonny dress. You're not doing him a disservice, quite the opposite.' But Josie said in firm voice that they could still take them off. Watching her grand-daughters troop dispiritedly from the room, Thomasin called to the eldest, 'Eh, it's your coming-of-age soon, isn't it?' The young woman turned and nodded, eyes lowered. 'In that case I should save your dress for when you're dancing with all those handsome beaux at your party. Don't waste it on us.'

Liz smiled for this little kindness and closed the door. At the girls' departure Thomasin met with further remorse from both her daughters-in-law, Josie adding that they could not possibly countenance a party now. Thomasin's voice showed how tiresome she found this. 'For God's sake, I've said it doesn't matter! Do we really have to look like crows just to show how much we thought of him? And you will not cancel that lass's party, that's the last thing Pat'd want . . . God, I wish Friday was over.'

* * *

Most of Thursday morning was devoted to tinkering with
the car which, after much swearing from Dickie, made a
bronchitic return to working order. Telling the others that
they were going sightseeing, Dickie and his wife drove to
Belle's after lunch and asked permission to take the children
out. It had not been Dickie's idea to include all of them,
but his wife said they couldn't possibly be so mean as to
take only the three. Consequently, the green and yellow
vehicle was dangerously overloaded as it chugged away down
Hull Road.

The drive lasted only for as long as Dickie could stand
Frederick's breath on his neck, the boy craning eagerly over
the seat in order to learn every aspect of driving. At the
first open space he hauled on the braking handle and made
the terse suggestion that they all go and stretch their legs.
Taking his wife's arm, he sauntered along the frost-furred
path, watching the children scamper from one discovery to
the next, bending and peering into the bushes, collecting pine
cones and beech masts. God, will ye ever look at him, came
the dismal thought. What a mawk. He had tried very hard
to find just one thing to like about the boy, but had failed.

However, he pretended he was enjoying himself for his
wife's sake – although there was no need for deception where
the girls were concerned; he found them quite beguiling. 'Ah,
aren't we the lucky ones to be blessed with such company,
Aunt Dusty!' He smiled broadly as the effervescent Julia
danced up to pile her 'treasure' into his hands for safe-
keeping, her more timid sister clinging onto Dusty's coat.
'Like two little flowers outta the hedgerow.' Julia asked what
sort of flower. 'A celandine,' came the prompt reply. 'Bright
an' golden as the sunshine.' He stuffed his coat pockets with
pine cones, while the recipient of his flattery giggled and
shrieked in her highly-strung manner.

117

'I like woses,' announced little Faith from behind her thumb.

'Well, isn't that remarkable?' Dickie donned amazement. 'Wasn't I just about to say that in your pretty pink coat you're the very image of a rose, an' twice as sweet.' He chuckled as Julia managed to persuade her sister to leave go of Dusty and the two pranced off to scavenge the countryside.

'What am I?' Frederick had taken possession of Dusty's fur muff which he was stroking as though it were a pet.

Smile paling, Dickie glanced down at the boy. 'How's that?'

'What sort of flower am I?'

It required little thought. 'Hogweed.'

Dusty hid her exasperation and patted the boy's shoulder kindly. 'Boys aren't meant to be flowers, Freddie. They're meant to be tough an' protect their womenfolk. And you look very tough to me. Go run after your sisters an' make sure they're safe.'

'They don't need protection,' opined Frederick. 'I'll stay here and look after you.'

Dickie glowered. 'Why would she need you when she's got me to protect her?'

The boy said in hoity-toity voice, 'I'll bet you don't know what an alchemist is.' Dickie muttered that he did, but it wasn't a fitting subject for little boys. Fred recognised the bluff and told him gleefully, 'It's a person who can turn ordinary metal into gold.'

'Oh, really? I thought he was just called a clever bugger – onward, little pilgrim.'

Frederick eyed him speculatively, then dashed off.

'If this is an indication of what you're going to put him through when we get home,' came Dusty's quiet remonstrance, 'then I'll give up all ideas of adoption.'

He hung his head. 'Ah, I'm sorry, darlin'. I really meant to be nice to him. It's just that when I open me mouth . . .'

'I don't think you ever intended being nice to him,' said Dusty. He protested that he had, but she stopped and pulled him round to face her. However, when he met her eyes, he saw not anger but apology. 'Look, I realise this has all been a bit one-sided. I've been thinking only of myself, not considering that you have as much right in the choice of our children . . . if it's anybody's fault that Frederick's being treated this way then it's mine, for forcing him onto you when you didn't really . . .' She groped for the right words. 'What I'm trying to say is, maybe we should wait.'

'We've *been* waiting, Dusty.' She smelt the kid of his gloves as his hands cupped her cheeks. 'Girl, you've put up with me for all these years, I'm sure I can put up with him.' Before she could object to his irrational statement, Dickie called the three children to him, telling the others to walk on. He bent and put his hands on his knees, saying in confidential tone, 'Now, is any of ye good at keeping secrets?' Faith wanted to know what a secret was but her sister and brother shouted her down with their positive answers. 'Good,' replied Dickie. ''Cause this is just between the five of us, no one else is to know. How would you like it if me an' your Aunt Dusty were your new mother an' father?'

Above the loud noises of approval from the girls, Frederick reminded him impatiently, 'I thought you said you weren't gonna be our mother and father.'

'Well, I had to say that in front of Sally, didn't I?' Dickie managed to look pleasantly upon the boy. 'Big secret an' all that. D'ye like the idea o' going to America with us?'

'Yes.' Frederick slipped a hand into the man's. 'Do I call you Dad now?'

'Er, no, better keep to Uncle Dickie until we get all the legal stuff sorted out with your Aunt Belle. A secret now, remember.' He smiled and winked at his wife. 'It's said now, Momma; we've committed ourselves.'

His wife embraced him with gratitude, but soon he broke free to grab Frederick and hoist him onto his shoulders, galloping madly along the country lane and back to his wife. Each in turn received their precarious ride. Dusty laughed at the expression her husband was pulling on his bouncy return with Faith. 'What a face! She isn't that heavy, I'm sure.'

Freed of his rider, Dickie presented his back for his wife's inspection. 'Is there anything on me shoulders that wasn't there before?' Receiving a puzzled no, he laughed ruefully and ran a hand over his neck before putting it to his nose and sniffing. 'A rose by any other name would smell as sweet.'

Dusty caught the inference. 'Oh . . . she hasn't really, has she?'

'Aye, a wee accident, methinks. But I'll leave that to you.' He patted her and smiled sweetly. 'That's what mothers are for, is it not?'

They returned home at three-thirty and found that Nick had arrived with his wife Winifred. She was a quiet and unobtrusive young woman, pliable to her husband's demands without being totally submissive. Introductions were made. Dusty's greeting was warm, but she could not hide the fact that her interest lay more in the baby whom Win carried. As any mother, Win did not begrudge the attention lavished on her infant, and handed him over willingly to the other woman, the better to greet Nick's uncle. Naturally, her awareness of the true relationship lent spice to the meeting.

Dick was his usual flirtatious self, kissing her hand and telling Nick what a lucky man he was, having no recourse to flatter, for Win was indeed very pretty. Her eyes were hazel with little flecks of light in them and had a slightly oriental tilt at the outer edges. Her nutbrown hair had been collected into a soft knot on her crown to form a cottage loaf; free from the attention of hot irons, it gleamed even in this poor light. The sickness that she had been suffering lately did not show in her complexion which bloomed with health, and neither had her last pregnancy spoilt her figure – as Dickie's eyes verified. At first Win found this attention from such a handsome man very pleasant, especially as she did not feel at her best. But his prolonged gaze soon became embarrassing and, feeling flushed, Win unconsciously linked her arm with that of her husband as if in need of his protection. It was at this point, watching the effect on his own wife, that Nick understood his father's potency. 'If you'll excuse us . . .' he murmured to Dickie, and led Win over to the sofa.

Dickie stood watching the couple for a moment, then noticed that his brother stood alone by the window, and wandered over to him. 'You all right, our kid?'

Sonny smiled at the old term of endearment. 'Aye . . . I've just been shifting Dad into the front room with Mrs H. for his viewing. Nick and John helped me to carry him down. God, we had a hell of a job with the lid being loose. I had visions of us tipping him out.'

Dickie gave a vacuous smile, more pertinent matters occupying his mind: one being the deep conversation he had not yet had with Nick, his son; the other being the baby boy over whom Dusty was still drooling . . . the one who was, in actuality, his grandson. Hell no! He felt much too young to be a grandad.

Sonny noticed the wistfulness in his brother's eye and followed its course. What he saw took him off-balance. He had always thought of himself as a secure man, but here was Nick's real father; what would be the outcome? It mattered little that Nick was a grown man, nor even that he had sworn he would never look upon anyone but Sonny as his father, Sonny knew how persuasive his brother could be. And then there was his grandson . . . but it wasn't his grandson, it was Dickie's grandson. Someone gripped his knee. He glanced down and a smile replaced the worry; no one could take Paddy away. He lifted the child into his arms. 'Ah, and what does this fine fellow want – a good hiding?'

'No, a good story,' answered Paddy with a cheeky smile.

Sonny groaned. 'Sorry, Uncle Dickie, this bloke's dragging me away.'

Seeing her husband was on his own, Dusty came up and held the baby out to him. 'I've just realised – Paddy is Johnny's uncle.' Dickie laughed and took hold of the child.

'Mind his little arms!' Erin warned her brother. 'You nearly pulled them out of the sockets.'

'He's all right, aren't ye, Johnny?' The moment Dickie spoke, the baby burst into tears and was quickly handed back to his mother. 'Dear God, ye'd think I was an ogre – Feen!' He noticed her eyes on him. 'Come and sit your sweet self beside me an' show your nephew I'm not so bad.' Shyness prohibiting any uninvited approach, Feen was delighted to imbibe of his flattery. Yet even whilst seeming to concentrate his entire attention on her, Dick watched the fair-haired young man and wondered how to approach him. There was scant chance here of a private conversation. To aid thought, he lit a cigarette.

'Oh, not another of those blasted things,' moaned Thomasin as Nick prepared to light up too. 'You've just put one out. It's like a taproom in here. I can scarcely breathe.'

It was the opportunity for which Dickie had been waiting. 'Oh see, Feen, even my own mother's agen me.' To her infinite disappointment, their cosy chat expired. 'Come on, Nick, we'll puff our weeds someplace else – is Dad's study OK?' With his mother's grateful consent, he rose and discarded the cigarette in the ashtray. 'On second thoughts, Nick, you can treat me to one of your cigars.'

Nick had been waiting for this too – not wanting it, but expecting it. With a reassuring wink at Sonny he followed the other man out of the room. Watching her husband exit with that handsome young man, Dusty felt insanely jealous of the woman who had borne Dick's son; then just as quickly repelled this madness – how could one feel jealous of a dead woman?

It was quieter in Pat's study. Dickie sat in his father's chair and bit the end off the donated cigar, spitting it at the hearth. The fire in here was low, but this being a small room it was adequate. 'Mm, very smooth.' He took an appreciative drag as Nick, standing over him, withdrew the matchflame and put it to his own cigar. 'D'you always buy such expensive smokes?'

The match burnt down before Nick managed to ignite his cigar; he struck another, filling his nostrils with sulphur. 'Not if I can get someone else to – these were a gift.' The end of the cigar began to smoulder and glow. With a flourish, he tossed the dead match at the fireplace, missing.

'I wish my friends bought me presents like this.' Dickie rolled the smoke round his tongue.

'Did I say they were from a friend?' Nick took a seat.

Dickie raised an eyebrow and tapped the cigar. 'No? Well, with enemies like that ye sure as hell don't need friends.'

There was a short silence while both concentrated on their cigars, then Dick said, 'I saw one of your advertisements in a magazine today; your Nan tells me it was your idea to have shopping by mail.'

'Most of the ideas are mine. I just let her think she's running the business.'

'Pretty smart.'

Nick made a gesture to show that he agreed. 'So . . . what have you been doing with yourselves while you've been in York?'

'Nothing much, just going round the old haunts. It's changed a bit.'

'I expect it will have. How long do you plan to be here for?'

'We haven't fixed a definite return date. We'll probably stay for a couple of months.'

Nick lifted his right leg, resting its ankle on his left knee, and nodded.

Dickie stared for a while at the young face opposite. If he needed more evidence than Peggy's word that this was his son – and he did, for she had been a promiscuous slut – then he had it here in the Feeney blue eyes which held his scrutiny without flinching. He wondered how this fine young man could evolve from such a sordid coupling as his and Peggy's. It had meant absolutely nothing to him, had been just another tumble, how could it yield such a son when the loving union shared by himself and Dusty remained barren?

On impulse, he leaned forward. 'Look, Nick, I want to . . .'

The young man forestalled him, still seated in casual pose. 'I don't expect any explanation.'

Dickie rolled the cigar between his fingers, meditating over this. 'Don't expect, or don't want?' Receiving only a phlegmatic shrug, he added, 'I couldn't blame ye if you were hostile towards me. I can't understand why you're not. I know I would be in your position.'

'What reason do I have to feel hostile?' Nick's free hand scratched the ankle which rested on his knee.

'Me clearing out an' leaving my brother to act the father.'

Nick unhooked his leg now and sat forward, too. His face was serious. 'Let's clear up a few misconceptions: he's not acting, he *is* my father. As far back as I can remember he was there taking an interest in me, making sure I was happy.

124

Now as far as I'm concerned, that's what a father is. I've not the slightest interest in biological details, your brother is my father, you are my uncle.' He rejoined his spine with the hard back of the chair.

After a moment's perusal, Dick nodded and stuck the cigar between his lips. He had expected some kind of conflict, some show of feeling but the only emotion on his son's face was that of mild contempt and even this soon blended into the usual fathomless mask. Dickie could not help feeling a certain malice for this apparent indifference and neither could he keep it from his tone. 'If the relationship was so special it makes me wonder why he left ye behind in your grandparents' house when he moved to Leeds all those years ago.'

Nick refused to bite a second time, recrossing his legs and making himself appear as relaxed as he could in this chair. 'There was no question of desertion. Rosie and I were given plenty of opportunity to go with him, but at nine years old it's surroundings that seem most important. We'd lived here most of our lives, our friends were here . . . I think it says a hell of a lot for Father that he didn't force us to go, he knew we'd be happier here. It's only since I've been a father myself that I realise how much it must have hurt him watching us turn to Grandad whenever we wanted something. But despite that and living twenty miles away he was still our father.' Make no mistake about that, said Nick's eyes.

'He's a lucky fella.' Not knowing what else to say on the subject, Dickie proffered with a smile, 'An' so are you, Nick, that's a fine-looking woman ye've got yourself.'

Nick returned a similar observation, but despite the compliments there was no warmth between them and as soon as the cigars were finished the two rejoined the others, Dick feeling a sense of deflation.

With their arrival, and the announcement of tea-time, it was suddenly noticed that little Paddy had disappeared. 'Oh, my God!' Erin clutched at her mouth. 'If he gets out of the front door he'll be straight over that road.' She stood up as if to go and search, infecting Josie with her panic.

Ever calm, Nick bade them sit down. 'Uncle Dick, will you take a look round the house while I search outside?'

'He hasn't got out that way.' Thomasin pointed at the french windows. 'They're still bolted. Little demon, I never saw him go. He'll probably be down in the kitchen, that's where they all make for. Liz, you lasses go look upstairs. Erin, stop worrying, will you!' She gestured forcefully for Erin to sit down while the searchers left the room.

First, Dickie made investigation of the kitchen, gracing Vinnie with one of his smiles and making her blush as he had intended. With the girls pounding from room to room overhead, there were only two other places in the house where Paddy could be. He hoped one of these was not the room containing the coffins. The door of this room was slightly ajar; he hadn't noticed before. With heart in mouth he crept over the hall and peeped in.

Paddy had lugged a chair up to Pat's coffin. By standing on its seat he could rest his elbows on the back and see his grandfather, to whom he was now chatting. When Dickie inched nearer he saw that in one hand the little boy clutched a bag, whilst the other hand was trying to feed Patrick with chocolate drops. The corpse's mouth matched Paddy's own; a brown sticky ring.

Seized with the simultaneous urge to laugh and cry, Dickie held back for a second. Then, not wanting to shock the boy into falling off the chair, he said softly, 'Hello, Paddy,' and moved closer to lift him down.

'Grandad's come back from Heaven but he won't wake up.' Paddy directed a stained finger.

'Ssh, let him sleep.' Dickie carried the child to the door. 'Ye shouldn't be in here.'

'There's a lady in that one.' Paddy's finger indicated the cook's resting place.

'I know, don't wake her up.'

Paddy looked deeply into his uncle's face, then attempted to press a chocolate drop between the other's lips. With a strangled chuckle, Dickie opened his mouth to accept it. 'Thank you!'

Paddy's responsive beam had a sudden braking effect on the man's legs. He compared this charming little fellow with the one he was meant to adopt, and damned Fate. It would have been nice to spend a lot longer with the child, but the others would be concerned. So, after opening the front door and calling Nick back from the road, he went back to the drawing room.

While Josie censured her son and confiscated the bag of sweets, Thomasin asked where Dickie had found him. 'He was in the front with Dad ... trying to feed him chocolate drops.'

There was a collective, 'Aw!' and not a few damp handkerchiefs.

Sonny sighed. 'I suppose this means more explanations. God help us.' After some hesitation, he unbolted the french windows. 'Come on, Pad, we'll go for a little walk down the garden.'

'He'll need his coat.' Josie began to rise. 'And it's nearly dark out there.'

'We won't be that long ... I hope.' Sonny took his son's hand and stepped out into the twilight, closing the doors behind them.

The family watched the pair wander a short way down the garden, saw Sonny's arm point to the dead flowers in the border, then at the sky. Paddy stopped walking to crane his head at his father, face searching ... then his arms stretched up to be held and Sonny bent to comfort him. When they came back both were distressed. Paddy strained for his mother who enveloped him in a fleshy cradle and rocked him while Sonny blew his nose, at the same time running the handkerchief round his eyes.

With a voice that was gruff, Dickie excused himself. 'I'll just go an' clean Dad up a bit.'

Standing once again in that room of rest, he spat on his handkerchief and dabbed away the smudges of chocolate from his father's mouth, then tarried there, simply to look. How could you fit all those years into one oak box? All that pride, strength, spirit, sexual passion, those hopes, dreams . . . how did they all condense into a few pieces of nailed-together wood? He became fixed with the body of his father on its bed of white satin and felt an overwhelming terror, seeing himself lying there. It seemed mere seconds since he had been sitting on that withered corpse's knee, listening to a fairytale. The ornate casket with its brass handles and crucifix screamed mortality. Since it had entered the house yesterday it had sprung to every idle thought, given him nightmares.

Tomorrow, when the last person had filed past in respect, the lid would be screwed down and the box lowered into a dank hole in a windswept boneyard . . . but Dickie would never be rid of it. Never. His gaze was involuntarily drawn to the plainer coffin where lay the dead cook, then with a shudder, he left the room.

7

She wished she could have given him one of his lively Irish wakes, but no one would have understood – oh, maybe Erin and the boys, but not the others. Thomasin followed her husband's coffin between the rows of black tophats and veils, a son on one arm, a daughter on the other. Behind her trailed Dickie and his wife, behind them Pat's grandchildren.

'Isn't it sickening how you have to wait till you're dead to see how popular you are,' she murmured. Every pew in the church was crammed full and some mourners were having to stand at the back. Her comment was not a bitter one, merely an observation on the absurdity of human nature. There were people whom neither she nor Pat had seen for many a year, among them Dominic and Edith Teale, Erin's parents-in-law. Since her husband Sam's death when Erin had moved to Peasholme Green, the Teales had seen little of her and Belle; they were not a closely-knit family as were the Feeneys, and Belle had not really looked on them as her grandparents. Indeed, thought Thomasin, the last time they met must have been at Belle's coming-of-age . . . almost five years ago. There was nowt so queer as folk. Still, she mustn't quibble, she would no doubt have been very hurt had none of them turned up to show their respects.

Thomasin suffered the lengthy Requiem Mass in silence, but swore to herself that this was the last time she would enter this church. Afterwards, the black horses with their head plumes carried Patrick to his grave, where the final act was performed, ironically, by Father Gilchrist, a man whom Patrick had detested. The priest, it seemed, was to have the last laugh on Pat by flinging the crumbs of soil onto his coffin lid. Even in midsummer this cemetery was a dreadful place. Today in the bleak and bitter cold of January it filled Thomasin with such intense despair as she had ever felt in her whole life. Was there really a Hereafter or was this the terminus? This bloody, detestable hole.

Nearby were the graves of her parents, William and Hannah Fenton. Somewhere in this place, too, were the bones of all their old Irish friends and Pat's first wife. But who knew where, with no stone to mark their paupers' graves. Long ago, when Dickie had died Patrick had bought a family plot where Rosie, too, lay . . . but Dickie was standing here beside her. For the first time it struck Thomasin that someone else was lying in there with Rosie. While the priest droned on, she began to wonder who he was. He couldn't have been loved otherwise his family would have come looking for him, would have traced him to that fire years ago. Anger stirred. He was an intruder, shouldn't be in there – bad enough if he had been any stranger, but to have the man who had committed adultery with Sonny's wife in the same place as her beloved Pat and Rosie . . . tears of rage mingled with those of loss, then dried just as quickly in the bitter wind. Too late to do anything about it now. A hand was trying to press something into hers. With a dull look at her daughter she accepted the crumbs of earth and cast them at the hole.

Stop! she wanted to shout. Fetch him up, I'm not having him in there with that wretch! He wanted to be in Ireland . . . but then she heard Pat's voice say, 'No, Tommy, Rosie's in there. Leave me be an' let the other fella lie.'

She felt another hand cup her elbow, steering her away from the grave; apparently it was all over. She didn't feel as if she were here. Her body was, yes, but her mind would not coordinate. She felt like . . . like she had when she was giving birth to Dickie. The pain had become so bad that her mind, her spirit, had come adrift from her body so that it seemed as if she were watching herself writhing in agony from some point overhead. Strange, to liken the pain of bereavement to that of birth, for with the latter there was a whole new life beginning . . . but then were the two so dissimilar? At this moment more than any other she yearned for Pat's surety in a Heaven.

Home from the cemetery, Thomasin's mind had returned to her body, but the disorientation continued. Most of these people were family, part of herself and Pat, yet she was assailed by solitude. She was no longer one of a pair. It wasn't that she thought no one would understand, for Erin had been through widowhood herself; she just could not articulate her grief. How could she talk to her children about how she would miss – already missed – the way his body curled into hers, the way, in his waking moments, he would cup a semi-conscious hand round her breast. Old people didn't feel like that, or weren't meant to. She herself had held this view when she had been young, wouldn't have understood if anyone had tried to tell her. And what did she do when all this was over, when all these people went home? The thought made her so desperately lonely . . .

A large hand scooped her fingers from where they rested on her lap and squeezed comfortingly. Of all the people she might have expected to see when she turned her head, the last on that list would have been Dickie, the most selfish, the most insensitive, the most callous of her children. 'You know,' she said to him, rubbing his skin with a thumb, 'I keep feeling I've done the wrong thing.' Her eyes searched his handsome face. 'Your father loved Ireland so much . . . maybe we should have taken him to be buried there.'

'Does it matter to him now what happens to his body?' Once more the old insensitive Dickie, thought Thomasin – but no, his next words surprised her yet again. 'He's gone somewhere better.'

'By . . . you'll never cease to amaze me!' She shook her head in wonderment.

'Me being the infidel?' smiled Dickie.

'D'you really believe that?'

'That I'm an infidel or that there's a Heaven? Doesn't really matter whether I believe or not; Dad thought there was.'

She gave a slow nod of acceptance. 'Still, I just keep thinking . . . I mean, he went to Ireland with the intention of dying there.'

'Did he ask for you to have his body shipped there?'

'No, neither of us wanted to talk about it. But maybe he was expecting me to know.'

'If it'd make ye feel better could ye not just take one of his belongings an' bury it in Ireland? Ye know, something he thought a lot about.'

'He thought a lot about you but I doubt you'll be volunteering for premature burial.' His mother gave a mordant smile and patted his hand. 'I never realised you were such a sentimental soul, Richard.'

He gave a self-denigrating laugh, but inside he felt quaky and sick. A look at his brother told him that Sonny was experiencing the same crisis, wondering how long it would be before the family was gathered for his funeral, wondering if there was anything afterwards. But added to this was the fact that when he died that was the end, there would be no continuity in his children, for he had none. He jerked his mind from such depressing thoughts. 'Ye know, there's something missin' here. I seem to recall that Erin used to play the harp at all the old wakes.'

'You've a good memory,' said Thomasin; they had made

the split from the Irish community thirty years ago, since when the harp had rarely been used for the same purpose. She peered around. 'Where is your sister? It's a good idea of yours. Go find her and tell her to give us a nice tune.'

Dickie went off to seek Erin, coming across her staring from the window of their father's den in a pose of misery. 'Hey, Sis, go an' fetch the harp an' give us a tune.'

She responded with derision. 'I'll play nothing for you!' then pushed herself sullenly from the window and flounced off. 'But I will play for my father.'

The harp was fetched and those funeral guests who had not seen it before remarked on the beauty of its carving.

'It was the only possession my husband brought with him when the famine drove him from Ireland,' explained Thomasin quietly as Erin got ready to play. 'He could never master it himself, though I understand his father was very talented. Apparently, it had been handed down through the generations.' Here she smiled, recalling Pat's opinion on the harp's ancestry, then sat back to enjoy the haunting music, remembering all the other times it had been played, both happy and sad. And with the plaintive melody came a decision; she would visit Ireland and take something of Pat's. She knew the name of the place where he had been born; someone would give her directions. In fact, she decided, they would all go.

The old cook's funeral in the afternoon was a much less crowded affair and the service not so lengthy as Patrick's Catholic one. Even so, it was torture to have to stand once more in that chilly graveyard. Afterwards, when they were warming their hands round cups of tea and waiting for the arrival of the solicitor who would be reading Pat's will, Thomasin spoke of her plan. 'I think your father would

133

have wanted you all to see where this family began; not in the slums of Britannia Yard but in a place of beauty.'

Erin was quick to respond. 'I'd love to go. I wanted to go with Dad . . . but o' course, we all know now why he refused to take me.' She had been so angry about that, had called him all sorts of names, for which she was now suffering guilt. 'Should we wait till it's a bit warmer?' Another pang: those were the words she had spoken to her father.

Thomasin was averse to raising the subject of her own death, but Pat's demise had shown her how quickly time sneaked up on one. 'I have to face it, Erin, I might not last much longer myself – o' course I could live another twenty years,' she said with a chirpy tilt of her head, 'but . . . who knows? It's best if we arrange it for as soon as we can all make the trip. I'm not talking about a long holiday, just a little trip there and back. Two or three days should be adequate. I know Belle isn't here, Erin, but there's nothing to stop you taking her yourself some day. I have to grab my chance while I can. What do the rest of you think?'

Dickie and his brother said they would go. 'But just us,' said Sonny. 'There's no need to trail Josie and the kids, is there?'

'John, you make it sound as if it'll be too much trouble,' reproached his wife. 'I was as fond of your father as anyone.'

'We know that, Josie,' Thomasin's voice soothed. 'And Pat loved you as well. This isn't going to be a pilgrimage, it's simply to satisfy a bit of family curiosity – I'm not implying that you're not a member of the family,' one had to be so careful in one's choice of words to Josie, she tended to take things the wrong way, 'but you've no personal interest in Ireland, it'd be a shame for you to drag yourself over there in this weather just because you thought it was the right thing to do.'

'So, you wouldn't think I was awful if I stayed at home.'
It was Win now.

Thomasin smiled at the pretty but drawn face. 'Good Lord
no, you've had enough sickness without having to suffer the
mal-de-mer variety on top. And there's no need for you to
go either, Nick.' She turned to her grandson. 'Unless you
especially feel you must. Stay home and look after Win. You
can go to Ireland any day. It's only us old'ns who're short
on time.'

'Hey, don't be lumping me in with that statement,' objected
Dickie, then looked at his wife. 'Dust, you might as well come
for the trip; it'll be a bit lonely here for you.'

'You mean how will I possibly last a few days without
your company.' She shook her head smilingly. 'I'll welcome
the rest. No, you go ahead. Anyway, it should really be just
for you and your mother.'

Of the same mind, Thomasin made no objection.

'We'll stay and keep you company, Aunt,' offered Win.

'Eh, hang on. I do have work to see to,' Nick reminded
her.

'A few days alone won't harm me,' vouched Dusty. 'I can
put it to good use.' That use remained a secret. Only Dickie
guessed that she would spend the time getting to know their
children. He laid an arm over her shoulder.

'Good, that's all settled then,' said Thomasin. 'Sonny,
will you make the arrangements, love?' He asked when for
and, swamped by the awful feeling that she was going to
die before she could see Pat's birthplace, she answered, 'As
soon as possible.'

'Are you all right, love?' Erin touched her arm.

'Aye . . .' Thomasin's mouth smiled, but her eyes showed
the truth. 'I'm just tired – oh, that sounds like the solicitor.
Better fetch the girls down, Sonny, they'll probably get a
mention.'

On everyone being gathered in the drawing room, the solicitor began the reading of Pat's will. Nick picked his nails idly, waiting for the real stuff to begin. He had no idea what was in that document – unusual for Nicholas who knew everyone's business – but it had not been drawn up until Pat's return from Ireland. Unlike his wife, Pat had been too superstitious to commit anything to paper until he had known he was actually dying.

'. . . *Everything to be left in the capable hands of my wife, who I know will dispose of it fairly in the event of her own testimony* . . .'

Nick's heart bounced. Surely he had misheard?

'*God bless you all, my loves, and forgive me. I am just too tired.*'

Nick was still waiting when the will was folded and the solicitor excused himself to go to another appointment.

Thomasin's eyes embraced him and the others apologetically. 'I wouldn't've dragged you all down if I'd realised . . . he never showed it to me.' She glanced at her grandson. His mood did not require clairvoyancy. 'Never mind, you'll all be looked after when I go.'

'Behave yourself,' chided Erin. 'We don't want your money.'

'I know, love, but I just feel . . .' Her tone changed to one of pique. 'Eh, your father never was one for making decisions, leaving everything up to me . . . I know why he's done this, so's there's no squabble over unfairness.'

Erin looked pained. 'He thought we'd only be interested in what he'd left us?'

'No, no, but even in the closest of families there's always someone who thinks he's been hard done by.'

'I'm sure there's no one here who . . .' Erin broke off to donate a penetrating glance at her brother. 'Oh aye, maybe you're right.'

Dickie replied caustically, 'Oh, give her a piece of leather to chew on, somebody.' Josie thought it wise to dismiss the girls.

'See!' cried Thomasin. 'You're at each other's throats even with nothing to fight over – that's exactly what your father wanted to avoid and you're doing it just the same. I think when I go I'll leave the whole bloody lot to charity.' There was silence. 'Aye, I thought that'd quieten you down. Well, you can just buck your ideas up else it won't just be an idle threat.'

Dickie consulted his brother. 'D'ye think we should do her in now while her will's in our favour?'

His joke broke the tension. 'I shouldn't bother,' said his mother tartly. 'You were cut out of it years ago.'

He laughed in acceptance of the truth and came to cuddle her. 'You bloody old villain, don't pretend ye won't enjoy doling Dad's cash out – sixpence for you, threepence for you, a kick up the arse for our Dickie.' He dodged her swipe. 'Well, if I'm not gonna benefit from the ould bugger's will, the least ye can do is pay my fare to Ireland.'

Thomasin caught hold of his hand and smiled sadly. Her next words were not just for him but for everyone. 'He did love you, you know.'

'We know, Mam,' replied Erin softly. 'We know.'

'I never for one moment imagined it would be like this.' Thomasin stepped from the carriage into the windswept Irish landscape and stared around her. 'The way he spoke of it, it seemed like . . . Paradise.'

Erin was staggered, too. Admittedly, it was a beautiful sweeping landscape with a granite mountain that looked purple in this light – but so wild, so forbidding somehow. Both of them found it hard to equate it with Pat's warm nature. There was virtually nothing here; no streets, no shops, no people, just wilderness. If Thomasin had hoped to alleviate her suffering by coming here then she had been misleading herself.

On the journey over from Castlebar they had been treated to one of the spontaneous downpours that are special to Ireland. There were no warning spots, just a deluge. Luckily, they had been in the carriage and the only inconvenience had been the loss of a view; the shower had been so heavy that it had blocked the windows as effectively as a curtain. They had been forced to look at one another and listen to the drumming on the roof. It had ended as abruptly as it had begun – though this was of no consequence to the poor driver and his horses who were still drenched now, a condition exacerbated by the cutting wind that had welcomed them to Pat's birthplace.

Dickie rubbed his hands together and hunched his shoulders against the cold. 'God, I'm bustin' for a pee,' he muttered to his brother whose face glowed red from the climate. He looked round for some cover, but the nearest bush was some distance away.

The womenfolk had begun to move in the direction of the imposing mountain. Looking back, Thomasin saw that her sons were not following and paused for them to catch up.

'You go on!' Sonny's voice competed with the wind. 'We're just having a wander down this way. I can do with one myself,' he added to Dickie.

'Men,' smiled Thomasin to Erin as they walked on. 'They can never hold their water.'

In the shelter of the clump of gorse, they relieved the pressure on their bladders. As he went about his business, Dickie's narrowed eyes spotted a few cottages. 'Christ, there are folk here. How the devil do they survive? it wouldn't do for me.' A cloud of steam rose around their feet.

'Me neither,' admitted Sonny, though he did have a sudden desire to paint the scene and damned the oversight that had allowed him to leave his colours at home. One day, though, he would come back. 'It might look more friendly in the summer.' He buttoned his trousers and refastened his overcoat. 'I wouldn't mind coming back for a holiday with Josie and the kids. They could stop a bit closer to civilization . . .'

'Civilization?' laughed Dickie. 'In Ireland?' He had made constant grumbles about their hotel which was fabled to be the most modern in Castlebar.

'. . . and I,' continued Sonny, 'could spend a few days camping out here.'

'Let me guess.' Dickie adjusted his clothes. 'Ye want to paint it.'

Sonny laughed with him. 'Well, I think it'd look rather good on the wall. You know,' he placed imaginary blocks of letters in the air, '*Here began the Feeney clan* . . . sort of thing.'

Dickie looked around. 'Mam's right. I never expected this, did you?'

Sonny shrugged. 'I don't know what I expected really . . .'

After this, the brothers seemed at a loss as to what to do. A sudden gust whipped the younger man's hat away. He chased it over several yards, pounced and jammed it back on his head, then turned towards his brother, anticipating more laughter, but Dick had a handkerchief to his nose . . . ah no, when Sonny came nearer he saw that the handkerchief was attending his brother's eyes. Dick felt the comforting hand on his arm, wiped his tears, blew his nose and made a joke. 'It was a bloody long way to come for a pee.'

'Aye . . . but at least we can say we've seen it. God, this wind's making my ears ache.' Sonny rubbed at them, but the moment his hands fell away they throbbed again.

'Mine too. C'mon, let's head back.'

They searched the landscape with their eyes, spotted two small figures which were Thomasin and Erin and began to head for them. 'When we get home,' said Sonny, fighting to get his words out as the wind fought just as hard to put them back in his mouth, 'you and Dusty might like to spend a weekend in Leeds.'

Dick took an extra long stride over a boggy patch. 'Great, we'd love to. I kinda hoped I might have an invitation from Nick, but no.' He caught his brother's unease. 'Don't worry, Son, I haven't come home to stir up any trouble. Nick made it very plain that he only regards me as an uncle.'

'And how do you regard him?'

After weighing the consequences of any admission, Dick was truthful. 'I guess I look upon him as my son, even though I was never a father to him – but that's kinda natural, ain't it? Anyway, as I said, as far as Nick's concerned he's only got one father. He had some good things to say about you.'

The path was made uneven by clumps of gorse and heather; Sonny veered to his right. 'Oh? Go on then, embarrass me.'

Dickie repeated Nick's statement, adding, 'You're a very lucky man.'

Sonny smiled. 'Aye, I know.' He watched his sister and mother hanging onto one another, stumbling through the heather, their black coats flapping like crows' wings. 'When I think of all the heartache our Erin's been through . . .'

'Ah come on, you've had your own share of tragedy, what with Rosie . . .'

'She was yours too,' cut in Sonny.

'I lost her years ago,' came his brother's dull reply.

'Aye well . . .' Sonny's expression was scarred by memory. 'I have to admit it was bloody terrible. You don't expect your children to die before you do. But, apart from the time I thought you'd died in that fire, Rosie's death's been the only real tragedy in my life,' – he seemed to have discounted the bad years of his first marriage – 'whereas Erin's seems to

140

have been full of loss and struggle of one kind or the other: she lost her husband, her baby, had to put up with Grandma saying that Belle was an imbecile . . .'

'An' now she's got her detested brother back from the dead.'

'Oh now,' coaxed Sonny. 'She doesn't detest you. Surely you can understand her anger?' His ears were purple now.

Dickie puffed out his cheeks then gave a wan nod. 'I'm sorry for what I did to everybody. Especially to you. I know it's been said in our letters to each other, but words on paper, they don't mean much, do they?'

Sonny smiled and clapped a hand to his brother's shoulder. 'I'll tell you, Dick, those words of yours meant a hell of a lot to me after thinking you were dead all those years.'

Dickie grinned, then heaved a sigh. 'Ah dear . . . it's a funny old life, ain't it? You with all those kids an' me with none.'

'What's so bloody funny about that?' asked Sonny in mock offence. 'You make it sound as if you didn't think I had it in me.'

Dickie gave a cheeky smile. 'Well, it did take ye a long time to find out how to use it.' He widened the subject. 'Did ye hear that Dusty wants to adopt some of Belle's children?'

'No – some, you said?' Sonny missed his footing and swore before righting himself.

'Three o' the buggers.' Dickie made a face. 'She must think I'm Doctor Barnardo. Keep it under your hat in front of Erin, though. 'Twas Mam's idea. At least, she told Dusty that Belle wanted to find homes for them. Dusty didn't need much encouragement. She's got it into her head that if we get to know them before Belle comes back we're over the first hurdle.'

'I don't want to disillusion her but I have a feeling she's

wrong there,' said Sonny. 'Belle can take a lot of convincing. Still, I wish you luck.'

'I'm not sure it's what I want – I don't mean luck, I'll probably need plenty of that. No, I mean the kids. See, they're not blood kin. Oh, they're nice enough little things, but I don't really feel anything for them, Son, not like I do for your wee lad an' Johnny.' He smiled at the thought of the latter.

Sonny felt a twinge of alarm, but suppressed it. He was being much too possessive. 'You might like them more when you get to know them.'

'Not young Freddie, I won't.' Dick was unshakable. 'The little . . . D'ye know what he called me? A bugger!' His brother laughed and Dickie had to join him. 'The little rat. I'd've clipped him if I hadn't thought it'd ruin Dusty's chances of adopting the girls. Anyway, hush up,' they were nearing the women, 'I don't want Erin sticking her two pennorth in and spoiling things.'

He took ten more steps then put an arm round his mother. 'Ye look freezin'. Was there nothing up that way for ye to see?'

'There's nothing much to see at all, is there?' Thomasin, face pinched with cold, gazed round her. 'I don't think I'll be setting up shop here. Well . . . I suppose I've done what I came to do. I'm off back to sit in the carriage where it's a bit warmer. You three don't have to go yet, if you don't want.'

But they too had seen enough. Leaning into the wind they fought their way back to the cart track. With his passengers huddled inside the carriage, the thankful driver steered his horses back towards Castlebar. All this way just for a ten minute walk in the heather – and at this time of year! But then he ought to have known he was in for trouble when he'd heard the English accents. Didn't everyone know the English were bloody mad?

Thomasin rolled sad eyes for one last glimpse of Patrick's birthplace. Somewhere back there, in a little pocket of turf nestled his favourite pipe. You're a daft ould biddy, she heard him say, before turning her eyes towards home.

When they got back to York it was to an empty house, save for the staff. According to the cook, Dusty had gone to visit Belle's children. Erin met this news with interest, and her brother prepared for some caustic remark, but none came. Their luggage was toted away and unpacked by the manservant, baths were drawn and clean clothes laid out, whilst Vinnie prepared a most welcome hot meal. Afterwards, Sonny told his mother that he had better transport himself home, 'Unless you particularly want me to stay?'

'No, you get back, love. Give those bairns a kiss from their Nan.'

'I will.' Sonny looked at his brother. 'Would you and Dusty like to come with me, stay at our place for a week? I don't mind hanging on till she gets back.'

'I'd like to,' Dickie showed enthusiasm, 'but maybe we'd better wait a while.'

His mother caught the inference. 'Eh! I don't know why everyone should think I need taking care of as though I'm an invalid. I've been looking after you lot for years. Get yourselves off if you want to. Erin, a break might do you good as well.'

'Aye, she'd no doubt feel better for breaking my neck,' whispered Dickie to his brother.

If Erin heard then she made no riposte. 'I've had a long enough break,' she told her mother. 'I've decided I'm off back to the factory tomorrow, if you'll be all right?'

'Will you behave!' reproved Thomasin. 'Anybody'd think I was senile.' Her younger son asked when she might be returning to work. Her reply was apathetic. 'I don't know as

I'll bother. Not for a while, anyway. Maybe I'll get together with Francis next week, just to check that I'm not on the verge of bankruptcy.'

'Well, if you need any company all you have to do is pick up the telephone,' Sonny told her.

Dickie excused himself to go upstairs and pack a few things for his stay in Leeds. 'Get John to do that,' his mother called after him. 'That's what he's paid for, the lazy article.'

Dick replied that the man could polish the brass on the car, tarnished by January fog. It wouldn't take him a moment to pack. Three minutes later, he answered a tap at his bedroom door with a shout of, 'Come in!' and looked surprised to see it was Erin.

'I only knocked in case you were prancing about in the buff.' His sister's voice was chilly. 'Not because you deserve the courtesy.' She closed the door and came up to him.

'Oh, do come in.' Dickie gave a mocking flourish of his hand.

She folded her arms under her breast. 'It won't take long.'

'I see.' Dickie smiled knowingly. 'Now the religious ceremony's over, the ritual slaughter begins. I wondered when ye'd get down to it.'

'Yes, well some of us do have respect for our dead father,' she responded, before launching straight into her planned speech. 'You come back here expecting us all to welcome ye with open arms – well, let me tell you that *this* one!' – she stabbed her chest – '*this* one is never going to forgive ye for what ye've done to our family. You killed him! Ye know that.' Before he could ask how she had worked that out, she told him. 'The times he an' Mother forgave ye, took ye back. When I think of the way they mourned you after that fire, called you a bloody hero! My God! And they each blamed themselves for your death. Would ye credit

144

that? I had to watch my parents grow further and further apart because of you! Mam spent every hour at her shop 'cause she couldn't bear the thought of being at home with him because he reminded her so much of you – though God knows the resemblance is only skin deep!'

'Why, Erin,' said her brother affably, 'I didn't realise I'd upset ye quite so much. You'll be giving me a refund next.' At her frown of incomprehension, he told her, 'The money I left ye in my will, remember? Ye won't be wanting it now if I'm so repulsive to ye.' Gritting her teeth, Erin sped from the room. 'Er . . . don't forget the twenty-six years' interest!' he called merrily.

She was back in no time at all to fling a cheque at him. 'There! You're right, I want nothing from you!'

Dickie smiled pleasantly and looked at the angry scrawl on the cheque. 'I can't quite make this out. *Pay A. Bastard . . .*'

'Ye've no conscience at all, have ye?' yelled Erin. 'You slither in after twenty-six years an' expect everybody to throw their arms around you! Well, I know your game . . .'

'Oh, do ye?' Dickie pocketed the cheque and folded another article of clothing into the case.

'Yes, I bloody-well do! I've realised what all this is about; all ye've come here for is to scout for some children because your wife can't have any.'

'Hogwash!' he sneered. 'If I wanted children I didn't need to come thousands o' miles, I could've got them in America.'

Erin mirrored his scorn. 'I don't doubt you've sired any amount, but not on your wife. Why else would she be visiting Belle's children unless she was after adopting one?'

Dick grabbed another shirt. 'Hang it all! She's had to have something to do while I've been in Ireland.'

'There's more to it than that! Well, let me tell you that if I have my say ye won't be getting your children from Belle or anybody else, because you're not fit to be a father!'

In the brief raging pause, her brother said in defence, 'Look, Erin, I can understand ye feeling that way about me, but taking it out on Dusty . . .'

'I have no cause to feel sympathy for Dusty! She's as much to blame as you are. She could've written to Mother an' Father at any time to say you were alive but she didn't, so don't either of ye expect me to feel sorry for yese, ye've got everything ye deserve.'

Dickie ceased trying to be reasonable. 'You ought to get married again, our lass. Being deprived of a man's turned you into a right bitch.'

'And you're a . . . shithouse!' she yelled before storming out.

Dickie stared at the door for a second, then, in angry fashion, resumed his packing. Who the devil was she to tell him he wasn't fit to be a parent? He was as good as anybody else, and if he wanted to adopt those children then he sure as hell would!

They travelled to Leeds in Dickie's car as, prior to their trip to Ireland, Sonny had come to York by train. The younger brother was given control of the steering wheel. Despite this occupation, he could not help noticing how unusually subdued Dickie was. After a few miles of silence, he just had to comment on it. 'I noticed our sister followed you when you went to pack.'

'Aye,' muttered Dickie, staring out at the winter fields. 'She's had her little word with me.' His brother said he hoped it was a forgiving one. 'Has "shithouse" become a term of endearment in my absence?'

His wife looked highly disapproving. 'Erin wouldn't be so vulgar.'

'Wouldn't she? If we're allowed to stay there long enough ye'll hear better words than that. She might look like a lady but somebody forgot to inform her gob. That bloody sister of ours, Son . . . she's gonna try an' put the kibosh on our adoption plans.'

Dusty sat upright, gripping the back of the driver's seat. 'You didn't say anything when I came in!' He had simply given her two minutes to throw some clothes into a bag and whisked her into the car.

'That's because I don't intend for it to make any difference,' he said blithely. 'It's not Lady Effingham who has the say.'

Dusty brushed the reassurance aside. 'Just tell me what was said, if you please!' When Dickie conveyed the brief details of the exchange, she groaned and covered her mouth. Her brother-in-law tried to offer some comfort, saying that Belle wouldn't be swayed by what her mother said, she would make up her own mind. Behind the worried green eyes, Dusty's mind fumbled for a solution. 'Maybe if I speak to Erin . . .'

'Don't,' advised her husband.

Dusty bounced up and down with the motion of the car over the rough road. 'I've got to repair the damage you've . . .'

'Just don't.'

'Why? Come on, Dickie, you haven't told me everything, have you?' Even under her glare, he refused to enlarge, but she guessed. 'I see,' she said slowly. 'She blames me as well.'

'There's no reason for you to take any notice o' what she thinks, Dust.'

'She still thinks it though, doesn't she?' Dusty looked at the back of her brother-in-law's head and asked softly, 'Do you blame me, Sonny, for not letting you know Dick and I were together?'

''Course not.' Sonny looked to right and left at the junction, then pulled across the road. 'I blame that wretch sitting

147

beside you.' His tone conveyed that it was not a genuine accusation.

Dickie took her gloved hand. 'Don't worry, darlin'. Son'll put in a good word for us with Belle, won't ye, Son?'

Sonny didn't answer. How could he honestly tell his niece that Dick would make a good father? He had no idea of the kind of living that his brother was making for himself in America, nor of his motives for wanting the children – was it just to please his wife? He had said himself that he felt nothing for them. Would Dick be as irresponsible to them as he had been towards the rest of his family?

He changed the subject. 'We'll cheer you up when we get to Leeds, Dusty,' he said brightly over his shoulder. 'Those girls of ours'll keep you occupied.'

Sonny's house was actually situated outside the borough of Leeds at Roundhay, away from the smoking chimneys of mill and factory. In this elevated position its eight gables were visible for some time before they reached it. It had been built for its previous owner in the early 1870s, making it a mere youngster beside Thomasin's Georgian residence. Even so, it lacked some of Peasholme's more modern facilities. It was smaller too, but here the disparity ceased for, being away from the city, almost every window displayed a section of rolling Yorkshire countryside.

The interior, as might be expected, was furnished with materials designed by the owner. The walls, too, held examples of Sonny's expertise – not simply the paintings but the wallpaper. Most of the furniture was modern and the visitors were surprised to learn that Josie was the originator of this; to look at her one would never dream she had such progressive taste.

They did have a marvellous time in Leeds. Weaned on Yorkshire hospitality, Josie was a splendid hostess and it was plain to see the root of her corpulence when dinner was served: barely an inch of table had been wasted, with enormous vessels of soup, steamed turbot, honeyroast ham, several types of fowl, huge and elaborately-sculptured pies, stacks of vegetables and a variety of rich desserts. Dick fell into raptures with each mouthful and swore that he would seduce Josie's cook home to America with him.

Overnight, snow fell and by morning there were several inches to provide much hearty occupation. The entire family joined in the fun, though Dickie only lasted an hour, which was his usual limit for concentrating on any one thing. Banging his hands together to knock the compressed snow from his gloves, he announced that he was frozen and asked if anyone was joining him for coffee. His wife hurled a snowball and called him a sissy. At which, he scóoped up a handful of snow and pursued her shrieking around the garden until he caught her and rubbed it all over her face. Amelia thought it hilarious to see two old people behaving in such a fashion. The sight provoked thought from her father, too: Dick and his wife were like a pair of young lovers, whereas he and Josie had grown too comfortable.

'Isn't any of yese coming to keep me company?' beseeched Dickie, backing towards the house.

'I'll come!' Feen, who had been hovering at her uncle's flank ever since his arrival stumbled through the snow, her face gleaming with cold and adoration.

'There y'are,' Dickie called to his wife. 'I don't need the likes o' you any more when I've got this scrumptious damsel.' He wrapped an arm around Feen's shoulders and led her up to the house.

'Hang on!' shouted Josie. 'I think I've had enough too. Come on, John.' When Sonny showed reluctance to follow she hissed through her smile, 'We're not leaving him alone with Feen, now come on.'

Sonny shook his head at the silly notion, but nevertheless he left the revellers to accompany her. Robbed of the opportunity to be alone with her uncle, Feen's smile waned to disappointment, compensated only by the large hand on her shoulder.

'Eh, knock that snow off your boots!' Josie pulled her brother-in-law back as he was about to march straight in.

He complied in exaggerated manner. 'D'ye want I should walk on me hands?'

Josie gave him a push, then laughed as he pretended to go flying. 'Just take your boots off at the door, please.'

'Give us a hand, Feen, darlin'.' Dickie raised a dripping boot on which Feen gladly hauled.

In stockinged feet, all padded from the kitchen entrance to find indoor footwear. 'Feen, your dress is soaked,' observed her mother. 'Go and change it.'

The girl bounded off and the adults retired to the drawing room. Once provided with cups of coffee by the butler, all three stood smiling at the window overlooking the garden, watching the others have the time of their lives, until the draught from the glass drove them back to the fire. Dickie settled his full length on the sofa and picked up a newspaper, balancing the cup and saucer on his chest while he rustled through the pages. Sonny smiled at his wife. 'Make yourself at home, Dick.'

'I'm just seeing if there's anything on at the theatre.'

'Don't waste your precious eyesight,' Sonny told him, 'it's all arranged. I telephoned the store and asked Nick to book us some seats at the Grand. I believe it's a farce, so it shouldn't stretch your intelligence.'

Dickie folded the paper into a manageable position and lifted the cup and saucer from his chest to take a drink. Feen, in a change of clothes, returned and came to sit on the arm of the sofa where her uncle lay.

'It's not Sunday, is it?' Josie looked her daughter up and down.

'Mother, you're always telling me I'm untidy,' argued Feen, and brushed at her best dress in embarrassment at being shown up in front of her uncle.

Josie sniffed the air suspiciously, then asked her husband, 'Have you washed your feet lately?'

'It's him!' An indignant Sonny stabbed a finger at his brother.

'Never,' said Dick vehemently. 'You can't smell them, can you, Feen?' She shook her head. After browsing over a few pages he grinned and said, 'Eh, you kept quiet about this, didn't ye?' Sonny enquired what it was and his brother waved the paper at him. 'This painting of yours up for auction at Sotheby's – fetched seven hundred an' fifty quid.'

Sonny snatched the newspaper. 'I never saw anything . . .' His eyes pored over the page.

'Well, I can't admit to having acquired a knowledge of the art world while I've been in America, it's just that my eyes naturally gravitate towards large sums of money. When's the shareout gonna be, then?'

Sonny was smiling; he had found the article. 'Sorry, it isn't mine – at least I don't own it any more. I sold it to a man called Lewis in the Seventies for ten guineas.'

Dick was scathing. 'You silly sod.' His sister-in-law buried her chin into her neck to mark her disapproval. Feen blushed and pretended not to have heard.

'I thought it was a fortune then.' Sonny's smile diluted as he read the next line. 'Oh, it's been auctioned as part of Lewis' estate. Poor man . . . I didn't know. I haven't seen him in ages.' He handed the paper to his wife for her to read.

Dickie was eyeing the walls which held a large collection of his brother's work. 'I wouldn't mind having one o' them if ye've any going spare.'

151

'Surely,' came the generous offer. 'Which would you like?'

Dickie shrugged. 'Any'll do.'

Sonny barked a laugh and shook his head in Josie's direction. His brother asked what was so funny. 'Don't you ever think in anything other than material terms, Feeney?'

'I don't see what's wrong in that. I'm proud of you doing so well for yourself. Wake me up when it's time to eat.' Dickie closed his eyes, crossed his ankles and went to sleep.

'Trying to figure out how much that one would bring?' Sonny had sneaked up on his brother who, on his way down to tea, had dallied to examine the huge family portrait which hung at the top of the first flight of stairs.

For once Dickie didn't seem in jocular mood. His eyes on the picture, he said dolefully, 'It kinda pulled me up, seeing all the family there . . . an' me not on it.'

'You are on it.' Sonny pointed out the picture within a picture; a portrait of Dickie hanging on the wall behind the group of people.

'Aye, I noticed that . . . but it's a picture of a dead man, stuck away behind the others.'

Sonny knew what his brother meant. When he had created the others' portraits there had been something, some*one*, missing from the group. He could hardly paint his brother in as if Dickie were still alive, so he had added the framed portrait to the backdrop, painting Dickie from memory and old photographs. His eyes wandered over the other characters. Two of those were dead now: Rosie and his father. After a little more thought, he said to his brother, 'I could always paint you in.' At Dickie's surprise, he added, 'You don't think I managed to paint the entire family at one sitting, d'you? I did them all separately.' He remembered the trouble he'd had in getting the ten year old Rosie to sit still. 'It'll be simple enough to squeeze you on. I'll have it taken down tomorrow. When I've prepared the canvas you can sit pretty for me.' Adding another body would put the picture totally out of balance, but his brother's pleasure made up for any technical shortcoming.

'As a matter of interest,' said Dickie, 'how much would ye charge for a family group like that?'

'To you . . . five hundred.'

'You're jokin'!'

'That's a ten percent discount for relatives.'

'Bloody hell.' Dickie was amazed. 'That's what artists are charging these days?'

'Only the famous ones like me.' Sonny grinned. 'I have to make the most of my talents. What with concentrating on design I don't have much time for portraiture these days.'

Dickie looked interested. 'But you were being serious when ye said you're famous?'

'A few people might have heard of me, yes,' said his brother modestly. In fact, he was highly acclaimed, both here and on the Continent – though it rankled that The Royal Academy had not yet seen fit to make him a member. Sonny believed that this oversight stemmed from sheer snobbery at his humble beginnings; it could certainly not be lack of talent. He spotted Paddy coming down the stairs and shouted to him, 'Hold onto the banister!' The child showed impatience, but reached dutifully for the support and came down to meet the men. 'Honestly, the times I've told him,' breathed Sonny to his brother. 'He'll be coming down head first one of these days.'

Dickie made a grab for the boy and swung him off the stairs, laughing. 'We have to show our manhood, don't we, Paddy? Can't be hanging onto the banisters for the rest of our lives.'

'Eh, don't you be teaching him your bad habits,' warned

Sonny as his brother galloped down the staircase, jiggling the child up and down.

'Tell your father he's an old fusspot,' said Dick, and laughed when Paddy followed his instruction. 'Me an' you are going to be great pals, aren't we, Pad? Will we go out for a snowfight before tea?'

'Oy, no!' Sonny intercepted the cry of agreement from his son. 'Josie'll go mad, she's just got him dry – oh, and I have to tell you to curb your language if you'd be so kind.'

Dickie groaned. 'Bloody women! Looks like we'll have to find something else to do, Paddy. What d'ye fancy?' They had reached the hall.

'Draw me a picture,' said his nephew.

Sonny laughed at the resultant expression and said he would fetch some paper. In the minutes that preceded tea, Dickie set about imitating his brother's skills, with not too great success. Paddy, sitting on his lap, studied the finished drawing. 'What is it?'

'What is it!' Dickie voiced his affront. 'Don't ye know a cow when ye see one?'

'Daddy doesn't draw cows like that.' Paddy frowned at the cow's underbelly. 'Where're its dumplings?'

Dickie tutted at the ripple of amusement from the others. 'It's a bullock.'

'Oh . . .' said Paddy. Then after a moment's ponderance asked, 'Uncle Dickie, what's the difference between a cow and a bullock?'

'Don't ye know that at your age?' cried Dick. He pointed to the drawing. Josie sat forward in alarm. 'A bullock's horns point frontwards an' a cow's horns point sideways.' He grinned at the others over the small auburn head, then admired his handiwork again. 'How much d'ye think I'd get for this, Son? Two-fifty?'

Sonny nodded. 'A worthy successor to Landseer.'

Paddy was reaching for a piece of paper of his own, saying he would draw his Uncle Dickie a cow. Whilst lying on the carpet he spotted a beetle and poked it. When, after a few goadings, it failed to move, Paddy looked up at his father and asked, 'Is that dead?' Sonny nodded. 'Is it going to Heaven?'

His father dodged the question, leaning over to ask, 'How much of that picture have you done?' and sneaking his hand over the dead beetle.

Some minutes later the picture was held aloft for inspection. Dusty tittered at her husband. 'It's better than yours!'

He grimaced. 'Paddy, ye've made me feel really great – being outdrawn by a four year old.'

Feen was cross at the others for mocking her uncle, and told him, 'It's better than I could do.' To which the ever-critical Sophia replied that anything would be better than Feen could do.

Dick screwed his own picture up and lobbed it at the fireplace. 'No, I have to admit I'm no artist. Just as well I've brought my camera – hey, don't let me forget, I want some snapshots of you all before we go back. Especially you, Feen. Have to show the folks back home what a true English rose looks like.' Sonny answered that their father would turn in his grave to hear this; the Irish blood might be diluted but it was still an important heritage.

'Look!' Paddy toured the assembly, thrusting the picture into each face. 'Look at my good painting. Look, it's better than Uncle Dickie's.'

'I fear we've a member of the Italian school among us,' the boy's father apologised. 'The Great Braggadocio – Paddy, true talent does not need to sing its own praises.'

Paddy argued that he was only repeating what his aunt had said, then asked out of the blue. 'Why did you put that beetle in your pocket, Father?'

Sonny was spared having to answer as the butler arrived to announce that tea was ready and everyone rose.

'Leave your pencils behind, Paddy,' ordered his mother. 'We don't want your handiwork on the tablecloth.'

'Bloody women,' sighed the little boy.

Josie stopped and wheeled in outrage. 'I *beg* your pardon?'

Paddy looked up at her artlessly. 'Uncle Dickie says it.'

'Oh, does he?' Josie glared at her brother-in-law who was laughing fit to burst. 'Well, I don't want to hear you saying it – nor anybody else in this house, else they'll be getting a cauliflower ear.'

'I don't like cauliflower,' sulked Paddy.

'Then keep your mouth clean!' Josie jabbed a thumb at the dining room.

'After you, Paddy,' invited his uncle. 'I'm not partial to cauliflower either – on second thoughts there's safety in numbers!' Grabbing Paddy, he used him as a shield as he jigged past his sister-in-law and ran laughing to the table.

'That brother of yours,' grumbled Josie as she and Sonny brought up the rear. 'I thought you were going to tell him about his behaviour. I can't have Paddy learning words like that.'

'Hey, Josie!' Dickie called from his seat at the table. 'This young fella wants to say something else to ye.'

'I don't wish to hear it!'

'Oh, ye do! Go on, Pad,' he whispered, 'say it like I told ye.'

'You've got lovely eyes, Mammy.' Paddy beamed.

When everyone laughed, Dickie winked and nudged his nephew. 'See what I mean, Pad? A wee bit o' flattery works wonders.'

156

8

On Sunday the family went to early Mass. Dick had been asked the previous night if he would be accompanying them, but he replied that he never visited church these days unless it was for baptisms, weddings and funerals. Josie was most relieved to be told this, knowing that any public appearance with her brother-in-law could only spell worse embarrassment. After returning from church Sonny disappeared. His wife and daughters went to take off their hats and coats and deposit their prayerbooks. On her descent of the stairs, Josie paused to weigh her surroundings; there was something missing but she could not think what it was. Slightly annoyed, she continued to the dining room. Sonny wasn't at the table when she arrived. Over their twenty-two years of marriage she had grown used to his whims. He'd be off painting somewhere.

She was helping herself from the tureen on the sideboard, when she felt two arms girdle her waist and squeeze. 'Ooh, Josie,' groaned her brother-in-law sensuously while his body pressed itself into her back. 'You're gorgeous – not like this skinny wench o' mine.'

'Tell him to behave himself,' was Dusty's advice as Josie squeaked her protest.

Dickie released her. 'Damn, just when I was going to enjoy meself. I knew she'd creep in.' He began to lift the tureen lids. 'Where's himself?' A pink-cheeked Josie smoothed her

157

clothes and said she had no idea. 'Oh aye, I remember now.' Dickie filled his plate. 'He told me he's got an appointment with this woman in Doncaster – oh God, I'm sorry!' He clapped a hand to his mouth. 'I forgot, he told me not to say anything. Josie, I'm *real* sorry.'

'Take no notice, Josie,' advised her sister-in-law with disdain. 'He thinks he's being funny.'

Dickie stuffed bacon into his grin. 'I do know where he is, though. He'll be getting that canvas ready for me. I noticed it'd gone.'

'*That's* what it was!' Josie looked satisfied. 'I knew there was something missing. Well, I hope he isn't planning to work on it all day and neglect you two.'

'No, I'm not then!' Sonny came in, dished himself some food and took a seat at the table. 'I was just getting it ready. I can't do anything till I've made some sketches – you'll sit for me later, Dick?'

His brother consented, then paused in eating. 'Ye know, I was thinking last night . . .'

'Oh God, here comes trouble,' said Sonny.

'That painting was done nearly twenty years ago . . . if you paint me as I am now, it'll be a bit odd, won't it?'

'He means it'll make him look older than his father,' smirked Dusty.

Sonny agreed that this was perfectly true. 'But don't fret, I'll paint out your bald patch.' He laughed as Dickie's hand went involuntarily to his head.

'Hah! Ye wouldn't laugh so loud if ye knew what I was doing with your wife before ye came in,' said Dick with a sly nod.

'You can do what you like with the old scold,' said his brother airily. 'I couldn't give a bent meg.'

Dickie held out his hands. 'See! I told ye he wouldn't mind, Jos – me an' him, we share everything.'

'Share this.' Dusty rapped his knuckles with a spoon. 'That's the way to deal with men, Josie.'

Then the banter was arrested as the girls came in to breakfast.

Their fast broken, Sonny took his brother off to begin sketching. Josie sat and talked with her sister-in-law and the younger ones went to read or draw. At one point the peace was broken by Paddy who howled that someone had stolen his plasticine, but he was soon silenced on being taken for a walk by his Aunt Dusty. Had the latter known the use to which the plasticine had been put, she might have been more concerned. Up in her room the culprit, Feen, saw her aunt going down the drive. Grasping the opportunity, she dashed to the guests' room, tugged some hairs from Dusty's brush and dashed out again. Back in her own room, she twined the hairs around the doll she had fashioned, then studied it in approval. She took a pin from the bowl on her dressing table and after a fearful hesitation, plunged it into the plasticine body. Then she waited for Paddy to come running up the drive alone.

Her aunt returned unscathed. Maybe you have to do it a few times before it works, thought Feen. In this hope she inserted several pins at once. There was panic when one of her sisters barged into her room to tell her that luncheon was ready, but she managed to hide the doll in the folds of her skirt until Amelia had gone. As the day progressed even more pins were inserted, but came the evening and her aunt was still looking remarkably healthy.

Normally, Sabbath at the Feeney house was spent in quiet obeisance, but Dick showed no such respect, linking arms with Sonny's girls whom he had dubbed The Nubiles, telling jokes and tales, rolling on the floor with Paddy and now this evening putting a record on the gramophone and asking Feen to dance. Josie was relieved when the impressionable Paddy was a-bed and her husband hauled his brother away to begin the painting in earnest, and thought it quite humorous when her sister-in-law asked, 'I hope you don't mind Sonny being dragged away like this.'

'Oh, he needs no excuse to paint,' returned Josie. 'Sometimes he just disappears for days on end. Still, I shouldn't complain,' she lowered her voice against eavesdropping girls and laughed confidentially into Dusty's ear. 'At least if he's using all his energy on painting he leaves me alone.'

Dusty found this attitude strange. She could not think of anything worse than Dickie 'leaving her alone' as Josie so delicately put it. 'Do you think you'll have any more children, Josie?'

'My goodness, no!' Josie chuckled, and made sure the girls were busy with their own conversation before whispering, 'I thought I'd finished with all that until Paddy came along. Thank goodness it's done with now. Still, as I said, I shouldn't complain, I realise how lucky I am. I feel so sorry for you, dear.'

Dusty nodded. 'Perhaps I shouldn't mention this, as Belle hasn't been consulted yet, but I'm so thrilled . . . We hope to adopt three of Belle's children.'

'Well, actually John did tell me,' confided her sister-in-law, smiling. 'I think it's wonderful. Don't worry, he warned me not to speak of it in front of Erin. Eh, I don't know, she can be very set in her ways can our sister-in-law. And she's always going on about how disappointed she is that she'll never be a grandmother. I can't understand her – well, I understand her disappointment, but I mean she's always trying to encourage Belle to marry and it's wrong you know, what with her deformity. She'd pass it on to any children – if she could have any, of course. Oh, I didn't mean . . .' She looked guilty and rushed on. 'It's just as well she's as stubborn

160

as her mother. If she's set her mind against marriage – or anything come to that – she won't shift for anyone.' She saw that she had put her foot in it again. 'Oh . . . well, I'm sure when it comes to considering the children's future she'll be sensible. Don't worry about it. We'll all speak up for you.' She noticed that the girls had gone quiet and cautioned Dusty not to proceed with the intimate topic.

The other woman reached for her bag. 'Would you like to look at some old photos we brought with us? I brought them for Mother's benefit really, to try and fill in the missing years.'

Josie put aside her knitting and sorted through the photographs, making suitable comments. 'I'll bet she had a little weep, didn't she – girls, come and look at your aunt's photographs.'

Dusty nodded. 'Let's hope we can make it up to her while we're here.'

Dick had reached his boredom threshold and began to shuffle in his chair. 'Have you nearly finished, Son?' Receiving an exasperated reply he strode over to the easel. 'Christ, is that all ye've done?'

'Maybe I'd get it done quicker if you'd sit frigging still!' Sonny threw his brush down.

'What a temperamental little soul you are – come an' have a drink, ye can always finish it tomorrow.'

'Tomorrow?' It came as a squawk. 'It'll take weeks.'

Dickie groaned disbelievingly, then had a sudden thought. 'Eh, you're not in cahoots with Mam are ye? Trying to keep me here?'

'Josie'd laugh at that.' His brother draped a cloth over the canvas.

Dick formed a crooked grin. 'Yeah, I kinda thought I was outstaying my welcome when Josie shoved some sandwiches under the bedroom door.' Sonny was quick to point out that no slight had been intended by his comment, and told his brother he loved having him here. 'But you'd love me even better if I went home.'

'Dick, I'm not saying this to hurt you, but when you've got children of your own you'll understand . . . you can't be saying the kind of things you do in front of them and expect Josie to be pleased.'

'Sorry, Son, I guess I just took things to be the same as they were when we were boys. I'm forgetting we're all meant to be respectable now. I'll go easy on the cussing for the next fortnight.' He guffawed at Sonny's undisguised shock. 'Don't worry, I'm only joshing yese. We'll be on our way back to York tomorrow morning.'

Sonny grinned. 'I think we can put up with you for another day. Anyway, I want to show you the houses I had built for my millworkers before you go back.' He closed the door on the painting and the two of them went to join their wives.

When her mother and aunt looked up to greet the men, Feen managed to slip a photograph of Dickie into the pocket of her pinafore before the snapshots were handed to her father. Dickie rubbed his hands. 'Gee, it was cold in there – feel.' He clamped his palms to his niece's cheeks. 'Come on, Feen, let's you and me sit in the cosy-corner.' He led her to the cosy-corner seat beside the fireplace, where he adjusted the height of a complexion screen to, 'guard that gorgeous skin from the roaring fire', then squeezed onto the seat beside her.

This closeness was all that Feen had been wishing for, yet at the same time she was frightened. He was so big, made her feel even more bashful and childish. Josie damned the man and hoped he would soon be gone. She announced that it was time for bed. Feen pretended not to have heard, and asked, 'Uncle Dickie, do you like horses?' He replied that

162

he did. 'Will you come riding with me tomorrow morning before breakfast? I'm not allowed to go out alone and no one will ever go with me on these cold mornings.' Josie said it would be dark but no one appeared to take note.

'It would be an honour, my dear – about seven?' He scooped up her hand and kissed it, whispering, 'Better go to bed now. Ye wouldn't have me take a hiding from your mother for keeping ye up so late?'

'You really shouldn't lead the poor girl on like that, you know,' scolded Dusty when they were in bed. 'She idolizes you – and you shouldn't've promised to go riding with her. You know what you're like at that time of morning.' Dickie muttered that if he had said he would go then he would go, that was if she didn't keep him talking all night. She snuggled up to him. 'How much longer are we staying, Dick?' He gave the opinion that it was usually him who got fed-up first. 'I'm not fed-up, I've had a lovely time. I just want to get back to the squiblings. I miss them.' Whilst the family had been in Ireland she had spent virtually the whole time at Belle's, helping Sally to wash and dress the little ones, telling stories, playing with dolls. 'Fred's not a bad little soul when you bother to talk to him – very intelligent, in fact. He was telling me things I didn't know. And he kept asking when you'd be back. He likes you, you know.'

'Does he?' Dick sounded pleased. 'Well, I guess he's not so bad himself . . . with a mask on. Ow! You little . . .' He rubbed his injured stomach. 'Right, that's the last time you strike me, woman, I'm exerting my rights. If it happens again, I'll . . . I'll get my pal Josie to come and sit on you – aagh! Mercy!' She had bent one of his fingers back.

'Then kindly stop demeaning folk. There's more to people than physical appearance.'

'Yeah, I realise that, darlin',' he replied sincerely. 'Otherwise I'd never have married you, would I?'

His loud laughter under his wife's tickling assault was the last noise Feen heard before she fell asleep. Throughout the night she woke several times with a start to shine her torch on the bedside clock, dreading that she would oversleep. In between naps, she pictured her uncle's strong arm encircling her waist, lifting her onto his steed, and the two of them galloping away. A dowdy old woman would rush out of the house and beg Dickie not to leave, and he would look down on her pityingly and say, 'I'm sorry, Dusty, but you see I've fallen in love with Feen . . . goodbye.'

She slipped her hand into her nightgown and touched the photograph which she intended to keep next to her heart always, wondering if he were awake too, and trying desperately to exclude the woman who slept beside him.

At six, Feen was roused by the light tread of the housemaid on her way down from her attic room. At six forty-five she was dressed in her brown tweed riding habit and tripping excitedly over the yard to the stable block. Uncle Dickie was not yet up, but she was fifteen minutes early and it was still quite dark. The groom had already received instructions last night from his master to saddle a horse for Mr Richard and a chestnut hack stood clinking his bit beside Feen's solid pony. At the groom's information that it was five to seven, Feen mounted and led the chestnut out into the slushy grey morning. There was light and movement at one of the windows. Feen smiled expectantly, but it was only a housemaid pulling the drawing room curtains. Seven came and went. The horses began to stamp and snort. Feen decided to walk them round the house; it would ease their impatience and also alert her Uncle Dick who surely must have overslept.

Through the muzziness of sleep, Dusty heard the crunch of horses' hooves beneath the bedroom window and felt for her husband, encountering hot flesh. Without opening her eyes, she tapped him, receiving a grunt. 'Dickie, Feen's waiting for you to go riding.' There was another more petulant grunt, then silence. As much as she shoved and pinched him, Dick remained oblivious. His wife gave up and snuggled under the covers for another half hour.

It grew lighter. Ignorant of the time, but knowing that her uncle was late, Feen continued to walk the bored horses around the house, searching each window. There was another flash of movement. Her mother was signalling for her to come indoors. Feen tried not to catch her eye but failed and, close to tears, gave her pony a sharp kick in the ribs, steering him back to the warm box.

As she had dreaded, there was a full dining room when she entered. Whether or not the assembly included her uncle, she did not know, for she had neither the courage nor the inclination to lift her eyes from the floor, such was the depth of her misery.

'I shall have to have words with your uncle when he comes in,' said her mother through taut lips – obviously Dick was not present, then. 'Keeping you out like this – you should be changed and ready for lessons. Sit down and get your breakfast.' Josie had not been a supporter of the riding expedition, but her husband had made it clear just what a goose he thought her. 'Did you enjoy your ride? Where did you go?' Feen mumbled something. 'Speak up, dear.'

'I didn't go anywhere,' said Feen, still not lifting her eyes.

Dusty explained to her sister-in-law. 'I'm afraid Dickie overslept. It's one of his faults.'

One of many, thought Josie, but felt relief rather than annoyance. At that point Dick sauntered in, 'Sorry I'm late, folks,' and went to help himself from the tureens on the sideboard with never a look in Feen's direction.

'Please may I be excused?' the girl asked her mother.

Sensing the desperation in her voice and the threat of tears, Josie permitted this and Feen was swift in leaving.

'That was unforgivable, Richard,' accused his wife. 'Not only do you break your promise to Feen but you forget you've ever made it.'

After much brain-racking, Dick slapped a hand to his forehead. 'Oh Christ . . . where is she? I'll have to go and make amends.' Ignoring advice to the contrary he want after his niece. 'Feen!' She had reached the bend in the stairs. Not wanting him to see her tearful face she stood with her back to him. He came bounding past the housemaid who was polishing the mahogany balustrade, planted himself in front of his niece to stop her going any further and took hold of her with gentle hands. 'My dear girl, I ought to be whipped. How can I ever make it up to ye?'

'It's quite all right . . .' She tried not to look at him but he bent his head down to hers and tilted her chin with a finger.

'No, it's not. I ought to be boiled in oil for missing our rendezvous. And me so looking forward to it. It's not much of an excuse, but ye see I didn't get to sleep till very late last night. It's your grandfather, ye know, I can't sleep for thinking about him sometimes. I guess you're the same.' She nodded. 'Aye . . . we all miss him – but it's no excuse for my sleeping in. I said I'd come with ye an' I shoulda been there. I shall have to be punished and you'll be the one to dole it out. What'll it be? Hot irons? The rack? I'm at your sweet mercy, Feen.'

Feen smiled into her breast and said there was no need for anything so drastic. Almost upon them, the maid was forced to keep polishing the same stretch. Over Feen's bent head Dickie looked her up and down, then winked, adding more vim to her elbow. The air was heavy with beeswax. 'Am I forgiven then?' For the first time she met his pleading eyes and the disappointment was flushed away. She smiled and nodded, drawing a sigh of vast relief. 'Ah, you're a wonderful girl! Give me a kiss so's I know ye truly mean it.' He held out his cheek to receive her shy lips. Then Feen slipped past him saying she must go and change for her lessons. 'Hey, hang on! Will ye be allowed to go out riding after these lessons?' With eager face she said that she might. 'I'll check with your father. He wants to show me around his mill this morning, but this afternoon we'll go for that gallop. OK?'

His twinkling eyes followed her dash up the remainder of the stairs. When she was gone he grinned at the housemaid, wiped imaginary sweat from his forehead, said, 'Phew!' then leaned on the section of balustrade that she was waiting to polish. 'And what's your name, then?'

With Feen trying her best to concentrate on her Latin, the rest of Monday morning was devoted to a guided tour of the millworkers' cottages and then the mill itself. For his brother's sake Dickie tried to show some interest, but finally the boredom began to creep into his face.

'. . . and I'm thinking of setting up a library for the workers,' Sonny's tongue appeared to be competing with the clacking looms. 'I think it's important to keep the mind occupied – don't you, Kelly?' He addressed one of the workers.

'Oh, aye, sir!' Kelly nodded respectfully and smiled. 'Very important.'

The party strolled on. However, Dickie went back to wink at a female who had caught his eye and in so doing overheard Kelly say, 'Bloody library – I ask you! What we need is proper shithouses, not reading books. I'm scared to death every time I go in ours in case t'roof falls in on me. He hasn't spent a farthin' on our house in years. Talk about Titus Salt? Titus arseholes!'

Dick found this much to his sense of humour and wasted no time in repeating it to his brother. 'You don't want to have so many hangers-on, Son,' he added at luncheon. 'They'll take ye for everything ye've got and still call you a skinflint.'

Sonny had begun to read the newspaper which he'd only had time to scan that morning. At Dickie's words he threw it down and without reply marched from the room. Dickie looked bemusedly at his sister-in-law who, after a moment, picked up the paper and ran her eyes over the print. Her face darkened and she, too, threw it down in disgust. 'Isn't it marvellous how a few lines can ruin an entire day. He'll be locked away till bedtime now.'

Dickie read the paragraph in which a critic spoke of last Friday's sale of Sonny's painting, saying that it was doubtful whether J. P. Feeney's more recent efforts would fetch such a sum in thirty years' time. '"*His latest style consists of lashing as much paint onto the canvas as one might use for a battleship and would compare with the first efforts of an infant. Where is the shape and form of his earlier works? One cannot tell now where his subject begins and ends . . .*"' Dickie stopped reading and gave the paper a derisive tap. 'But he doesn't take any notice of these blokes, does he? I'd've thought the money his pictures bring speaks for itself.' Ignoring Josie's opinion that it wouldn't do any good, he said he would go and talk to his brother.

It was unnecessary to search far; Dickie had only to follow the sound of crashing. He came to the room where the noise was loudest and tapped on it. Sonny spared him two words. Tapping again, he was asked if he hadn't heard. 'I heard the last word right, but I wasn't sure of the first. I didn't think you'd use such a word to your brother.' There was no responsive laughter. Dickie shrugged and went to rejoin the others.

As Sonny's wife had prophesied, he remained closeted

for the rest of the afternoon, making it impossible for him to grant Feen leave to go riding. With Josie gone shopping accompanied by her sister-in-law, Feen was most concerned that once again her dreams were to be dashed. But Uncle Dickie laughed away any problem and said that she had been granted permission to go riding this morning, hadn't she? And was it her fault that her silly old uncle had overslept? Telling her to climb into her riding togs, he went over to the stable and when she came out of the house he was mounted.

Josie was furious when she came home to the news that her daughter had disobeyed instructions to finish the embroidery she had started last year. There were many chilling looks when the exhilarated pair finally arrived home. Feen was banished to her room and told not to emerge before breakfast – at which time her mother expected to see the embroidery completed – and Dickie was totally ostracised from the female conversation. After many attempts to ingratiate had been rebuffed, not just by Josie but also his wife, Dickie grabbed his small nephew's hand and loped off to another room, where he spent some time playing rough and tumble before collapsing in exhaustion on the sofa. 'Right, Pad, ye've worn your old uncle out, I think I'll take a nap. Run along now.' He closed his eyes.

But Paddy, overexcited with the game, climbed onto the man's chest and bounced up and down shouting and whooping. Dick grew annoyed under the assault. After several attempts had failed to calm the boy, he swung his legs down, sat Paddy on his knee and said he would teach him a song. The ditty was repeated until Paddy was word-perfect. 'Now, d'ye think ye can remember all the words? Good, well you go and sing it for your mammy and show her how clever you are.' The boy scampered off, leaving Dick to close his eyes in peace.

Paddy took the stage before his mother and aunt and

performed the song: *'It's only me from over the sea said Ballocky Bill the sailor . . .'*

. Dickie heard the howl for which he had been waiting. Saved from further interruptions, he grinned and went to sleep.

Thomasin's behaviour after her sons had left caused Erin to change her plans about going back to the factory the following day. It wasn't fair of the boys to go swanning off leaving their mother to her grief; someone should be here to comfort her. Giving the weather as an excuse, she sat with Thomasin round the fire, leafing through albums of old photographs, browsing through memories, though sometimes she had the feeling that her mother didn't know she was here.

The snow barely lasted the weekend. With the rise in temperature great chunks of it began to slither down the roof and fall onto the garden with a thud.

Thomasin jumped as yet another section fell. 'God, there can't be much more to come down, surely? It's been at it since dawn. I bet the river's right up.' After a quick thaw like this the river could not cope with all the water that teemed down from the Dales. 'You might be canoeing to work tomorrow.'

'Ah well, I don't suppose the factory'll close down if I leave it another day or two,' returned Erin.

'You're staying at home for me, aren't you?' said her mother. There was denial, but it did no good. 'Yes you are! I've told you I'll be perfectly all right, now tomorrow you can get yourself off.'

They were briefly interrupted by the arrival of Nick. 'Just called to see how you are, Nan.' He came to the fire, saying hello to his aunt.

Thomasin said she was fine. 'She's not fine,' contradicted Erin. 'She needs cheering up.'

'We can find plenty of work for you to do, Nan.' Her grandson turned his back to the fireplace to warm his cold rear.

Thomasin shrugged apathetically. 'What's the point of working yourself into the ground when all you've got to look forward to is death.'

Erin felt like weeping. 'Mam, don't get too depressed. Ye'll see Dad again one day, ye know.'

This was met by cynicism. 'I wish I had your faith, love. I've been thinking about it a lot lately. Huh! can't get it out of my blasted mind. I mean, when you go to Heaven, always assuming there is such a place, are you still able to see what's going on down here? See every hurt inflicted on your children, your grandchildren? If so, then how can it be Heaven? Tell me that one if you can.'

Erin couldn't, and Thomasin felt sorry she had asked. 'Nay, don't let me get you down too. You go back to work if it'll do you good.'

Erin did not argue – it would benefit her to get out of the house – but said that she would probably only work until lunchtime if the river looked likely to burst its banks and cut off her route home.

Thomasin formed a smile for her grandson and looked up at him, but Nick's eyes were meandering about the room. Why, oh why did she always get the impression that Nick was taking an inventory whenever he came to visit? The thought gave tongue to a pressing issue. 'I shall have to get round to altering my will sometime, what with Dickie being alive and Pat leaving all his assets for me to sort out.'

Nick paid instant attention.

'You're going to include Dickie?' Erin gaped. 'Well, I think you're wrong.'

'Oh, well . . . we'll see.' Apathy returned. 'I can't seem to think straight just now.' She asked Nick, 'Have you seen much of your uncle while he's been in Leeds?'

171

'Very little. He came to the theatre with us one night.' Her grandson's mind was anchored to the will. Why should Dickie share the inheritance after all the pain he had caused? He sought to blacken the man's hopes. 'I fear he's been wreaking havoc at Roundhay. Mother looked very harassed when last I saw her.'

The ploy failed. 'It doesn't take much to harass your mother,' said Thomasin, before asking him to ring for some tea.

It was odd being in the house alone. Oh, there were the servants, but Thomasin only ever saw them when she ordered a pot of tea – which she did quite frequently just to have another human being in the room. Then there was the pain. She hadn't told anyone about it, nor had she consulted the doctor, but she would have to for it was worsening. It had woken her a couple of mornings ago, a nagging ache in her knees. Now it had spread to other joints. Every step had become excruciating. To take her mind off it, she decided to sort through Pat's clothes; this was painful in itself, but was better done now and not left. Once the clothes were on their way to the Salvation Army, she sought out some other occupation to distract her mind, but finding neither the energy nor the enthusiasm, she limped back to her fireside chair.

She was rather glad when Erin decided to come home for lunch and remained there for the rest of the day, and even more glad when that same evening, Dickie telephoned to say he and Dusty would be returning earlier than anticipated, tomorrow afternoon, Tuesday. At least their battling would take her mind off her pain.

It was while she and Erin were awaiting his homecoming that someone else visited. Peter Rufforth, her insurance agent, called to collect Patrick's death certificate in order to fulfil the duties of the life assurance policy she had taken out on her husband.

'Mrs Feeney.' He clasped her hands, face suitably composed. 'May I offer my deepest sympathies on Mr Feeney's passing.' He had been told of Pat's death by the manservant when he had called a week ago to collect the monthly premium and this was the first time he had seen Thomasin to offer his condolences. 'I didn't wish to trouble you earlier, but neither did I want to prevent you from claiming what's rightfully yours.' When Thomasin looked puzzled, he said, 'The policy on Mr Feeney ... I wouldn't want you to think I was being negligent in putting your claim forward.'

'To tell the truth, I'd forgotten all about it, Mr Rufforth.' Thomasin gestured at a chair then accosted Vinnie before she closed the door, asking for a pot of tea.

Vinnie tutted mentally about the amount of tea she had had to brew lately. However, she had found a girl who was starting tomorrow so there would be no more traipsing up and down with tea after today. As she was about to close the door someone came in by the front entrance and she turned back to inform Thomasin, 'Mr and Mrs Richard are here, ma'am,' before going to help remove their coats.

'Oh, good, thank you, Vinnie,' called Thomasin from the bureau where she was in the act of getting Pat's death certificate for the insurance agent. She stared at it for the umpteenth time, this piece of paper that told her Pat was dead, then handed it to him. 'There you are, Mr Rufforth.'

He thanked her and tucked it into his pocket. 'It shouldn't take too long to come through.'

'There's no rush.' Thomasin folded her spectacles and eased herself back into the chair.

Rufforth, who had remained standing out of courtesy, now sat down too and rubbed both hands over the shiny knees of his brown trousers. This short, slightly-built man had been calling here for a quarter of a century and Thomasin had seen his hair retreat from his brow year by year until now it was a mere fringe around the back of his skull, though he could not be much more than forty-five; what remained of it was light brown, as was his sparse moustache. He had a weak mouth and a receding chin which at the moment was partially hidden by his scarf, though his obsequious manner was very evident; this aside, Thomasin found him not unpleasant.

'I'd like to be the one to bring you the money but I'll be moving to another district very soon,' Rufforth told her. She said what a shame this was. 'Oh no, not really,' he looked brighter. 'It's promotion. I'm going to miss my old customers, though.' He looked to the door as Dickie and his wife entered.

'Ah, let me introduce my . . .' *My God!* Thomasin couldn't stop an involuntary hand from clutching at her chest. Here was her son who was meant to be dead – in the same room as the insurance agent who had handled the policy on his death! With all the other upsets it had never occurred to her that she could be in drastic trouble over this.

With her reaction and the pallor of her face, Erin had leapt to her mother's chair. 'Mam, what is it?'

Thomasin stared at her dumbly, then at the insurance agent who had also come to her aid, and then at Dickie. She fought to recover. 'Nothing. It's all right. I just got a . . . touch of indigestion or something.' She realised with another twinge that this was the excuse which Pat had always used to explain away his bursts of pain, and she sought to reassure Erin. 'I mean real indigestion. I'm quite all right, it's gone now.' She played for time by examining her spectacles to see if her panicked grip had damaged them; then somehow forced a smile. 'I'm sorry, Mr Rufforth, I was just about to introduce my nephew and his wife, Mr and Mrs Feeney.'

174

Dickie's mouth fell open when he saw that her hand was directed at him. He looked at Erin who was equally perplexed, but nevertheless he reached out and shook the man's extended hand.

'They're here on a visit from America,' said Thomasin, hoping he wouldn't hear the panic in her voice. 'Not a very auspicious time for them to choose for a holiday, I'm afraid.'

'Indeed no, very regrettable.' Mr Rufforth waited for Dusty to sit down, then did likewise. 'And the weather isn't too conducive to enjoyment, is it?'

'Oh, we've managed to get about,' said Dickie, trying to decode the waves that were coming from his mother. The look in her eyes did not require interpretation: she was scared stiff. He decided it was better to keep his words to a minimum so as not to drop any bricks.

Rufforth was trying to make out the strange accent. 'Were you born in America, Mr Feeney?'

'No, me an' the wife emigrated some years ago,' explained Dickie. When Rufforth asked in what part of America he lived, he answered, 'New York.' Rufforth smiled and said he imagined that it was very different from the Old York. Dickie said that it was indeed, and was temporarily rescued from further grilling as Vinnie entered with the tea.

Rufforth felt that there was something amiss here, but attributed it to the recent bereavement. After taking a sip of tea he continued the polite chat. 'And will you be spending all your holiday in York?'

'No, we've just been at Leeds staying with my ... with relatives.' Dickie supped deeply, scalding his throat.

'That would be your son, Mrs Feeney,' guessed Rufforth.

Thomasin froze and stared at him.

'The relatives at Leeds.' He took her expression to mean confusion. 'Your son resides at Leeds, doesn't he?' They had often enjoyed discussions about their respective families.

'Oh, I'm sorry! Yes, yes my son is this Mr Feeney's cousin, of course.' How long can I keep this up, thought Thomasin. Erin, I wish you'd stop looking at me as if I'm round the bend. 'I'm glad to see this snow's not hanging around.' With the change of subject she glanced out of the window.

Rufforth heartily agreed. 'It's taken me much longer to get round my customers – which is why I'll have to rush my tea, I'm afraid, and be on my way.' He took a few quick gulps, left the cup still half-full and rose. 'I'll ensure the policy is attended to promptly and I'll call on you again as soon as it is: providing I'm still attached to this district. Goodbye, Mrs Feeney. Again, I'm most sorry about your loss. Mrs Teale, Mr and Mrs Feeney, good day to you all.'

As soon as the door closed, all wheeled on Thomasin, demanding to know what was going on.

'Shush!' She held up her hand and listened for the sound of the front door, while everyone else waited impatiently.

In the hall, Rufforth snatched his hat from the stand and put it on as he made for the outer door. Vinnie was coming down the staircase and he smiled up at her. Unfortunately, his raised vision missed Dickie's carelessly-placed valise. He tripped over it and had to grab at a table to steady himself.

Vinnie rushed to support him, though it was an unnecessary gesture. 'I'm sorry about that, Mr Rufforth, have you hurt yourself?' When told that the man was perfectly all right, she grasped the valise and shoved it into a more sensible position. 'It's that there Mr Richard's!' She hooked an exasperated thumb at the door of the drawing room. 'I don't know! He expects everybody to run about after him. I'll be glad when he's gone back to America. Are you comin' down for a natter?' Usually, the agent would sit in the kitchen for half an hour and chat to Mrs Howgego.

Vinnie wanted to show off her new status, hold court like Mrs H. had done.

Rufforth massaged his ankle. 'No, I'll have to fly, Vinnie, else I'll end up being late for my tea. Anyway, I expect you'll have your hands full with Cook passing over and Mrs Feeney's nephew and his wife here to stay. Have they got any family with them?'

'Neph . . . ?' She frowned, then looked amused. 'Oh, you mean Mr Richard! No, there's just the two of 'em, thank God. Anyway,' she took the opportunity to preen, 'it's not too bad 'cause I've hired a girl to help me. From tomorrow you won't see much of me upstairs, only to discuss the menus with the mistress.'

'Oh, *Cook* is it,' said Rufforth in grand manner and elbowed her. 'I'll have to pay you a visit and sample your dishes, see if you're as good as Mrs H.'

'I'll have you know I knock spots off her.'

He laughed and said his wife would knock spots off him if he stayed here flirting with Vinnie and, repositioning his hat, he left.

Thomasin heard the door go and chanced a peep into the hall. Vinnie turned and smiled courteously. 'Did Rufforth have anything to say, Vinnie?'

The young woman cocked her head. 'Nothing important, ma'am, just passing the time o' day.'

'He seemed to be talking a long time,' replied Thomasin dubiously.

'Ah well, he tripped over Mr Richard's case,' Vinnie informed her.

Her mistress sighed. 'You didn't mention anything about Mr Richard, did you?'

'Like what, ma'am?' Vinnie had become uneasy.

'Like him being my son?'

Vinnie thought carefully about this. 'No, ma'am . . . I don't

177

think so. In fact, Mr Rufforth, he seemed to think Mr Richard was your nephew.'

'He is,' said Thomasin firmly and to Vinnie's further astonishment drew her in front of an audience – who appeared to be as confounded as she was, judging by their faces. 'I'm going to ask you to do something for me, Vinnie . . . I'm afraid it involves lying.' Erin demanded to know what was going on but Thomasin silenced her. 'Your turn in a minute, Erin. Vinnie, from now on if any visitor comes to the house – I don't mean family like Mr Sonny, but people like Mr Rufforth – you are not to tell them that Mr Richard is my son. He is my nephew. Got that?'

After an unsure pause, Vinnie said with a frown, 'Yes, ma'am.'

'Thank you,' said Thomasin. 'Now, I don't expect you to lie without giving you good reason . . .' She drew a deep breath. 'I know it happened before your time, but you'll probably have heard the story of how we thought Mr Richard died in the fire that destroyed our house in Monkgate.' Gossip was always rife among servants. 'Well, at that time, I laid claim to an insurance policy.' She glanced at her children who were now beginning to understand. 'I was given quite a large amount of money. If the insurance people were to discover that my son is really alive . . . I'm in very serious trouble.'

'Oh, I see! Oh, well you can count on me to keep quiet, ma'am,' vouched the cook.

Thomasin was considering asking Vinnie whether she valued her job, but decided that that would be cheap and distrustful; Vinnie had always been a loyal servant. 'Thank you, Vinnie. That's all, then – and send John up, he'll have to be told as well.'

Erin waited until the cook raced off before spinning on her brother. 'Not content with killing my father ye want to put my mother in prison!'

'Erin!' cried her mother. 'Nobody killed your father.'

'Yes they did! Him!' Erin whisked her finger in the air as if conducting an overture. 'He ruined your lives and he killed Dad with the worry.'

'Your father was an old man,' said Thomasin wearily. 'Eighty is a damned good innings. If anything ruined him it was Rosie's death.'

Erin would not be deterred. 'No! It started well before that, Mam. You know full well that after the fire things started to get bad between you, both of ye blaming yourselves for the way ye'd brought him up – and all the time he's sitting pretty in America, telling himself how clever he is. Well!' she yelled into Dickie's face. 'Aren't ye going to say anything? Give us one of your famous excuses?'

Dickie took the abuse in silence. His wife had moved to the window where she stood looking out, her face as bleak as the view.

Erin noticed her. 'An' don't think you can turn your back on all this! You're as much to blame. Couldn't you have had the decency to stop him from coming here? Couldn't you?'

Dusty made no retaliation, just kept looking out of the window. Erin was about to go and snatch her arm, but Dickie snatched hers instead. 'It's nothing to do with Dusty! You leave her alone.'

'I will not leave her alone! The pair of ye've got my mother into this an' I want to know what ye're going to do about it – in fact I know what you're going to do – you're getting on the next boat home!'

'No!' said Thomasin hastily. 'Erin, calm down. I wish I'd never said anything now. We're all making too much of this.' She put her palms together as if praying. 'I hardly think Mr Rufforth's going to remember something that happened twenty-six years ago. Think of all the claims he'll have had

179

to deal with every week, hundreds and hundreds of people's policies, endowments . . . no, I'm just being daft.'

'Then why did ye nearly have a seizure a moment ago?' demanded Erin. 'I don't think ye're being daft, I think ye're being rightly cautious.' She thought hard for a while. 'Couldn't ye just be honest and offer to pay the money back? Say ye genuinely believed Dickie was dead?'

Thomasin considered this. 'I could do . . . but then what reason am I going to give for lying and saying he was my nephew?'

Dickie, sensing more personal danger, persuaded his mother not to change her story now and she sided with his argument that it would make things worse, telling Erin, 'Besides, I've just remembered about the will Dickie made.' The will that had brought her son's trickery to light . . . Some twelve years ago, when Sonny had finally been forced to tell Rosanna and Nick that they were not his natural issue, they were in fact his brother's children, they had told him something about that day of the fire which had planted the idea in his brain that Dickie might not have died, after all. This had precipitated a visit to his brother's solicitor where he asked to see Dickie's will. He had read it several times with increasing despair, until the discrepancy had leapt out at him. Dickie had made a mistake with his address: he had said, *To my dearly loved brother I leave my house on The Mount* . . . totally forgetting that according to the date on the will, 20 September 1874, he should not yet have ownership of that property! After learning that Dusty had emigrated to America around the same period it hadn't taken much guesswork to trace the pair. Fearing that the shock would kill his ageing parents, Sonny had kept the secret until last year when he had received Dickie's letter out of the blue saying he was on his way home.

Thomasin looked at her elder son. 'That's always been a puzzle. I'd like to ask you why you wrote that will when it could have incriminated you. We'd've got your money anyway ... *My*, Dickie, I never thought to see you blush!' Her son looked most uncomfortable. 'Never mind, your face just told me the answer: you didn't want your parsimonious old mother to get her hands on your cash.' The distribution of the Feeney wealth had always been a contentious issue. Dick had been very bitter about his allowance as a young man.

'It wasn't so much that, Mam ...' He played with the fringing on an antimacassar. 'I felt rotten about how I'd treated our Sonny. I wanted him to have the lion's share, that's all.'

'And you knew he wouldn't get it if you didn't make a will.' Thomasin wasn't angry.

Erin was. 'Why in heaven didn't you *think* when ye wrote the date on it? Why did ye have to put September? Ye could have just dated it a few weeks before the fire.'

'Oh, that'd look good, wouldn't it? I make a will then pouff! – two weeks later I snuff it. That wouldn't've looked suspicious, I suppose?'

'You haven't the intelligence ye were born with!' accused Erin. 'Wait till I tell Sonny, he'll flatten ye.'

'Behave!' cried Thomasin. 'You're not to worry anyone else about this, and I'm sick of hearing ifs and buts. Just because we know Dickie's not dead doesn't mean that Mr Rufforth knows. Why should he? I introduced him as my nephew, didn't I? If he continues to think that then all's well.'

Erin glared menacingly at her brother. 'And let's hope for your sake that he does, because if you bring this family's name into disrepute just one more time ...' She didn't finish. There was no point in saying she'd kill him when there was little likelihood of her being able to carry out the threat. But that didn't remove the urge. She spotted something which her mother had overlooked – a photograph of Dickie as a young man, donated from Erin's own album when her mother's had been destroyed by fire. 'And we'd best shift this for the next time Rufforth calls, don't ye think?' Grabbing the silver-framed photograph, she shoved it in a drawer, and wished that she could dispose of her brother so effectively.

Rufforth didn't know why the episode should keep pestering him, yet it did – all evening. He sat indulging in his pipe, listening to his wife fingering the piano while his children played cards on the rug. It was Vinnie's face which was most prominent in his mind. Not simply because it was a very attractive face, but for its expression; she had been confused when he had mentioned Mrs Feeney's nephew. So had the nephew, come to that. Rufforth tried to imagine what the reason could be and pondered over the American Mr Feeney, or Mr Richard as Vinnie had called him. He remembered then that he still had Patrick's death certificate in his coat pocket, and went to put it in his case ready to take to the office tomorrow. He stared at it, wearing an ironic smile. What a strange coincidence that the very first time he had called at the Feeney residence as a young agent twenty . . . what? twenty-six years ago, it had been to handle their claim on the life policy for their son, and here he was winding up his dealings with them by paying out on the old gentleman. Wasn't life funny?

He had been the one to deal with the fire insurance, too, for their house at Monkgate. He remembered it so well because it had been his first big claim. He had been ambitious in those days, but his hopes of promotion had taken a very long time to achieve. It wasn't anything to do with his efficiency; he just seemed to be one of those people who spend their lives being overlooked. Well, that had changed now; he was on his way and, who knew, this promotion could lead to much bigger things. What a sad parting with this old customer, though.

He tucked the certificate into his case and went back to his chair and his pipe.

But uncannily, the Feeneys remained in his mind. When the children had gone to bed, he discussed the morbid coincidence with his wife. 'I can remember accepting their claim for that fire as if it were yesterday. Dreadful it was for a callow chap, as I was then. I didn't know what to say to them about their son.' He tried to think of the boy's name, but couldn't remember. His wife saw his eyes suddenly narrow, and asked what was wrong. He emerged from his brown study. 'Oh . . . nothing really. I just keep getting the feeling . . .' His face twisted in concentration. 'Well, I've been in this job a long time and I've grown used to people evading me, sending their children to the door to say Father's not in, when all the time he's hiding behind the kitchen door 'cause he's spent the insurance money on booze. Not that I'm accusing Mrs Feeney of that o' course.' He laughed, then returned to his thoughtful pose, scratching his brow with his pipe-stem. 'But I swear there was something worrying her.'

'D'you mean she's trying to get some money she's not entitled to?' asked his wife, Judy.

'Ooh no.' He looked shocked at the suggestion. 'Mr Feeney's death is genuine enough, poor old chap. No . . . everything was fine until that nephew of hers came in. Tut! It'll keep me awake all night. Come here and sit on me knee an' take me mind off it.' He opened his arms and grunted contentedly as she snuggled against him.

He was right about it keeping him awake. It niggled him for a good hour after he'd fallen into bed, his tossing and turning letting the cold air into bed to keep his wife awake too. 'I'm sorry, Jude.' He reached out to pat her thigh. 'I just know there's something . . .'

With a heavy sigh she sat up, pushed and thumped at her pillow, then snuggled down again under the warm covers.

'You say it's something to do with this American nephew? What's his name?'

'The maid called him Mr Richard, so it must be Richard Feeney.' His half-open eyes turned to look at her. 'I don't know why I've got it into my head, I never gave it a thought at the time . . . I just have this feeling that Mrs Feeney had to think twice before she introduced him as her nephew. I get the idea that she was going to say, "This is my son."' His wife said he had lost her, and he explained, 'I've known her for over twenty-five years and talked a lot about families. She only ever had the two sons: one I've seen several times called John; the other one died in that fire . . . or was meant to.'

She tumbled at last. Her mouth fell open. 'But what evidence have you?'

'None whatsoever.' He drummed his fingers at the horse-hair mattress. 'Only they were lying about something, I'm damned sure.'

'Can you remember what the dead son was called?'

'No, but I dare say I'd be able to find the claim if I dug far enough back.' Excitement was beginning to churn; what a propitious beginning to his new office! He cuddled up to his wife, feeling elated. His career had been painfully slow in taking off, but if he could help bring this scandalous fraud to court, his position with the company might go much, much higher.

9

The family waited. Maybe I'll die before they have a chance to clap me in gaol, thought Thomasin, plagued by the fact that two people close to her had died and there had yet to be a third. So firmly had she convinced herself that this was to be her, that the tears she shed on reading of Queen Victoria's death on the twenty-second of January were more for herself than for the monarch.

'What a relief!' She dabbed behind her spectacles and looked again at the newspaper. 'Eh, I shouldn't say that really, poor old lass. I'm just that glad it wasn't me.'

But was she? Apart from the agony of her rheumatism, her loss had really begun to bite; she was very depressed and often short-tempered with her family. It might be better for everyone if she was dead . . . the thought was just so frightening.

Still in mourning dress for her husband, she was suitably attired for the demise of the Victorian Era, but the crow-like garb made her more melancholic than ever. Even worse was seeing every other member of the public dressed in black too. Yet it was different for them; underneath the mournful faces lurked a hint of gaiety. For Thomasin there was a sense of glories past, of fear for the future. The Queen's death seemed to set the seal on the permissive way of life that had grown out of recent years. Everyone around her was young, it made her feel weary just to watch them. It was her grand-daughter

Elizabeth's coming-of-age tomorrow; she would have to shake herself out of the doldrums by then – but how?

She had been seated in front of the dressing table mirror for the last five minutes, mind full of these thoughts, trying to find enough energy to pin up her hair. 'Come on, frame yourself, girl.' She raised her hands, but could not hoist them above her shoulders without crying out in pain. She got mad then. *Look at the agony Pat must have been in yet we never heard him cry out once.* She tried again, without efficacy. 'Right, I'll bloody-well sort you out!' Raking about in the top drawer, she found a pair of scissors and after much sawing and hacking, the white plait came away in her hand. There was instant regret. She watched her mouth turn down like that of a scolded child. Tears came.

'Oh, Mam! Whatever have ye done?' Erin sighed at the forlorn sight.

'It's my hair, I can do what I like with it!' She did not mention the pain. 'I got sick of having to fasten it up day after day, I decided it might as well come off.'

'But ye shouldn't ought to have gone to such extremes! One of us or Vinnie could have done it up for ye.'

'I've done my own hair for seventy odd years, I'm damned if I'm being treated like a bairn now!'

'I'm not suggesting anything of the sort. Ladies have their maids, don't they? Just because you've never considered having one doesn't mean you're not entitled to change your mind.'

Braving more abuse, her daughter made her sit down and with gentle hands set about repairing the damage.

She felt sorry now that she had treated Erin so. The sight of that chavelled stump must have brought back old nightmares for her daughter. As a twelve year old, Erin had had her lovely hair hacked off by a cruel employer. But Thomasin had never given that a thought. She would have to be nicer when Erin came home from the factory.

The solitude of the drawing room closed in on her, making her want to run. But the ache in her joints shackled her to the chair. Several times she tried to rise, but on each, pain held her in its vice. She cursed her ailing body and thumped at her knee in frustration. You will get up, damn you, you bloody useless old cripple! You've got to keep going otherwise you're done for. Her rise from the chair brought a moment of triumph which was too brief. She paced up and down for a moment, then for no reason other than to escape this room, made for the stairs.

Maundering about the bedchamber, she was inexplicably drawn towards her wardrobe. With aimless fingers, she trailed the row of hanging garments, twice back and forth. Then something took control of her hand. Not quite knowing why she had chosen it, for it was very old, she lifted a dark green dress from its hanger and held it against her. For one strange moment the depression lifted – she felt almost happy. Someone was smoking a pipe upstairs, she would have to remonstrate with them ... even so, the smell of pipe tobacco brought comfort, reminded her of Pat, made her feel as if he were holding her. She hugged the dress for a few thoughtful moments, before hooking it back over the rail. Her depression flooded back and she slammed the door of the wardrobe, marching out onto the landing.

Here she bumped into the manservant. 'John, will you please not smoke your pipe upstairs!'

He looked put out. 'I haven't been smoking, ma'am.'

'Don't argue! I can smell it. You're the only one in the house who smokes a pipe. I don't mind you puffing it downstairs but I won't have it up here – do I make myself clear?'

'Yes, ma'am.' John watched her stalk away. It didn't do

to contradict the mistress at any time and even less in her present mood. He sniffed and shook his head – not a whiff of smoke. She was going barmy.

The Queen's death put the dampers on Elizabeth's coming-of-age party. Nick was especially piqued that the burial would take place on a Saturday and traders had been asked to regard it as a day of mourning. 'She would choose our busiest day,' he complained to his grandmother. 'I don't see why our takings should suffer just 'cause the old girl's finally pegged out.' His grandmother enquired if that was the way he would talk about her when she had gone. 'Yes, I shall demand they bury you on a Sunday.' Nick smiled as he said it; being pleased that she had not yet altered her will.

'You would, too. She's been our Queen for over sixty years, Nick. If only for that she deserves our respect. One Saturday won't ruin us . . . anyway, the store could close every day as far as I'm concerned.'

A month passed. Under guise of mourning, the Edwardian Age came tumbling in like a precocious infant. Thomasin raged at the hypocrisy, her anger magnified by the rheumatism that bored ever deep into her joints. Sleep oft elusive, those winter months spanned centuries, her days spent muffled shroudlike by the fire. All resolution to keep moving seemed to have dried up.

Erin grew increasingly worried about her mother's mental state. Everyone was still missing Patrick dreadfully of course, but Mother had always been an outgoing sort, now she hardly left the fireplace. She appeared to be limping, too. 'Are ye not going to your YAS meeting again this week?' she asked as the two of them sat alone one damp February evening, sipping glasses of sherry.

'YAYAS,' mumbled Thomasin, pronouncing it as one word. 'They've changed the name. Every blasted thing's changing, they can't leave anything alone. I'm not going.

It's too cold.' She tugged her shawl more tightly around her.

'Ye never let the weather put ye off before.'

'I've never been seventy-four before.'

'If . . .'

'Look, Erin, if I want to go out I'll go, if I want to stay in I'll bloody well stay in!' She emptied the glass and slammed it down.

Shocked, her daughter went back to reading her book. 'All right, all right . . . though it might have been nice if my brother and his wife had asked you to go to the theatre with them.'

'They did ask me as a matter of fact. I didn't want to go. I thought I'd stay in and have some peace but it seems that the only place I'm going to get that is in bed! Goodnight!'

But, lying sleepless in her bed, Thomasin began to see the validity of her daughter's concern. She must do something, she couldn't just sit around the house waiting to die . . . Tomorrow she would have a little ride down to the Parliament Street store. Taking the staff unawares might provide a lift to her spirits. A moment's calculation told her that it would be time for a stock check shortly; organising that would take her mind off Mr Rufforth. After that she would arrange a board meeting. Yes . . . that's what I'll do . . . if I wake up tomorrow.

'We can't wait forever,' complained Dickie. 'The meal'll be cold and she probably won't be eating it, anyway.' He, Dusty and Erin had been sitting at the table for fifteen minutes and still Thomasin had not come down. Erin had begun to chitter her concern.

'That's all you're worried about, isn't it?' she snapped at her brother. 'Your blasted guts. You couldn't give a damn that your mother might be lying helpless.' She squeezed her cheeks between the fingers of one hand.

Dickie laughed. 'Helpless! Our mother?'

'She is seventy-four, you know!'

'She was fine last night when . . .'

'When you two swanned off and left her for me to look after, yes I know!'

'We did ask her to come, Erin,' said Dusty.

'I notice ye didn't ask me, though!' Erin rubbed her hands over her face. 'God. D'ye know what I caught her doing the other day? There were all these sacks of clothes and shoes and what have yese piled on the landing. I ask her what they are and she says, "I'm having a sort out so's none of you have to do it when I die"!'

'She's bound to be depressed, Erin,' ventured her sister-in-law.

'No, 'tis more than that. Sometimes I catch her frowning as if she's in pain, but when I ask her she throws a fit. God, I don't know what I'll do if she's . . . I'm going to give her a knock!' She sprang up and left the room.

'I've never known anybody like her for worrying.' Dickie shook his head and reached for a tureen. 'Ah well, might as well have a mouthful before she comes back to give us heartburn.'

But he had scarcely served himself when Erin came rushing back into the room. 'She isn't answering! I've knocked dozens of times . . . oh, Jesus.'

Her mood was infectious. Dickie put down his fork. 'Did ye go in?'

'No, I daren't – oh, Dickie, come up with me.' She gripped herself in fear.

Both Dickie and his wife rose from the table and accompanied Erin up the staircase. On the way to their mother's room they encountered the new maid and asked her if she had seen Mrs Feeney this morning. On her negative reply, they proceeded swiftly to Thomasin's room. Erin knocked again, but still there was no answer.

'I can't go in – you go, Dickie.' She shoved him forward. He looked at his wife, stood there for a second, then grasped the door handle and entered.

Thomasin was in the act of pulling her nightgown over her head and the onlookers were treated to the sight of her stark naked form before she realised she had an audience and let out a shriek. 'What the bloody hell – will you all get out of my room!'

Dickie backed away rapidly, treading on his sister's foot and stumbling. 'Sorry, Mam! Erin thought . . .'

'Get out!' Still naked, a furious Thomasin staggered over to the dressing table looking for something to throw, white breasts swinging round her waist, dimpled haunches quivering.

The three retreated onto the landing with a hasty slam of the door, whereupon Dickie started to laugh. His wife turned her face away lest Erin should complain about her mirth, but she needn't have worried, for Erin was unable to stop her own laughter and was soon making as hearty a sound as Dickie.

'I can bloody-well hear you!' yelled their mother. 'Just you wait till I get dressed!'

Still spluttering, the three made their way back down to the dining room where their laughter was given free rein. Even when a more presentable Thomasin hobbled in to reprehend them they could not stifle their merriment.

'I did knock dozens of times, Mam.' Erin mopped her eyes and tried to look repentant.

'Aye, I heard you!' Thomasin gripped the back of a chair to steady herself.

'Then why didn't you answer?' asked her son.

'Because I'm sick of people checking up on me all the time! Being treated like a child! My bedroom is the only place where I haven't got some bugger wittering at me and I intend to keep it that way – at least I did until someone decided it should be open to the public!'

'We were only concerned about ye,' reproached Dickie. 'Thought ye were lying dead or something.'

'Well, I'm not! And I'll thank you all to stay out of my room until you're invited! All right?' Erin and her brother nodded sheepishly. 'Good!' Thomasin began to clash tureen lids. 'Now I'm going to have my breakfast then I'm off down to the store. If nobody minds, that is.'

Nothing more was said on the subject of the invasion, the talk confined to what Dickie and his wife would be doing today, which would include going to see 'their' children. With Dusty's amusing anecdotes about what Freddie said and did, Thomasin gradually cooled down and at the end of the meal said that she was sorry she had been so harsh with them and realised that they were only concerned about her.

'That's all right, Mam,' replied Erin. 'I'm sorry we embarrassed ye.' She folded her napkin. 'Right, I'll get my coat and away to the factory with me.'

Thomasin rose with difficulty. 'Aye, I'll be going too. Have a nice time, you two.'

'We will,' answered Dick, going to the door and opening it for his mother. A mischievous glint came to his eye as she passed him. 'Take care ye don't slip on that ice now, I'd hate for ye to damage that beautiful body.'

His mother eyed him menacingly, but once the door had closed she imagined what she must have looked like to them and was forced to chuckle. 'Ah dear, Pat,' she sighed. 'That a body once so passionate could now be such a source of ridicule. Oh well, it made our Erin laugh and that can't be bad. I must say, I feel a wee bit better this morning too.'

Throughout the day her spirits fluctuated. She spent the morning harrying her staff at the Parliament Street store, then telephoned Francis and arranged to have luncheon with him. The company of her old friend was ever precious to her these days; only he could understand the experience of being old, knew her feelings without having to ask. In the course of the afternoon he even managed to restore some of her interest in the business . . . that is, until she came home and found Mr Rufforth waiting for her in the drawing room.

Vinnie, who had been hovering at the entrance to the kitchen, anxiously awaiting her mistress' return, whispered the news to her the second she was through the door. 'Mrs Teale's in there keeping him occupied, ma'am. Mr and Mrs Richard are hiding upstairs.'

Thomasin sighed and hoped that Vinnie had not been so furtive in Rufforth's company. Thanking the cook, she steeled herself and went in.

The moment the insurance agent turned to greet her she knew something had happened. His smile was too tight and his eyes were too watchful of her reaction. This isn't Pat you're dealing with, she mocked herself, how can he read your mind? Just keep your voice casual. Apart from resorting to torture he can't prove that Dickie didn't die in that fire, otherwise there would have been repercussions years ago.

'Your cheque, Mrs Feeney.' He smiled as he handed it to her.

That was reassuring; if they had judged her guilty of fraud they would hardly be handing her more money. 'Thank you, Mr Rufforth.' She didn't even look at the amount on the cheque. 'Have you been offered tea?'

'No, but that would be most kind.'

Erin tightened her lips. She hadn't offered tea because that would keep him here and she could not understand why her mother wasn't trying to get rid of him as fast as she could. Thomasin rang the bell. John appeared and took her order down to the kitchen. While they awaited its arrival, Rufforth initiated the chat.

'Is your nephew no longer with you, Mrs Feeney?' He had the fear that his quarry might have escaped back to America whilst the investigators were kicking their heels. It was infuriating – all those hours he had spent up to his neck in dust, ploughing through archives of documents, and when he'd found the one he had been seeking and presented it triumphantly, what had they done? They'd filed it for future investigation. 'He's going to get away!' Rufforth had pleaded. 'You must act now.' He had been told that it was out of his hands now, he could get on with his job and leave it to the experts. Experts! Sitting on their backsides while time was ticking away. Their inefficiency had decided Rufforth to do some investigating of his own. He had already made a start by calling on some of the more elderly residents of Monkgate and had been rewarded with a perfect description – if a somewhat younger version – of the man purporting to be Mrs Feeney's nephew, plus some interesting comments on his behaviour. Please God he was still here. There was a motor car in the drive which had been there on his last visit, but he couldn't be sure it belonged to the nephew.

Thomasin answered, 'He's out sightseeing, I believe,' and put the cheque into the bureau.

'Nearby?'

'I beg your pardon?'

'He must be sightseeing locally; he hasn't taken his motor car.'

'Oh yes, locally – ah, here's the tea.' Thomasin tried to veer the subject onto the weather whilst pouring from the pot, but Rufforth was not about to let go.

'Yes, it's still terribly cold. Your nephew must have a stronger constitution than I have to go tramping round

194

sightseeing. I expect you'll miss him when he goes back to America? How much longer does he intend to stay?'

Thomasin said that her nephew and his wife were enjoying themselves so much that they had no immediate plans to return.

'Did I hear Mr Feeney say that both he and his wife had been born in York?' Rufforth received a nod. 'Then Mrs Feeney will be enjoying reunions of her own, no doubt.'

'Sadly not, my . . .' Damn! She had nearly said daughter-in-law; best stick to names. 'Dusty's father passed on many years ago and she has no close relatives.'

Rufforth smiled. 'An unusual name for such an attractive lady.'

Thomasin smiled back. 'Only a nickname.'

'For a miller's daughter, perhaps?' Rufforth was still cheery, but his motive for this line of questioning was very clear to Thomasin now; it was no mere small talk.

'D'you know,' she replied with a frown, 'I'm really not sure how it came about and I've no idea of her given name. Isn't that a dreadful admission? But we've always known her as Dusty. More tea, Mr Rufforth?' She tipped the spout at his cup and managed to deflect all Rufforth's further enquiries however doggedly he tried.

When he had gone, her body flopped in the chair and she stared at Erin. 'He knows.'

Erin nodded fearfully. 'That was pretty obvious. What're we going to do?' When her mother failed to provide the answer, she got up and marched from the room, shouting up the stairs, 'Dickie! Get yourself down here!'

On being told of Rufforth's inquisition, Dickie looked at his wife. 'Looks like we'd better skedaddle.'

Thomasin felt a stab of fear and snatched his arm as if to keep him here. 'There's no need for that. It isn't you who's in bother, it's me. I made the claim.'

195

Erin sighed exasperatedly. 'It's him who's brought all the bother though, isn't it? She glared at Dickie. 'Didn't you pay any consideration at all to what would happen if you came back? I mean, you obviously never gave a fig for what it would do to Mam and Dad but surely ye saw the legal implications?'

'How the hell could I see this?' replied Dickie. 'What do I know about insurance? I never bothered with that rubbish.' He stared for a moment at his mother's worried face, then approached her. 'I'm sorry, Mam, I never woulda come back if I'd seen any o' this happening. 'Tis no good, we'll have to go home. I think maybe you're wrong about it just being you who'll be in trouble, they might see it as a conspiracy. Anyway, without me they can't prove a thing.'

Thomasin tightened her hold. 'No! They can't prove it anyway. If we stick to the claim that you're my nephew it'll all be fine. Don't go . . . remember the children.' She turned a pleading face on Dusty.

The children were all Dusty had been thinking about. This was her last chance of becoming a mother, and it was in danger of being aborted.

Dick saw the distress on his wife's face and removed his arm from his mother to put it round her. 'Ye won't lose them. We can come back when all the fuss has died down.'

Her answer was cold. 'When – in five or six years' time? I'm old enough to qualify as their grandmother now, I'll be totally decrepit by then. Your mother's right, they can't prove anything. We shouldn't go rushing off until we're sure they can.'

'By which time my mother could be in prison!' Erin stormed out, rather than have them witness her tears.

The three of them let her go in silence. Dickie was thoughtful. 'I'm off to pay Sutcliffe a belated visit, but I think we can guess what his advice'll be. He could be in trouble over this as well. He'll want me as far away as possible.' The solicitor had been party to his client's dishonesty.

When her son had gone, Thomasin took her daughter-in-law's arm. 'You have to keep him here, Dusty, please.'

'But what about the repercussions?'

'Hang the repercussions! They can't do anything to hurt me at my age except rob me of my son again. You talked about your last chance of being a mother, Dusty. Well, it's my last chance too. I don't have many more years. I want them to be happy ones with my family round me. Help me, Dusty. I promise I'll do everything in my power to persuade Belle to let you have those children.'

'You must think I'm very self-centred.' Dusty looked chastened.

'We can all be self-centred when there's something we want badly enough, lass. I suppose I'm risking Dickie in wanting to keep him here, but I can't let him go, I just can't.'

Dusty was racking her brain for a way to obstruct the departure. She had to make the prospect of returning to America less inviting than staying here – but how?

Thomasin saw something pass over her face, and asked eagerly, 'Can you do it?'

Dusty's answer was cautious. 'I may be able to stall him for a while, though I don't know how long.'

'Whatever the delay I'll be grateful,' said Thomasin, then asked what she intended to do.

Dusty appeared to lose interest, turned and walked away. 'Right now I'm going for a walk.'

Thomasin opened her mouth to object, but Dusty had closed the door. Alone, the old woman writhed in discomfort and pressed a worried hand to her cheek. She was going to lose her first born again.

Dickie bore grim news on his return, telling them that his

prediction of the solicitor's advice had been correct. 'I'm sorry, Dusty,' he told her up in their room. 'I'll have to go and book the passage tomorrow.'

'What about your mother – don't you owe her a few more days at least? Just until we know what's happening. I mean, that's just it, we don't know anything *is* going to happen.'

'I'd rather not wait till the investigators are here with the warrant,' said Dickie.

'And what about me? Don't you owe me anything?'

'The kids? I've got that all worked out. We take them with us.'

'Kidnap them?'

'Ssh!' He covered her mouth with a kiss. 'I can't see that it matters; nobody else wants 'em, do they? We act as if we're taking them for the usual outing then just go.'

Her response was derisive. 'And I suppose nobody's going to notice the packed suitcases in the back of the car?'

'We'll have to leave them behind, just take what'll go under the seat.' He grinned. 'Good, huh?'

'Oh, don't be so bloody childish! I sometimes wonder why I want children when I've already got you. We're not playing games, Dickie.'

'I thought ye wanted these kids?'

'I do! But legally. Even if we succeeded I'd never rest knowing what we'd put Belle and your mother through. Erin despises me enough as it is. God knows what she'd think if I were to resort to your underhand tricks.'

Dickie put his hands on her shoulders. 'Ah, ye don't take any notice o' that fat old dumpling.'

'Yes I do! Unlike you, I care about what people think of me. I couldn't live with myself if I'd done what you're proposing.'

He sighed in defeat. 'I can't see what other answer there is.'

She wheedled. 'Just hang on a wee bit longer, a day or two can't make much difference.'

He gave a soft laugh. 'I suppose if they come for us we can always climb out o' the window.' Then he had another idea. 'Hey, what's to stop us taking Mam to America? That'd solve everything.'

'No, it wouldn't, clot. She's trying to keep this family together. Heaven knows why, all you ever seem to do is fight.'

Sonny came over a few days later, primarily on business, but a brief visit to the house for luncheon turned into a much longer one when Erin informed him of their dilemma.

'I told you not to bring your brother into this!' Thomasin laid down her knife and fork with a clatter.

'I'm glad she did,' cut in Sonny before his sister could answer, then looked accusingly at Dick. 'God's truth, I thought the emotional upset you brought with you was bad enough – I could thump you! Well . . . what are we going to do now?'

'We can't do anything till we know what the insurance people're up to,' said his mother, resuming her meal but merely to pick at.

Sonny was stunned. At that point the doorbell sounded, making all jump. The manservant went off to attend, returning with a scrap of paper on a tray. 'For Mr Richard, ma'am,' he told Thomasin, and presented it to her son.

Dickie stared from the cablegram to his wife who urged, 'Get it open then! It must be urgent.'

On reading it his face changed. 'It's from one of our staff,' he told the gathering. 'Seems there's been a bit of a problem at home.' Thomasin's heart lurched. But the fear that he was being summoned back to America was soon to be allayed. 'We've had intruders,' he spoke mainly to his wife now. 'They smashed the place up pretty bad.'

'No!' Dusty put her napkin over her mouth, then removed it to ask anxiously, 'Is everyone all right, and Lurk?'

'Who the devil's Lurk?' demanded Sonny.

His sister-in-law explained that he was the dog. 'He's real old, I hope they haven't hurt him.'

'No mention of it,' said her husband, frowning over the words. Dusty asked had they stolen much. 'Er, no . . . doesn't look like it. Apparently they weren't in there to rob us . . . seems they were looking for me.' He had the frightening vision of Stone's men going to work on him with a meat cleaver.

'But who were they?' His wife's loud query broke his trance.

He looked sheepish. 'Well . . . I was in a spot of bother with these gentlemen before we left – over some business. I had hoped my absence would make their hearts grow fonder but . . .'

'I might have known!' Dusty slammed the napkin down on the table, vibrating the glasses. 'All this rubbish about wanting a holiday.'

'I didn't arrange it just to get away from them!'

Thomasin listened concernedly to the argument, yet hope was rising. 'Might these men be waiting for you when you get back there?'

Dickie tore his face away from his wife's and nodded uneasily. 'Looks like we're going to have to stay here a while after all.' He saw joint relief as his mother and Dusty locked eyes. This provoked thought as the meal was resumed.

When the luncheon plates had been cleared and the womenfolk left them, Sonny leaned his elbows on the table and asked his brother. 'These men . . . was one of them the person you mentioned in your last letter, the one whose wife was a friend of yours?'

'Maybe.' Dickie puffed a cigar, still thinking.

'You don't have much to say for yourself today,' observed his brother. 'Growing bored with us, are you?'

Dickie only half-emerged from his reverie. 'Sorry, I'm just wondering if it was a wild guess or whether Dusty actually knew about this guy Stone when she got the maid to send it.'

'Send what?'

'The cablegram.' Dickie glanced at him. 'It's a sham. Oh, I admit I was taken in at first ... till I saw the look that passed from me mother to me wife. They've concocted this to keep me here, at least Dusty has.'

Sonny laughed. 'That's a bit unlikely. Have you questioned her about this theory?'

'No need to, it's not theory. I know exactly why she's done it – because of the kids. She wants to keep me here till Belle gets back. As I said, the thing that worries me is whether her choice of subject for the cablegram was just guesswork or whether she knows about my fling with Stone's wife.'

'You never learn, lad, do you?'

'Oh, I do, Son. I made my decision: she was the last one. I'm finished with women.'

His brother showed that he didn't believe him. 'So what're you going to do? Risk going back on the premise that Dusty did send that cable or risk staying here and face an insurance fraud?'

Dickie grimaced. 'It's a short and curly job, Son, ain't it?'

In the front sitting room, Thomasin was issuing her relief. 'I'm really sorry about your house being broken up, Dusty, but if it had to happen it couldn't have come at a better time.'

'Don't be too concerned about the house.' Dusty was straight-faced. 'It was a lie. When one lives with Dickie one has to be as devious as he is.'

What a marriage theirs must be, thought Erin, sipping her coffee. But Thomasin gave an admiring smile. 'I rather thought the coincidence was too lucky. How did you do it?'

'I got in touch with Mary, my maid, and told her what to put – used Dickie's fear of physical violence.'

'So there are no men after him?'

'I'm quite sure there're plenty who'd like to get their hands on him.' Dusty chose not to look at Erin who had sniffed loudly in agreement. 'That's what gave me the idea. But no, these were fictitious.'

Thomasin sighed, then heard the crunch of gravel as a vehicle came up the drive – an ominous sound after recent developments. Edginess took her to the window, but when she turned back to the other women she was smiling. 'It's Belle!'

Erin wrapped her arms round her daughter then drew back to behold her tearfully. 'You look worn out – come on, come on, inside! Oh, 'tis lovely to have ye back. You too, Brian!' This afterthought was flung over her shoulder at the bespectacled doctor who had been Belle's companion for several years; in what capacity Erin was not quite sure. Oh, she knew that Brian worshipped her daughter, but Belle had sworn she would marry no one. The relationship was something of an enigma.

'It's good to be back.' Brian Dyson grinned and paid the cabbie. He was a man in his early thirties, of average height and build. In fact Brian was average everything, virtually nondescript, other than to say he had brown hair and eyes, spectacles and a pleasant smile. His character was easier to define than his looks; he was approachable, caring, generous and kind, and though his lack of diplomacy had sometimes made him unpopular with Belle's family, in general they liked him.

Picking up his and Belle's luggage, he followed the women into the hall where Thomasin was welcoming her grand-daughter home, her sons being unaware of the arrival yet. He failed to notice Dusty who slipped along to the room where her husband and brother were. But Belle caught the retreating back and asked, 'Who's that?'

Erin glanced over her shoulder, then said, 'Oh . . . ye'll meet her in a moment – now come away in by the fire!' She suggested they go into the larger room at the back of the house. 'Look at your tanned face. We'll have to get some lemon juice on it.'

Belle moved into the drawing room with a pronounced limp, the effect of having one leg shorter than the other. This was offset to some extent by the wearing of a surgical boot, though nothing could be done for her twisted spine. These genetic defects had undoubtedly helped to mould Belle into the strong-minded character she was. The insults she had suffered in childhood had caused her to resort to some form of camouflage, both in clothing and hairstyle; the latter was a dark bush of curls that fell almost to her waist, helping to disguise the hump of her shoulders, and the rest of her body was draped with Bohemian robes of autumn hue.

Paradoxically, the style she had adopted tended to draw the eye rather than avert it, though if the onlooker saw an eccentric rather than a cripple then it served its purpose just as well. However, no camouflage was required for her face. The bright blue eyes and elfin features of her mother were further enhanced today by the kiss of Jack Frost. She looked truly beautiful.

Eschewing her mother's invitation to take off her mantle, Belle moved shivering to the fire. 'Gosh, I'm really feeling the cold after all that sunshine!' There was no Yorkshire or Irish accent here; her speech from childhood had been most refined, to the puzzlement but pleasure of her mother. 'We haven't been home yet. I wanted to come and tell you and Grandfather all about the tri . . .' It was impossible to miss the sudden change in their faces at the mention of her grandfather. 'What's the matter?' When no one responded she looked round.

Until this point she had assumed their mourning apparel to be for the Queen, but now it became sinister. 'Where is Grandfather?'

Thomasin, trying her best to smile, hobbled towards her and grasped her arms. 'Belle . . .' The glisten of tears spoke for her.

Her grand-daughter uttered a gasp of shock, but remained standing where she was. Brian moved into action. 'Come and sit down, Belle.' He coaxed her to a sofa then sat beside her, arm around the deformed back. Unlike Belle, his clothes were very sober – Norfolk jacket and green tweed trousers. To the family this couple had always appeared ill-matched and, juxtaposed, they seemed even more so. It wasn't just their clothes that were at odds but their characters, too. Their only shared trait was a great sense of philanthropy, and even this was performed with totally differing aims. While Brian sought to comfort, Belle did not appear to know he was there. Her piercing blue eyes were dazed. She wanted to ask, *when?* But the word wouldn't come.

Thomasin seemed to know. 'He died on New Year's Eve, dear.'

'What!' Belle found her voice now and jumped from Brian's embrace. 'But it's nearly March! Why did none of you write?'

'It would've been too late for ye to do anything, darlin'!' Erin came bustling over to comfort, but an agitated Belle evaded her and limped around the room, leaving her mother to clasp helpless hands and look on.

Thomasin spoke to the doctor. 'Brian, maybe we should leave them on their own for a while.'

He looked at Belle who ignored him. Pushing himself from the sofa, he escorted Thomasin from the room.

Erin struggled to speak, twisting her fingers. 'He was very ill, Belle. None of us knew, naturally,' she added at her daughter's angry, enquiring glance. 'He'd kept it to himself for some time.'

Belle cast her frantic mind back. There *had* been something wrong with him, but when she asked why he kept screwing his eyes up he had said he needed glasses. Why hadn't she seen the lie? For a spell she stared from the window. The manservant had been collecting ice from a pond which he was now transporting in a barrow to the domed building at the end of the garden. It took Belle's mind back to when one of her foundlings had fallen through the ice on the river . . . poor May. 'What was it?' she asked her mother woodenly.

'Something to do with his liver.'

Belle threw her face at the ceiling and gave a bitter laugh. 'The drink was it?'

'Well . . . that's probably what started it,' said Erin quietly. 'It finished up as a growth.'

'Cancer?' Her mother's reluctance to use the word caused Belle's perversity. 'The times I told him.' She suddenly bent her head and covered her grieving face. Erin tried once again to comfort, but was in for more abuse. 'Well, thank you very much for having the decency to tell me, Mother!' Belle shook herself free of the embrace. 'It's a marvellous homecoming, I must say!'

Erin used the rejected arms to beseech her daughter. 'Darlin', I've told ye . . .'

'I know! There wasn't time! And how long before he died did you learn about it?'

'Not long, just over a week.'

'Time enough for you to have sent a cablegram! I could've made it!'

Erin refrained from pointing out the impracticability of this.

'Ye wouldn't've wanted to see him like that, dear.'

'Don't tell me what I want! I've had enough of you knowing what's good for me!'

'Don't speak to your mother like that.'

An angry Belle spun to face the stranger in the doorway. 'And who might you be?'

Erin groaned and wrapped her arms about herself as Dickie came in. 'Oh, no . . . everything seems to've happened while you were away. This,' she said distastefully, 'is your Uncle Richard – my brother.'

Belle's anger was displaced by confusion. She gaped at the tall man with the striking good looks. 'But I thought he was . . .'

'An' so did we all.' Erin sighed heavily. 'But the Devil's sent him back to haunt us yet again.' She spoke sharply to her brother. 'Richard, will ye please go 'way and give us some privacy!'

'Sorry.' He retreated behind raised palms, face contrite. 'It just sounded like ye needed an umpire.'

Belle was still watching the space where he had been even after the door closed.

'If I'd known when you were arriving I'd've met ye an' told you all about your grandfather,' said Erin softly. 'I'm sorry, Belle.'

Belle tore her puzzled eyes from the door, glared at her mother, then said abruptly, 'I'm going home,' and began to march.

'Wait! Don't ye want to know . . .'

'You've kept it from me this long, Mother, I don't see that another day is going to make that much difference!' Belle spoke without turning and yanked on the door handle. 'I'll be back in the morning for an explanation.' She yelled into the hall, 'Brian!' and the doctor appeared in the company of Thomasin and Sonny. The latter came forward with the obvious intention of kissing her, but she eluded him and headed straight for the outer door. 'Save all your sympathies! You'll put the words to better use by forming an explanation as to why none of you had the decency to tell me about Gra . . .' She swirled away before she broke down and limped off down the drive.

'Brian!' Erin intercepted him before he could charge after Belle. 'Try an' make her see 'twas for her own good.'

Brian contributed nothing save a telling look, then seized the suitcases and hurried after Belle, calling for her to wait for him.

Dusty, having gone upstairs to look for her husband, closed the door on Belle's noisy exit. 'A very good impression you made, I'm sure!' she snapped at Dickie who lounged on the bed. 'You're meant to be wooing her! Where's all this charm that women seem to find so irresistible?' She dismissed his manufactured forlornness with a flick of her hand. 'Oh, put that face away! It won't wash. I don't know why you had to poke your nose in; it was between mother and daughter.' The intoxication she had felt on Belle's return was now causing a hangover.

'I'll make it up when she comes tomorrow,' promised Dick. 'I'll be Prince Charming himself.'

'Well, not too charming. We don't want her to see what a lecher you are.'

10

Belle arrived with Brian at nine o'clock the following morning, dressed in the black robe-like creation that had been made for Rosie's funeral. There were cool introductions between them and the couple from America. When all were seated in the drawing room and none seemed eager to voice the first sentence, she asked cryptically, 'Would you care to draw straws?'

Her mother's face crumpled. 'Belle, please don't make it any harder. We did it for . . . no, I'm not going to say for your own good – though your feelings were a priority – but we did it as much for your grandfather's sake. He didn't want you to see him in pain, didn't want any of us to know, come to that. That was the reason he went off to Ireland for a so-called holiday at Christmas – so's we wouldn't see him in his final wretchedness. He thought it would be better if you remembered him as he was.'

Belle's eyes did not waver. Only Brian had seen the full strength of her emotion last night. 'And did he suffer very badly?'

Erin glanced at Thomasin, then said in gentle honesty, 'While he was keeping it to himself he must've done, yes. But once we got him home the doctor did everything he could for him.'

Digesting this, Belle didn't speak for a while, just stared rigidly at the black and gold lacquered sideboard.

'If ye like,' offered her mother, desperate for forgiveness, 'I'll take ye to see his grave this afternoon.'

'Much good that'll do him or me,' mumbled Belle. Erin looked away. 'And what about him?' Belle's eyes were on Dickie now. 'Where did he spring from?'

'If you've a few hours to spare, I'll tell you,' said her grandmother. 'It's a very complicated story.'

'It must be,' came Belle's tart utterance. 'For somebody who's been dead and buried for twenty-six years he looks remarkably healthy.'

'Doesn't a good Catholic like yourself believe in miracles?' quipped her uncle, blue eyes twinkling.

Thomasin butted in. 'The brief details, Belle, are: your Uncle Sonny discovered his brother was still alive eleven or twelve years ago . . .' Belle interrupted to ask how. 'Oh, you'll have to ask him when you see him,' said Thomasin. Sonny had gone home. She carried on with her theme. 'For reasons of his own he kept the knowledge to himself but the two of them stayed in touch by letter until the end of last year when your Uncle Richard decided that he wanted to come home and see his family.'

'And if Uncle Richard wants something he has to have it,' scathed Erin, receiving a glare from her mother who then went on.

'Naturally, Sonny had to warn me that he was on his way . . . and at the same time Francis divulged your grandfather's real reason for creeping off to Ireland.'

Why could he tell somebody like Francis, anguished Belle, and not me? 'So presumably someone went over to Ireland to fetch Grandfather back?'

'I did,' Thomasin smiled sadly. 'Though when I got there he'd already made his decision to come home to us. I think he realised that home isn't a certain country but the place where your loved ones are.'

'So that's what he meant.' Everyone turned to look at Brian, who was cleaning the lens of his glasses. 'Just before we went to South Africa, he said to me, "Things might've changed when you get back, Brian. I hope you'll be here to look after her . . ." I didn't catch the implication then, but I do now.'

Belle reared again. 'You didn't say anything to me!'

'Oh, stop trying to pin the blame on somebody, Belle,' said her grandmother tiredly. 'What if Brian had told you? Would you have interpreted the remark correctly? Of course you wouldn't. Don't you think we've all been asking ourselves how we failed to miss the signs, the telling little comments? Your Uncle Sonny found a bottle of stomach and liver tonic stuffed behind the cushion a year ago – yes, a year! He's been going on and on about how he should've realised. If I as Pat's wife didn't twig then why should anyone else? Because we weren't meant to, that's why. There's no call for any of you to blame yourselves or anyone else.' *But I do*, she agonised. Me and Pat used to be able to read each other's mind, why didn't I read his suffering? Because I was too busy moaning about his embarrassing displays of drunkenness in front of my friends.

Belle's mind still lingered over her grandmother's earlier comment. A year. Uncle Sonny had found the medicine bottle a year ago. She saw her grandfather's face wrinkle in pain . . . Forcing herself to return to the topic of Uncle Dickie, she said, somewhat tightly, 'I have another question for you, Grandmother. When I arrived home yesterday I was told by my nursemaid that a certain Mr and Mrs Feeney had been making it a regular habit to take three of my children on outings. The permission for this seemed to have come from Mrs Feeney senior.'

Dickie spoke up. 'I'm sorry if we stepped out o' line. We were just so impressed with your achievement that

Mam suggested we come along an' have a look. They're fine kids. Me an' Dusty were really taken up with them, weren't we, Dust?'

His wife nodded eagerly. 'I imagine you'd have a surprise to see the baby; he's adorable, isn't he?'

'I could have thrown him through the window,' replied Belle without humour. 'He didn't stop crying all night.'

Dickie sought to appease. 'If we've caused any offence by giving 'em treats I'm really sorry, Belle.' He gave her his best Dickie smile.

Belle speared his artless blue eyes with her own. 'It's not so much the treating I object to, it's that they're going to miss it when you go back to America.' Her manner became airy. 'They seem quite taken with you both. I almost had to gag Freddie, I got so sick of hearing about these splendid people. He seemed to be under the impression that you were his new parents.'

'I'm sure we never intended that,' said Dickie.

'Yes we did.' Dusty leapt in. 'Belle, I won't lie to you . . .'

'And your husband will?' Belle treated her uncle to one of her head to toe scourings.

'I didn't mean that.' Dusty shook her silver head impatiently, sending a loose hairpin to the carpet. 'Dickie's just trying to make amends for getting too involved without your permission, but I think it's best we're open from the start. What I mean is, I do — *we* do want to adopt them, if you'll let us. Your grandmother said you were looking for a suitable home for them.'

'That's true.' Belle was still aloof.

'Then would you consider us?'

'I'll consider you, yes,' said Belle politely, but far from reassuring.

Erin spoke now, picking up the hairpin and giving it to

her sister-in-law. 'There's one more thing you should know before you make your consideration, Belle.' Her mother guessed what this might be and said there was no need to bring that up. Erin said there was. 'She's complained of us keeping her in the dark, we might as well be frank about the other revelation.'

'Ye're just tryin' to ruin it for me!' complained her brother angrily.

'If I do, then all to the better. I doubt Belle would forgive me if I let her hand over the children to someone who'd put his own mother in gaol.'

'Erin, stop being petty,' warned Thomasin. 'And stop exaggerating. Nobody's going to gaol.'

Belle's face demanded an explanation. Against Thomasin's wishes, her mother provided it. 'Your grandmother could face serious charges relating to the insurance money she collected from your uncle's supposed death.'

'We've no indication of that being about to happen,' argued Thomasin.

'Nevertheless,' Erin was insistent, 'I think you should see what a load o' trouble he's landed us with, Belle. If you still feel like considering him as an adoptive parent then that's up to you. I'm just being open.'

Dusty was crippled by a new emotion: helplessness. She had always been able to hold her own in any argument or crisis, but this was very different. If she struck back at Erin it could jeopardise her chances with the woman's daughter. She must show Belle that she was capable of remaining calm, must keep on good terms with her . . . though at this moment she had never detested anyone more; hated her arrogance, her condescension, her superiority and, most of all, the way Belle made her feel weak. She must leave the room; if she stayed here she could not keep those feelings from her eyes. 'If you'll excuse me, Mother,' she said, twisting the hairpin in her fingers, 'I don't think I wish to listen to any more. Belle, I hope we can resume this conversation in a more sensible climate.'

Dickie barely heard his wife's parting remark, still concentrating on Erin's disclosure. 'You vindictive bitch.'

'That's enough of that sort of language,' rebuked his mother.

'Ye'll hear some language in a minute!' Dickie's stance was menacing.

'Then you'd better leave the room as well,' said Thomasin. 'Go on, look after your wife, she's obviously upset.'

'An' have her make defamatory remarks behind my back?' Dick wagged a finger at Erin. 'I bloody will not.' He sat down stubbornly, face brooding. 'She'll doubtless have plenty more slander up her sleeve.'

'About you being a thief, a cheat and a womaniser?' asked Erin.

'Oh, don't stop there! Ye forgot to tell them about the necrophilia.'

'I'm not familiar with that word,' said Erin haughtily. 'And I'm surprised you are, seeing as it's got more than four letters. But whatever it is I'm sure you're capable of it.'

'Will you both please stop!' cried their mother, banging her fist on the chair arm.

'I've said all I have to say,' said Erin, nose hoisted in the air. ''Twasn't done out of spleen, I just thought Belle should be aware of what she's dealing with.' She looked at the clock then turned to her daughter. 'Anyway, I'm sorry but I'll have to go to the factory now, I'm late enough already. Will you come round for dinner tonight? We haven't heard any of your news yet.'

Belle was ungracious. 'Not tonight. I've things to do.'

'Well, maybe later in the week then,' pressed her mother.

'Maybe.' Belle remained aloof.

213

Erin compressed her lips at her daughter's attitude. *I knew she'd blame me for all this*, her eyes said to Thomasin, before she left the room.

Her entrance to the hall disturbed her sister-in-law who had been standing head bent, arms gripped tightly around herself. 'I can't see why Belle's so hostile towards me,' she mumbled at Erin who was putting on her coat.

'Don't think you have the sole privilege.' Not looking at her, Erin did up her buttons. 'Ye heard the way she talks to her own mother. Think yourself lucky ye have no children. Sometimes I wonder if the pain outweighs the pleasure.'

Dusty bridled at the casual utterance. 'I'd give *anything* to sample that pain!' she said with feeling. 'It's nothing compared to the pain of being unable to bear Dickie's child!'

A stupefied Erin watched her dash up the staircase. 'I didn't mean to be . . . I only meant . . . Sorry!' But Dusty slammed the door on her apologies. Erin bit her lip, then called to John to bring the car round and went outside. But all the time she waited and stamped her boots against the cold, she could not get Dusty's words out of her mind, and by the time the car arrived she had actually begun to feel sorry for her sister-in-law.

Thomasin was speaking to her grand-daughter. 'Don't set too much store by what your mother says, Belle. It's true, yes, that I could be in trouble, but Dickie didn't realise I had an insurance policy out on him. What I'm saying is, take him as you find him yourself and don't let your mother colour your judgement. She's very upset with him at the moment but she'll come round. If you want my opinion I think Dusty will look after those children admirably.'

'I should take your opinion and ignore Mother's?' But there was a tinge of humour to Belle's words. 'You know me, Grandmother, I only ever listen to my own advice.' She noticed that Dickie had handed a silver case of cigarettes to Brian and was now putting a match to one of his own. 'But were I to take my uncle's manners as an example of his character it wouldn't get him very far.' When Dickie looked blank, she told him, 'I smoke too.'

'Oh, sorry.' He fumbled for the case, flicked it open and extended his arm.

She took one and waited for him to light it, smiling at her grandmother's scandalised expression. 'I started while I was in South Africa; so did Brian. We found it calmed our anger.' She forced the smoke through her lips. 'Some of the things we saw . . . Anyway, I'll save all that for next time. You sound as if you've had enough upset.'

'You haven't heard the rest of it.' Thomasin told her about Mrs Howgego's passing.

Belle shook her head in disbelief. 'The Queen too . . .'

Thomasin gave a sad nod, but did not feel much like dwelling on the matter of death. 'So . . . will you come for dinner on Saturday? You'll be settled back in by then. I'd like to invite Sonny and the others over for a welcome home party.'

Some welcome, thought Belle, picturing her grandfather, but said that she would. Her grandmother was pleased. 'I'll get Vinnie to cook something special. In fact, I'd best go and see her now so she's got time to prepare. I want it to be really nice for you.'

'Sit there,' said Brian. 'I'll ring.'

'No, I'm not stopping here with you lot puffing clouds at me and your mother will have a fit when she sees what disgusting habits you've brought back with you.' This last was said for Belle. Wincing, Thomasin pushed herself from the chair. Only Brian stood and waited until she had gone.

When he turned back he looked at Belle but her eyes were on Dickie. In fact, her eyes were all over Dickie. In an attempt to douse his qualms, Brian took a long drag of his cigarette and sat down. 'How long do you intend to stay, Richard?'

Dickie kept his gaze on Belle as he answered. 'We're not sure.' She was a beautiful-looking girl – pity about the handicap. He was still enjoying a lustful fantasy when Brian distracted him again.

'Belle, I'll have to be going. I've a patient to see.'

She tore her eyes away from her uncle. 'I though Doctor Barley said last night that he'd handle things while you got straight at home?' Brian had previously been in partnership with the said doctor until Barley had decided to sell up and retire, when Brian had continued the practice alone. However the other had kindly agreed to act as locum while Brian was in South Africa.

'He did, but he also told me he's got Mrs Hepworth on his list this morning and she can be very difficult. I said I'd see her.'

'Oh well, you go and I'll see you this evening. I'd like to grill my uncle for a while.' Her eyes abandoned him.

Brian persisted. 'I didn't say exactly what time I'd call on her. I can wait till you've done here and give you a lift.'

'I'm not incapable of putting one foot in front of the other, Brian,' she chided. Before the doctor could say more, Dickie offered to take her home in the car. 'There you are, I've got an escort. Now go and see to your woman.' Belle waved him away.

Brian had no option but to leave, stubbing out his half-finished cigarette and cursing himself for inventing the patient – it was just the way Belle was looking at the other man that had spurred him to do it. She had never looked at him like that.

'You've got beautiful hair.' Dickie exhaled a chestful of smoke and brushed the front of his clothes to remove a sprinkling of ash. It was an instinctive and involuntary act;

216

one designed to draw the onlooker's eyes to his physical form, which was still in very good condition. Old habits never died. He answered his urge to flirt with her.

This one didn't blush, but drew on her cigarette and eyed him through the haze. Belle had the urge to flirt too; a new experience for her. She felt both anger and amusement at the same time for the man who had provoked it.

'In fact, I have great admiration for you in many ways, Belle.' She asked him why. 'Oh . . . your Christian activities for one.'

'Christian?' She frowned.

'Taking in other people's mistakes an' . . .'

'You're referring to the children?'

'Yes, an' those ye want to help in Africa. You're a very compassionate lady.'

She simply laughed and puckered her lips around the cigarette again. He laughed too, and asked what he'd said that was so funny. She answered with a shake of head and studied him unblinkingly for a long time. Under her stare, Dickie had the unusual sensation of having a woman make him feel uncomfortable. To cover this, he leaned forward and ground the cigarette into the ashtray. It broke her concentration. She too stubbed out her cigarette and when she sat back it was to gaze into mid-air.

After a span of silence, she made a weird comment. 'Some-times . . . sometimes, I loathe and despise people.'

Dickie looked bemused. 'But ye do so much to help 'em.'

'Not because I like them.'

He chuckled. 'Then why bother?'

'To stop them from destroying each other,' said Belle. 'To make their offspring into decent human beings. Educate them so that when they grow up they won't spend their time putting other people into concentration camps – that's what

217

they're doing in South Africa,' she explained. 'And all under the British flag. It made me feel ashamed.'

'I don't know much about the cause,' said Dickie. 'But surely in a war . . .'

'These aren't just soldiers we're talking about; they're women and children. I'm not so concerned about the women, they're a tough lot and they've brought half of it on themselves by smuggling weapons to their men, but the children have no say in the matter. They're rounded up in a frenzy of politics and allowed to rot.'

Dickie showed an interest he did not really feel. 'From starvation?'

'Partly. I'm told they receive the same rations as our soldiers – which isn't saying much of course, the Army never did overfeed its men. But no, it's disease that's claiming the majority of them, having to be cooped up together like pigs.' Dickie asked what she planned to do about it. 'There's little I can do except raise funds. I see no point in going back to South Africa where I'm banging my head against a wall. I might as well be here organising relief parcels.' She added in mock officiousness, 'I shall be asking all the members of this family to dig deeply, of course.'

'Oh, naturally I'll do everything I can,' promised Dickie and seeking his wallet, provided her with a substantial contribution. After she had taken it with thanks, he asked, 'Well, does that prove how willing I am to be a father?'

She replied like a schoolmarm, 'Good gracious, you'll have to do more than flash your wallet!'

'And so I will!' he vouched theatrically. 'I'll prove it to ye when I drive ye home. Ye'll see how the kids like me.'

Belle folded the money into a square and said whimsically, 'My mother doesn't seem to like you very much.'

He did not deny this statement, but after a moment of silence, asked, 'Has she ever told ye about me?'

'A little, but what I find puzzling is that it conflicted with the information she gave me a moment ago; I was always led to believe that you were some sort of hero.'

'Ah, that was when I was dead,' supplied Dickie. 'Now that I'm resurrected I'm the swine again.' After a soft laugh he became pensive. 'Ye know, I always had the feelin' right from being very small that your mother resented me, as if I'd taken something that was hers. God knows what it was.'

'And when did you become the cheat, the liar and the womaniser?' asked Belle.

'Oh, tried and convicted, am I?'

Belle made an elegant gesture. 'I'm granting you the right of reply, Uncle.'

The skin around Dickie's eyes crinkled. 'Ah well, I suppose I was a bit of a bad lad in me youth. But as ye can behold,' he tugged at his greying hair, 'that was a long time ago. Ye see, your mother forgets that twenty-six years have gone by. She doesn't know me as I am now.' He fixed penetrating eyes on his niece. 'You, on the other hand, not having met me before, have the privilege of making up your own mind.'

Belle did not flinch under the stare, her own eyes amused. 'Oh, I will.'

Dickie held her gaze smilingly, then looked thoughtful. 'Fred and his sisters aren't very much alike, are they?'

'That's because they all have different fathers.'

He laughed. 'Their mother was a pro?'

His indelicacy did not seem to bother her. 'No . . . but she's a very generous sort.'

Dickie looked concerned now. 'She isn't dead then?' This might affect his plans to adopt.

Belle distorted her mouth. 'No, and I shouldn't really be making fun of her. Her name's Ann. She's thirty-five but has the mind of a child – is totally incapable of looking after herself, let alone offspring. Until recently her own mother had been caring for them all and doing an admirable job, but she's a sick old woman and Ann takes more looking after than Freddie and the girls put together. So, when she sneaked out and got into the family way yet again . . . her mother felt unable to cope any longer and put her in the Workhouse. She did try to continue looking after the children for a time, but her health deteriorated and she could see that if she didn't do something about it then the children would be taken into the Workhouse, too. Living just up the road she was familiar with our aims and so . . .'

Dickie grazed on the information for a while. 'With the mother being loco, is there any chance o' the kids . . . ?'

'She didn't start out as an imbecile!' snapped Belle. 'She was quite normal until some fool ran over her head with a cart.'

Dick said he had heard the children talk about their grandmother and asked if she ever came to see them. Belle told him she did. 'Would there be any trouble from her if we wanted to adopt them?'

'Not from a legal standpoint. She's signed their guardianship over to me.' Belle saw his face relax. 'So, you only have me to contend with.' Her gimlet eye warned that this would be no easy task.

A glance at the clock told her she should be getting back for the children's lessons. 'Right, Uncle, enough dalliance. I believe you mentioned a lift home?'

Playing the gallant, Dick made a circle of his arm, guiding Belle to the automobile. Dusty saw them from the bedroom window and was bolstered by the sight; enough to think of rushing down to accompany them. Then she saw the way Belle was gazing into Dickie's face. A wife's presence would obviously be superfluous.

Belle gave one of her rare smiles as the children made a fuss

220

of her uncle. 'You certainly didn't lie about them being fond of you.'

'You wound me, Belle!' He faked offence. 'I never lie.' Picking up Faith, he took Julia by the other hand and followed his niece through to the parlour. The next half hour was devoted to proving what a good father he would make, telling the children jokes and stories. When Belle said they really must get some work done, he showed what a wrench it was for him to leave by hugging and kissing the girls and even patting Freddie's lank hair. Ordering them to have their books ready for her return and pleading with the nursemaid to cork the baby's howling mouth, Belle went with her uncle to the door.

Dickie leaned on the jamb and ran his eyes over her. 'What's it to be, then? Do we get Faith, Hope and Chattery?'

She held his eyes. 'You're determined I'm going to make up my mind today, aren't you?'

'An' why not? Isn't two hours in my company enough to make an impression – if ye say no I'll commit suicide.' He flashed his teeth.

'I think I have your measure.'

'So?'

'You don't like Freddie, do you?'

He was startled, having come to believe he had won her over. 'How can ye say that when I've just spent half an hour spouting all my good tales to him?'

'I'll compliment you on your performance; it was very good . . . if a little forced.'

'But they like me!'

'Oh, I agree they do. They also like the coalman because he lets them ride on his horse and the woman who brings the milk because she conjures toffee from her ear, but that doesn't mean I'd allow them to go and live with either.'

'Listen, ye haven't had a proper chance to speak to Dusty yet. She's marvellous – she'll convince ye.'

'It wouldn't matter if she were the best mother in the world – those children are not going out of this house until I'm positive they'll have a stable home.'

'Why don't ye try Joseph an' Mary?' muttered her uncle sarcastically, then tried again. 'Look, don't decide now. Let me take ye out to dinner an' we can discuss it more intimately.'

'You're too frivolous, Uncle Richard.'

He stared at her. Suddenly this took on an extra dimension. It wasn't simply that he had to have those children to please his wife, but that he had to master Belle. He donned his hat at a defiant angle. 'Can I ask ye something, Belle? What makes you so bloody special that ye feel ye have the right to run people's lives for them? I'm not talking about me, but about those kids. What makes ye think that you know better than they do in their choice of parents?'

She merely smiled. 'I must tell you than I abhor bad language . . . and now I really must say goodbye, Uncle Dickie.'

She was about to shut the door, but he put on an imploring face. 'Drop the Uncle.'

'Why – don't you care for the responsibility of a niece?' she asked flippantly. 'If you don't then you'll hardly be fitted to cope with parenthood, will you? Until Saturday.' She closed the door in his face.

Seething, Dickie strode to where he had parked the car, beating the air with every swing of his cane. He was bending over the starting handle when a cry of, 'Uncle Dickie!' brought his head round. The sight of Frederick produced an oath, 'Oh, shit,' but he waited for the boy to run up. 'What d'you want? Your Aunt Belle'll be mad if she catches you out.'

Freddie sprawled on the car's bonnet. 'Aren't you and Aunt Dusty taking us out today?' When Dick replied negatively, the boy asked why.

''Cause . . .' Dickie sought for a reason, glaring at the child. Fred knuckled his snub nose, regarding him with anxiety. Even with the impetigo healed, he was no picture. Christ, what a repulsive little sod you are, thought Dick. Why the hell my niece is being so choosy beats me. She ought to be thankful that anyone wants to take the boy, there'd be few volunteers. ''Cause your Aunt Belle says not!'

'But you're still going to be my new dad, aren't you?'

'Just get back home!' Dick gave the boy a shove. 'On second thoughts, I'll take ye; show madam just how wrong she is.' Cupping a rough hand round Freddie's skull, he propelled him forward. A sharp series of raps brought Sally to the door. Dickie elbowed his way in, shoving the boy ahead of him. 'There y'are!' he told a surprised Belle. 'See how much he thinks of me? See how responsible I am? We coulda swanned off, the pair of us, but I knew how worried ye'd be so I brought him right home – though he was devilish keen to go with me, I can tell ye.'

Belle gave a gracious inclination of her head; it was clearly a mocking gesture rather than an appreciative one. 'That was most conscientious of you, Uncle,' she said as if to a pupil. Dickie left.

Dusty had been sitting at the window of their room awaiting his return. When the car trundled up the drive she hurried down to meet him in the hall. 'Did you enjoy yourself?'

The tone made him wince. 'D'ye mind if I take me coat off first?' He did so, then headed for the drawing room.

'Upstairs!' Dusty picked up her skirts and began to climb. 'Your mother's in there. I don't want anyone butting in.' When they were in private, she folded her arms. 'Well, what did she have to say?'

Dickie sat on the bed. 'Nothing of any import.'

'And it took all morning to say it? Were the children even mentioned at all?'

'Of course they were! What d'ye think I've been doing there?'

For answer, she thrust her tongue into her cheek. 'So, are we to be allowed to adopt them?' Her husband told her Belle was thinking about it. 'Maybe I can aid her decision when I go round tonight.'

'That's not such a good idea, Dust. She isn't expecting to see us till Saturday.'

'Then she'll have a nice surprise, won't she?'

If the surprise was pleasant, Belle didn't show it when she answered their knock that evening. 'Oh . . . I'm just bathing the girls.' There came the sound of merry splashing along the passage. With an impatient glance over her shoulder, Belle decided to let the visitors in. 'Would you mind waiting in the front parlour with the boys until I've got them dressed. It's only the younger ones, I won't be long.'

'I'll help,' said her eager aunt, as Dick entered the front room to a loud welcome from the boys. Belle told her there was no need, but Dusty was already rolling up her sleeves. On coming across the roomful of naked female flesh, she covered her face in pretend shock, 'Ooh, four bare gollies! My goodness gracious,' and whipped a towel from the fireguard to swaddle the dripping Julia. Sally, lifting Faith out of the zinc bath, smiled a welcome. She had come to like her employer's aunt, particularly for the way she had reduced the workload in Belle's absence. Dusty bundled the little girl onto her knee and patted her dry, singing all the while.

'Look at this water on the carpet!' complained Belle. She grabbed the last girl, Lucy, out of the long bath and began to rub her vigorously with a towel. Dusty thought she was much too rough on the delicate skin. She also wondered how the children could hold such genuine affection for this woman – they behaved so warmly towards her. Dusty could only think that they were more perceptive than she was.

After all were dressed in nightgowns, Belle and the nursemaid lugged the bath away whilst the other woman ran a gentle comb through the damp locks. On returning, Belle announced that they would never get the girls to bed at this rate and, grabbing a brush, hauled it roughly but effectively over screeching heads until all were ready for bed. Dickie was allowed in then, to tell the children a story over cocoa.

When, looking exhausted, the nursemaid went off to wash the cups, Dusty asked if she might accompany the children upstairs to tuck the little ones in. Belle was all too grateful for someone to save her legs and in her aunt's absence sat by the fireside to chat to Dickie.

Having kissed each one and supervised prayers, Dusty came down to find her husband sitting very close to Belle and the pair of them enjoying some joke. Temper flared, but reminding herself that she had been the one to prescribe her husband's charm as an antidote to Belle's obstinacy, she bit her tongue and sat down. For the next half an hour she conversed quite politely, until she could no longer stand the looks that passed between Belle and her husband. Consulting the clock, she said that they should be getting back for dinner and, fury thumping at her temples, she led the way out.

The couple had been gone an hour when Belle received another caller. Condemning himself for the unfounded jealousy he had entertained earlier, Brian arrived carrying a bottle of good wine.

Belle eyed the label approvingly. 'You haven't got some illegal trade set up, have you? You're usually moaning about having no cash.'

He kissed her and hung his coat on a peg in the passage.

'It was a sacrifice, but your grandmother's idea of a welcome home party got me to thinking along the same lines.'

Belle asked him to uncork the bottle and put it on the sideboard while she went to the kitchen. 'I'm sorry but there's nothing very special to go with it.'

Brian sorted noisily through the contents of a drawer for the corkscrew. 'I didn't realise you had such a low opinion of yourself, dear.'

'I was referring to the food. I wasn't sure you'd be coming.'

'I said I would, didn't I?' He gripped the bottle between his knees and employed the corkscrew.

'You said you might, and it is nine o'clock. I'd almost grown sick of waiting.' She finished bringing the food in, and made loud lament as the cork popped out, bringing half the wine with it. 'You'd make an excellent wine waiter, Bri.' She used a napkin to mop first at his trousers and boots, then at the carpet. 'I don't think we'll wait for it to breathe, do you? It's on its last legs already.' They both sat down.

'Ooh, you are a critic, Belle.' He smiled and poured the wine. 'Tell me what you think.' She sipped it and said it would pass, then laughed and told him it was excellent.

As they ate, she spoke of her aunt and uncle's visit. 'You know, I asked the children just what it was they liked about Uncle and his wife, expecting them to give some deep meaningful reason for wanting them as parents. Julia said she liked Aunt Dusty because, "She wears nice clothes", and Uncle Dickie, because "he sings rude songs while he's driving the car".' Brian showed amusement then, trying to make his voice casual, asked what she herself had though about Uncle Dickie. She inserted a forkful of chicken. 'He's one of those infuriating people whom you can't help liking even though he is full of himself.'

Brian's fork toyed with his food, 'Yes . . . I had the feeling that you were pretty impressed with him.'

She looked up from her plate, frowning. The gaslight fell on his spectacles, making it impossible for her to see his eyes. 'And what did you make of him?'

'I wasn't particularly enamoured with the way he was behaving towards you.'

She took a sip of wine and went back to her meal. 'I can't say I noticed any impropriety.'

'That could possibly be because you were too busy admiring him to notice.'

She laughed and continued to chew for a while, then a glance at him warned her his comment hadn't been intended as a joke. 'Doctor Dyson!'

'Doctor Dyson, what?'

She lowered her fork. 'You know what!'

'And why shouldn't I be jealous?'

She chewed rapidly to get rid of her mouthful and swallowed. 'Brian, he's my uncle! And he's twice my age.' Her face was still half-amused.

'He's a very attractive man.'

'Then you have him!' Her mood changed now. 'Brian, you're being utterly ridiculous.' Her cutlery savaged the chicken.

'If it's ridiculous why are you annoyed?' Brian shook his head sadly, then snatched a mouthful of wine which he had hoped to use in celebration – not of a marriage proposal, for he had accepted Belle's decision to remain single, but they had discussed the possibility of him moving in with her. In the past this had been delayed because she feared it would upset her grandfather. Now Patrick was dead and Belle didn't care if any of the others thought her a scarlet woman, Brian had hoped that tonight the plan might come to fruition. He would have liked that fruition to be complete – ached for Belle to bear his child – but he knew in his heart that she never would. Despite her charity towards other people's children she had few maternal feelings.

The meal ended in disharmony. Belle dabbed at her lips with a napkin and, snatching his unfinished supper, took the plates away. 'Men!' she hissed at the nursemaid who had been sitting in the scullery reading a novel. When she went back into the parlour, Brian was wearing his brown caped overcoat. She did not ask why he was leaving.

'Goodnight, then.' The last button was fastened and he observed her unaffectionately. 'Shall I call tomorrow?' She reflected his dispassion, saying he could if he liked. He turned his back, took two strides . . . then stopped and presented a naked face. 'I'm frightened I'm going to lose you, Belle.'

Dispassion turned to anger. 'I'm not yours to lose!' With a resigned nod he headed once more for the exit. 'Oh . . . hang on, Brian.' Her attitude mellowed. 'I'm not averse to having a row over something important but this is totally absurd.' He had rotated to look at her again. 'I was just so mad that you thought I could be influenced by an attractive man . . . I apologise for what I just said.'

His face didn't alter. 'You were right; you're not mine to lose.'

'Not in the possessive sense, but we do have a partnership and I was making it sound as though that counted for nothing when it counts for a great deal. Come back and finish your wine.'

Brian unbuttoned his coat and slung it over a chair. Belle handed him a glass of wine as atonement. 'I expect it's the shock of Grandfather's death that's making me so quick-tempered.'

Brian hoped it was. But he still had the fear that her anger stemmed from being caught in the act of desiring a man, and later when she said, 'Take off your specs, Bri,' – which was her jocular prelude to their making love – he could not help thinking that she was doing it because she felt sorry for him.

228

11

'Ah, Bellissima!' Dickie was the first to greet his niece when she arrived in the drawing room at Peasholme Green on Saturday evening. The entire family, plus Francis, had been summoned together by Thomasin to welcome her home, but Dickie was the one who reached her first, bending low over her hand, then drawing her nearer the fire with a further display of linguistics.

Belle allowed herself to be led through the smiling throng, enjoying being the centre of attention. 'You speak Italian, Uncle – and such a beautiful accent.'

He speaks sufficient to get him into some signora's knickers, thought Erin, unimpressed.

'In a cosmopolitan society like New York one manages to pick up all sorts.' Dickie glanced slyly at his brother who responded with an admonishing smile. As her uncle straightened, Belle noticed the bruising around his left eye and remarked upon it. 'Oh, the cupboard door is a bit stiff,' explained Dickie. 'I gave it a tug the other night and smacked myself in the eye.'

'Don't let him fool you,' joked Sonny to his niece. 'I'll bet your aunt did it.' Everyone laughed and Sonny donated a welcoming kiss. 'I'm sorry we didn't have the opportunity to talk the other day, Belle.'

Her smile shrank. 'I didn't exactly feel like talking to anybody.'

'No . . . have you been to the cemetery at all?'

'Not yet.' It had barely sunk in that her grandfather was dead. She looked at Erin who, unsure of her reception, had hung back. 'Mother, I'd like to go if you're still willing to come with me.'

Accepting this as an apology, Erin came forward and linked arms with her. 'Of course I will . . . and if you get chance of a few days' holiday in the summer I'll take you to Ireland to see where your grandfather was born, too.' It would be more welcoming in the summer.

'I'd like that,' replied Belle, then went back to appraising Dickie, his red silk handkerchief an obscenity among all this black. So intent was her study, she did not immediately notice that Dusty had moved up close beside her husband. On encountering her, Belle smiled politely. The return smile was cool. There seemed to be some warning in her aunt's eye. Good grief! thought Belle, she can't possibly have the same idea as Brian. My God, I believe she does. Notwithstanding her shock, Belle greeted her aunt in friendly manner.

'Good evening, Belle,' returned Dusty. 'Was Brian unable to come with you?' Belle explained that he was with a patient.

'A pity,' said her aunt. 'He's a nice young man.'

'We all think that but she still won't marry him,' said Erin.

Belle's face censured, then turned back to Dickie who had produced something from his pocket.

'We brought everyone a gift from America, Belle. Hope ye like it. May I pin it on for ye?'

He did not even wait for permission, and was attaching the ornament to her left shoulder, when Belle observed, looking directly into his face, 'It's very pretty, but rather inappropriate to wear with mourning, don't you think?'

His lips parted, 'Ah yes . . .' and his hands withdrew,

retaining the brooch. 'My mistake. Well here, you take it and put it in your bag.' He handed it over.

'Thank you, Uncle ... Aunt.' Belle nodded graciously then put the brooch into her jet-encrusted bag. She looked round at the other participants and laughed at Feen. 'Good gracious, whatever has she got on?' The girl was trying to keep balance on the two blocks of wood which she had tied to her feet. Her hair was pinned into a bun and skewered by two knitting needles. She wore a length of flowered silk tied with a wide sash, and an oriental fan completed the outfit.

Sonny put on his oppressed father look. 'She's in her Japanese period this week.' His daughter often entertained such fads, using the costumes as a cover for her shyness. Last month it had been her Russian period, when she had gone about the house dressed in her father's old trousers, a pair of knee boots and a fur hat. 'I suppose I should stop her really, but they're all missing their grandfather, I don't like to be mean.'

Feen spotted her audience and came over, taking little shuffling steps in imitation of what she imagined to be that of a Japanese lady. 'Ah, who eeze thees?' The costumes might vary but the accent was always the same. Her long-suffering father underwent the pretence and introduced Belle. 'I am very plizzed to meet you.' Snapping the fan shut, she tucked both hands up her sleeves and bowed low.

Her aunt from America laughed delightedly and said to Erin, 'Isn't she cute?'

It was obviously taken as gross insult. The Japanese lady gave her a withering look and departed. But Dusty's eyes had strayed back to her husband. He was paying far too much attention to Belle. 'Come on, Dickie, don't hog your niece. I'm sure someone else would like to talk to her.'

Belle examined her aunt's face. There could be no doubt about the warning now. Despite her adult bearing, there remained enough of the child in Belle to make her do the complete opposite of what was required of her. A look of defiance came to her eye.

'And how's my erudite cousin?' Nick stepped forward and severed the women's examination of each other. He, too, had sensed the air of enmity.

'Do you always let him insult you like that?' asked her uncle, before being firmly removed by his wife.

Nick added a 'Welcome back.'

Belle pulled a face, still watching her uncle who was now over by the french windows canoodling with Feen. 'Not so good a welcome, was it?' she said miserably. Her mother patted her hand and drifted away. 'What went wrong? You normally know everyone else's business, why didn't you see he was ill?' When Nick shrugged uncomfortably, she softened. 'Oh, never mind, I'm just trying to make sense of it all.' Feeling tears burn, she gestured at her uncle from America. 'I suppose it must've been a big shock, finding out he was alive?' Belle was aware of the father and son relationship.

'Well . . . I did know actually,' Nick divulged.

She asked how. 'He's been reading my flaming letters,' growled Sonny, overhearing.

Belle gave a warped smile, then greeted Win and asked, 'How are you? I do hear you've plans to increase your brood.' Dusty had mentioned this the other night.

Win held her stomach. 'I don't feel so bad at the moment, thank you, Belle. Late evening's the worst time. And I get ill bumping up and down in the carriage – but I just had to come and find out how you fared in South Africa; you're so intrepid!'

'She'll tell us all about it over dinner,' called Thomasin, rubbing her knee. 'Come on, somebody, help me up.'

Erin approached her mother's seat with the intention of helping. 'That leg's troubling you, isn't it?'

'No, no, I've told you! I'm all right.' Thomasin turned grouchy. 'Francis, come and rescue me, I beg you.' Shaking off her daughter, she clung to Francis' thin arm, and pried herself up, the pair of them leading the way to the dining room.

Her offices rejected, Erin sauntered beside her daughter and asked, 'Well, what d'ye think to him?' Dickie and his wife were some way ahead and out of earshot.

'I presume you mean my uncle? I like him. He makes me laugh.'

'Oh, he's good at that, especially when the laugh is at someone else's expense. Be very mindful of those children, Belle. He's not to be trusted.' Erin restrained herself from further soothsaying as they reached the table.

'Feen, that's your Aunt Dusty's place,' scolded Thomasin as her grand-daughter jostled her way to the seat beside Dickie. 'I thought you four girls could sit over that side.'

'I am sorry but I do not understand Engleesh.'

'You'll understand when it comes to asking who wants more meringue though,' laughed Thomasin.

Feen barely managed to conceal her disgust at her silly old grandmother's treatment, but waited in the hope that her aunt would give way. When Dusty merely smiled, she set her mouth and flounced round to the other side of the table, inwardly swearing her hatred of both women.

While the meal was being served, Belle was pressed for her adventures by the rest of Sonny's girls, Amelia asking excitedly if she had bumped into any tigers. 'I don't believe they have tigers in Africa,' said Belle. 'If they do then I certainly didn't see any. I saw elephants, and a monkey . . . though he was on top of a barrel organ outside King's Cross Station.' Her smiling mouth imbibed of the soup. Amelia snorted and dipped into her own, leaving the quizzing to others. Elizabeth asked how on earth their cousin had managed to survive in the jungle for all this time. Belle chuckled. 'I haven't been any-where near a jungle. Where I've been it's a huge open space.'

'Like a desert, you mean?' asked Sophia.

'Good Lord – Uncle, if I were you I would seriously question your governess' credentials. No, Sophia, it's a very beautiful country – but what they don't have in South Africa is delicious meals like this so if you'll excuse me I'm going to tuck in and enjoy it and let someone else provide the conversation for the time being.'

Thomasin was the one to do so. 'I've been wondering whether to buy somewhere smaller. It's silly, this big place with just the two of us. If we want to get together we can all go to your house, Sonny, or Nick's.'

Nick was horrified. 'I don't want Belle's mob smashing up my new furniture, thank you kindly! We've just got the place looking nice.'

'Stop slandering my children, you big snob,' said Belle.

'If I'm a snob in not wanting my home wrecked then I'll admit to it.' Nick averted any similar suggestions. 'Nan, I've been doing some research into the possibility of us acquiring a tea plantation. I've brought the figures with me, you could take a spez at them later. It looks quite viable.'

'That's a matter for the boardroom, Nick, not the din-ner table.'

'And when was the last time you visited the boardroom?' enquired Nick. His grandmother reminded him sternly of her loss. 'I didn't mean to sound uncaring, Nan, I miss Grandad too, but the business has to be run and I really do feel that this tea plantation is a matter we must discuss. It could save us an awful lot of cash in the long run and the coolies work for next to nothing.' Thomasin told him they would speak of it later; her tone brooked no further attempt.

The diners ate in silence for a while, then Belle asked, 'Have you been sightseeing today?'

With the question unprefixed by any form of address, Dusty was unaware that Belle was speaking to her and so continued eating until her husband nudged her and she looked up. 'Oh ... yes. We've been to Aysgarth Falls.' Belle said it was a place she had not seen and asked if it was worth a visit. 'It's lovely.' Dusty stirred thoughtfully with her soupspoon, a dangerous spark to her eye. 'Though you can get too much of beauty. I feel as if I ought to be getting back to routine.'

'Personally, I never tire of beauty,' said Dick and tried to retain his smile as, beneath the table, his wife ground her heel into his little toe. 'But Dusty's right of course, we should be getting back to business I suppose.' He managed to extricate his tortured foot.

'You don't need to go to America to find business,' said Thomasin, trying to veil her concern with cheerfulness. 'I could find you a job here.'

Nick's spoon poised ever so slightly in its passage to his mouth. Win felt his alarm.

Dick blotted his lips and smiled over the napkin. 'I'm not a shop-keeper, Mam.'

'Beneath you, is it?' Thomasin watched the bowls being collected and replaced by plates of meat.

'No, but . . .'

'I do not eat dead animals!' Feen informed the new maid. She was rebuked by her mother for her discourtesy to the servant and for interrupting her grandmother, and told to eat it.

'You want to think yourself lucky, Miss Dolly Daisy Dimple,' said Thomasin. 'I never got big meals like this when I was little.'

'And your poor grandfather only had taties,' said Erin. 'Taties for breakfast, dinner and tea.'

Sonny joined in the fun. 'And he had to kill his own spuds.

Eat it up and you'll grow big and strong like your mother. On second thoughts no, I don't want another one pushing me around.'

Stupid, stupid! cursed Feen at their laughter. Why do they all insist on treating me like a child? Especially silly old Nan. *Dolly Daisy Dimple!* She wanted to stab at the meat, but knew what this would bring, and so had to content herself with imagination.

Josie insisted that her daughter eat the meat, but Thomasin waved the episode way. 'Oh, let her leave it, she's only a bairn.' Sonny objected that he had been forced to eat things he didn't like by his mother. She ignored him and tried to change Feen's sullen expression. 'Eh, do you know what your father used to say when he was little? If I said, d'you want some pork, he'd say, "Is it pig pork?"'

Feen took a mouthful of vegetables so that she would not have to laugh with the others. Her grandmother underwent a private sigh and asked herself what was wrong with today's children, then said, 'Now, where was I?' She put a hand to her face and looked cross. 'I seem to be forgetting all the time these days. My mind must be going.' Her brow screwed up in concentration.

'The business,' Francis reminded her.

'Oh yes, the business.' Thomasin turned back to her elder son. 'It's not just the small concern it was when you left. I've got branches in York, Leeds, Bradford, Scarborough and I'm considering opening one in Sheffield . . . Least I was till your father died.' She picked up her cutlery, staring down at her plate. 'I don't know if I can be bothered now – but you could do it for me.'

'I really can't see me managing a shop.' Along with every-one else, Dick set upon a fresh course.

'I'm not asking you to, just to set it in motion for me. You'd have a seat on the board, of course.' Here, Erin said

236

she hoped the rest of them would be consulted about this first, but Thomasin didn't reply. 'I might even abdicate my Chairmanship.'

Nick looked at the morsel on his fork, then lowered it, unable to swallow.

'Oh, Nick, can you help me, dear, I feel really faint.' Win began to sway and grasped his arm to steady herself. 'Help me upstairs.' She looked woefully at Thomasin. 'I hope you'll excuse me, Nan?' Thomasin projected concern, as did everyone, and asked if she wanted Vinnie to mix her something. 'No, thank you, I just need to lie down.' Win leaned on her husband's arm. The other men stood as she was escorted from the room, Dickie running ahead to open the door.

'Poor lass.' Thomasin passed a sympathetic smile to Erin. 'I'd forgotten how awful it can be.'

And I've never known, thought Dusty. Erin, more sensitive to her sister-in-law's feelings now, caught the stricken features and tried to change the subject by asking for more vegetables.

In the hall, Nick delivered a supportive kiss to his wife's cheek and led her gently to the stairs. 'Poor old Win, I thought you were over the worst of it.'

'I am.' She took her weight off his arm. 'I just thought I'd better get you out of there before *you* fainted.'

Nick stopped and gave a bitter gasp. 'D'you think anybody else noticed?'

'That you almost sawed your plate in two? I shouldn't be surprised. Come on,' she urged him onwards up the staircase. 'I might as well carry out the pretence. I'm not hungry anyway – especially for fatty pork.'

'Me neither,' said Nick. Arm in arm, they wandered up to the room in which they would be staying. 'Leave it for the boardroom, she tells me, then in the next breath she's offering him the Chairman's job. It'll be just my luck for her to leave him the lion's share of the store in her will, when she gets round to doing it. How can she do this to me, Win?' he appealed to her. 'After all she put me through before giving me the directorship.'

'Maybe she still thinks you're too young to run the company,' replied his wife as they left the landing.

He loosed his hold on her and she went to lie on the bed. 'For Christ's sake I'm almost twenty-nine – I'll be thirty next year! Do you have to be an old fossil before you're worth anything round here? And the nerve of asking him! What the hell does he know about commerce?' He flung himself on the bed beside her.

'Don't swear, dear.' Win went on to comfort. 'He didn't look that enthralled.'

Her husband wasn't listening. 'I don't think Nan realises just how much I've been doing lately. I've been carrying both her and Francis. I thought . . . well, when Grandad died she lost all interest, I thought she might pass the Chair over to me. Francis is ready to pop his clogs.' Win said he would just have to prove he was capable of doing it. 'I've just said I have been doing it!'

'Then you'll just have to keep on doing it unless you want to lose your position altogether.'

'Prove myself all over again.' Nick closed his eyes in exasperation.

'Or . . .' Win closed hers too, suddenly feeling queasy.

'Or what?'

'Or get rid of your Uncle Dickie.'

He opened one eye and squinted at her. 'Kill him, you mean?'

She giggled, 'You daft idiot,' and rolled over to curl her body into his side.

Nick chuckled with her, but wondered what they were talking about downstairs.

Despite Erin's attempts to spare her sister-in-law, the talk remained on babies. 'Your father used to say when anybody died there'd always be one born to replace them,' said Thomasin. 'Well, there's three gone – Pat, Mrs H. and the Queen. So far we've only heard about Win's baby, but there'll be two more I don't doubt.'

The maid, Barbara, was at her mistress' elbow when the comment was uttered. As she leaned over to collect the plate, she confided, 'I hear Miss Cecilia from next door's expecting a happy event in June, ma'am.'

Thomasin rose up at the gross impertinence which at one time might have been overlooked. 'Just do the job you're paid to do and less of your tittle-tattle! We'll have dessert.' Everyone stopped speaking as the unfortunate maid scurried round with plates of meringue before being dismissed. 'Have you ever heard the like!' exclaimed Thomasin. 'She'll have to go.'

'Grandma Fenton,' mouthed Dick to his brother, who covered a smile.

Catching the interplay, their mother was bent on rebuke, when she touched on the full implication of their joke. *Surely* I'm never as bad as my mother was? To compensate, she dredged up a little risqué humour. 'Oh well, we only need one more baby then – has anyone else an announcement to make?'

Josie bit her lip in silent reproof, Elizabeth and Sophia looked coy, Amelia asked what her grandmother meant and the subject was changed.

Nick returned while the dessert was being consumed. 'Excuse the long absence but I thought I'd best stay with her.' He raised a declining hand at the offer of meringue, saying he couldn't manage it. His grandmother laughed and said she had heard of men like him. He frowned. 'Sorry?'

'Being infected by your wife's delicate condition. You look really green.'

Everyone laughed. Nick allowed them to think this was the case, when inside he boiled with frustration. Josie, too, laughed from politeness, but wished that her mother-in-law would stop airing the subject so openly.

Sonny guessed his wife's discomfort and, finishing his meringue, turned to Belle. 'So, my dear, are you going to tell us all about these exploits of yours?'

Josie delayed the answer. 'First I think it's time Feen and Amelia were in bed.' There had been enough unfitting topics already without the children being exposed to war. 'Make sure Paddy's still tucked up when you go.'

'Mother, can't I stay up, I am almost fifteen.' Averse to being parted from Dickie, Feen sat tight.

Dusty saw the annoyance rise in a blush from her sister-in-law's neck, and sought to cajole before violence was done. 'You realise that it's beauty sleep which keeps us all envious of that marvellous complexion, don't you, Feen?'

Stupid woman, thought Feen. Don't you realise that I'm going to take your husband away?

'Feen doesn't need beauty sleep.' Dickie smiled gallantly at his niece and pushed his chair back. 'All she requires is an escort – come on, you two, I'll see you safely to bed.'

With a niece on either arm he left the gathering. Whilst Josie nibbled her lip and counted the moments to his return, Feen clung to her uncle's side, wishing that the staircase could be a hundred miles long, but unfortunately she found herself on the landing in no time at all. Dickie bent to kiss Amelia who reared away in alarm. 'I don't kiss people nowadays!' Her uncle laughed and turned to his other niece. 'Well, I don't want to insult anybody . . .'

240

'I won't be insulted!' replied Feen eagerly and lifted her face to be kissed.

Dickie looked down at her, saw the sexuality that was invisible to her family and envied her her youth. He lowered his handsome head. She inhaled his warm breath, felt his lips on hers, *he actually kissed me on the lips*, tasted the wine he'd had with dinner . . . and then he was gone down the stairs, leaving her shiny-eyed and throbbing. She floated after her sister into the room they were to share, not hearing a word of Amelia's grumbles. Only when the younger girl had tripped along to the bathroom did she return to life. Fumbling amongst the contents of her valise, she took out the voodoo doll and pierced its breast with yet another pin.

Dickie marched back into the room with the gay announcement that the girls were a-bed, allowing Josie to relax. He asked had he missed anything gory while he'd been playing the gallant.

'I've been telling them about the awful conditions in the camps,' said Belle. 'And I was just about to inform everyone that I'm starting a fund for the refugees.' She looked around the table. 'I shall expect all of you to contribute.'

'I'm afraid I shan't be giving anything,' said Thomasin bluntly.

Belle looked shocked. 'After what I've just told you? Why?'

'Because of what they're doing to our lads,' said Thomasin firmly.

'But these are children I'm talking about!'

'Yes! The Boers' children! The Boers who're torturing our men, burning them alive – aye you might scoff, young lady! You haven't been here reading the press reports.'

'Grandmother, how can you be so heartless.'

'Look, Belle.' Thomasin leaned on her elbows in the manner that she used for the boardroom. 'When you traipsed off

241

to South Africa I made no accusations about conspiring with the enemy so don't you accuse me of not caring.'

'Conspiring with the enemy?' Belle had to chuckle.

'Oh, you might laugh, but that's how some see it,' her grandmother told her. 'A lot of people consider you to be unpatriotic and would like to see you and your friend Emily Hobhouse in gaol. Now, I admire you for wanting to help people, Belle, but from what I gather the life in those camps isn't very different from the way they live normally.'

'With respect, Nan, you don't really know what you're talking about . . .'

'Belle, don't be rude,' warned Erin.

'. . . you haven't witnessed the overcrowding, the terrible rations.'

'Maybe I haven't,' said Thomasin. 'But I was speaking to someone who's lived in South Africa and they told me that every summer the Boers camp out at the seaside – the entire family in one tent, so that puts paid to your theory of overcrowding for a start. As for the diet, aye, I've heard the rumours about the ground glass in the flour, well I say it's propaganda – but then if you tell me you've witnessed it with your own eyes, I'm bound to believe you, Belle.'

'I haven't witnessed it.' Belle was impatient. 'And there's propaganda on both sides. I'm not concerned with that, nor am I concerned about the politics of this blessed war, what I am opposed to is children dying. That I *have* witnessed and I can tell you, Nan, you wouldn't want to see it. The camps are rife with disease – measles, dysentery . . .'

'Aye, because the Boers are a filthy lot.'

'I shall swear in a minute!'

'Oh come on,' Sonny pretended to rise. 'We'll all have to go out if Belle starts swearing.'

'It is not amusing! Some of the poor little devils are living skeletons! If Grandfather were here he'd have something to say on that score; he experienced starvation. I think it's disgraceful to see you all at this table, stuffing yourselves silly, making facetious remarks about it being like a seaside camping holiday!'

'So this is what I've been missing for twenty-six years,' smiled Dickie.

'Oh shut up, you!'

'Hey, is that any way to speak to your only contributor?'

'Don't tell me ye managed to get money out o' him?' said an amazed Erin. 'It's like milking a hedgehog.'

'Yes, and it was a most generous contribution as a matter of fact,' informed Belle, 'At least one member of this family has some morals,' and could not understand why most of those present broke into laughter. But at least her unintended humour had averted a serious argument and the meal was allowed to continue under a different topic of conversation. After dinner, Thomasin and the other women withdrew, leaving Dick, Sonny, Francis and Nick to smoke and chat. There was little garrulity from the young man, who was far too incensed over the Chairmanship to indulge in small talk with his enemy. Francis, also, said little, feeling almost too tired to open his mouth. He was beginning to abandon hope of catching Thomasin's firstborn alone, when Dick excused himself to visit the lavatory. Saying that he must be on his way, Francis bade adieu to Nick and Sonny and followed his prey into the hall.

'Richard, if you'd spare me a moment.' Dick paused in his ascent of the stairs and asked what he could do for Francis. 'Will you come back down, I don't want to have to shout.' When Dick had complied, he said, 'How much will you take to drop the idea of joining the company and go back to America?'

Dickie laughed. 'That's blunt I must say.'

'Don't waste time.' Francis wasn't smiling. 'I don't want your mother to hear this.'

'I'm not surprised! Trying to get rid of her beloved son when she's trying her damnedest to keep me here. Can I ask why?'

'In brief, I don't like you.'

This had little effect on Dickie, who said casually, 'I know that.'

'You probably won't wish to hear my reasons, but I shall tell you all the same: it's because I know how much you've hurt your mother in the past and I believe that if you stay here you'll hurt her again. I want her last years to be happy ones. Also, I want Nick to have what's rightfully his.'

Dick was still smiling but it was a nasty expression. 'Ah, come on now be truthful, Fran. It's yourself you're looking after. Now Dad's dead ye expected to get your feet under the table.'

'How dare you suggest that!' Francis gripped the handle of his cane.

'I don't know what you're getting so aeriated about, ye don't even belong to this family – why should you care?'

'Might I inform you that during your long years of deception I have been regarded as a member of this family. I helped build that business into what it is. I'm concerned about who's controlling it but I care a great deal more about your mother and I won't let you hurt her.'

'You silly old buzzard.' Dickie sneered. 'I didn't come here to hurt her. I came 'cause I wanted to see how she was – how they all are.'

'But you never intended to stay.'

Dick grew angry. What gave this old codger the right to imply that he didn't know how to treat his own mother? 'How in hell d'you know what I intended?'

'I read you very well, Richard.' Francis' sherry-coloured

244

eyes blazed. 'I can see that you have not one shred of regard for the business but you might take what Thomasin offers just to spite Nicholas.'

'Why in God's name would I want to do that?' sighed Dickie.

'For some obscure, childish reason of your own. Now,' Francis reached inside his jacket. 'How much?'

'Shove it up your arse,' replied Dickie. 'I'm not having anybody telling me what to do. I'll go back when I'm good and ready. In the meantime if I feel like it I might just take up Mam's offer.' Without excusing himself he turned his back and went upstairs.

The old man tried to control his palpitations before seeking out his hostess and begging his leave. 'I can't keep the hours I used to do in my youth, Thomasin.' He clutched her hand and kissed it. 'If I'm not in bed by ten I'll fall asleep on one of your sofas and you'll never wake me.'

Thomasin dragged herself painfully to the hall where John helped the old man on with his coat, then went to open the front door. Francis still held her hand and looked her in the eye. 'D'you think he'll accept the offer?'

'Who – oh, Dickie. I hope so.'

'You realise that Nicholas expects to get that Chairmanship when you relinquish it.'

She nodded. 'Poor Nick . . . I'm going to disappoint him yet again. But I have to have some carrot to keep Dickie here, Fran.'

'I know he's in some sort of business in America, Thomasin, but where is his experience in retail? Isn't it a bit rash to put him in charge? Just remember how long it's taken us to build that business up. Nick knows the company inside out. You really are being unfair on him.' At Thomasin's shrug, he gave up the argument. 'Well . . . I trust you know what you're doing.' His words lacked conviction. 'Goodnight, dear.'

When the door closed on Francis, instead of going back in to join the others, Thomasin went into Pat's study, lowering herself into his chair. 'I don't know what I'm doing at all, that's the trouble, Pat. I feel more confused now than I did at Feen's age. I don't want to disappoint Nick after all he's done for the business, but I'll do anything to keep Dickie here.'

She sat there thinking of Pat, wondering for the millionth time if the consequences would have been different had she made more effort to stop his drinking earlier. Then – what the hell am I feeling guilty about? she asked him forcefully. You brought it on yourself, no one asked you to drink so much, did they? Look at the times you embarrassed me. You wouldn't mix with my friends, you just wanted to go your own stubborn way and expected me to conform – I don't know why I'm even talking to you! I won't feel guilty, you awkward old bugger, I damnwell won't!

The door opened. Belle looked surprised to see her grandmother and after apologising made as if to go.

'No, come in, love.' Thomasin crooked a hand to draw her back.

The young woman entered the room and, closing the door, stared around at her grandfather's belongings. 'I just wanted to . . . feel close to him.' She hugged her arms round herself, looking rather perplexed.

'And do you?'

'Yes – isn't it strange?' breathed her grand-daughter in wonder. 'I feel as if Gramps is in this room.'

Belle stared at the old woman who sat in her grandfather's chair. She and Thomasin had never shared the bond enjoyed by the other grandchildren, though in these past few years things had improved tremendously between them. Now, though, there was a new feeling. It was as if this wasn't Nan sitting in that chair, but Grandfather. Belle had a sudden desire to sit on the chair arm beside

246

her. On doing so, she felt Patrick's presence even more strongly.

The move surprised Thomasin, as did her own impulse, which was to link fingers with those of her grand-daughter. In the space of two minutes, an intimacy had sprung up between them. Both were rather moved by it and did not speak for a while.

Thomasin employed humour to mask her intense emotion. 'I thought you might've come here to make a confession – you know, what I was saying earlier about there having to be three births.'

'Nan, what a thing to say to your unmarried grand-daughter!' Belle smacked her hand reprovingly.

Thomasin put on a knowing face. 'Why is it that every member of this family thinks I'm daft?'

Belle laughed lightly . . . then looked into her grand-mother's canny smile and realised that Thomasin knew all about the intimacy between herself and Brian. The revelation drew a gasp. Then she sobered and asked worriedly, 'Gramps didn't know, did he?'

'Not from me, he didn't.' Thomasin's smile grew sad. 'We didn't seem to get very much time to talk . . . at least I didn't. I doubt he knew, though. I think you would've heard something from him if he had.'

Belle nodded, still rather mystified as to how her grand-mother had come to learn of her relationship with Brian. 'How long have you known?'

'That question implies that it's been going on for quite a while,' answered Thomasin. Belle merely smiled. The old lady tilted her head in shrewd manner. 'Not going to tell me, eh?'

Belle gave a half-hearted shrug. 'I don't mind. It's three years actually.'

'Three years,' mused Thomasin. 'I really am losing my

wits. I only guessed on the morning after you came back from Africa. When you rolled up so early with Brian . . . well, you were like a married couple. I thought it might have started while you were away. Three years, eh, and still no plans to marry?' When Belle shook her head, she quizzed, 'Would you marry Brian if he gave you a baby?' Belle said there was no chance of that. Her grandmother replied that this was not what she had asked.

'No, I wouldn't marry him.' For once Belle was at a loss to explain. 'You wouldn't understand, Nan.'

'Oh, and why wouldn't I?' demanded the old woman tartly. Belle said that things were different in her day. 'Eh, you young'ns! Every generation thinks it's the one to discover the difference between men and women. I might tell you, young lady, that I had a good deal of practice before I married your grandfather – good God, I've shocked the girl!' She laughed at Belle's expression, then whispered, 'Don't tell your mother. You're the first I've ever told.' How remarkable was this new bond! Belle was experiencing it, too. She gripped Thomasin's hand, feeling for all the world as if she were holding Patrick's. 'Your grandfather'd like to see you happy, Belle.'

'For me happiness doesn't have to mean marriage, Nan.'

'But you are happy with Brian?'

Belle's eyes toured the rows of books: red, green, blue spines, some with gold lettering, some with silver, leatherbound, all well-thumbed. 'Yes.'

'It took you a long time to think about that.' When her grand-daughter did not respond, Thomasin looked at her carefully. 'You said earlier that I wouldn't understand.' It was formed as a query.

Belle hesitated, then divulged. 'I don't love Brian – at least, not in the romantic sense. We're just very good friends. You must think me awfully shameless. Sometimes I feel guilty about it.' She sighed. 'It's hard to put into words.'

'You don't have to,' said Thomasin. 'I've had such a relationship myself. Well, not quite the same but very similar in that there was no romance. I knew this man . . . was his mistress as a matter of fact. I wouldn't have married him even if he'd been free because I didn't love him in that way, but we did have a very good friendship.'

Belle gave a disbelieving laugh. 'I can't get over this – Nan, you're outrageous! Mother would never understand.' Erin had nearly fainted when her daughter had lit a cigarette.

'I'm sure she wouldn't and I'm sure she doesn't know about you and Brian so don't even think of making it public. You'll only hurt her.' She gripped Belle's hand more tightly. 'But just because I understand, doesn't mean I don't worry about you, so do be careful, Belle. I wouldn't want to see you forced into marriage by pregnancy – yes, I know what you said but opinions haven't changed that much, Belle. An illegitimate child is still a creature of scorn – not to mention what folk would call its mother. You wouldn't want to inflict that on a child of yours, would you?'

'You may be right,' concurred Belle. 'People set great store by appearances. If I did fall for a baby I'd probably conform like all the rest, much as I'd despise myself. It's just as well it's a hypothetical question; I have no intention of bearing a child.'

'That's what they all say. It might be less of a risk for you with Brian being a doctor and knowing about such things, but he's only human.' Thomasin clutched her hand and shook it. 'I don't want to harp on about it, love, it's just that I want you to visualize what it'd be like if you were forced to marry Brian and then someone came along who swept you off your feet like your grandfather did me.' Her voice trembled.

The young woman laid her head against her grandmother's and gave her a loving squeeze. 'Oh, Nan, I'm sorry about the argument before. I know how upset you still must be – I am.'

Thomasin patted her. 'Nay, don't start burning your soapbox just because you reckon I'll be upset. You can't change your nature, Belle, and I wouldn't want you to. You carry on with your cause . . . I still think you're bloody wrong, mind.'

Belle tutted, and laughed but did not argue. She sat thinking for a time, then ventured a question. 'Nan . . . what happened in eighteen-sixty?'

'Eighteen-sixty?' Thomasin's white eyebrows puckered.

'Grandfather once told me it was the year that you and he almost split up – he didn't go into details, of course . . . I just wondered what could have happened; it must've been something very drastic.'

Thomasin's smile had gone. 'It was, but I'm not sure I want to tell you about it, Belle.'

'Oh, if I'm being nosey . . .'

'No, you're not being nosey.' Thomasin moved her head slowly from side to side. 'It's just something I'd rather forget. Let's just say that he thought I'd betrayed him and I thought the opposite. That was half the trouble. Your grandfather and me, we were too much of opposites, we liked different things, had different values . . .' Belle apologised for raking up old hurts. 'That's all right, love. It wasn't all bad. In fact it was quite a passionate year.' From the look in her eyes, she was far away.

'That's what Gramps said, too.'

Thomasin's mind came back to the room and she smiled again. 'Tell me, have you decided whether or not you're going to let Dickie adopt those kids of yours?'

Belle shook her head. 'I like him, but I'll reserve judgement for the time being. It would make it a little easier if they intended to stay in this country.'

'Well, I'm doing my best in that area,' said Thomasin. 'But there's still this insurance thing hanging over our heads. Dickie was all for going back to the United States but his wife persuaded him to stay. She and Dickie want those children badly.' There was a tap at the door. 'Oh God, who's that come to pester us?'

Belle limped over and twisted the knob. It was Lol who said he was looking for her grandmother. Thomasin called for him to come in and asked what she could do for him. He seemed reluctant to speak in front of Belle.

'Oh, private is it?' she said airily.

'No, it's just . . .'

'Don't worry, Mr Kearney, I'm not interested!'

'I hope I haven't upset her,' said Lol as the door closed on Belle.

'Surely you've known her long enough to realise you can't upset her, Lol.'

He grinned, but was soon looking awkward again. 'Mrs Feeney, I thought you should know, well it's only right . . . Me an' Sarah, we're gonna have to bring the wedding forward . . . like next week.'

'Been a naughty boy, have we?' said Thomasin sternly. 'I was wondering who the culprit would be.' When Lol hung his head she chuckled. 'Oh, don't worry lad. You won't be the first.'

He raised penitent eyes. 'I'm sorry I've let you down.'

'Don't talk daft, Lol! You haven't let anybody down.'

'Oh, but Mrs Feeney, you don't . . .'

'For heaven's sake, Lol, if you tell me I don't understand I'll swing for you! I do know what it's like to be in love, you know.' She studied his forlorn posture and said more kindly. 'Are Sarah's parents very upset?'

He nodded. 'Her dad thumped me.'

'Aw! Still, it could have been a shotgun – and he hasn't marked your face.'

Lol managed a laugh and rubbed his sore belly. 'That's what he said. Didn't want me appearing in front of his

251

relatives sporting a shiner.' His amusement was shortlived. 'I really am sorry about showing you up like this. You're not going to sack me, are you? If I lose me job I . . .'

She was baffled. 'Why should I sack you? And how can it be showing me up?'

'Well . . . Sarah's dad, he said it were the way I'd been brought up.'

'He did, did he!' She feigned outrage. 'I might have a few things to say about him if he isn't careful – oh don't worry, Lol, I'll wait till after the wedding to sort him out. Next week, you said?'

He nodded. 'A week today. Her dad's goin' frantic 'cause he had it all worked out how much he needed to save. Says he can't afford the sort o' do he'd planned an' people'll known it's a rush job.'

'I'll speak to him,' said Thomasin. 'I understand that he sees it as his responsibility, but as I'm Sarah's employer I don't think I'd be out of order in offering to hold the reception here, d'you?'

'I don't know if he'd let you . . .'

'Just tell him if we have a big posh do then Sarah's relations'll be that impressed they'll have something more to talk about than his daughter's condition. Besides, I always said I'd like to give you a good send-off. We're all very fond of you, you know.'

'Eh, Mrs Feeney, I feel so guilty. I mean, a week, it doesn't give you much time to prepare.'

'Next week or next year, if the caterers are any good they'll fix it. Tell Sarah not to worry, nothing's going to spoil her wedding. To let you into a secret, Lol, I'm glad it's been brought forward. I could do with something to cheer me up.'

'Oh, thanks, Mrs Feeney.' Lol beamed. 'She'll be that relieved.'

Well, I'm glad somebody is, thought Thomasin.

12

In spite of the wedding being a hasty affair, it was an enjoyable one for all concerned, giving the Feeney womenfolk an opportunity to put aside their black for one day. Sonny's daughters wore the dresses which their aunt had bought them, with black hats and gloves as a token of mourning. Erin was in deep crimson, her mother in grey, both with the obligatory black trimmings. The rest of the women showed similar respect, though of course the family of Lol's bride had no such commitment. Sarah's parents had been slightly miffed at not being the providers of what was to them a lavish reception – it made it look as if they couldn't do right by their daughter – but Thomasin had informed them that for today this wasn't her home, they were the hosts and she was glad for once to stay in the background whilst they toured the assembly of guests.

In this pose she was able to take in more of the proceedings than if she were having to entertain, and so was privy to the antics of her elder son. Dickie, resplendent in his morning suit with a totally incongruous purple cravat, had his arm round his brother's wife, trying to coax her away. 'Come on, Josie! Have a dance with a handsome bloke for a change.'

Sonny issued a mocking laugh at this effrontery and said his wife had better be mindful of her feet. However Josie, like almost every other woman in the room before her, allowed herself to be swung around the dance floor. The modest number of guests had removed the need to hire a ballroom; with the furniture pulled back and the big double doors to the hall open, there was ample room for cavorting.

Dusty, used to her husband's flirtations, watched placidly, while Erin, from a seat near to Thomasin's, made acid observations. 'God, will ye look at Buffalo Bill there. Strutting about like a rooster and all those daft hens clucking round him.' She tapped her foot to the scratchy music. Her mother had declined to hire an orchestra when she had a perfectly good gramophone. Feen had been placed in charge of this and sat winding furiously, waiting for her uncle to get around to her. 'He's even got Josie at it. I would've thought she'd have more sense.'

'He is gorgeous though, isn't he?' replied Thomasin. 'I'd think so even if he weren't my own son.'

'Aye, he's that all right,' conceded Erin thoughtfully.

'You're not still harbouring that grudge, surely?' said her mother. 'It's you who'll suffer from it, not Dickie.'

'Oh, I realise he couldn't give a hoot what I think of him.' Erin looked across the room at Dusty. 'No, I'm just thinking how hard I've been on her. It must be murder being married to my brother.'

'She doesn't look too unhappy,' smiled Thomasin. Belle's children were among the guests and the two girls whom Dusty hoped to adopt were sitting talking to her, though Thomasin could not see Freddie at the moment.

Erin was still cogitating over her sister-in-law. 'I think I'll just go over and sit with her for a while. Ye'll be all right on your own now?'

'Get away before I clatter you,' ordered her mother and turned her attention to her grandson and Francis. Nick was apparently trying to convince the older man of something, making gestures and leaning forward intently. It had to be business; Nick didn't wear that look of enthusiasm for anything else. Poor Sonny, now sitting with them, had a glazed expression on his face.

The subject of Nick's eager chat was a profit-sharing scheme. 'It's like this, Fran.' He motioned with his hands. 'Each month we set aside a section of the profits, dividing it amongst the staff, according to how long they've been with us and the hours they work. At the end of the year, say Christmas, we pay it out in a lump sum.' Here Francis voiced amusement that Nick was actually proposing giving away the company's money. 'It's not a gift, it's an incentive, Fran. The harder they work the higher the profits to be shared. From the point of view of the factory it's a more effective scheme than piece work because it improves the quality of their output. On the shop side, it'll make them more keen to catch pilferers. What d'you say? Will you back me?'

Francis agreed it was a sound idea and said he would discuss it with Thomasin. 'Not today though.'

Nick threw up his arms. 'It's always not today with her! She's too busy trying to persuade Uncle Dick to take my job.'

His father introduced a note of optimism. 'Don't worry too much on that score, son. He's more bothered about getting the children. Once the decision's been made he'll be away.'

'I wonder if Fred realises how privileged he is.' Nick tapped his patent leather boot.

Dismayed at his own lack of tact, Sonny fell silent. Nick caught the implication. 'Oh no, I didn't mean it like that, Dad. I've told you he's nothing to me. No, it's my bloody future I'm worried about, not the past.'

Sonny examined the young man's face. Like his brother he found it hard to believe that there was no bitterness present. It was nigh impossible to read Nick, but he tended to favour what his son had said. Nick had little time for emotion of any kind. He wished he could set the young man's mind at rest over the Chairmanship, but he could never be sure which way his brother would turn.

Erin made her way through the wedding guests, surprising Dusty with her cordial approach. 'Ye looked left out, your husband dancing with all the other women, so I thought I'd come and keep ye company.'

'Don't worry about me.' Her sister-in-law's green eyes sparkled. 'I've got these two to keep me on my toes – but come sit down, Erin.'

Erin did so, smiling at Faith and Julia. 'I expect you're getting quite attached to them.' Dusty was spending more and more time at Belle's lately.

'We are. I do hope Belle realises that.' Dusty glanced at Belle who was sitting with Brian, watching the dancers. Dickie was now twirling Feen around the room while one of her sisters took over the gramophone. The young girl's face was ecstatic.

'I'm sure she does. And I hope it works out for you, Dusty.'

Dusty offered a surprised smile of thanks. 'I'm forgiven, then?'

'You are.' Erin settled back to watch the dancers. After a period of deep thought, she said 'Dusty . . . do you think I'm fat?'

Her sister-in-law spoke kindly. 'You're nowhere near fat. Don't let Dickie nettle you.' She looked across the room at Thomasin. 'Your mother's still very low, isn't she?'

Erin snatched glances of her mother's frowning face between the milling guests. 'Aye . . . still, it's not three months since Dad died. And she's worried over this insurance thing. So am I. I can't say I won't be glad when you go back to America.'

Dusty thought about this. Though her husband was keen to be on his way, she herself had no yen for America. With the dilution of Erin's venom, she had found herself growing used to being part of this large family. 'Your mother wants us to stay.'

'Ye know that's not really feasible. That insurance man's onto Dickie, I'm positive. The sooner you're gone the better.'

Dusty had to agree, although it wasn't just the insurance fraud that worried her, but her niece. 'We can't go until Belle's made her mind up.'

'Ah well, I don't know if it'll help but I'll speak to her in your favour.'

Dusty thanked her, kissing the top of Faith's blonde head as the child slid off her lap to romp with her sister. 'But it's Dickie who's the main stumbling block.'

'Isn't he always?'

Dusty turned on her. 'That's rather unfair. It was you who coloured Belle's judgement against him in the first place.'

'Expected the big homecoming, did he?'

Her sister-in-law replied firmly, 'No, he knew you'd have plenty to say and that he deserved it, but neither of us expected it to be so prolonged. He's changed a lot since last you saw him, Erin, and he's as fond of the children as I am.'

'I don't believe that for one minute,' replied Erin. 'But much as it galls me I'll speak on his behalf. Anything to get rid of this dreadful threat that's hanging over us.'

Dusty might have a quick temper, but she lacked Erin's capacity for bitterness. There was no trace of acrimony on her face now and the thanks she issued were sincere.

Erin flicked her head. 'Ye know, I have to admire you, Dusty. Ye've managed to hold onto him all these years. How, and more to the point *why* did ye do it?'

'It might surprise you to know that I didn't have to do anything. Dickie is the one who's had to do the holding on.

And I stay with him because I'm married to him and I love him, Erin.'

The boisterous Julia was calling. 'Watch me! Watch, Aunt Dusty!'

Erin smiled affectionately at the other woman's reaction. 'Ye want them very badly. don't ye?' With her sister-in-law's nod, she regressed into memories. 'People are so funny, aren't they? I remember wanting a dozen babies when I first got wed, but if I couldn't have had one, then I wouldn't have wanted anyone else's. I only wanted Sam's – oh, Dusty, I'm sorry, that was cruel.'

Every day, thought Dusty, every single day there's someone who'll remind you what a failure you are. But she employed the banal shield that had served her for many a year. 'It doesn't matter.'

'Ah dear, I'll never see Belle in a wedding gown. And I'll never be a grandma . . . I'm grateful I've got her, though.'

The brass horn of the gramophone fell silent. Dickie bowed to his adoring satellite, forsook her, and set his sights on Belle.

Up until now the latter had been content just to watch the dancing. When Dickie approached she waved him away, blowing her red nose. As a result of the sudden drop in climate on her return from Africa she had incurred a heavy cold which she had passed to the children. The room hummed of camphor, completely drowning the scent of the bride's sweet bouquet. 'You deedn't ibagine you can dance with every female in the roob and leave me as a last resort.'

'Nonsense!' cried Dickie. ''Twas merely a case of leaving the best until last.'

'I'm sorry, Uncle, but I don't dance.' Belle glanced at Brian who was plucking tetchily at his pin-striped trousers. She tucked the sodden handkerchief back up her sleeve.

'Everybody dances,' responded her uncle. Discounting her

refusal, he grabbed her and began to twirl, holding her much closer than either decency or his wife allowed.

Feen was mortified. Neglecting the gramophone, she rushed off to her room. No one noticed until the voice on the record developed a low drawl and Sophia rushed over to wind it.

Feen could have felt no more anger than Brian. His nostrils twitched as he put a match to his cigarette, but it was more than the sulphur that irritated. Belle had been watching her uncle all afternoon. Her mouth told Brian that he was being ridiculous, but her eyes spoke otherwise. He cast a look at Dusty. She was talking to Erin but her expression showed that he was not alone in his assessment of the situation. It made him even angrier. He looked back at the dancers. Belle and her uncle had vanished.

Dusty saw the doctor craning his neck anxiously and wondered whether to tell him that she had just seen his beloved being danced out through the french windows. Instead, she decided to handle this herself.

Brian became alert as Dusty stood, said something to her sister-in-law and the girls, then made for the french windows. He waited a few minutes after she had gone into the garden before following. On the terrace he shaded his eyes; the March sun held little warmth but reflected off the paving flags it was blinding. He peered down the garden, wondering which of the many paths Dusty had taken. She was nowhere to be seen. He set off along a route lined with spring bulbs, searching every bower along the way.

Dickie had waltzed his niece all the way around the path that skirted the garden, humming a continuation of the tune. His niece, awkward in her surgical boot, gave up the protestations for him to stop, and made the best of things. While her aunt and Brian searched, she and her uncle were already re-entering the party, where the crackling record was just coming to its close. Catching her breath, Belle laughed and forced herself out of his embrace. 'Oh no! You're not doing that to me again. I'm going for a rest, and you should too at your age.'

'Cheeky wench! I'll be back for another one later.' A smiling Dickie watched her limp exhaustedly to her seat, then decided to go and answer the call of nature.

On finding an empty chair, Belle looked round, then went over to ask her grandmother, 'Have you seen Brian, Nan?'

Thomasin, having been thinking of her husband, looked askance. 'He was there a minute ago, love.'

Belle sat down, still trying to regain her breath. 'Never mind. He's probably in the garden. I'll go and find him in a moment.'

Brian had almost caught up with Dusty. He hung back, not wanting to admit to her that he harboured the same suspicion. At each secret cranny he watched her pause to listen for whispers. But the garden yielded nothing save the chirp of sparrows.

She sauntered on, pausing uncertainly at the ice-house beneath the group of budding trees, ear cocked at the door. Brian shared her indecision: should she go in? Her hand hovered over the latch for a second, then pulled. The door fought against her, scraping the pebble-strewn ground. Brian held his breath as she went inside. But she emerged within seconds and, ramming the door on the frozen interior, marched on.

He followed her right around the snaking path to the house. Instead of re-entering by the french windows, she took the front door: Brian did not know why, but copied her. When he edged round the door and into the hall she was nowhere to be seen . . . but Dickie was.

Brian watched his carefree jog down the stairs, saw him pull his clothes into place. He ignored the bright greeting that Dickie gave on spotting him, uttering stiffly, 'Can I have a private word with you, please?'

'Sure!' Dickie indicated his father's study and, once they were in there, said, 'What can I do for ye, Bri?'

Brian clasped his hands behind his back and looked down at his spats. 'I don't know if you realise that Belle and I have more than just a platonic relationship?'

'I gathered as much.' Dickie grinned and gave him a conspiratorial tap on the shoulder. 'Don't worry, your secret's safe with me.'

'Oh, I don't worry,' replied Brian. 'Not about that . . . however, one thing does concern me. I can understand that a man of your years might feel certain insecurities . . .' The other's smile began to fade. '. . . Might find the need to prove he's still virile. Well, I can sympathise with that, but I'd prefer it if you practised on someone other than Belle.'

'Wha . . . you . . . I don't bloody believe what I'm hearing!' Dickie was thunderstruck, but came to life now as Brian reached for the door. 'Hey, just hold on a minute, you! Ye can't go around accusing a man of that and then walk out!'

'I've nothing further to add,' said Brian curtly. 'I just want you to keep your hands off Belle.' Before Dickie could speak again, he had closed the door.

Dickie stood there nonplussed. By the time he thought to go after Brian the hall was empty. He glared for a second through the open doors of the drawing room at the happy throng of guests, then decided it would be unwise to rejoin them in his present state. Charging up the stairs he burst upon his wife who had been examining their room in search of him.

'Oh, there you are!' She looked most annoyed.

'That bloody little shit of a doctor!' He slammed the door, then kicked at a piece of furniture. 'D'you know what he's just said to me?'

261

'I can guess.'

At her icy tone he looked at her more closely. 'Bloody . . . ye don't think . . . Christ!' He strode about like one demented, cursing and swearing his disbelief. Dickie didn't often get mad with her, but when he did it was quite a spectacle. He kicked at another piece of furniture, then changed tack, pleading, 'Surely Dusty, you don't think . . . ?'

'How the hell do I know! But I am not prepared to sit down and watch the pair of you carry on as if there were no one else in the room!'

His temper reboiled. 'That's bloody daft!'

'It's right!'

'You were the one who told me to turn the charm on! I'm doing it for you, to get ye those kids.'

'Well, you're making too good a job of it, I want it to stop!'

He saw her bunched fist and was quick to ward her off. 'Don't you dare mark my face for this weddin'!'

With great difficulty she refrained from striking him, but said through clenched teeth. 'Just you take heed.'

'All right, all right! I won't even bloody talk to her!' He was still furious that anyone, especially Dusty, could believe he'd sink to such depths.

'It's not the talking I mind.'

'Ye know your trouble?' He pointed at her. 'You're too bloody possessive.'

She was calmer now, though still dangerous. 'All this anger worries me, Dickie. Usually when you're found out you behave like a whipped dog.'

'What're ye talking about *found out* – there's nothing going on, I tell ye. Oh . . . sod ye!' He stormed from the room.

Belle, having failed to find Brian, was investigating the hall and looked up at her uncle's thumping descent. 'Oh hello, have you see . . .'

'Yes I have!'

'What's the matter?' She came to the foot of the stairs.

'The matter is, my dear,' Dickie completed his descent and spoke right into her face, 'your doctor friend has just accused me of having carnival knowledge of you.'

Belle groaned. 'I'll kill him. Where is he now?'

'I don't know an' I don't care, but I would like to know how he got the impression that there was something between us.'

Belle gaped at him. 'You think I told him? You've got a nerve!'

'He got it from somewhere!'

Belle was furious. 'Well, not from me!'

Through the open doors of the drawing room, he saw heads beginning to turn towards the altercation. Erin came bustling out to hiss at them, 'Do you two mind! There's a wedding going on in here. What's all the noise about?'

Belle tore her steely eyes away from Dickie, saying to her mother, 'Sorry . . . there's just been a misunderstanding between Brian and my uncle.'

'What about – and where is Brian?'

'About the children's adoption,' said Belle, for want of another answer. 'I have no idea where Brian is. In Hell for all I care. I'm not going to let him spoil the afternoon.' She marched back into the drawing room.

Erin narrowed her eyes at Dickie, then told him, 'We're about to throw the pennies to the children, are ye coming to watch?'

Calming himself, he donned his normal devil-may-care expression. 'Don't mind if I do.'

'Well, give Dusty a shout then.' Erin went back into the room.

A shovelful of coins had been warming over the coals. When Sonny ascertained that everyone was present he lifted the shovel and led a procession to the front door. Outside, a horde of ragged children were assembled, having being forewarned of the happening. With a whoop, Sonny tossed the shovelful of pennies high in the air – and what a scrambling and fighting and jostling did this provoke as the waifs tried to catch the hot pennies.

'Oh, God, look at him!' Dickie had caught sight of Frederick, who had sneaked into the crowd of children and was effortlessly collecting the coins – with the aid of gloves. 'Dusty, come here an' look at him!' Apparently forgetting their argument, he pulled her forward, laughing at Fred's ingenuity and shouting to everybody, 'That's my lad!'

Sonny approached his wife, who guessed he had something funny to tell her from the hand that kept creeping to his mouth. He could hardly eject the words. 'You know . . .' he broke off to snigger, then began again. 'You know when Dickie had that black eye and I made the joke about Dusty doing it? Well . . .' he snorted again and tried to look straight-faced. 'I think she really did do it!' His shoulders shook and he turned his face to the wall lest Dickie read his mirth.

Josie's jaw dropped. 'Aw, she never did!'

He nodded, eyes watering. 'I've just been upstairs and I heard him shouting – "Don't you dare mark me for this wedding"!'

The pair fell into clandestine giggles.

The wedding festivities continued until early evening. Belle asked Sally to take the children home to bed so that she could enjoy a supper with her family – though it was hardly enjoyable, knowing what was going through her Aunt Dusty's mind every time Belle so much as looked at her uncle. Nevertheless, she stayed if only to avoid a row with Brian, who would most certainly have been waiting for her had she gone home earlier.

By this time, ten o'clock, she calculated that he would have grown sick of hanging round.

He hadn't. When she entered her parlour there he was to greet her. Seeing him, she pulled up sharply, then marched on, easing off her gloves and slapping them onto the sideboard. 'And what are you doing here?'

He had risen, face contrite. 'I've been waiting to see you.'

'Oh really? Well, now you have done you can get out. Sally!' she called into the kitchen. 'Make some cocoa will you – for one.'

'Belle . . .' He tried to take her arm.

She looked at him coldly. 'I'm afraid if you require cocoa, Doctor, you'll have to take it elsewhere.'

His brown eyes pleaded. 'I only did it because I care for you so much.'

'Did what? Stormed off like a truculent child leaving me to escort myself home? A fine way of showing you care!'

Brian lost his temper. 'I'm sure there were plenty of volunteers to accompany you!'

'Ah, so that's why I find you here,' she rasped. 'Not to apologise but to learn which one of them might have jiggered me after you left.'

'If you're not prepared to talk about this sensibly . . .'

'Sensibly! You accuse my uncle of . . .' She uttered a mew of suppressed fury. 'I can't believe that you could think anything so despicable. If my mother could hear this . . .'

'She probably saw it for herself! You were openly flirting with him!'

'And where's the sin in flirting? I'm twenty-six, not an old woman.'

'So you admit it?'

'Admit that he's a very attractive man? That I find his attention flattering? Yes, I do. What's wrong with that?'

'Because I love you and it hurts me, that's what's wrong!'

She studied his anguished face, and after a long hesitation, said, 'I think we've come to the parting of the ways, Brian.'

He was too shocked to answer.

'I just can't cope with all this. I haven't time to waste on answering these interrogations every five minutes. You knew how it was when we started this relationship.'

Brian found his voice which emerged in a tone of disbelief. 'I knew that you didn't love me, yes! But I certainly didn't think you were going to flaunt yourself at other men.'

'I'm sorry if my bit of enjoyment has hurt you; it certainly wasn't intended to. But I think it's shown both of us how futile this relationship of ours is. The longer it continues the more you're going to expect of me and the more you're going to be hurt. You want too much, Brian . . . it's better if we end it now.'

'Oh, Belle . . .' He clapped a hand to his dismayed brow, searching for an answer. 'We can't throw all these years away on something so . . . Look, just forget I came here tonight and what I said today. I was wrong and I'm sorry. Let's just go back to what we had. I swear I won't try and possess you. I love you.'

She almost blushed for him. 'Don't grovel, Brian.'

'Grovel!' His eyes flew to hers. 'I tell you I love you and want to keep you and you call it grovelling?' He looked disgusted. 'For someone who complains so much about people's inhumanity to each other, you're a cold cruel bitch sometimes.' He spent three seconds glaring at her impassive face, then spun on his heel. 'Goodbye, Belle.'

She turned away uncaringly as he walked out.

In the ensuing quiet, Sally opened the kitchen door a crack and peeped through. 'Is it safe to come in with the cocoa?'

'Damn the cocoa!' Belle glanced at her, then sat down. 'Sorry.'

'What was it about this time?' Sally being a friend as much as a nursemaid, was permitted this familiarity.

Belle gave her a cynical look. 'Missed the odd word, did we?'

'Fancy accusing me of eavesdropping!' Sally put the cocoa on a tablemat.

'I can see the impression of the keyhole on your cheek.'

Sally raised an involuntary hand, then laughed. 'If I were you I'd be flattered.'

'Flattered that my employee cares enough about me to listen to all my private conversations?'

'Tut! I mean that he's jealous!'

'And did you happen to catch what he was jealous about?' said Belle. 'I fail to see anything flattering in that.'

'Well, I agree it was unthinkable but it shows how much he cares for you.'

'I was already aware of that – that's the trouble.'

Sally gave another sound of irritation. 'I don't know! Most women'd be glad to have somebody like Doctor Dyson care for them. All you seem to want to do is drive him away. I can't think why he keeps coming back.'

'He won't be back this time.'

Sally studied the expressionless face. 'I really don't understand you. I mean, I know I'm not supposed to know what you and him get up to on a nighttime – but I am in the room next door, I can't help what I hear . . . You must love him so much and yet you act . . .'

'Why must I love him?' demanded Belle.

'Well, a woman doesn't allow herself to be compromised like that if she doesn't have passionate feelings for a fella.'

Belle laughed pityingly and shook her head. 'Sally, we're living in the twentieth century now. A woman doesn't have to pretend to all that romantic tosh just to satisfy her basic needs.'

267

Sally's brow furrowed. 'But how can you . . .' She didn't mention sex by name, but a gesture showed her meaning, '. . . if you don't love him?'

Belle laughed again. 'Because I enjoy it.'

Shock flooded the nursemaid's face. 'Why, I think that's . . . that's disgusting!' When Belle demanded why, she spluttered, 'You're supposed to love the person!'

'Oh, come, Sally. Don't tell me you never looked at a man and . . .'

Sally docked the question. 'No, I do, I think it's awful! I made allowances for you and him not being married 'cause I thought you were in love with each other, but . . .'

'How magnanimous of you!' came Belle's sarcastic retort.

'But to do it coldly . . .'

'There's nothing cold about it!'

'All these years you've had me thinking you loved him . . . I don't know if I should stay here, now.' Sally looked most offended.

Belle was abrasive. 'Don't be stupid!'

The maid narrowed her eyes. 'You think I'm stupid 'cause I don't believe in letting a man have his way with me before we're wed?'

'Of course I don't! I admire you for sticking to your principles, but you know perfectly well that I have no intention of marrying and I see no reason why I should remain celibate just to have your prudish sanction. You're as bad as Brian — in fact you'd make the perfect couple; the next time I see him I'll suggest it!'

'You said you weren't going to see him again,' taunted Sally.

'Thank you for reminding me!'

Sally was still dumbfounded by the revelation. She put her head to one side and looked at Belle closely. 'What the doctor said about you and your uncle . . . is it true then?'

268

Belle gave an outraged laugh. 'For God's sake!'

'Well, you've just admitted to something I never thought possible, how do I know what you might descend to?'

'You don't!' said Belle sharply. 'Now goodnight!'

'I'll take your cup . . .'

'Goodnight, Sally!'

During March, Belle saw nothing of the doctor; that surprised her, for after each of their previous disagreements Brian had always come creeping round to apologise. She supposed on this occasion their parting had been a little more final than the others; she had never actually told him before that it was finished . . . still, it was an odd sensation. She paused to wonder how she really felt about him, and came to the conclusion that though she did miss him quite badly some nights, she was glad it was over. None of the family were aware of it yet. Since the wedding, she had only seen them briefly, having so much work to do. She would see them for longer today though: it was Mothering Sunday and she was going to a church service and afterwards for luncheon at Peasholme. This latter thought spurred her into motion and Brian was shoved from her thoughts.

'Sally! Where are my . . . oh, Freddie don't creep up on me like that!' She scooped him out of the way in her search for her gloves.

'Where're you off?'

'I am *going* to church.'

'What you off there for?'

'Don't make it sound like such a rare occasion in this house. I'm going because there's a special service for Mothering Sunday when all the sons and daughters should be with their mothers – where are my gloves?'

'I'd better get my coat then.' Freddie turned.

'Why would you be going?' asked Belle carelessly, still

269

searching. Then realising how thoughtless that remark had been, turned to him and said, 'You always get restless in church, Freddie. I thought you could stay with Sally and then we'll all go out this afternoon.'

'But you just said all the sons and daughters should be with their mothers, so I should be with mine. I'll get me coat.' Before she could stop him he had run off.

Belle slapped a hand to her forehead and waited for Freddie to return. 'There'll only be me and my mother there, none of the others . . . still, I don't suppose it would harm for you to come to Peasholme afterwards.' She sighed at the state of him and grabbed hold of his lapels to put him in order. 'They won't allow you into church looking like that. Look at you! Where's that comb?' Finding it, she scraped his hair forward over his brow and drew a parting, ignoring his complaints that the comb scratched. 'You'll be scratching even more if you continue to neglect your hair! And look at your neck for heaven's sake! Go and wash it if you insist on coming with me.' She pushed him at the door and went back to searching for her gloves.

'I'll tell our lasses to get ready an' all,' he shouted over his shoulder.

'Oh no, Freddie . . . oh do if you must! And you can tell the others to get ready, too. If I'm to be lumbered with you three I might as well go the whole hog and let Sally spend the day at her mother's.'

Not being churchgoers, Dickie and his wife had remained at home with his mother, who had not set foot in a church since Patrick's funeral. By lunchtime it seemed as if the entire Feeney clan was congregated in the drawing room. There was Sonny with his sons and daughters, Nick with his son, Erin with her daughter . . . and Dusty with no one. She looked at them all and wondered if any of them guessed how much the sight hurt her. But then of course they wouldn't; none of them knew the torment of childlessness.

There followed presentations of bouquets – from Belle to Erin, Erin to her mother, Josie to Thomasin . . . Dusty prayed for the day to end. She tried to salve her pain in conversation, asking Sonny if his recent birthday had been something to celebrate or to forget – though, of course, not mentioning that he was forty-seven in the presence of his daughters.

'Oh, a celebration definitely,' replied her brother-in-law. 'And thank you for the card – but I'm afraid it was wrongly addressed. It should have said *J. P. Feeney, RA*.'

'Oh, Sonny, congratulations!' beamed his mother. 'And not before time too.'

Dickie finished blowing his nose – he had caught Belle's cold – and reached for his brother's hand. 'You've showed them, Son.' He turned to Josie. 'Did you get anything out o' this, Jos?'

'He tret us all to a new hat each,' said his sister-in-law, and was immediately corrected by Sophie.

'Mother, it's not tret, it's treated.'

'A new hat?' cried Dick. 'Glory be to God, you were a bit extravagant there, weren't ye, Son?' In almost the same breath he pulled a face and looked at the others. 'Christ, can someone tell me what that stink is? It's been up my nose since this morning. I can smell it even with this blocked-up conk.'

Sonny got his own back. 'If it's been following you around then chances are it's coming from you.'

Dickie chastised him, adding the opinion that it was 'bloody horrible'.

For once Erin agreed, then suddenly realised that the smell emanated from her mother. 'It's you!'

'I don't know why you're all kicking up such a fuss about a drop of embrocation,' muttered Thomasin bad-temperedly.

Erin clicked her tongue. 'I knew there was something

271

wrong with that leg! Why did ye not tell us before, ye naughty girl. Have ye been to the doctor?'

'There's no cure for old age,' snapped Thomasin. 'And I'll thank you to stop patronising me, I am still your mother!'

Erin looked at the others and threw up her eyes. During the conversation that followed, Dickie sidled from the room with a mischievous glint to his eye. On his return he was carrying something.

'Got a present for ye, Mam.' He waved his grandmother's walking stick which he had previously noticed tucked away in a cupboard in his bedroom. 'Well, you're beginning to sound like Grandma Fenton, ye might as well look like her, too.' He folded her hand around the stick.

The result was like an eruption of Mount Etna. 'I'm damned if I'm using that!' Thomasin hurled the stick at the window. Luckily it did not hit the pane head on and glanced off without damage, but this served to make Thomasin angrier than ever.

'What's all the stink about – if ye'll pardon the pun,' laughed Dickie. 'Don't I have a walking cane?'

'Yours is to make you look like a dandy!' retorted his mother. 'This one'll make me look like a cripple.'

Dickie looked for Belle's reaction to this but she didn't bat an eyelid. He put his hands together and began to recite a child's prayer. 'I thank you angel dear tonight, for helping me in doing right.'

'You soft monkey!' His mother's face was still cross.

He propped the walking cane in a corner. 'Ah well, I'll leave it here for when ye feel ye need it.'

'The only need I'll have for that is to lay it across your back!'

Dickie leaned towards his sister and whispered, 'At least I managed to provoke some sign of life.'

Erin had to smile in agreement and tempted another

outburst from her mother. 'I'm sure the doctor must have something for the pain. Brian would have told you if you hadn't kept it to yourself – where is Bri, anyway?' she asked of her daughter. Brian, whose own mother was dead, often shared in this family occasion.

Belle had been dreading this, but had never been one to shy away from the truth. 'Brian and I are no longer together.'

Erin gave a disappointed cry which drew the others' attention. 'But why?' she asked. 'When did this happen?'

'A few weeks ago,' replied Belle.

'You never said anything before,' scolded her mother.

'I've barely seen you since Lol's wedding,' said Belle. 'Besides, why should I have told you? It's hardly of world importance.'

'That poor man!' keened Erin. 'So, what have ye done to him, then?'

'I've butchered him with an axe and melted him down in an acid bath.' Her mother said there was no need to be clever. 'Well, must I tell everyone my private affairs?' demanded Belle. 'Brian and I decided that the relationship could no longer continue and . . .'

'I'll bet it wasn't Brian!' interjected her mother. 'He worshipped you. It must've been your fault. Was it the disagreement ye had at the wedding?' Thomasin asked what disagreement. Erin informed her, 'They had a row over the children – it's all right, they're not listening, they're playing upstairs.' She turned to Dickie. 'I believe you were at the root of it.'

'It was nothing to do with the children or Uncle Dick,' said Belle flatly. 'And it's nothing to do with you, Mother or you, Nan. My life is my own and if I choose not to see Brian then that's up to me.'

'Well, I'm sure we'll all miss him,' said Erin and the others agreed. 'He was such a nice fellow . . . like a member of the

273

family.' She looked at Belle coaxingly. 'Oh, can't ye make it up, darlin'? You must miss him too, surely?'

'I don't miss him at all,' said Belle quickly – too quickly.

A knowing smile twitched Erin's lips. 'Now don't tell fibs. I'm sure ye'll make it up with each other whatever it was.'

Belle looked wearily at her grandmother who silently expressed condolence then moved her eyes back to Dusty whom she had been studying.

Dusty sensed the attention, and fought to divert it, asking, 'Have you found a home for the baby yet?'

Belle answered, 'Yes, as a matter of fact he goes tomorrow.'

Dusty felt naked in her disappointment, felt their pity, smelt it above the overpowering stench of liniment . . . She stood up quickly and, not looking at anyone in particular, informed them, 'Well, I think I'll just go and wash my face before luncheon,' and hurried from the room.

Even outside in the hall, the family atmosphere was stifling, with children's coats on the stand, children's gloves on the radiator, a child's wooden horse grinning at her . . . Dusty brought her hands up to her face and rubbed vigorously, trying to exorcise the frustration. The lifetime of childlessness had been bad enough in itself, but this uncertainty was ten times worse, not knowing if the children would be hers or not, not wanting to get too attached to them just in case . . . but failing. There was a little cough. Dusty jumped and removed her hands from her face to see Frederick standing before her, hands behind back. She sighed, then smiled and put out a gentle finger to flick his snub nose, saying nothing. Returning her affection Frederick brought his hand into view; it was holding a bunch of daffodils.

He waited for praise. But his gift produced the opposite effect. 'I thought you'd like 'em,' he said with puzzled face, as Dusty's eyes filled with tears. She was quick to drop into a squat and deliver a reassuring hug, though she could not speak for many seconds.

Frederick allowed himself to be squashed for a moment, then pulled free. 'D'you like 'em?'

Dusty sat back on her heels and brushed her wet cheeks with a palm. 'They're beautiful,' she told him with a sniffle. 'Thank you.'

'The girls are picking some an' all,' he told her. 'But I wanted to get here first.'

'That's very good of . . .' Dusty paused. 'Fred, where did you get them from?'

'Garden. Them two don't know how to pick 'em properly, they've just picked heads.'

'Oh no.' Dusty put a hand to her mouth. 'You shouldn't have picked them from Mrs Feeney's garden.'

'Oh, it's all right, I didn't pick them from hers – there's loads in that garden next door. Are you gonna put 'em in a vase like them in there?' He gestured at the room she had just left, which was where he had got the idea.

She hesitated, then bit her lip and laughed. 'Yes, but we'd better find the girls before they pick too many.'

The girls took little finding, Dusty had only to follow the trail of abandoned daffodil heads. She had intended to apologise to the owners of the decimated gardens but on seeing the extent of the damage, conscience was overthrown by cowardice. Grabbing the girls, she rushed back into the house.

At Frederick's insistence, two separate vases were sent for, 'I'm not having theirs in with mine,' and Dusty was begged to take them into the drawing room to put with the others. Holding the vases rather self-consciously she went in. On hearing that the daffodils were a gift from Fred and his sisters, the other women thought it very touching. Dusty looked more guilty than the culprits as she told Thomasin where the blooms had come from. 'I think you might be getting a few complaints.'

Belle took hold of Fred and shook him. 'You naughty child!'

'You brought flowers for your mother,' he objected.

'Bought them! Not stole them from someone else's garden. For that you can scrub the step every morning this week.'

'Why just me?' he demanded. 'Why not them?'

'Because they're too little to know better. They were just copying you. Now you can do as I told you or I'll double the punishment.'

'Don't be too hard on him, Belle,' entreated her aunt. 'He was only thinking to bring me a gift.'

Belle opposed her. 'He has to be taught that stealing is wrong.'

'I wouldn't say it was stealing really,' coaxed Dusty.

'Well, I would, and as Freddie is in my charge I think I am capable of dealing with his punishment, thank you, Aunt.'

Thomasin intervened. 'I hope you haven't picked any from my garden.' The children said forlornly that they hadn't. 'Oh that's all right then, I won't have to smack any bottoms. Did anybody see you picking the flowers?' Dusty told her she did not think so. Thomasin turned to Belle. 'Well, it's not so bad after all then, is it – and it was done with the best of intentions, Belle. The children were just trying to show us that they'd made up their minds about who they want as their new mother. Have you made your mind up yet?'

Belle was annoyed at being coerced and showed it. 'I don't think it's an appropriate time to discuss it.'

'On the contrary,' said her grandmother. 'I can't think of a more appropriate time than Mothering Sunday.'

'You're being sentimental, Nan,' replied Belle. 'You're not seeing it from my point of view.'

'What is your point of view?' demanded Dickie. 'Ye want

the best for the children, don't ye? Well, so do me and Dusty.' He pulled his wife into his side.

'I just don't think we should be discussing this in front of you-know-who,' said Belle.

'It seems to me that you-know-who have already made their minds up,' said Sonny. 'It's you who's . . .'

'Don't think that by ganging up on me you'll provoke a decision!' warned Belle, then started exasperatedly at the collection of pleading faces and clicked her tongue. 'What a family!' Her eyes moved down to Frederick's face. It was true, she couldn't keep him and his sisters waiting forever. They spoke of nothing else but their new mother and father. After instructing them, 'Go play in the garden,' she told the gathering, 'Look, I realise that you all have great difficulty in understanding how a cold-hearted woman like me can be doing such work, but just consider this: where were all the soft hearts when those children needed help?' Her accusation hit home and several pairs of eyes were diverted; Belle had faced much opposition when setting up her home for waifs and strays. 'Yes, it's all too easy to say, "Oh, dear isn't it a pity?", but not so easy to translate that pity into action. Well, I don't just offer sympathy, I *do* something about it. And I haven't worked myself to death educating them, scrimped and saved to feed them, just to let them jaunt off to America with someone about whom I know precious little. Having said this . . . if things are still going as smoothly by the end of the month, then Fred and the girls can move in here and I'll start drawing up contracts.'

Whilst the others gasped their delight, Thomasin declared, 'Well, I must say that's awfully generous of you to let them live in my house, Belle.' At her grand-daughter's smile of penitence, she allowed herself to add her good wishes to her son and his wife.

Dickie was cautious. 'What's so important about the end of the month? What difference can a week or so make?'

'By that time I should have received the information I've been waiting for,' said Belle. 'I contacted a detective agency and asked them to investigate your business affairs.' Her uncle looked aghast and his mother threw Belle a suitably reproving look. 'Well, I had to make sure that you lead a pure life, Uncle, and that your finances are secure.'

'The damned cheek of it!' Dickie turned away and passed a worried look to his wife who made synchronous accusation. What hornet's nest was this going to stir up? 'Is it the Pinkertons?' Belle said no and, after a moment or two came up with the name of the agency.

'I'm sure they'll find everything in order, Belle,' said Dusty, praying this were true.

'Well, once I receive their confirmation then I can be more positive,' said Belle. 'Well smile, someone! I've just given in to your threats, haven't I?'

'Am I going to live here now?' Fred had crept back to listen.

Belle turned on him. 'You most certainly are not! I've told you you've got that front step to clean every morning for a week.' At his look of disappointment, she softened. 'But at least you'll soon know about your new father and mother, one way or another.' She turned brisk again. 'Now that we've sorted that out, could we think about getting luncheon ready? I'm starving.'

As was customary on Mothering Sunday, the staff had been granted the day off to go and visit their own mothers, hence someone else had to cook luncheon. Sonny's girls volunteered, but left such an impact on the kitchen that their mother declared she might as well have done it herself for all the washing up she had to do afterwards. There was much jollity at the table – not least over the disastrous meal.

Liz and Sophia took the jibes in good part, though Amelia was stung by the reception to her pudding.

'It looks scrumptious, darlin',' salved her Uncle Dick as the bowl of indeterminable pudding was set before him. There was a twinkle in his eye when he tried to dig his spoon in. Amelia asked, didn't he want custard on it?

Eyeing the lumpy mess in the jug, Dick said he would just try the pudding without. 'I don't want to swamp the flavour.' Never the diplomat, he made it plain this was a joke. The spoonful was almost to his mouth when Fred refused the custard too on the grounds that, 'It looks like snot.'

Everyone groaned and lowered their spoons. Thomasin started to laugh. Unable to speak, she laughed and laughed till the tears came, infecting those around her – with the exception of Amelia who was mortally hurt.

'It's just as well it's Lent!' wheezed Sonny behind his napkin.

The first to recover, Dusty poured a generous helping of custard over her pudding and assured Amelia that it was the best custard she had ever tasted, most of the adults agreeing. When the meal had been digested, Josie went off to see her own mother, accompanied by her husband and offspring. The moment their car was out of sight of the house, she began the frantic task of examining her daughters' hair for signs of lice, as she did every time they had been in contact with Belle's foundlings. Win, Nick and Johnny, too, departed in order to spend the rest of the day with the Cordwells in Leeds. Those who remained were entertained by Belle's children, who played the piano, danced and gave recitations till Thomasin felt utterly exhausted and wished that Mothering Sunday was over.

Erin had thoroughly enjoyed her day, apart from the news about Brian. Later when her daughter was leaving, she sought to assume the role of arbitrator. 'If it's too hard for ye to go round and make it up with Brian, I'll go and smooth the ground, if ye like.'

Belle thought this amusing. 'I can remember when you did everything you could to deter Brian's attention from me.'

Erin helped yet another child into his coat. 'That's a long, long time ago, before I saw how good he was for you. Go on, go see him . . . you miss him really, don't you?'

Belle was silent for a moment, then nodded. 'I suppose I do.' She did not tell her mother just how she missed Brian; the sexual need he fulfilled.

'Well, go on and see him.'

'What is this, Benevolent Sunday? Just because I've done one good deed doesn't mean to say I have to be nice to everybody.'

'I'm glad you decided about the children. I feel so sorry for Dusty now, he's led her a merry dance.'

'Well, prepare to feel sorry for her again if the investigation shows anything criminal.'

'So you really are having Dickie investigated?'

'Of course.' Belle frowned at her mother's naïvety.

'I thought maybe you were just saying it . . . well, it was wrong of you to raise Dusty's hopes if there's chance of her being let down – not to mention the children's feelings.'

'Mother, you are the most contrary woman! Weren't you amongst those bullying me into a decision this morning? And weren't you the one most opposed to the idea of your brother adopting the children?'

Erin conceded that this was true. 'But I've been watching him and he does seem to get on well with the children. We'll have to wait and see what the detectives turn up . . . oh, do go and make it up with Brian, darlin'.'

Securing her hat, Belle replied, 'It's far too late to go this evening . . . however, I may just call some time this week.' She smiled and received her mother's kiss then gathered her children and left.

13

There was scant chance of sleep for Dusty now that Belle had voiced her decision – nor for her husband either. For an hour or so he listened indulgently to her excited patter before begging her to shut up.

'Sorry.' She settled down and made as if to sleep. But a moment later began again. 'I think it's awful, Belle making poor Freddie scrub the step in this weather.' Dickie mumbled that it would hardly kill him. 'But he's only little. Never mind, once he's with us he won't have to do things like that.'

He pleaded with her again to shut up. She did, for a time. Dick was just rolling over the verge of unconsciousness when he heard her sobbing. 'For Christ's sake, what's wrong now?'

She sobbed and laughed at the same time. 'I'm just so happy!' The excitement was so acute it had become unbearable. She could hardly draw breath. 'I can't believe they're almost ours.' He enveloped her in muskiness and ordered her to calm down. 'I just keep thinking – what if Belle changes her mind?'

'She won't. Now stop.' His embrace, his scent and his kisses had a tranquillising effect. Her chest began to rise less frequently and soon her breathing returned to normal. Dickie fell asleep. She herself could not remember doing so, but she must have done for it was now morning and the sun was shining through the curtains. Dickie had turned over. Slipping from the bed, she dressed, made herself as presentable as she could, then went downstairs. It was seven o'clock. She hoped she would be in time.

When she arrived at Belle's house a small figure was kneeling on the pavement scrubbing half-heartedly at the step. Hurrying up, she forestalled his greeting with a finger to her lips and knelt down beside him. An amazed Fred allowed her to take the brush from his hand. 'Oh, look at your poor little fingers,' she whispered. 'They're all blue – here, put my gloves on.' She dipped the brush into the bucket and exclaimed, 'Why, it's cold water too! Whatever is she thinking of on a day like this? I wouldn't even make a servant use cold water.' She set to scrubbing at the step. 'Never mind I'll soon have it done. I'll come and do it tomorrow for you too.'

She had just dipped her brush into the pail and sloshed water onto the step, when a pair of feet appeared on the doormat – one of them wearing a platformed boot. Hardly daring to raise her eyes, she stopped scrubbing.

Belle looked down her nose, but didn't say a word. After a moment of staring, she turned and went back along the passage. Dusty lifted her head and stared after her, then glanced at the boy. Fred wore an expression similar to her own. She spluttered a laugh and pressed the back of her raw hand to her mouth – then laughed again. Fred laughed, too. Before long the pair of them were giggling uncontrollably.

Able to hear them in the back parlour, Belle was compelled to smile herself at the memory of her aunt's face – it had been a picture.

Every morning that week Dusty came to relieve Fred of his chore. After that first confrontation, Belle had decided to pretend not to know she was there. If her aunt wanted to make a rod for her own back then she must find out the hard way. Belle had other matters to sort out.

Brian expected to see a patient when his housekeeper announced that there was a visitor, but when he looked up from his *Evening Press* he was surprised to see Belle. Standing, he directed her to a chair and waited for his housekeeper to leave.

Belle didn't care for this room. It was far too cluttered with furniture and ornaments, and the dark wallpaper made the walls close in on one. With the velvet curtains drawn and the gas lamp at its lowest, it was most claustrophobic. She chose a green velvet button-backed chair and sat down, looking not at him but at the array of medical books that lay open on the carpet. 'I hope I'm not disturbing you?'

'No, I'd just broken off to read the *Press*.' He was still holding the paper, but now folded it and laid it on his lap.

'How are you?' asked Belle.

'I'm fine . . . and you?'

'I'm fine.' She waited for him to add something, but when he didn't she said, 'I thought you might have called to see me.'

He frowned. 'And what reason would I have to call – oh, to say I'm sorry, you mean? Like I did all the other times we fell out?'

She nodded sheepishly. 'I realised that it's always you who has to apologise first whenever we've rowed. That's why I'm here now. It should be my turn. I'm sorry, Brian.'

'Why?'

Belle looked puzzled. 'I've just told you.'

'Yes, but I'd like to know your reasons for this apology; it all seemed pretty final when you told me to leave.'

Her expression was one of remorse. 'I know . . . I lay awake that night for ages thinking.'

'Thinking about me or Uncle Dickie?'

The remorse vanished, but she managed to entrap the natural retort. 'About you, and how I missed not having you there.'

'Yes . . .' Brian crossed his arms and looked deeply thoughtful. 'I know the feeling. I smashed a particularly useful jug last week.'

Belle rose stiffly and limp-marched to the door, expecting him to cry out and stop her; but he didn't. Her hand on the white glass doorknob, she looked round. There seemed to be no regret on his face. 'Well . . . I've made my apology.'

'Yes, you've done your duty, Belle, you can run along.' He unfolded the newspaper and started to read.

She hauled furiously on the door and exited, slamming it behind her.

Brian's nonchalance collapsed. You bloody clown, he told himself.

When Belle reached home, she was still livid over the way he had humiliated her and was about to give Sally a diatribe on the doctor's true character, if Sally hadn't butted in first. 'Your uncle's here.' When Belle looked round, the nursemaid added, 'He's upstairs tucking the girls in.'

Belle's mood altered. 'Good, I can do with some company who doesn't argue.'

'I don't know if you'll be quite so pleased to see him when you know what he's done,' said Sally. 'The landlord called for the rent and your uncle let him in.'

Belle groaned, just as Dickie appeared with Fred at his heels. 'Why did you let him in? I've managed to keep him out of here for years so's he won't see how I've improved the place and try to put my rent up.'

'Improved the place?' Dickie laughed rudely and looked around.

'It might not be a mansion,' retorted Belle, 'but it was

almost derelict until Grandfather got to work on it.' She hung up her cloak and smoothed her black clothes. 'My rent's been the same for years – but I'll wager it won't be much longer now he's seen what he's got.'

Dickie apologised and watched her set up her painting equipment on the table. 'I'll go if you're busy . . .' He took out a watch and looked at it. 'I just came to see the lad here.'

'No, stay,' she said hastily. 'I must get this illustration finished but I'd welcome the company while I work.'

'Call that work?' Dickie grinned.

'It pays the rent,' she censured. 'Or did do till you . . .'

'All right, all right.' He looked over her shoulder at the half-completed painting. 'How much will that bring?' He was told to mind his own business. 'Huh, touchy. What sorta person'll put that on their wall then?'

'It's not for a wall, it's an illustration for a children's book.' She dipped her brush into water and swished it round. 'Normally I only do pictures for journals, but someone saw my work and offered me a commission. Freddie, it's time you were in bed.'

'It's not my bedtime yet.' Frederick took the watch out of the man's hand and studied it. 'It's only – eh, this clock's got no hands.'

'Neither will you if ye bust it.' Dickie tried to retrieve the watch but the boy held it away from him.

'How d'you tell the time if it's got no hands? Where's it come from?'

Dickie told him it was Swiss and explained the process. 'Now give us the darned thing back an' go to bed.'

'Will you buy me one? It's my birthday next week.'

Dickie said yes, but Belle forbade it. 'It's far too expensive a gift for a little boy. Now go to bed.'

At the crestfallen look, Dickie said, 'I'll buy ye something more useful – a rugby ball like Paddy's – now hop it.'

When the boy had gone, Dickie turned to the pictures on the walls and asked Belle, 'These yours too?' She told him they were. 'Mmm,' he sounded impressed. 'Everyone in this family seems artistic 'cept me.'

'I'm sure there's something at which you're gifted,' said Belle. At his silence, she looked over her shoulder to catch him grinning. Overlooking the innuendo, she added, 'Languages, for instance. You seem very fluent in more than one.' Being multilingual herself, she recognised his talent. Apart from Italian, she had heard him speak French and Spanish. It had been meant to impress and it had done.

'Ah, I don't see that as a gift. I just like to talk to people in their own lingo; it promotes good relations.'

'When you say people, do you mean women?' Belle stroked colour onto the paper.

Dickie laughed and came to sit at the table with her. 'You ain't heard my German yet – it sounds like I'm trying to cough up a hairball.' He watched for a while, then asked, 'Have ye made it up with Brian?'

She was irked at being reminded. 'No and I don't intend to. Neither do I wish to talk about him.'

'Let's talk about our love affair, then.'

'I don't think that's in very good taste, Uncle.'

'Well, what do ye want to talk about?' Using his elbow as a prop, he leaned his chin on his palm and gazed at her.

'Something, anything . . . I do miss not having Grandfather here to talk to. We used to have some lovely bits o' crack, as he called them.' Her bush of dark hair got in the way; she tossed it back.

'Well, I'm a good listener,' he said softly.

'Ah, but can you be trusted to keep a confidence like Grandfather could? I should hate to tell you my secrets then find that all the family knew.'

'It may interest you to know, young lady, that back home

I have such a reputation for discretion that I even have the President's ear.'

'Really?'

'If ye don't believe me I can show you it, I keep it in a little box on my bedside table.' He laughed and dodged as her paintbrush was jabbed at his face.

Belle went back to her painting. 'I believe you were the last one to speak to Grandfather. Did he . . . did he say anything about me?'

'Such as?'

'He didn't, then . . . it doesn't matter. Huh, it's funny the things you think about when someone dies, isn't it?' She gazed into mid-air. 'When I was a child, I used to love the smell of whiskey on his breath. If I'd known then that it was the stuff that was going to help kill him . . . I can't rid myself of the vision of him lying there on his deathbed and me thousands of miles away . . .' She went back to her painting. 'Speaking about foreign parts, there's something on the mantelpiece which should interest you.'

Dickie brushed past her and took hold of the scrap of paper that she had indicated. After reading it he turned on her. 'How long have ye had this?'

'It came this morning.'

'An' it was gonna sit there for another week by the looks of it – why didn't ye tell Dusty when she was here? Ye know how keyed up she is.'

'Dusty? Oh, you mean my charwoman.' Her uncle's face begged an explanation. She told him about his wife's arrangement with Fred.

Having believed Dusty had only been helping with the children, he took great umbrage at the news that she was scrubbing steps. 'Ye should get somebody to do jobs like that!'

'I had someone, but if Aunt chose to take on his punishment

– and not even to announce her presence – then the blame lies with her. Where is Aunt, by the way?'

'She's caught my cold – the one you so generously gimme. She's got Erin faffing round with goosegrease and brown paper. The two of them are hitting it off better these days. Though I expect Sis'll be glad when we've gone.' Face inscrutable, he read the cabled report from the detective agency, which stated that the subject had no criminal record and that he had applied to several orphanages but had been turned down on the grounds that he and his wife were too old. Investigation into his business had thrown up nothing sinister, and he enjoyed considerable income.

Dickie folded the report. 'Sorry ye had to waste your money when ye've so little, Belle. Especially when it could have been used to better purpose – like hiring someone to scrub your step.'

Belle said she didn't consider it wasted and contrary to what he might believe she was glad to hear he led an honest life in America.

'Ah well, ye see, if you'd only taken our word for it, it would've been a lot cheaper. We said ye wouldn't find anything.' Dick congratulated his friendly detective in New York with whom he had made urgent contact after Belle had dropped her thunderbolt in his lap. Thank goodness her man had used the cable; if his report had been in the form of a letter it would have already been on the boat and there would have been no way to alter its contents. As it was, a word into the ear – or rather a few hundred bucks into the pocket – of the agent working for Belle, and Dickie's more nefarious dealings slipped from memory.

'So, we shall have to arrange for the children to move into Peasholme – perhaps at Easter.' Easter Monday fell on 8 April this year. He asked when he and Dusty could take the children home to America. Belle said that she would prefer an interim of three months before signing the contracts, but as they had already spent considerable time with Freddie and the girls, then she would be willing to let them go by the end of April.

He was much pleased, not only for the adoption but because he would be glad to get home, back to the big brash city. His demeanour changed to concern. 'Our leaving is gonna hurt Mam. I don't know how to break it to her.' He came and sat back at the table, looking pensive.

In his presence, she had made little progress on the illustration. She put down her brush, rubbed her eyes, then began to side her equipment away.

'I'm putting you off,' said Dickie.

'Yes you are, but that doesn't take much doing. I need little excuse to stop painting.'

'It's not a passion like it is with my brother, then?'

'Far from it.'

'What is your passion?'

'I'm not the passionate sort.'

'Neither am I,' he said approvingly. ''Tis a waste of energy.'

She finished putting her equipment away. 'Come on, we'll sit on the sofa.'

'Not passionate, she says an' here she is inviting me to share the couch with her.' Dickie brought his long legs from under the table and went to sit beside her. 'I really should be getting the news back to Dusty . . . ah, what the hell, it's waited all day, it can wait a few minutes longer.'

The sofa being a small one, and Dickie being a tantaliser, his thigh pressed against hers. Belle made no attempt to act the besmirched maiden and did not move away. It was probably the closest she would get to a man for some time.

March went out with a heavy fall of snow. It was five inches deep in the streets and deeper elsewhere. Dickie was bored. There seemed nowhere to go and nothing left to see. His wife was happy enough now that the contracts were being drawn up for the children's adoption. She would be happier still if he'd agree to remain in England. They had fallen out over it last night. 'You never think of asking me what I want to do!' she had thrown at him. He had pointed out that hers was the only dissenting voice – Freddie and his sisters were keen to go. 'America's only a name to them!' she had argued. 'They don't have any measure of distance.' He had replied that it might only be a name to them, but to him it was home.

'Life's too slow here, Dusty. It'd drive me nuts.' He had taken hold of her and spoken earnestly. 'I know the real reason ye don't want to go back. You're scared those guys who smashed the house up are gonna be lying in wait for me, aren't ye?' She had looked at him sharply, receiving one of those slanting leers that told her he had seen right through her subterfuge. Devoid of ammunition, she had laughingly capitulated. He watched her for a while, playing in the snow with Frederick, Julia and Faith who were here on a visit, then came away from the window, sighing heavily.

'Getting fed-up of us, are you?' asked his mother, the only other person in the room.

'No, not of you. It's just that I can't sit round all day with nothing to do.' He looked at her apologetically, shuffling his hands inside his trouser pockets. 'Ye know, I really will have to go back home and sort things out.'

Thomasin shifted in her chair. It was pleasant to be able to move without pain shooting from every nerve; she had at last visited the doctor who had prescribed Salicin powders. They could be considered quite effective, if one didn't expect to be able to do somersaults, though walking still presented a problem and she rarely went anywhere without the motor car. 'The Census returns have to be in tomorrow. I was hoping I could put you down as a resident.'

'Oh, Mam . . . I can't lie to ye.'

'You never seemed to have much trouble in the past.' Her lips twitched. 'I'm sorry, that was a bit cheeky. You've turned into a decent man . . . well, not too bad anyway. Eh, I don't know . . . I'd hate to ruin your life by forcing you to stay in England, love. I just don't want to lose you again.'

'Ye won't lose me.' He came to perch on the arm of her chair. 'We'll come over regular for holidays – an' you can come to us.'

'But it's the other side of the world,' bewailed Thomasin. 'I can't just pop round for a chat whenever I feel like it.' She looked sly. 'Dusty's happy here.'

'She'll be happy in America,' he reproved. 'Don't be using her to get to me.'

'Ah dear . . . I can see I'm wasting my time.' She patted him and wrinkled her nose. 'But just stay a wee bit longer, eh? At least till after Easter. This cold weather won't last long, then we can all get about a bit more and you won't be so bored.'

He laughed. 'Belle won't let us go till the end of April anyway – but straight after Easter I'm off to book our passage, okay?'

'Right, we'd better make it a damned good Easter then,' said Thomasin.

. . . After which, I'll have to try and find some other excuse to keep you here, she thought.

Following Good Friday Mass, in which Erin was the only Feeney amongst those who queued to kiss Christ's feet, she and her mother went to take flowers to Pat's grave. Getting into the car, she was interested to see that her mother had begun to make surreptitious use of the walking stick, and smiled to herself – though she refrained from any leg-pulling. Once the blooms had been arranged, both stood there for a while, watching two young gravediggers at work. 'Always someone to bury,' remarked Thomasin. 'Those lads'll never be unemployed.'

Erin nodded, then said quietly, 'I think I'll go take Sam some flowers tomorrow.' Her husband was buried fifteen miles away where he had been born. 'Unless ye want the car to go anywhere.'

Thomasin said she didn't and leaned heavily on her cane. 'I don't know why I bother coming. Your father isn't here, is he?'

Erin gave a bleak smile and shook her head. 'Look at us . . . two old widow women together.'

'It's been a long time for you, hasn't it? How did you ever get over losing him, Erin?'

Erin linked her mother's arm more tightly. 'I don't think I ever did. I still sometimes have a little weep over him.'

'So you wouldn't ever marry again?'

Thomasin's daughter looked down at her with interest. 'This isn't a feeler, is it? You're not trying to tell me you're going to marry Francis?'

'Marry a dried-up old stick like Fran? Good God, no!' Thomasin actually laughed. 'Oh, that sounds rotten, Fran's a wonderful pal and we share a great deal of interests, but I could never imagine sleeping in the same bed.'

Erin thought what a strange comment this was for an elderly lady to make, but chuckled anyway, 'At least I made ye laugh.'

'Aye, I do feel a bit better today.' Thomasin's eyes focused on the young gravediggers again and she nudged her daughter. 'Eh, which one d'you fancy?'

Erin made a sound like a donkey. 'What have I started! Just stop this naughtiness or I'll kick that walking stick from

293

under ye – ah, ye thought I hadn't noticed!' She pointed a teasing finger as Thomasin looked found-out. 'Well, I can see it's doing ye no good at all. Come on, let's have you home before you get me into trouble!'

Passing the gravediggers on their way out, Thomasin offered a smile and a coquettish 'Good morning!' setting herself and Erin laughing again all the way to the car.

The snow was washed away by April showers, swelling the river. Undeterred, the Feeneys and hundreds of others converged on the boatyard at Lendal Bridge on Easter Monday to take a trip down the Ouse. Belle, having a detestation of water, was not among them, but the three adoptees had been allowed to come. They had not been told yet, but apart from the thrill of this morning's Easter eggs it was to be an especially exciting day for them, and Dusty too. Belle was coming over to Peasholme for a celebratory luncheon, when the children would learn that they could now regard this as their home until their departure to America. In preparation for this, their grandmother had been rationing her visits lately. There would be tears at the final parting, but knowing they were going to a better life, she had given the adoptive parents her blessing.

Now, Dusty caught her husband's eye and exchanged a loving look. Before the children had arrived this morning, he had presented her with a coloured pasteboard egg filled with chocolates, to which she had responded, 'I don't suppose I'll be receiving so many presents now I'm to be a mother at last.' He hadn't understood at first. When she had explained her meaning he had been truly bewildered. 'You think I bought ye presents to make up for being childless? Dusty, of course I didn't! I buy ye things 'cause I love you. You're the most important person in the world to me.'

Thomasin stared at her son and his wife who were rowing

the boat. She should feel as happy as they obviously did. The sun had come out to warm her rusty joints, she had a new hat for Easter – even if it was black – here and there along the way an explosion of yellow forsythia heralded spring . . . but how could she be happy when Dickie would soon be gone. A majestic flotilla of swans drifted by. She turned to watch them as far as her neck would allow. Erin was just commenting on the lovely sight, when something landed in the boat with a thud. All looked up as they passed under Scarborough Bridge and caught a glimpse of some merry faces. When the boat emerged the other side there was another thud.

'Blasted little hooligans!' Thomasin shook her stick at them. 'Children nowadays – pull to the side, Dickie and let me get my hands on them!' Several more stones plopped into the brown water, splashing all their clothes.

'Mam, sit still!' Erin held onto the sides of the boat as it rocked from side to side. 'You'll have us all in!'

'Christ, ye little bastard!' A wedge of brick had grazed Dickie's brow.

'Dickie!' chastised his wife, then immediately put down her oar to tend the frightened girls, whilst with a great deal more cursing, her husband began to row to the bank. There, he leapt from the boat and headed for his assailants.

He didn't catch them, of course. The ragamuffins spent some moments jeering at him before pelting off and were gone before the man had a chance to get within fifty yards of them. Freddie experienced a sense of disillusionment in his father's prowess.

'I don't know what children are coming to!' complained Thomasin as her son came back to retrieve his oars. 'They'd never have dared to do a thing like that in my day.'

'I'll bet he did.' Erin pointed at her brother who, after a moment's indignation, laughed and rubbed his head.

'Oh, they've cut you, the little devils!' Dusty had seen

blood on his hand as it came away from his brow. He said it was nothing and taking both oars began to row.

'Well, I don't want to go any further,' complained his mother. 'Your last few weeks and them little arabs go and spoil it!'

'Never mind, Mam.' He strained at the oars, turning the boat round. 'We've still got the party to look forward to.' His mother had said she couldn't possibly let them go without one.

'Aye . . . Eh look! There's a policeman – pull over, Dickie.'

The officer promised to attend to the hooligans at once and the family proceeded on their homewards journey without mishap. Due to aborting their trip they were rather early for luncheon and so spent the meantime drinking tea and chatting about the children who had been allowed out to play in the garden.

The doorbell rang. 'Oh, that'll be Belle,' said Erin, and Dusty sat forward in anticipation.

Barbara came in. 'There's two policemen, ma'am.'

'By, that was quick work!' crowed the old lady. 'They must've caught the little blighters. Send them in, Barbara, and fetch more cups.'

But the moment she saw the men she knew that they had not come about any street arabs.

When Belle arrived expecting luncheon her mother was demented. 'Oh God, at last you're here!' She hurled herself at her daughter.

'Mother, calm down, I can't tell what you're saying!' Belle gripped Erin's shoulders and led her to a sofa. 'Sit down and take a deep breath.'

Erin gulped in air. 'Your grandmother's been taken to the police station!' She put a hand to her heaving breast and swallowed.

It was Belle's turn to be disturbed. With an exclamation she planted herself on the sofa beside her mother. 'When?'

Erin closed her eyes and tried to compose herself. 'About a quarter of an hour ago. Oh, God! A couple of men came . . . said they were detectives. We thought they'd just come about the boys throwing stones . . . I knew, I *knew* Dickie would bring this on us! They took him into a room on his own for questioning, your Nan too – they even questioned *me*! Then after a while they carted the pair of them off to the station . . . they were very nice about it. I told Mother this was going to happen!' With Belle stunned she was free to rush in. 'I'll kill him! I'll kill that brother o' mine! My own mother in a prison cell!'

The hysterical tears jerked Belle from her stupor. 'Surely the police won't keep her there, an old lady like that. Have they actually been arrested or are they just there for questioning?'

Erin gave a wet sniff and rubbed at her eyes. 'I don't know what the hell's going on! I've telephoned Sonny, he's coming over right away.' Her daughter asked if Dusty had been taken too. 'No. They questioned her here for a while. She's gone to the police station to find out what's happening.' Erin covered her mouth, eyes wild. 'I was all on me own, I didn't know what to do . . .'

Belle took command, hugging her mother and attempting to calm her. The maid had appeared with a cup of tea which Belle put into Erin's shaking hands. 'Drink that up, Mother, and don't worry, I'll stay with you until Uncle Sonny gets here. Then if Aunt Dusty isn't back we'll all go over to the police station – but I'm sure she will be. Where are Freddie and the girls?' Her mother said that they were being looked after in the kitchen by the cook. Excusing herself for a moment, Belle slipped down to the kitchen and asked the manservant to drive the children home.

There followed an anguished wait. It was one-thirty and still no word. When the front door eventually sounded, both women shot to their feet ready to face Dusty's news. Alas, it was merely Sonny. After a few tearful sentences from Erin he echoed his sister's sentiments, 'I'll bloody kill him!' adding, 'Shouldn't one of us go and find out what's happening?'

'Aunt Dusty's gone,' Belle informed him. 'But she's been away hours. I said to Mother we should wait for you then go ourselves.'

'Better for someone to stay here in case Dusty gets back to an empty house,' said her uncle. 'I'll go on my own.'

On arrival at the police station in Clifford Street, he strode up to the desk and announced in masterful vein, 'Good afternoon. My name is John Feeney, I believe you have my mother and my cousin here for questioning.'

The desk sergeant observed his bearing for a moment, then slipped off his stool. 'Ah yes, sir. Would you care to step into this room. I won't keep you a moment.'

With only a table and two chairs for company in the small dingy room, the ten-minute wait was more like an hour and nerves began to erode his mastery. Nevertheless, when two men in plain clothes came in and one of them very politely introduced himself as Detective Inspector Croft, he remained sufficiently confident to demand, 'I want to know why you're holding my mother. How is she?'

'Perfectly well, sir, she's just having a cup of tea. Please, take a seat.' Both he and Sonny dragged chairs from under the table and sat down. Croft placed a sheaf of papers in front of him and laced his fingers over it. His black hair was slicked from its middle parting with grease. He had a waxed moustache, a pointed nose and hairy nostrils. His eyes were deep brown and unlike his colleague who stood watching, showed no suspicion, his manner most respectful. 'The gentleman with her, he would be your . . . ?'

'My cousin,' contributed Sonny.

The detective appeared to think he had misheard. 'Not your brother?'

The response was immediate. 'No, why do you say that?'

Croft stroked the end of his moustache. 'Well, it's just that Mrs Feeney has made a statement to say that he's her son. If he is, wouldn't that make him your brother?'

The residue of mastery evaporated. Sonny felt sick.

'Rather confusing, wouldn't you say, sir? The Yorkshire Insurance Company thinks so too, that's why they've asked me to investigate this matter. Perhaps you wouldn't mind helping to fill in a few points.'

'Yes, of course.' Sonny leaned his elbows on the table. 'Anything to sort out this idiocy.'

The inspector took personal details, then told him that allegations had been brought by the Yorkshire Insurance Company, relating to a fire that took place in November, 1874. 'You know which fire I'm referring to, sir?'

'I presume you mean the one which destroyed my parents' home.'

'That's correct. The one in which your brother was purported to have died. It is your brother who we're holding, isn't it?'

Sonny hesitated, then decided that continuing to lie would be the worst possible thing. He nodded guiltily. 'Yes.'

'Why did you say he was your cousin?'

Sonny rubbed at his hands nervously. 'I don't know.'

Croft's approach changed. 'I must tell you, sir, that you are not obliged to say anything, but anything you say may be given in evidence. Do you understand? Now, were you aware that your mother claimed several hundred pounds on Richard Feeney's purported death?'

299

'Yes.'

'Did you receive any of that money?'

'No!'

The officer went on, 'I know it's a long time ago but can you tell me what you remember about your movements on that day?'

Sonny told him that he had spent most of the afternoon at his studio painting. Later he had met his brother in a public house, then both had gone to the family home . . . 'When we arrived the house was already ablaze. My parents and my grandmother were standing outside with my sister, her husband and many of our neighbours. My father was attempting to get into the house, but all the doors were locked. He told us that my wife and children were inside and I began my own attempt to break the lock on the front door, aided by my brother.' The police officer cut in here to ask whether there were any windows open and Sonny replied in the negative.

'Eventually we succeeded in breaking in. Richard, my brother, went in, managed to find the children and brought them to safety. He said he had seen my wife unconscious and dashed back in for her. There was an explosion. We were informed later that a gaspipe had ruptured but we didn't realise this at the time. Everyone had to run into the road to avoid falling debris. I never saw my brother again . . . until he turned up last December.'

'Didn't he communicate with you in any way?'

Sonny decided that some lies were necessary. 'No. Not until I received a letter from him last year saying he was coming home.' He was asked if he still had the letter and replied that he had burnt it.

'Mr Feeney, I believe you were the one to identify your brother's body and also that of your wife.'

Sonny corrected him. 'They were too badly burnt to be

able to tell who they were. My wife had been wearing a locket which I had bought her and which was used in identification. In the case of the other body, there was a gold hunter watch which I knew my brother to own. Naturally I assumed that the body was Richard's.'

'You had no reason to doubt that your brother was dead?'

'None.'

'When your brother came out of the house with the children and told you that your wife was unconscious, did he say he had seen anyone else in the house?' Sonny said he had not. 'And yet there must have been a body, must there not?'

'Yes.' Sonny looked down at the table.

Croft rubbed his chin. 'You see, sir, if this body wasn't your brother's, then it must have been somebody else's, mustn't it?' Old police files had been uninformative. There had been no male reported missing around the time of the fire. Possibly the victim was from another town or his family just couldn't give a damn that he had never come home. Croft didn't particularly care either about an incident that had happened before he was out of frocks, even if it might reveal murder, but he had been asked to investigate this and he would do so with good heart. 'Have you any idea who it might have been?' Sonny shook his head. 'Surely in the present knowledge that your brother is alive you must have wondered who it could have been?'

'Yes, I have . . . But it's only theory.' At the officer's smiling nod of encouragement, Sonny disclosed his assumption. 'Well . . . I can only think that my wife must have had someone with her. A man.'

'Forgive the indelicacy, sir, but you mean a lover?'

Eyes averted, Sonny nodded. 'That's the only explanation I can give.'

'Uh huh, so you were aware that your wife was in the habit of bringing her lover into the house.'

301

'I most certainly was not!' Sonny's face reddened. 'I had no idea.'

'Yet, you've just put this forward as an explanation for the other body being there.'

'Up until last year I still believed that it was my brother's body. It was only when I found out he was alive that I began to wonder who it could be – but I have no proof and I definitely didn't realise that she'd brought her lover into my house otherwise I'd have . . .' Sonny broke off and studied his nails.

'Otherwise what, Mr Feeney?'

Silence.

'Otherwise you would have killed her?'

Sonny jumped to his feet. 'That's monstrous! I was going to divorce her – I had no need to kill her!'

The officer's voice remained calm. 'On what grounds were you going to divorce her? You just said you had no proof she was unfaithful.'

'I want to see my mother,' announced Sonny in firm tone though his insides were churning.

'All in good time, sir. I'll send someone to see if the lady has finished her tea . . . When did you first discover your wife's infidelity?'

Sonny shook his head in exasperation. 'I really can't see that this is relevant but I'll tell you if it helps to clear up this madness. A couple of months before the fire I came home earlier than usual and my wife wasn't there. When she arrived she said she'd been to visit her mother but from her state it seemed she was lying.' He was asked what he meant by her state and made haphazard gestures around his head. 'Her hair was all tousled and her face flushed . . . as though from excitement. When I questioned her she denied she'd been with a man, but later admitted it. I didn't divorce her immediately, but after she made no

302

effort to mend her ways I decided I couldn't live with her any longer. Look,' he beseeched the policeman, 'what has this to do with the fire?'

'You say she made no effort to mend her ways – did you ever actually see her with another man?' Sonny shook his head. 'And did you know whether she brought any men into the house in your absence?'

'I can't say for sure. It did cross my mind but then I discounted it because if she'd been doing that it would have reached my ears somehow. For one thing, the children would have noticed.'

'Ah yes, the children . . . Had you been aware that they were in the house on the day of the fire?'

'Naturally, they were always there. At one time my wife would take them out in the afternoons but she gave that up . . . that was another reason how I discovered she'd been meeting other men instead.'

'Were the children unconscious too?' Croft was told no. 'Didn't you think that was odd?'

Sonny looked bewildered. 'They were in a different part of the house where the fire wasn't so fierce.'

'Mr Feeney, divorce is an unpleasant business, isn't it?'

'It certainly is.'

'Wouldn't it have been far more convenient if your wife were to depart some other way?'

Sonny was horrified. 'Are you saying I set that fire? You're mad! Even if I'd wanted to, would I have done that with my own children in the house?'

The inspector spent several minutes referring to a document on the table. 'I see from the assessor's report that the fire had been smouldering for some time . . .'

'Do you see anything in that report that says it was started deliberately?' volleyed Sonny. The inspector did not reply, but seemed to be studying the document intently. 'Well –

do you? Because if you don't I'd be pleased if you'd allow me to go.'

The man continued reading. 'Just a few more questions, sir . . .'

About an hour after her brother-in-law had gone, Dusty returned; with her were Francis, Thomasin and her elder son.

'Oh, glory be to God!' Erin flew to her mother, who looked desperately frail, and led her to a seat. 'Ye've been gone so long I feared they were going to keep ye there.'

'We're remanded on bail.' Thomasin raised a weak smile as she sank into the chair. 'Your father'd think it was hilarious.'

'So you've been charged?' Erin bit her knuckle.

'Oh, we've been through everything short of torture,' replied Thomasin. When Erin shook her fist under Dickie's nose and snarled that they should have left him locked up, her weary mother begged her not to start all that again. 'What we need is some construction . . .'

'How about a gallows?' sniped Erin.

Belle tried to inject some sense. 'Top priority is a lawyer.'

She was told by her grandmother, 'It's all in hand. While we were still at the police station, Dusty went to see Francis and he contacted my solicitor.' She reached for her friend's hand and squeezed it. 'Otherwise we might still be locked up. I've been released on my own personal security of five hundred pounds. Dickie had to have an extra surety of two hundred and fifty.'

'Francis helped there,' Dusty told the listeners. 'We're going to have to wire America for some more cash, we've hardly any left.' She and the others paid homage to Francis for his support.

The old man felt undeserving of their thanks. Where now was his determination to prevent Richard from hurting his mother again?

Erin turned to Dusty. 'I'd like to know why you weren't charged. It seems to me you're more guilty than Mother.'

'I was rather surprised too,' admitted Dusty. 'I asked your mother's solicitor and he explained, but don't expect me to repeat it. I think it's something to do with the Law regarding husband and wife as one person.'

'Huh! I'll wager it's the only time being married to my brother could be classed an advantage.' Erin pumped her mother for more information.

'Well, I continued to swear Dickie was my nephew for a while ... till they told me he'd been identified by a person who once worked for him. I'll give you three guesses who that was.' When her daughter looked irritated, she told her, 'Amy Forsdyke.'

Erin shot an astounded look at her brother. 'My God, where did they dig her up from?'

'It wasn't hard when you think about it,' replied Thomasin. 'She was the last person to work for Dickie, her and the other maid. Of course once Amy'd poked her oar in there was no point in continuing the charade. I was rather glad, truth be known. I feel as if a lot of the weight's off my shoulders, even if there is worse to come.' But it hadn't all been relief. Unmasked, she had offered to pay the money back but the police officer had looked at her with near scorn and said it was far too late now. The shame!

'So what about Sonny?' asked Erin. After a show of blank looks, her alarm soared. 'He went down to the station to see what was happening!'

'But ... we never saw him.' Thomasin's eyes widened and took in her other son. 'Nobody told us. He must still be there!' She made to rise but Francis argued that there

305

was no point going back, they would just have to sit and wait.

And wait they did. Eventually, Francis decided that perhaps Thomasin had been right and he himself went down to the police station.

Much later he returned with Thomasin's younger son who looked as if he were suffering from a dose of influenza.

'Oh, lad, what have they done to you?' Thomasin held out her arms in pity. 'Erin, send for some tea for him.'

Sonny capsized into a chair and sat head in hands. 'Thank God you're all right,' he said to his mother. 'They said you'd been charged.'

'We have – but why did they keep you there so long?'

'Because I've been charged, too.' Sonny passed a tart look to his brother. 'I'm lucky it was only conspiracy to defraud; for a moment I thought it was going to be murder.' At the sounds of horror his attempt at nonchalance collapsed. 'God, it was awful . . . *awful*! They were trying to say I set the fire deliberately to kill Peggy and her fancyman.'

'But how did they know that that's who he was?' asked Thomasin.

'I had to tell them.'

'Sonny, you daft eejit!' Dickie was exasperated. 'They asked us that an' all, we just insisted we didn't know.'

'It's all right for you!' yelled Sonny. 'But I didn't know what the hell was going on. I was worried about Mother. I started off by saying you were my cousin, but when they told me that Mam had confessed I thought I'd better come clean too. I thought if I told them everything it'd take the heat off . . . but I just got in deeper and deeper.' He rubbed his hands vigorously through his hair. 'Was I glad to see Francis. I thought I was going to be there all night.'

After the cries had died down, he looked at his brother again. 'Are you still classed as a British citizen?'

306

Dusty answered for her husband. 'We've both been naturalised.'

'Pity he wasn't done years ago,' lunged Erin.

Sonny looked vexed at her petty interruption. 'So you hold an American passport. Have they taken it off you?'

Dickie raised a grin. 'No, they appeared to overlook that.'

'Don't you dare entertain any ideas about skipping the country!' shot his brother. 'You're not leaving us to clean up your mess this time – and I hope you haven't got that pettifogger who dealt with your will handling your defence, otherwise I don't give much for our chances.'

His brother beheld him warily. 'Ye didn't say anything about seeing my will?'

Sonny's head moved in negation. 'I maintained that I didn't know you were alive until last year.'

'Thank Christ for something.'

Sonny jumped to his feet. 'Anyway, I'd better telephone Josie and let her know what she's in for.' He left them to mull over the gravity of the situation.

'So, when's the fire going to be?' Erin gave a sarcastic look at her brother. 'My God, I hope you're proud of yourself.'

Dusty came to sit beside her husband, laying an arm over his shoulders. Everyone else was against him, a wife should show some support.

Erin seemed to want to make everyone smart, turning now on Belle. 'Now ye've got full evidence of what sort o' person he is! I don't see ye doing too much laughing.'

Belle, used to her mother's histrionics, ignored them. 'When will the trial be?'

Her grandmother said they had to go before the magistrate to be given a date. 'We'll find out more the next time we see the solicitor . . . ah, here's the tea.' The tray of tea which the maid brought provided Dickie with a brief respite from his sister's rantings.

307

Erin sipped from her cup, then turned to her daughter. 'I forgot to ask in all this, did ye go and see Brian?'

Not wishing to go into detail at this moment, Belle lied and said she hadn't. She glanced at Uncle Dickie over her cup. The incident seemed to have bled his attractiveness. He looked quite deflated, poor man.

At last, Dickie spoke. 'We have to work out what we're gonna say.'

'What lies you're going to tell, you mean!' Erin's tea slopped over the sides of her cup and she issued a curse, spending the next few seconds trying to dispose of the puddle in her saucer.

'We have to make sure we all say the same thing,' reasoned her brother.

Thomasin looked stern. 'We want no more inventions, Dickie. I know I've been to blame for a lot of this, telling Rufforth you were my nephew, but I told the truth in my statement to the police and I hope to God you did.'

'Sonny didn't though, did he? I'll have to get onto Sutcliffe and warn him.'

Thomasin had to agree on the point about the will, but said that apart from this they would just have to keep on insisting that she and Sonny truly believed that Dickie died in that fire. 'We must be able to dig up witnesses from Monkgate to tell the jury that our grief was genuine.'

'But what about him?' Erin gestured at Dickie. 'How does he explain the fact that he *is* alive? And what reason had he for wanting us to believe he was dead? It's better we should hear it before the trial.'

All looked at Dickie. 'You've never really been specific on that, Richard,' said his mother. 'Isn't it time you were?'

Dusty left her seat and wandered to the french windows. She did not want to give the game away with her face when her husband lied – as he was bound by nature to do.

He began, 'This is just for your ears, I haven't put it in my statement. The York cops know nothing about it . . .'

'Just what did you tell them?' asked Erin.

He bit his lip. 'I'm sorry, Mam, I had to tell them about my little brush with the magistrate – OK, OK, I know it'll look bad in Court . . . but not half so bad as the real reason, and they'd probably have dug it up themselves if I hadn't volunteered it.'

'I'm glad you've warned me,' said his mother acidly. 'Now, would you care to divulge the true story?'

He hung his head. 'Ye know when I was missing for those three years an' I came back well-off?'

Thomasin nodded. 'I didn't quite believe the explanation you gave us then.'

He looked pained. ''Twas true enough! I was left that money in the old lady's will, but . . . well, I didn't mention this, but the police got their teeth into it, thought I stole the cash. One o' them came looking for me – don't worry, he was a West Riding fella, there'll be nothing to connect in the local files, specially with it being twenty-six years ago. Anyway, that's when I saw the fire as an opportunity to escape.'

'Well, there'll be no fires this time,' sighed his mother. 'We're well and truly in it. Dickie, I wish you'd told me this earlier. Your inheritance may well cost us all very dear.'

More dearly than you imagine, thought Dusty, feeling numb. In all this turmoil the three children seemed to have been overlooked. She rose. 'I'd better go and relieve Vinnie of the children, they'll be driving her mad.'

'Don't bother,' said Belle. 'I've sent them home.'

'If the truth gets out, you realise what the consequences will be?' murmured Dusty, lying beside her husband that night, neither being able to sleep.

309

'I couldn't tell them, could I?' He let his hand lie on her breast.

'You could've done but you didn't. If it comes out at the trial . . .'

He covered her mouth. 'It won't. Christ, it was twenty-odd years ago!'

'So was the fire and the truth about that's come out.' She turned her head into the pillow. It wasn't until a shuddering intake of breath emerged that he realised how badly this had affected her.

'Hey,' he grasped her shoulders and tried to pull her towards him. 'Don't cry, it'll be all right. I'll get off.'

She uttered a bitter laugh. 'Isn't that typical of you, only ever thinking about yourself.'

He misunderstood. 'If I get off the others are bound to.'

'What do I care about them!' She showed instant remorse. 'Oh, will you listen to me. That's what comes of living so long with you. Of course I care about you all – but you must see that this ruins our chances of adoption.'

'Not necessarily . . . it could help in the long run.' She asked how the devil he had come to that preposterous conclusion.

'Dusty, I could easily have run back to America, couldn't I? But I've stayed to face the charges. That must show Belle how responsible I am.'

She granted him this much. 'But what help will that be if you're convicted?'

He didn't have an answer for this, and wondered how long the sentence could be. ''Tis all that bastard solicitor's fault!' At her incomprehension, he added heatedly, 'If he hadn't let Sonny see my will then my brother wouldn't've worked out that I was still alive an' you an' me would be sitting nice an' cosy in New York.'

'With a dozen beautiful children,' she replied sourly.

'Look, if we don't get these three we'll get 'em from somewhere.'

'Dickie, how can you say that? You've been behaving as if you're their father for the last few months, how can you shrug them off so simply? I thought you'd grown close to them – I certainly have, and I *won't* give them up.' She raged at Belle for taking them away.

'Then we'll get them,' he swore to her. 'One way or another, we'll get them, darlin'.'

At Thomasin's next meeting with her solicitor, she told him that he must 'Get the very best lawyer available for me and the boys whatever the cost.'

'That I shall do, of course,' he replied. 'But you do understand that it would be advisable for you to have separate counsel.'

'But why can't we have the same?" demanded Thomasin.

'My dear lady, I would not be averse to acting for your son, John, but from what you have told me of your elder son, I would urge strongly against his inclusion.'

Reluctantly, she agreed to follow his advice. 'But I have to say now that I won't have us set against each other and I don't want Dickie sacrificed just to get me off. You must make that clear to the barrister.'

'In that case,' replied her solicitor, 'on looking at the evidence I feel it only fair to tell you that your son may drag you down with him.'

'Then we'll go together,' replied Thomasin nobly.

Whilst this was being said, Dickie was speaking to his own solicitor in less heroic terms. 'Look, shyster, you just make certain no mention is made of that will otherwise we're both in the shit. 'Cause if I go down, you go down with me.'

311

14

When Thomasin had sought excuses to keep her son in England she had not envisaged anything so drastic. The trial would take place at the Summer Assizes in July – over three months away. The one comfort was that this gap would at least give their Defence a chance to find their old kitchen staff who might be able to help them.

Unfortunately, they discovered that one of the maids was now dead. Hope hinged on the other, Abigail, who lived in Germany but who had written occasionally with her family news. Her last letter had been two years ago. They must bank on her being at the same address. What could they do in the meantime but wait and pray?

This was one year when Erin welcomed the Budget. Hearing her mother's grumbles over the increased Income Tax and levy on sugar was preferable to watching her worry over the impending court case. She herself had a separate grievance; when pressed, Belle had come clean about her visit to Brian and said that he did not want a reconciliation. Erin had expressed her wish to crack their two silly heads together, and refused to believe that it was over. Brian would turn up in a couple of weeks.

The remainder of April and beginning of May was taken up by spring-cleaning, during which the four residents went to stay at Scarborough – after of course informing the police of their temporary address. Thomasin had a house here which was used to give her employees a chance to recuperate after illness before returning to work. It would stand them in good stead for their coming ordeal. But their holiday had its sad moments. Young Paddy, who had been brought to the seaside as a special treat, spent half the time looking for his grandfather.

At the next family gathering in York, Dickie announced that he had decided to accept his mother's offer of a senior position with the firm, taking perverse enjoyment in the ill-disguised antipathy from Nick and Francis. It would only be a stop-gap, he hastened to add – not to put them out of their misery, but to prevent his mother from false hope. Temporary or not, Francis and Nick both agreed that in the two remaining months up to the trial it was possible that he could bring the firm to bankruptcy. But what redress did they have when Thomasin had given him carte blanche? Nick was especially irked that the coming trial had hastened the alteration of his grandmother's will. More infuriating than anything was being in ignorance of its content; knowing her grandson's penchant for espionage, Thomasin had left the will locked in the solicitor's safe. Indubitably, his uncle's name would be on it; the question was, at what price to the other beneficiaries? Nick opted to press on with his detrimental jibes about his uncle, hoping that she would not die before he had swayed her to his way of thinking.

For Dickie this was a gleeful interlude in what was otherwise a disturbing time. Within the month he had succeeded in losing two valued customers, decimating the staff, countermanding Nick's orders, misplacing accounts and throwing the entire system into disarray – and then cool as you please, he had declared, 'I don't think I'm cut out for this after all,' and had left them to rebuild their shattered industry as best they might.

His wife knew full well the reason behind this disruption:

he couldn't bear his son's indifference, had wanted to provoke him, and had succeeded. She despaired of his juvenile tricks, preferring to spend as much time with the children as she could, praying that this devotion would pierce Belle's cold armour. It broke her heart to hear them keep asking when they would be coming to live with her.

Feen was overjoyed that her uncle would be staying on indefinitely – though to be in Leeds when he was in York was as bad as if he were in America. When they were apart she couldn't concentrate on anything but him, picturing him with Aunt Dusty and hating her for it, mooning over his photograph. The voodoo doll became so laden with pins that by now it resembled a porcupine. But to no avail; her aunt continued to thrive.

Feen drove the image away and dwelled instead upon the coming weekend, when she and her uncle would be together. Nan had arranged a family picnic. A picnic meant the countryside, where there would be plenty of space to wander off together, away from stupid comments and dowdy old wives. Then Feen would find the courage to tell him how she felt. Standing by her dressing table, she gazed at her reflection in its mirror, then slowly leaning forward, pressed her lips to those in the glass, trying to pretend that the coldness was warm flesh. It was a poor substitute. With a sigh, she pushed herself away from the mirror and wandered along the landing, fantasising on their conversations, feeling his warm lips, his arms around her . . .

Reaching her eldest sister's bedroom she knocked and went in. Liz and Sophia had been granted the day off work to make ready for their weekend in York, though there appeared to be little activity. Amelia was there too, sprawled over the multi-coloured rug, while Sophia sat at the dressing table, attempting to bleach her freckles. Liz was propped up on the bed, ankles crossed, reading the *Girls' Own Newspaper*.

On seeing this, Feen wailed, 'Haven't you finished it yet?'

Elizabeth did not take her eyes from the page. 'I don't know why you're getting so steamed up, I'm not taking any longer than usual.' Feen said she had had the paper for half an hour. 'I bought it! If you don't shut up I won't let you read it at all.'

Feen turned to her other sister. 'Please can I have my turn before you, Soph?' The paper was handed down in order of age.

Sophia examined her efforts in the mirror. 'How much will you pay for the privilege?'

'Oh, don't be mean! You know I haven't any money.'

'Hard luck then.' Sophia picked up a comb and dragged it through her frizzy auburn hair.

Feen threw herself on the bed in frustration.

'Stop bouncing! How d'you expect me to finish it when you keep blurring the words.' Elizabeth turned a page and read on while Feen sulked in a pile at her feet.

After a while Liz started to giggle. Sophia asked what was so funny. 'I'm just reading the answers on the letters page. Goodness . . .'

'Don't tell me,' complained Sophia, dropping the red combings into a bag attached to her dressing table. 'I like to read them myself.'

'Oh, just this one, it's a beauty – listen. It's addressed to Cleopatra: *"We cannot decide if you are wicked or completely mad, although the pseudonym which you have chosen speaks for your egotistical nature. To harbour such indelicate thoughts about your uncle – let alone submit them to paper – is truly disgraceful for one of such tender years. Naturally, it is inconceivable that we answer your query in detail; it is far too disgusting for a refined paper such as this. Suffice it to say that a fourteen year old schoolgirl should be concentrating on her lessons and*

315

her handwriting, which in your case is absolutely appalling. You ought to be thoroughly ashamed of your evil thoughts towards your aunt."' Elizabeth snorted in merriment. 'Poor child!'

Feen rose swiftly from the bed and, face averted, made for the door.

'I've nearly finished now, Feen,' Liz called after her, but the door was slammed.

I wish I were dead. Feen slouched about her room, looking for some means with which to end her agonising humiliation. It had been stupid of her to rush out like that, her sisters would guess that she had written the letter. She heard gales of laughter as the dawning came to Sophia and she shared the joke with Elizabeth. How different would the reaction be, were they to come in here and find her hanging. She visualised herself swinging from the gaslight with its pretty pink globes, or prostrated on the ground thirty feet below her window. Sagging onto the bed, she lifted the lid of her musical box and sang with the plaintive tune. But before the first line emerged, tears were bulging and she was too choked to continue. *Oh, Dickie.*

Later in the morning, Sophia poked her head round the door to hand over the *Girls' Own*. 'You might at least say thank you!' she cribbed. Then looked sly. 'I thought you'd enjoy reading the letters page.'

As soon she had gone, Feen ripped the paper to shreds. Gorged on self-pity, she had not gone down to luncheon. When Amelia came to demand her turn of the paper, she had been met by the yell that, 'It's a stupid blasted paper, written by idiotic old people! If you must know I've ripped it up.' Amelia had returned with her oldest sister who said that she would buy another and Feen could pay her back out of her allowance when she received it. If Feen did not comply, then she would tell Mother who would bar her from the family picnic – not to mention what she would do if told about the letter. Faced with the threat of not seeing her uncle, Feen had to give in.

'Where are we going on this picnic?' Sonny asked his brother. The two were alone after Sunday lunch, the females having departed.

Dick, eyes closed, mumbled that he didn't know and didn't care. 'By the time the women are ready I'll have dropped off.'

Sonny snuggled back in his chair. 'D'you remember that picnic we took with poor old Bones when we met that girl?'

Dickie pursed his mouth, trying to recall it. 'Yeah ... yeah, I think so. Was it in a wood or somethin'?'

His brother smiled. 'That's right. There was this track that led off the main footpath and we found this lovely lake. I never did find that place again, you know. I've been once or twice since, but no luck.'

'Ye had no luck on that day either if I remember rightly,' said his brother with a sleepy grin.

'No, you little bugger. You and Bones ran off after her and left me to cuddle a twisted ankle.'

'An' the next day poor ol' Bones was dead,' said Dick.

'Aye ...' Sonny gave a sad frown.

His brother sat up impulsively. 'I bet I could find it.'

'I'm not sure I want to,' replied Sonny. 'Places you visited as a child never live up to expectations.'

'Aw, come on, it might be our last chance before we're all banged up in the Castle.'

'That's reserved for Military nowadays,' Sonny informed him dryly. 'The riff-raff go to Wakefield.' At Dickie's insistence he capitulated. 'Oh ... all right. But I'm not trailing all over the wood to find it. That's always considering these bloody women are ever ready.'

The hold-up was due to one of Sonny's girls. Three of them

were suitably dressed, the youngest in white lace dress, white stockings and white doeskin shoes, the elder two in striped shirts with cravats and dark skirts – their period of mourning was over now – but the fourth was confronted as soon as she entered the room where the rest of the family waited.

'You are not going out dressed like that!' Josie stared at her daughter who had obviously entered a Spanish period; her hair was draped with a piece of black lace secured by a gardenia above her left ear; from some trunk in the attic she had dragged a couple of red petticoats which she wore over her skirts arranged in tiers in an attempt to look like a Flamenco dancer, and her bosom had increased in size, due to the aid of some rolled-up stockings. 'And what have you got on your face?' demanded Josie, bending to glare at the black smudges that marked her daughter's eyes. 'You look like a pugilist.'

'It's the stuff they use to clean the fireplace,' answered Feen petulantly. 'Spanish dancers always have dark eyes.' Her mother said she was to scrub it off at once. 'You never complained before,' objected Feen. After a couple of days the pain of the scathing magazine article had lessened. Why should she take notice of a crabby old editor who had probably never known romance? She was once again set to woo her uncle and now her mother was intent on spoiling it.

'I don't mind you dressing up in the house but you are not going out in public like a . . . just go and scrub it off!'

Feen looked pathetic. 'I won't go on the picnic, then.'

Without another word, Josie grabbed her daughter by the scruff of the neck and hauled her off to the bathroom from where emitted screams as the leaden eyes were scrubbed and scoured. After the hold-up the outing proceeded with a red-eyed, red-faced Feen clad in white dress and stockings, sulking all the way to the countryside.

Apart from Sonny's family, Nick and Win were over

with little Johnny who had just taken his first steps. With Belle and her children being invited too, the cars were rather overloaded, and so some of the young adults pedalled behind on bicycles. When the procession of vehicles stopped there followed a walk down a woodland path which seemed never ending.

'I hope one of you knows where you're leading us,' puffed Thomasin, hobbling along with the aid of Erin's arm, the prodigious clan marching ahead, laden with picnic hampers and rugs. The Salicin was not strong enough to combat the pain of this trek, but she was determined not to give in.

'I did offer to get you a bathchair, Mam,' called Dickie from the head of the column. He laughed at her retort and grinned at his brother. 'I like to make her mad, it keeps her going.' He assured her it was not much further now, then pointed to a track to his left. 'Hey, I think this is it, Son, isn't it?'

'If it were that easy I would have found it years ago,' replied Sonny, but turned off the track after his brother.

'Where's he leading us?' asked Erin.

'God knows,' replied Sonny. 'But there should be a lake at the end of this path.'

'Well, if there's any wild geese on it,' grumbled Thomasin, swiping at mosquitoes with her stick and stumbling in the undergrowth, 'they'll get damn-well throttled.'

They seemed to be going nowhere, growing hotter and more bad-tempered by the second, when all at once the track opened onto a clearing. Dick stood with his brother to examine it. 'This can't be it surely,' murmured Sonny.

'Well, if it isn't it's damn-well going to be.' Thomasin poked her sons onwards with her stick. 'Come on, get that rug spread, Erin.'

Sonny wandered further into the clearing. There was little doubt that this was it, for the layout was familiar. But the

319

place they had visited as children had been enchanted and secret; here was just an ordinary, if quite pretty clearing with a small weed-laden pond. He felt a twinge of annoyance that his brother had helped to wreck a childhood illusion.

However, he was forced to smile as Belle's children made a beeline for the water and began uprooting reedmace to use as swords. It was obviously as magical to them as it had been once to him.

'Paddy, come away from the pond!' called the child's mother.

'Want to go pee-wee,' said one small body, whilst Thomasin was asking, 'Who's got my chair? Come on, Sonny, don't just stand there, I'm ready to drop.'

Her son rushed forward and set up the chair, into which she promptly collapsed. 'Oh, that's better.' After a few deep breaths she recovered somewhat. The rest of the family buzzed about her like workers round their queen, spreading rugs and cloths, opening hampers. 'It's not a bad place, is it? When did you say you'd come here, Dickie?'

'Oh, a long time ago, Mam.' Dickie took up a boxing stance and faced his nephew who was complaining noisily about being dragged away from the water. 'Come on, Pad, let's see if ye can scrap as good as your dad.' He pranced around on the balls of his feet, feinting and swiping while little Paddy swung out at his legs with bunched fists. Frederick, not to be left out, started punching too.

'Just look at him,' murmured Dusty to her brother-in-law, shaking her head. 'The big daft clot.' Sonny observed that he was trying to recapture his childhood. 'Recapture it?' Dusty sighed. 'He never lost it. D'you fancy taking a stroll round the pond while this lot calm down?'

Dickie noticed the pair ambling off together. 'Hey, stay away from the woods with my wife, Feeney!'

Sonny smiled at his partner, who was wearing a close-fitting lilac skirt with a minute waist and a train that brushed the grass, a matching bolero-style jacket with embroidery and guipure lace and a wide-sleeved blouse with a bunch of frills at her throat. 'You know, you look younger than Josie – but don't tell her I said so.'

Dusty smiled back at him from under the shade of her straw hat; its white feathers dipped gently in time to her saunter. She was silent for a time, then gave a little laugh. 'You didn't like me very much when we first met, did you?'

'Oh . . . it wasn't that I disliked you, Dust. It was just . . . well, Mam seemed to favour you more than Peggy, that was all. Gosh, it's hot!' The black mourning garb attracted the sun. He took off the jacket and slung it over his arm.

Dusty continued the theme. 'I used to think you were a real dope over her.'

'You'd've been right. As the saying goes, love makes fools of us all.'

'I'd be the first to agree with that. But you've learned from your encounter, whereas I'm still being made a fool of.' She saw him flush slightly. 'I see you understand my meaning. Has he said anything to you about her?'

Cornered, Sonny rubbed the back of his neck uncomfortably and shook his head. He had noticed how his brother's voice lowered an octave when he was talking to his niece. 'But it's not serious though, Dusty. It's just . . . Dickie being Dickie.'

'Josie's worried too, isn't she?'

'About Feen? Ah well, Josie's just being daft.'

'I'm glad you think so. Everyone else has such a low opinion of Dick, apart from your mother. But he'd never . . .'

Sonny stopped her. 'I know that, Dusty. And I know he'd never do anything with Belle either.'

Her face showed dubiety. 'Erin's noticed. Oh, she hasn't said anything, but I know she's concerned.'

'And what does Dickie have to say to all this?'

'What one might expect him to say – what he always says.'

'D'you want me to speak to him?'

Dusty shook her head, making the feathers on her hat shiver. 'No, it'll fizzle out. They always do. I hope I haven't spoilt your afternoon by mentioning it.' They walked on.

Dickie had ceased his pretend fight with the boys and flopped onto the long grass next to Belle and her mother, gasping his exhaustion. For a while he lay flat on his back, shading his eyes against the sun. Belle knew he was looking at her. So did Erin, who censured, 'You'll get grass stains on that white suit.' Her annoyance stemmed partly from the fact that he had already abandoned his mourning clothes. 'Why don't ye go sit on the rug.'

Dickie hoisted himself on an elbow and grinned. 'She doesn't like me sitting next to her,' he whispered close to Belle's ear. Pulling at a blade of grass, he sucked on its root. A disturbed moth flittered round his head.

'Moths round a flame,' observed Belle. She, too, had cast her black, but the floating chiffon creation she wore was still respectful, in the colours of sweet peas.

The moth became an irritation. Dickie snatched it from the air and tossed it aside, leaving a gold smudge on his palm. It still fluttered pathetically in the grass. Amelia had seen the action and said indignantly, 'You've left it half-dead!'

'He has that effect on most of us, dear,' said her Aunt Erin.

Amelia scooped the moth up and examined it. 'One of its wings is broken. I wonder if I can mend it.' With an accusing look at the culprit, she wandered off, still looking at her cupped hands.

Dickie had been still for long enough. He leapt up. 'Right, who's for a game of hide and seek?' The younger children immediately gathered round enthusiastically. 'You too, girls!' he called to Sonny's daughters.

'I'm a bit old for games, Uncle,' smiled Elizabeth from the shade of her parasol.

'My God, decrepit at twenty-one,' scoffed Dickie. He took off his white blazer and threw it down. 'What about you, Feen?'

Up until now, Feen had been very morose, but at her uncle's invitation the sulk was abandoned. Jumping to her feet, she joined the game.

Dickie rolled up his sleeves. There were white scars on his forearms where a pig had once bitten him. 'We'll have a slight change of rules. I'll hide, you lot count to a hundred and try to find me – you too, Belle.' He pelted off towards the wood calling over his shoulder. 'The first girl to find me gets a kiss!'

'I hate to think what the loser gets,' breathed Erin as a sour-faced Amelia muttered some insult whilst trying to fix the moth's wing.

Belle clambered to her feet and smoothed her chiffon robes. Her mother squinted up at her. 'You're not deserting us, are ye? Who's going to get tea ready?'

'There's plenty of you, isn't there?' Belle pointed to the other women and began to count with the children.

Josie came to sit by Erin. 'Mother's looking well today, isn't she?'

'What?' Too busy watching her daughter, Erin frowned. 'Sorry, Josie, what did you say?' When the statement was repeated she only half-agreed. 'It's a wonder she does, what with all the worry. But yes, she's good for her age.'

'Oh yes,' said Josie. 'If her legs weren't so bad she'd be very good.' She looked at Erin who had chuckled, then realised what she had said and laughed herself.

323

'That must be the shortest hundred ever,' remarked Erin with a smile as Feen, much to her mother's consternation, dashed off into the woods. Seeing this, the others stopped counting too and streamed after her, Belle taking up the rear. For a time the clearing was peaceful.

Dickie looked down from his perch in the tree and watched the seekers thrashing about the undergrowth. Julia and Faith had stopped to pick bluebells. Fred whacked and poked amongst the elder bushes with a stick. Belle had caught up with Feen, though the latter tried her best to shake her off. Eventually she made a quick dash to her right, shouting, 'I'll go this way, you go the other!'

Belle continued alone. There was no urgency in her performance as she dipped into every hiding place. Dickie kept very still, draped over the branch, watching. Somewhere above him, a chaffinch warned of invaders. Belle came nearer. He would have jumped down and surprised her, but she saw him first and stood at the foot of the tree, hands on hips.

He swung like a gibbon from the branch and planted himself before her, spreading his arms. 'I surrender. Claim your prize.' When she simply laughed and made to turn away, he waylaid her. Still she just looked at him, a taunt in her eye. With a swift grab he pulled her to him and murmured into her face, 'Come on, ye know you're dying for it,' then dealt her the most passionate kiss she could ever hope to have. Instead of struggling free as he had expected her to, Belle returned the kiss with a ferocity that shook him. Unprepared, he had widened his eyes when Feen burst upon them. He saw the look of excitement turn to dismay before the girl swivelled and ran back the way she had come, leaving him to be the one who struggled free.

'Too much for you, am I?' asked Belle triumphantly, then saw that his gaze was not directed at her and turned to see Feen's dark hair flying out behind her as she ran. Her gleam of devilment faded as she turned back to him. 'Oh . . . now look what you've done!'

'Me? It was you who was making a meal of it.'

'And why shouldn't I?'

'I'm a married man.'

'That doesn't seem to make much difference to you, why should it to me? Because I'm a woman?'

'Well, I would've thought that'd make you pay some consideration to Dusty.'

She gasped. 'You really are the most hypocritical pig!'

'You enjoyed it though, didn't ye.' The puckishness was back in his eye.

'As I said before, why shouldn't I? I have to make the most of these little acts of charity – doesn't everyone keep telling me how starved of love I am.'

'Like a bit more?' He made a grab for her.

Belle smiled, then did something she hadn't done for a very long time: she drew back her surgical boot and gave him the most horrendous crack on the shin.

Dusty looked round in surprise as a red-cheeked Feen plonked herself down on the rug beside her and said, 'They're so childish, aren't they? Especially Cousin Belle. One would think she'd be here helping with the picnic – can I do that for you, Aunt?' Still breathless, she reached for the pack of sandwiches that Dusty had been transferring to a plate and took over the arrangement.

'Why, thank you, Feen, that's very good of you.' Dusty smiled through her confusion. 'You didn't find Uncle Dickie then?'

'No, I got tired of looking for him.' Feen spoke airily. 'Belle found him first.'

Dusty looked up as Belle emerged from the wood alone. A fraction later Dickie burst from a different exit surrounded

325

by laughing children. His wife poured him a cup of tea and asked casually, 'Who won?'

'Faith.' Dickie flopped down beside her.

Dusty turned to look up at Belle who, though not outwardly perturbed, did not meet her eye. 'Oh? The runner-up must have got a kiss too, then.'

Dickie knew that tone and immediately leapt up again. 'Right, we'll get a game of Rugby in while the women are organising tea! Where's that ball, Fred?' As promised, he had bought this for the boy's recent birthday. 'Come on, let's sort the teams out. Son, you and me are the captains. I'll have Nick, Eddie . . .'

'Aye, don't tell me,' sighed his brother. 'I get Paddy, Baby John . . .' Dick laughed and conceded to fair play.

Josie had been watchful of events and had seen that all was not well with Feen. She came up to ask, 'Are you all right, love?'

'Of course,' snapped Feen, still angry at her mother for the earlier episode.

'We're still one short on my side,' called Dick. 'Feen, come on, you can . . .'

'I'm not playing stupid games,' replied Feen.

Her mother heaved a sigh of relief that the infatuation was over and went to sit down again.

'Aren't you going to play?' Erin asked her daughter.

'Don't be silly, Mother.' Belle had felt her mother's scrutiny ever since she had returned from the woods.

'What's silly about it? Ye played hide and seek, didn't ye . . . or whatever else the pair of ye were playing in there.'

Belle simply looked at her mother coldly.

'Well, whatever you're playing, Belle, remember he has a wife.' Erin turned to watch the match.

Sonny was demanding to know why his team's goalposts were thirty feet wider apart that Dickie's. His brother told him not to split hairs and the game began with Elizabeth as upholder of rules.

'Don't get too rough!' shouted an alarmed Josie as her small son became enmeshed in the scrum.

Dick made a gentle pass to the boy. 'Come on, Pad, run!'

Everyone pretended to chase Paddy while he, face abeam, ran for the goal. 'Come on, come on!' Dick scooped the child off his feet, tucked him under his arm and ran for the goal himself, setting him down and bawling, 'Try!'

'Foul!' objected Sonny and grabbing the ball set off at full tilt.

Dick streaked after him. Sonny came within a foot of the goalpost when he felt his legs clasped and crashed down onto his belly. Indeed, it was some minutes before he could gasp, 'Bloody hell, you're still fit!'

'I have to be, Son.' Dickie clambered to his feet, still panting. 'I've always got some bugger chasing me.'

Whilst they were still laughing, Paddy came up to stare at his father on the ground, asking, 'Is he dead?' Fred sneaked up and seized the ball. Elizabeth shouted that if they continued to flout the rules she was not going to waste her time umpiring. When the game proceeded she stalked back to sit with the women.

Fred was still running when Eddie performed a flying tackle on him. Both hit the ground heavily. Fred screamed and burst into tears. Dusty ran to comfort him. 'Oh, come here, let me rub it better, love – where does it hurt?'

Fred clutched at his groin and sobbed. 'There!'

'Oh . . .' Dusty's hand faltered and she hid a smile. 'Come on, let's leave these big bullies, there's some chocolate cake in the hamper.' She led him away.

After a few more skirmishes and cries of cheat! and foul! the players were called to eat. Dick, avoiding his wife, sat beside Feen, but she removed herself to the far side of the circle and did not speak to him for the rest of the afternoon. Neither did Amelia, whose attempts to heal the moth had ended with it being smeared over her palm.

While they ate, Sonny spoke about next month's exhibition at the York Art Gallery. 'I'm looking forward to it, but there'll be a lot of packing to do.'

Dusty said, 'Oh, Dickie'll help, won't you, dear? He's quite good at making exhibitions, expecially of himself.' So saying, she took a bunch of grapes from the hamper, looked her errant husband in the eye and, with a pair of scissors, very deliberately snipped off two of the pendulous fruit. Dickie grimaced and crossed his legs.

After tea everyone relaxed and enjoyed what was left of the sunshine. Thomasin sat like a queen on her throne while they lounged at her feet on the rugs, posing for Dickie's camera. Then Elizabeth and Sophia wandered off to talk of make-believe paramours and the children took their last chance of play before it was time to leave. Sonny produced a drawing pad. 'I think I'll get a few sketches while you're sitting still,' he told his brother. 'Otherwise I'm never going to get that portrait finished.' Since January there had only been two sittings and those had been brief.

'Had I known it was going to take this long I'd never have mentioned it,' grumbled Dickie. 'If ye wait till after the trial you could take a deathmask and save us both the . . .'

'Don't make jokes like that!' interrupted Thomasin angrily.

'Sorry, Mam.' Dickie looked chastened and played with his bootlace. He turned his eye on Dusty, then Belle; both were regarding him as though he were a leper.

'Why do I bother?' Erin asked the sky. 'We organise this picnic to take everyone's mind off the wretched business and one stupid thoughtless remark from you . . .'

Sonny was put out too, murmuring, 'Dick, keep your voice down, the children might overhear.'

'We've still got it to face though, haven't we?' said their mother. 'Pass me one of those sandwiches, love, we don't want to take them home.'

Erin complied, then fixed her eyes to the silver locket that dangled from Thomasin's throat. 'That's a pretty little thing, Mam. Is it new?'

'This? It's the one your father bought me the first Christmas we were wed. Don't you remember?' Erin shook her head. Thomasin lifted the sandwich. 'I thought I'd wear it for him. It's our anniversary soon . . . forty-nine years. Would've been our Golden Wedding next year.' She bit into the sandwich and made a face. 'God, I think this pig's celebrated its Golden Wedding, too. I can't get my teeth through it.'

There was a long silence. Then Dickie frowned. 'Hey . . . if you got married at the end of May and I was born in December . . .'

'You were earlier than expected,' said his mother swiftly. 'Pass me a bit of cake, someone please, I can't eat this.'

Dickie spent a moment staring at his sister. Erin wanted to giggle at the wounded expression. Instead she told him sternly, 'You can get your hair cut before the trial; ye look like a poet.'

'Now who's mentioned trials,' quipped her brother before saying to Thomasin, 'Don't look so worried, Mam. I know we're going to get off.'

'All right!' His mother suddenly came alive. 'If you're so confident we'll have a little bet on it.' When he laughingly agreed she put the terms, 'If we get off, you stay in England.'

'Eh, now hold on, Mam.' Her son was dismayed, and for the first time Nick was in total unison with his uncle.

'You can't welch on it now, I've got witnesses!'

Dickie looked amused at being so easily cornered. 'Talk about heads I win, tails you lose – if I'm found not guilty I have to stay, if I'm found guilty then I'll be staying anyway.'

I hope he is found guilty. Feen had isolated herself from both children and adults, but sat near enough to catch snippets of the latter's discourse. She was not sure what the trouble was all about, for Father and Mother clammed up about it whenever their children came near, but she knew that there was to be a trial. A loud screech from Julia postponed her eavesdropping for the moment. Ripping up handfuls of grass and casting a malicious glance at Belle, she wished her uncle was being tried for murder. *I'd rather him be dead than see him with her.*

'Still, we have to look on the bright side,' Dickie was saying to the others. 'Even if we are convicted the sentence shouldn't be more than a couple o' months' hard labour – are ye good with a shovel, Mam?' His sister told him he was stupid. 'It's the law that's stupid. Ye'd think it was hardly worth their bother trying us for the measly amount that Mam claimed.'

'Well, I've every faith in British Justice,' declared his brother, hand sketching rapidly. 'I'm going to book a holiday in Ireland for August.'

'You both seem to have forgotten the adverse publicity that comes with this,' said Erin. 'Even if you're found not guilty there'll be wagging tongues.'

'Can I have this, Dad?' Fred staggered up under the weight of an enormous grey cat with blazing orange eyes and tail that twitched.

'Put it down!' urged Belle. 'The blessed thing's wild.'

'No, he likes me.' Fred clung onto his squirming prize and turned to Dusty. 'Can I have it, Mam?' He and the girls now dared to use the more familiar titles in front of Belle, hoping that it would hurry their adoption along.

'I want it.' Paddy made a grab for the cat.

'You always want what I've got.' Fred held it out of reach.

'Go on, Mam, can I take him home?'

When Belle said that it probably came from a farm and would be missed, Dusty turned to her niece and whispered, 'Let him take it, Belle, please. You can always throw it out when he's asleep and say it's escaped.'

Belle did not normally yield to persuasion, but this time guilt over her uncle's kiss modified her stance. She gave her aunt a mute nod and began to clear away the leftover food.

Whilst his wife was busy elsewhere, Dickie shifted towards his niece. 'Dusty knows.'

'I couldn't give two hoots,' rasped Belle. 'I'm more concerned about what you've done to Feen. The poor child . . . I know exactly how she feels.' For that moment, there resurfaced the humiliation of seeing her first and only love in the arms of her cousin Rosie. She left him and in a spirit of compassion approached Feen to make reparation. But the girl deliberately turned her back and went to help Dusty.

There's something gone on there. Thomasin watched Belle and her daughter-in-law closely. They had never exactly been compatible, but something had happened to nudge mere dislike into antagonism. She cast her mind back over the afternoon, pinpointing the game of hide and seek as the catalyst. Whatever had occurred included Feen. Hitherto, she could always be found in the vicinity of her uncle, but several times this afternoon she had displayed alienation. Thomasin tried to picture what had happened in that wood, and came to a worrying conclusion. She watched Feen wander away from her aunt to stand alone by the lake, and suddenly realised with some shame that she was guilty of that which she complained about in others: she had been treating Feen as a child when in fact she was almost a woman. Asking Sonny to pull her out of the chair, she limped over to stand beside her grand-daughter.

'It'll be your birthday soon.' She leaned painfully on her stick.

Feen nodded, but continued to stare at the water. The expression in her eyes told Thomasin that her version of the scenario had not been far from the truth. She wanted to offer comfort, but there was little one could say to someone whose first experience of love had been shattered.

'We have a lot in common, you and me, Feen. They treat us both like kids.' Feen looked at her and formed a watery smile. 'You know, I haven't told anyone this,' Thomasin shifted her weight onto the other leg, 'but when the Queen died I kept seeing it as something drastic, all this change . . . Only recently I came to see that it's not the world that's changing but me that's grown old. I hate it, Feen. It frightens me. It seems to hit you with a bang. Until your grandfather died I felt the same inside as I'd done at your age – oh, I know, you think this old twig can't possibly have entertained the same emotions as you, but I did. That's why I came to offer my apologies. I've been so busy complaining about folk treating me like a bairn that I didn't see I was guilty of the same.' She turned round slowly, presenting her back. 'Here, unhook this locket for me, will you? I can't get my hands that far any more.'

Feen lifted the wisps of grey hair from her grandmother's neck and applied her nails to the clasp. Thomasin cupped her hand to catch the locket as the girl lowered it on its chain. She looked at it warmly for a second, then pressed it into Feen's hand. 'There you are. That's your birthday present.'

Acquainted with its origins, Feen gasped at the honour and gazed down at the little silver locket. Both this, and the way Thomasin had confided her adult thoughts, brought anguish over the dreadful things she had said of her grandmother. Tears welled up. She pressed an impulsive kiss to the downy cheek. 'Thank you, Nan.'

Thomasin put an arm round her, returning the kiss. 'Bless you, love. I only wish it were that simple to give you a life without heartbreak.' She looked up at the shout from her son – 'We're going without you!' The rugs had been lifted, leaving flattened patches in the long grass. 'Have you heard him?' demanded Thomasin. 'Treating us like bairns again.' Feen laughed and, linking her grandmother's arm the two made their way back to the gathering.

Dickie expected his wife to confront him when they got home. But she said nothing. 'You're mad at me, aren't ye?' he said when they were getting undressed for bed and she had hardly uttered anything other than sarcasms all evening. She asked what reason she could possibly have for being angry. ''Cause ye think I got up to something with Belle this afternoon.'

'I don't think that – I *know*.'

'It was only a game, Dusty, honest.' He opened the door to place his boots on the landing to be polished.

'Isn't everything a game to you? The adoption, our marriage, everything.'

He approached her with arms outspread but she raised her fist and he backed away. 'Remember the trial's coming up! I don't want to appear with a black eye.'

'Thank you for reminding me,' said Dusty, and thumped him in the gut instead. While he was still doubled over, she asked, 'Did you mean it about staying in England?'

He nodded painfully, hand clutched to midriff. 'For the time being. I'm not gonna sell the house, though.'

'What you mean is, it'll be there to go back to when your mother dies.' At the look on his face her harshness melted and she came to tend his injuries. 'Oh, I'm sorry, that was low.'

'It's right, though, isn't it?' sighed Dickie. 'It'll be just like I'm waiting for her to die. But I've promised her and that's

333

that. I'll have to wire Faulkener,' this was Dickie's lawyer in America, 'tell him to sort things out for us and send some more cash.' He finished undressing.

Dusty let out a gasp. 'Look at your shin!'

Dickie looked down at the large purple swelling. 'No more rugby for me.'

July arrived. Nursed back to confidence by her grandmother's frequent tête à têtes, Feen was now more enamoured of the new horse her father had given her for her birthday, than Uncle Dickie. Since the picnic, Thomasin had become concerned at the amount of time her son was spending with Belle. Of course it was natural that he and Dusty would want to keep visiting the children, but Thomasin felt that on Dickie's part it was just a convenient excuse. Today, Belle had come over for tea with the children, who were informally gathered in the drawing room. At least here she could keep tabs on her.

Erin shared this view, though she was unaware that her mother had noticed. She passed a plate of bread and butter to the adults and then to the children. 'Don't touch the cat, dear, when you're about to eat.' Freddie's cat had defied all Belle's attempts at eviction. Each time she opened the door on a morning, in it would stroll to be fed. The children's arms were covered in scratches from its assaults. Belle had threatened to drown it, but then a new baby arrived which was more troublesome than the cat and Fred's pet was safe for the time being. Erin only wished the child would not fetch it with him whenever he visited. She didn't care for cats and even less so when they were not housetrained.

Whilst they were eating, the animal leapt up onto the sofa beside Dusty and had the audacity to lick the bread in her hand. She lashed out at it, knocking it to the carpet.

'Aw, he was only tasting it for you to make sure it wasn't

334

stale, weren't you, Pussy?' Dickie leaned over to fondle the ruffled feline.

Erin ordered Fred to take it out and tea continued in a more orderly fashion. Afterwards, when the children were playing in the garden, she asked her daughter, 'Have ye seen anything of Brian lately?' Belle picked up a newspaper to deflect this, saying she hadn't seen him at all and didn't expect to. 'I wonder how the poor man is. I've a mind to go call on him myself.'

'I'll thank you not to.' To make her mother talk of something else Belle gave an angry flick of the newspaper. 'Just listen to this! It's headed: "*When Women Should Rule*".' She read aloud. '"*That women should rule to a certain extent we all allow – just as far as man's natural gallantry prompts him to place the reins in her dainty fingers. In little things, in everything that pertains to her own sphere let her authority be supreme. But in everything of importance man must govern for the good of all concerned.*"'

'Quite right too,' said her uncle. 'But they left out the bit about chaining them to the bedpost.' He gave a droll smile to his audience.

'You need someone to teach you what women could do if ever they were granted the chance!'

'I *know* what women are capable of.' He gave an oblique look at his wife. 'Anyway, what would women do if they were given the vote?'

'We'd stop all these stupid wars for a start,' retorted Belle.

'You don't stop bullets with feather dusters.'

'No! you usually stop them with a part of your body,' volleyed Belle. 'The real way to stop them, the sensible way, is at source, with the politicians who get us into these skirmishes, and to do that we have to have the vote. I mean, what makes men so special? What makes them look upon us as simply wives and mothers? Why should I with a First Class Honours Degree be denied a say in my own future while the man who shovels the contents of the privies has his?'

'Ah well, that's where you academics fall down, ye see. Ye think that just 'cause ye've been to university and passed a few exams ye're experienced enough to handle the country's future. Exams are useless when it comes to real life. The other man might be as thick as the stuff he shovels but he knows what real life's all about.'

'He knows about *his* life! He knows how much it costs for a pint of beer and a twist of tobacco . . .'

'That's rather patronising, Belle,' cut in Erin. 'Just because someone's poorly paid or roughly spoken doesn't mean he's uncaring of the wider world. You're forgetting that this family wasn't always as wealthy.'

'I'm not forgetting and I didn't mean to imply that all his kind are uncaring or unintelligent – though plenty of them are. I'm just pointing out the absurdities in the system. Everyone should be entitled to a vote and I mean everyone.'

'I dread to think what life would be like if that Hobhouse woman got the vote,' said Thomasin.

Belle defended her friend. 'The world would be a better place.'

Thomasin looked over her spectacles. 'For our enemies.'

'Oh, come! It's women and children she's concerned about.'

'It might be nice if she showed a bit of patriotism and compassion for our own soldiers who're being slaughtered by the husbands of the women she's helping.'

Erin agreed. 'Look at what happened to Rosie. She thought she was helping a cause. It's the same with these interfering Americans who send money to Ireland thinking they're doing good when all it's doing is subsidising murder.'

Dickie flared. 'Are you saying I helped kill my own daughter?'

For a moment there was acute tension in the room, then Erin sighed, 'Did I say that?'

'When ye say Americans ye usually mean me!'

'Well, I didn't. I doubt even you are that stupid. I was just making a general comment on the way people's interference in something that doesn't concern them often makes things worse.'

'Mother of God!' spat Belle. 'Where would we be if nobody interfered in atrocities just because it didn't concern them. What's going on in South Africa concerns all of us. If the French Army were to march in here and drag us all into concentration camps you'd have plenty to say.'

'That's a ridiculous analogy,' said Thomasin. 'The French don't have the same connections with us as we do with South Africa – they'd be invading a foreign country.'

Belle gave a growl of impatience. 'That's the sort of colonial attitude that's central to this war. You've no idea, any of you. You should have come and listened to Emily at yesterday's meeting. She'd convince you.'

'God forbid,' said her grandmother. 'Anyway, it'll all be academic soon, Kruger's about to surrender.'

'I doubt it,' said Belle. 'But even if that were true there're other battles to be won. There's a meeting of the York Women's Suffrage Society on Saturday afternoon. Why don't you come, Nan? You too, Mother and you Aunt. We need a few authoritative voices.' Her mother said they had too much on their minds with the trial. 'Then this will take your minds off it,' argued Belle. 'It would do you good to listen to some sense too, Uncle.'

'I don't think it'll be my cup o' tea somehow,' said Dick.

'Well, I agree that there might be some long words that you may not understand but I could explain them to you.'

337

'May one ask who'll be looking after the children while you swan off to this meeting?' asked her mother. 'Didn't I hear you mention that you'd granted Sally this Saturday off in lieu of yesterday?'

Belle replied that Sally could have another day off instead.

'And why should she?' enquired Erin. 'Hasn't she been put upon enough recently?' Belle asked what she meant. 'Well, you have been to rather a lot of meetings since you got back from Africa. The poor girl had to cope virtually alone until Aunt Dusty came, she might at least expect a bit of respite now you're back. Not to mention that she's probably up half the night with that new baby.'

'She gets paid for it, doesn't she?'

'Oh, that's a very philanthropic attitude, I must say!' scolded her mother.

Dusty jumped in. 'I don't have to come to the meeting. I can come round and keep an eye on them if you like.'

'I don't see why you should have to stay at home when your husband's gallivanting,' opined Erin.

'I enjoy being with the children,' said Dusty.

Are you trying to drive them together or what, fumed Erin. Here I am giving you the opportunity . . .

'That's settled then,' said Belle.

Political meetings were not Dickie's usual idea of entertainment, but he allowed Belle to drag him along. As it turned out the afternoon was more eventful than he might have imagined. From the outset there was a great deal of heckling, though the main speaker managed to deliver her speech without a waver. As it progressed however, the heckling grew to such a pitch it was almost impossible to hear her. Belle could stand it no longer and jumped up to confront the man behind her who was one of the noisiest contributors. Dickie shrank into his seat as she harangued the man loudly.

'Why don't you take control of your woman?' demanded a fellow sitting nearby.

'She's not with me.' Dickie looked offended and as inconspicuously as he could, made for the exit. He waited outside for her until the arrival of a police van, at which point he deemed it politic to make himself scarce.

Belle caught up with him some time later. 'Deserter!' She brandished a handful of leaflets at him. 'Just for that you can deliver some of these.'

The leaflets were delivered under duress. Belle told him he was a good boy and offered to buy him tea. He agreed to this, but made loud protest when on her way Belle purchased a sheep's head. 'Christ, that's not my tea, is it?'

'Don't be silly. We're just going to take a little detour, get our own back on that lout at the meeting. I know his address, he's always disrupting our talks.'

Arriving at the man's house, Belle put the sheep's head on his doorstep. She took a piece of paper from her bag, scrawled on it *Votes For Women Not For Sheep* and fixed it as best she could to the sheep's head. Then, satisfied, she took Dickie to the Coffee House in High Ousegate where she treated him to a plate of sausage and mash.

On Monday morning, Dickie learnt from the newspaper that a black magic coven was thought to be operating in York: a sheep's head had been found on someone's doorstep. Belle and he laughed uproariously when he told her about it the next time she came over. 'The note must have blown off!'

Erin did not share the hilarity. 'I think you ought to make your mind up just who and what you are, Belle. Are you a campaigner for women's rights? Are ye for the people of South Africa or are ye going to stick with the responsibilities you've already made for yourself – the children.'

Belle was put out by this attack. 'It's not a matter of choice.

The three are interwoven. The same people are responsible for all these injustices.'

'But it's the amount of time you're spending in fighting them! You complain about injustice but you're just as guilty of it. You shuffle Sally's free days about to fit in with your life, you're quite content to let Dusty take care of the children when it suits you but you drag your feet when it comes to letting her have them permanently.'

'You know I can't sign them over until after the trial.'

'Why not? Have they any more stability with you when you're out campaigning every night? You're going to have to buck your ideas up, my girl.' She was about to leave the room, when she noticed a pile of excrement behind a chair. 'Oh, who's done that!'

'Well, don't look at me,' said her brother, drawing more laughter from Belle. Her mother stalked out.

'What did I say to bring that on myself?' Belle asked her grandmother, whilst going to ring for the maid.

'It's the worry of the trial, and of course she's always a bit on edge at this time of year,' replied Thomasin softly. 'It's the anniversary of your father's death.'

'Oh . . .' Belle looked guilty. 'I forget, you know.'

'Well, you were only three when he died, you can't be expected to remember him.'

Belle did not contradict her, though she had not meant to imply that she had forgotten her father, for she often thought about him; it was merely the date of his death that did not hold the same poignancy as it did for her mother. 'I should have known . . . I'll have to go and find her.' The maid came in and was told to move the cat's deposit. Belle waited for her to go, then asked, 'Nan, do you think I've been neglectful of the children?'

'I do.' It was her aunt. After all these months of being afraid of Belle whose hand controlled her future, Dusty decided it was time to speak out. 'And your mother's right. You sit in judgement of us, but when it comes to your responsibilities it's, "Oh, but that's justified!" It's justified to leave the children because it's all in a good cause. Can't you see how hypocritical you are? I've spent more time with those children this month than you have in three!'

'Ah! So this is where it was leading.' Belle nodded sourly. 'All this, "I don't mind, I enjoy being with the children" rubbish – it was just ammunition for your gun.'

'No it damn-well wasn't!' Dusty was furious. 'I genuinely love Freddie and his sisters, Belle.'

Belle studied her indignant face, and acquiesced. 'Yes, well . . . I know you do, otherwise I'd never have drawn up those contracts. But you can't say that *his* prospects have improved in that sphere.' She jabbed a thumb at Dickie.

'You're a fine one to talk! It's you who's been encouraging him to join in your activities – when would he find the time to show parental responsibility? I'm getting a bit sick of your dog in the manger attitude, Belle. It's spiteful and cruel . . .'

'Spiteful? What reason have I for spite?'

Dusty held her eye. 'You know that best. But I can vouch for the cruelty, not just to me and Dickie but the children. They don't know where they stand. Either you want them or you don't, and if you don't here's someone who does!' Dusty stormed out, her husband following close behind.

Belle tried to involve her grandmother in the argument, but Thomasin said she was feeling tired and so Belle left.

When the door closed so, too, did Thomasin's eyes, but she did not sleep. She thought of her sons who might soon be in prison, she thought of her daughter-in-law desperate for children, she thought of the baby she herself had lost forty years ago. And all these thoughts led to Patrick.

341

15

'Looking forward to your retirement, sir?' Detective Sergeant George Palmer laid a newspaper on his superior's desk; it was folded in such a manner as to display an article about a recent acquittal, one which had cost the force months of hard work. Both the article and the remark were intended to sting.

Detective Chief Inspector Scholes Nettleton of the West Yorkshire Police raised penetrating eyes. It rankled with Nettleton that the sergeant couldn't wait to get rid of him. He himself detested the thought of retirement, had turned down the chance to quit after twenty-five years' service on a third pension, and had done the same after thirty years. Many of his colleagues had taken the opportunity to set themselves up as private investigators, but second-rate detective work was not for him. Alas, now he had reached the age of sixty there was no choice, he was classed as an old man, past his best, ready for the knacker. He studied the newspaper article with venom. 'I'd've preferred to have had this one under my belt before I clear my desk out . . . all that bloody evidence. I felt sure we'd got him, George.'

The sergeant placed a cup of tea on the desk and left the other to peruse the print. While he drank, Nettleton shook his grizzled head over the page. He was a whippet of a man with shrewd pale-blue eyes. His face had the purplish-red colouring of one with a heart complaint, and was deeply lined. At this moment, the lines around his mouth were especially pronounced, emphasising the disappointment he felt at leaving his post on such a note. Thirty-five years in the force, and to be outsmarted by a devious little tyke like that . . . One of his hands came up to pull distractedly at an ear that had been badly managled in a fight when he was a copper on the beat; most of the lobe had been ripped off by someone's teeth. That same person's teeth had left an imprint on his ankle before being smashed out by a truncheon. During his long career he had suffered an impressive collection of disfigurements, some of which had nearly killed him: a nine-inch scar near his groin, a small puncture mark under his left breast, a dent in his skull from a hammer which had left a legacy of headaches. He should be glad to be out of it – would have been, had this most recent villain been tucked away in Wakefield Gaol . . . sickening it was, sickening. And this heatwave didn't help matters. Nettleton ran a finger round his collar, his upper lip and brow dappled with sweat.

Once he had read the offending article, he tried to keep his eyes from it, turning the pages back to proper sequence. Taking another gulp of his tea, he set upon reading the rest of the paper, starting at the left-hand column and working his way across to the right, before turning onto the next page. Here were several crimes to interest him, some on which he had worked himself, others from the surrounding area. After shaking his head over grossly dramatized 'facts' of a murder, his eyes roamed on to read of the latest appearances at the York Summer Assizes. There were only two cases: one, a charge of murder; the other an insurance fraud. The Grand Jury had returned true bills against both. In the following column was a fuller account of the murder trial. The case of fraud would be heard tomorrow. Neither held any personal interest. After Nettleton had browsed idly through the passage he took another sip of tea and moved on to the next paragraph.

However, something lured his sharp eyes back to the previous section – a name. Admittedly it was a very common name, but it provoked him into reading the article more thoroughly. Some minutes later, after racking his brain for yet another name, an excited Chief Inspector was giving his sergeant orders to seek out a file. The sergeant, on learning that the file in demand was more than twenty-five years old, put a young constable to work in the archives. Much later, an exhausted, dust-covered constable staggered from the record vaults and held aloft the desired file for the sergeant's praise.

'Took your time, didn't you, Slaithwaite?'

The constable grimaced and stuck two fingers up at the sergeant's back.

'No, it's three o'clock actually, constable.' Without turning, Sergeant Palmer went into his superior's office, leaving the constable to gawp. 'And get smartened up, you look as if you've been down a cellar.'

At his entry, Nettleton seized the aged file and studied it at length. That evening, when he dropped his belongings into a paper bag and said goodbye to his colleagues, he did not feel the anticipated depression. There was a pair of handcuffs in his pocket which should have been surrendered, but he still had use for them. Packing an overnight bag he took a train to York, in order to be bright and early for the next day's sitting at the Assize Courts. And then just let them tell me I'm bloody past it, thought Nettleton delightedly.

'Court rise for the Lord Chief Justice, Lord Alverstone!'

Flanked by prison officers, Dickie stood as the judge entered the courtroom. He looked very respectable today, having thought it politic to return to mourning wear. At his sister's dictum, he had visited the barber; the back of his neck was now visible above his white collar and his hair neatly groomed. He cast a glance at his fellow accused,

344

then with casual eye examined the room: much of its lower half was panelled in oak, but overhead was an elaborately plastered dome supported by eight gilded columns. In front of Dickie was his solicitor, Sutcliffe, who was most fortunate not to have been called to the stand himself. The police had questioned him, but had been unable to produce anything untoward in his dealings with Feeney. It had been mutually agreed amongst the family, that nothing would be mentioned of Sonny's visit to the solicitor in 1888; as far as the Court was concerned, until their recent acquaintance, neither he nor the family had seen Sutcliffe since the latter had read them the contents of the will. Thomasin felt uneasy at having to lie, but if Sonny were to change his statement now it would be even more damning.

In front of Sutcliffe was Defence Counsel, John Haig. Dickie's heart had sunk on meeting the barrister for the first time – he didn't look old enough to be tackling the school bullies, let alone these heavyweights representing the Crown. Dickie had remonstrated with Sutcliffe over not hiring a KC, but the solicitor had told him that the silk gown did not necessarily mean the Prosecution was any cleverer. 'Don't be misled by that freshness of face, Mr Haig is a very competent lawyer.'

'Competent?' Dickie had brayed. 'Dammit, for the fee he'll be charging I expect something more than a snot-nosed kid.'

Thomasin and Sonny shared counsel, a man named Fox who had had many years of experience at the Bar. She hoped he lived up to his name.

The Judge settled himself beneath the royal arms next to his Judge's Clerk and the black-velveted High Sheriff of Yorkshire. On the front row of one of the three galleries that flanked the courtroom sat Belle with her mother, her two aunts and Francis. Nick had seen no point in coming –

his presence would be of little help – and anyway, someone had to see the business didn't collapse. Dickie had surprised Erin by forbidding his barrister to put his wife on the stand, so saving her distress.

The atmosphere in Court was sultry and pervaded by sweat. Those bewigged suffered most, their faces pink and glistening. Occasionally a handkerchief would come out to mop quickly at a brow. Ladies' fans wafted constantly, bringing the gallery alive with butterflies. The Clerk of Court was announcing the names of the Jury, while nearby a shorthand writer was scribbling on a pad. After much rigmarole, the case began. After the charges had been read out there were pleas of Not Guilty. The judge looked at Prosecuting Counsel and said, 'Yes, Mr Lindley.'

The barrister for the Crown rose and bowed to the judge. He was a stocky man with harsh lines to his face and a broken nose, sustained during his rugby-playing days. Belle had just decided he would look more at home in the dock, when he began to speak in beautiful English, his calm and precise manner holding everyone's attention. 'May it please Your Lordship, Members of the Jury. In this case I appear to prosecute with my learned friend Mr Bertrand Hilton. Mr Clive Fox appears for Thomasin and John Feeney, and Mr John Haig appears for Richard Feeney . . .' He went on to explain what was expected of the jury, then outlined the facts of the charges.

'The prisoners are charged with conspiracy to defraud the Yorkshire Insurance Company, that is, they concocted a plan to fictionalize Richard Feeney's death in order to benefit from his life assurance policy . . .' He spent a further period giving details of the alleged crime, saying that on the date in question it had been presumed that three people were in the burning house: two small children and their mother, Margaret Feeney, and that one of the prisoners, Richard Feeney, went into the blaze to try and save them. The children were rescued and Richard Feeney went back into the house for Margaret Feeney who was purported to be unconscious. Shortly after he had entered the house there was an eruption of flame and the roof collapsed, supposedly trapping Richard Feeney inside. In addition to the reimbursement for her house and contents, a sum of eight hundred pounds was later paid by the Yorkshire Insurance Company to Thomasin Feeney, who had taken out a policy on her son's life.

'We now know that Richard Feeney did *not* die in that fire; he stands before you in the dock along with his co-accused. For the past twenty-six years he has been living in the United States of America . . .'

The Court heard technical details of the fire. A gaspipe had ruptured due to the intense heat and the ensuing explosion scattered evidence of how the fire might have originated, but as the main body of destruction was in the hall, underneath the staircase, this suggested that a small fire must have smouldered for some time in the area of an understairs cupboard where the main gaspipe was situated. The fire assessors had found no evidence of a combustion agent in the debris and it was not the Crown's suggestion that the fire was started deliberately; the charge related solely to the falsification of Richard Feeney's death.

What no one in that courtroom would ever know was that a three year old child was responsible for her father, uncle and grandmother being in the dock today. Rosanna, an inquisitive and extrovert child left to an afternoon of boredom, had played 'houses' with her brother Nick in the cupboard under the stairs. A real house needed a fire. Rosanna had provided one with the box of matches so carelessly left within her reach. The resulting flames had scared them. Shutting the cupboard door they had run upstairs, hoping that the fire would go away. But instead it had almost killed them. Mercifully, the incident had been blotted from their infant memories. Right up to her own death, Rosanna had been ignorant that she was responsible for the death of her mother.

The Court then heard statements made to police by the three prisoners. Among those giving evidence was Peter Rufforth, whose occupation was given as 'Life Inspector for the Yorkshire Insurance Company'. He had obviously gained a further promotion since the last time Thomasin had spoken to him. She glared at him now – you little Judas, coming into my house, accepting my hospitality then betraying me to further your own career. For a brief moment, Rufforth met her antagonistic eyes and looked away shamefully. Thomasin felt sorry at once. The lad was only doing what she herself would have done. Good luck to him if he got his promotion. In the eyes of the insurance company she *was* a criminal. She was just going to have to prove them wrong.

Rufforth told the Prosecution of his connection with Thomasin Feeney, that he had been visiting her house for twenty-six years in order to collect the premiums on her insurance policies, and how he had been introduced to Richard Feeney on one of these visits.

'And what was it about Richard Feeney that provoked your investigation?' asked Lindley.

'Mrs Feeney introduced him as her nephew, sir.'

'Why did that make you suspicious?'

'Not that in itself – he could have been her nephew as far as I knew – it was the sudden change in her behaviour when he entered the room.' Rufforth was asked to elaborate. 'She grew very agitated when she was halfway through introducing him to me. She started to say, "This is my . . ." then stopped and went all white as though with shock. After she recovered she resumed the introduction and said, "This is my nephew," but it seemed to me as if she had meant to say, "This is . . ."'

'Objection, M'Lud!' Thomasin's defence lawyer, Fox, ejected himself from his chair.

'Sustained.' The Judge turned to address Rufforth. 'Witness must confine himself to the facts. You cannot speculate as to what was on the mind of the accused.'

Rufforth was chastened. 'Sorry, My Lord.'

He was then asked by the Prosecution what occurred after he had been introduced to the man, and then what had led him to the conclusion that this was Richard Feeney on whose supposed death Thomasin Feeney had received compensation. 'On my way out, I mentioned Mrs Feeney's nephew to the maid. She looked confused at first, then she said, "Oh, you mean Mr Richard." Up until that point I had only known the man as Mr Feeney. I just had the feeling that something was amiss. You get a nose for such things after years of experience. Going through old files I discovered that Mrs Feeney's son had been called Richard, too. On my next visit to the house I looked to see if there were any photographs of Richard Feeney, but there didn't seem to be. So I visited several houses in Monkgate where the Feeneys had previously lived, hoping to speak to anyone who might have known Richard Feeney and could give me a description. I was given a very good description by one of the residents and it matched that of the accused – oh, allowing for age of course.'

'Quite,' said Lindley. 'Thank you, Mr Rufforth.'

When the Prosecution had finished it was the turn of the defending barristers to cross-examine. Fox stood briefly, 'No questions, My Lord.'

Dickie's barrister echoed him. This response was repeated with the next of the prosecution witnesses, a woman from Monkgate who testified as to Dickie's identity. Dickie leaned forward and hissed at his solicitor, 'Christ, what's the silly little twat playing at? All that money he's charging – give him a poke an' tell him to get some questions asked.'

349

Sutcliffe found his client's use of improper language offensive at the best of times, but even more so upon this hallowed ground. 'For pity's sake, be quiet!'

But Dickie was not alone in wondering when the barristers were going to start earning their money; his mother was growing increasingly nerve-racked by their tactics. The Judge, too, seemed taken aback at the lack of questioning and, after the prosecution had finished with the current witness, he asked, 'Are you certain you do not wish to cross-examine, Mr Haig?'

Haig stood and said pleasantly, 'My Lord, it appears from my learned friend's examination of the witnesses that it is the Crown's intention simply to prove that one of the accused is Richard William Feeney and by that definition he must be guilty. May I put it to the Court that the identity of my client is not in dispute. Therefore I see no need to waste the Court's valuable time by cross-examining this witness.'

'Bloody hell,' grumbled Dickie. 'We might as well've saved some money an' only had the one lawyer, the amount mine's doing.'

Thomasin looked hopefully at her own Counsel but he, too, declined to cross-examine. It was most unnerving. The next witness for the Crown was called to the stand: Dr William Sayner, the pathologist responsible for the autopsies on the two bodies retrieved from the fire. He was an elderly man, but of upright appearance, wearing a black frockcoat and winged collar.

Lindley asked, 'Doctor Sayner, can you tell the Court exactly what your examinations revealed?'

The doctor's steady gaze bespoke authority. 'I am afraid I could not recall the case from memory, but I do have the official notes here. Shall I read the findings?' Sayner looked at the Judge and was told, 'Please do.'

He cleared his throat, though his speech still emerged

rather croakily. Up in the gallery, Belle wanted to cough for him. 'From the deceased's position between layers of burnt rubble, it appeared that they had been in an upstairs room but when the explosion occurred the floor of that room had collapsed, taking the bodies with it. Cause of death was shock due to burns. The bodies had been partially dismembered by the explosion and were very badly charred. From the material which remained, I had great difficulty in even determining the gender of the deceased, but I did finally ascertain that one of them was a man, the other a woman.' He gave sickening details of the latter corpse, before going on to that of the man.

'. . . Again, using his teeth as indication, I would put his age at a little older than the woman, certainly not less than twenty-one. The face had been burnt away and the skull had burst open with the intensity of the heat . . .'

Thomasin recoiled and glanced at her son for reassurance that he hadn't been the victim.

'. . . skin destroyed on chest, abdomen and upper limbs . . .'

In the gallery Josie wafted herself furiously with a fan and muttered, 'Oh, that poor man.'

'. . . internal organs of abdomen exposed and burnt . . . left foot and lower leg dismembered . . . as in the case of the female his height was impossible to determine exactly, due to the natural rigor of the limbs and the distortion caused by the intense heat, but I would estimate it at over six feet, a very tall man . . .'

These and the following details were absorbed by Lindley, who at the end of the doctor's testimony, said ponderously, 'So, it was quite impossible to say that the corpse which you examined was not that of Richard Feeney?'

'Impossible to say it was, impossible to say it wasn't. I can only present you with my findings.'

'But he was a very tall man, you say, around twenty-one

351

years of age – in fact of similar stature to Richard Feeney at that time.' Lindley thanked him and sat down.

There were no questions from Haig – further annoying Dickie – and few from the Fox, save to establish if there were any signs of injury to the deceased other than those caused by the fire. With Doctor Sayner's negative reply, he was given permission to stand down. Next on the stand was a former employee of the Feeneys and the witness they were dreading most. Amy Forsdyke was sworn and gave her occupation as shopkeeper. A quarter of a century on, Amy looked like a grandmother and was more richly-attired than when Dickie had known her. This raised an inner smile – he wondered how much she had managed to loot from his house before she had been given notice by Sonny.

After Amy had identified Richard Feeney as the man for whom she had been housemaid, Lindley asked, 'When was this?'

'In eighteen seventy-four, just for a few weeks. But I must stress that it was after he got rid of the brothel. I wouldn't like anyone to think I was frequenting such a . . .'

'Objection!'

Amy didn't give the Judge a chance to speak. 'It's right, Your Honour! It was in the paper he was found guilty, he had to sell up and find a new place, that's when I asked for a job as a maid.' Though censured for this unsolicited stream of information, she could not resist a triumphant smirk at her old adversary, Thomasin.

Haig begged for this to be stricken from the record, saying that it had no relevance, but the Prosecution said that it might prove helpful in showing why Feeney chose to disappear and so the accusation stuck. In fact, the Defence had been expecting this. Sutcliffe had agreed with Dickie that it was better to have the jury think this was why Feeney had absconded, rather than come to hear of his real crimes.

'Now tell us, Miss Forsdyke, when did you last see your employer?'

'Two days before his mother's house burnt down – I remember so well 'cause that was when the detective came looking for him.' She was asked if she knew what the detective wanted of Feeney but said that she didn't. 'It must've been summat serious though 'cause . . .'

'Objection!'

'Sustained.' The Judge asked the Jury to disregard this and for Amy to confine herself to the facts. At the back of the gallery Nettleton slid lower down in his seat, hoping this line of questioning would not persist. He wanted this one for himself. Attempts had in fact been made by the Prosecution to trace him, but there was nothing in police files to suggest the detective had been from the York force.

'Well, anyway,' went on Amy, 'when he heard the detective was waiting for him he paid me and the other girl off, dashed upstairs, packed a bag and climbed out the window. And that's the last I saw of him, Your Honour.' She was told to refer to the Judge as My Lord. 'Sorry, My Lord.'

Lindley proceeded. 'Did you know that he was supposed to have died in the fire?' Amy said she had read it in the paper. 'Were you then surprised to be told that he was still alive?'

'No, I wasn't. He was always in trouble, that one.'

Lindley sat down, and for the time being Fox left cross-examination to Haig. 'Miss Forsdyke – I am correct, am I not, it is Miss and not Mrs? Was Richard Feeney the only member of that family for whom you worked?'

'No, I once worked for his mother – but that was quite a few years previous to my employment with him.' Haig asked how many years and Amy said about four. She was asked why she had left Thomasin Feeney's employment. 'I didn't like it.'

'Is it not true that you were dismissed for stealing?'

353

Amy compressed her lips. 'I was accused, wrongly might I say, of taking a brooch, but it was Richard who stole it off his grandmother and gave it to me as a present.'

The schoolboy face assumed a look of reproval. 'You accepted it knowing it was stolen?'

'No! I wouldn't've worn it, would I, if I'd known. But when his grandmother saw it she accused me and he let me take the blame.'

Haig looked puzzled. 'Was it then not a strange move to later seek employment with a man who had blackened your character?'

'It wasn't a case of choice but of necessity. His mother dismissed me without reference. I had to scratch a living where I could. I was almost destitute when I read about Richard Feeney in the paper and decided to go and ask him for a job.'

More incredulity from Haig. 'Believing that he had been prosecuted for having a house of ill-repute?'

'I told you! He'd sold that when I went to work for him. I was a respectable girl who needed a job and I felt he owed it to me.'

'Before this you had been without work for almost four years?' His question received a yes. 'How did you feed yourself?'

'Oh . . . well, I did odd jobs and suchlike.'

'Can you be more specific?'

'It's difficult to say . . .' Amy scratched her head.

'Take your time, Miss Forsdyke,' said Haig kindly. 'I do understand how daunting it can be when one has not appeared in Court before. We do not want to confuse the facts by rushing you. I am right in saying you haven't appeared in Court, am I not?'

Amy looked uneasy. 'Not this kind.'

'Which Court then?'

Amy looked up at the elaborate plaster frieze and paused for a time before mumbling. 'The Police Court.'

'As a witness?'

Amy shook her head and looked increasingly uncomfortable. She was asked to answer verbally. 'I was charged.'

'What was the nature of that charge?'

Amy clammed her lips together.

The schoolboy had suddenly taken on the role of master. 'Miss Forsdyke, I put it to you that during the four year interval between working for Thomasin and Richard Feeney, you were a common prostitute.'

Amy swung on the Judge. 'He can't say that!'

'Furthermore, the real reason you were dismissed from Thomasin Feeney's employ was not simply because of the brooch, but for the theft of several items of linen and food, and also that Mrs Feeney was concerned about the bad influence you were having on her son.'

'That's a lie!'

Leaving no pause, Haig raced on. 'And that the only reason you are here now is to besmirch the man who took pity on you and gave you employment and a home, because you blamed him for your dismissal several years previously, a dismissal brought about by your own greed and no one else's!'

There was a vociferous objection, but the point had been made. By the time the Court adjourned for luncheon Thomasin felt a little more confident.

This feeling peaked and troughed throughout the afternoon, as the remainder of the Prosecution's case was put. It was not until late afternoon that the Defence lawyers made their opening speeches, giving the Court the first opportunity to see Fox's style which up to this point had seemed very undistinguished. Watching him step forward to address the Court, Thomasin felt little conviction. His gown hung on shoulders that seemed bowed by apathy, his dark eyes were vapid. But when he began to present his case, his demeanour suddenly came to life, the Jury appeared to hang on his every word as he told them what folly it was that this case had ever been brought before them.

After he had finished his speech, the Judge decreed that they were not going to complete the hearing today and said that the Court would reconvene at eleven o'clock the next morning.

On Wednesday morning, Sonny was the first of the defendants to step into the witness box. Hauling nervously at his cuffs, he took the oath.

'My Lord, Members of the Jury,' said Fox after Sonny had stated his occupation as mill owner and artist, 'you will no doubt be aware that Mr Feeney is an artist of international repute.' Lord Alverstone nodded in recognition – he had one of Sonny's paintings on his wall. 'Mr Feeney,' continued Fox, 'I want you to tell the Court what happened on that fateful day in November eighteen seventy-four.'

Sonny cleared his throat. 'Following my normal programme, I'd worked at my mother's store in the morning and spent the afternoon in my studio painting. Usually I would be there until dinner, but on that particular day I wasn't having much success so I packed up in the late afternoon and visited a public house where I met my brother. We took a glass of ale together and then he accompanied me to the family home in Monkgate. When we arrived, some time between five-thirty and six o'clock, the house was already well alight. My parents and my grandmother were standing outside on the footpath along with my sister, her husband and many of our neighbours. My father was attempting to enter the house but all the doors and windows were secured. He told us that my wife and children were inside and I began my own attempt to break the lock on the front door, aided by my brother . . .'

Fox broke in. 'Did no member of the family possess a key?'

'It wasn't normal practice for any of us to take a key when we went out as the maids would always be there.'

Fox drew the Court's attention to the investigators' notes which said that when they sifted through the debris they found that the locks did not have keys on the interior, but four keys were found together on a ledge, and because, to his client's knowledge, there were only four in existence, this would indicate that the doors had been locked from the inside. 'Please go on, Mr Feeney.'

'Eventually we succeeded in breaking the lock. Richard, my brother, prevented me from going in and said he would go.'

'Did he give any particular reason for this?'

'I suppose he thought . . .'

'Objection, My Lord!'

The Judge instructed Sonny to ignore supposition. 'I'm sorry. I think he said that there was no point in us both taking the risk, but I can't be sure of his exact wording . . . He disappeared for a short time. The draught from the front door made the fire spread. I feared he'd be trapped inside and wanted to go in after him but my father held me back. Richard managed to find the children and transported them to safety. All of them were badly affected by the smoke. My brother told me that while he was rescuing them he had seen my wife upstairs, unconscious. I tried to push past him and go into the house, but before I could stop him he had dashed back inside.' Sonny hung his head. 'There was an explosion. I never saw my brother alive again, until he turned up last December.'

'How many entrances were there other than the front door?'

'There was a side entrance that led to the kitchen, but this was locked too, and because of its position it would have

357

been difficult to get a run at. There were also french doors in the drawing room which led into the garden but these could only have been reached by climbing over a high wall and this would have wasted time, that's why we chose to break in the front way.'

'If someone had escaped through either of these exits would it have been possible for you to have seen them from where you were standing?'

'No.'

There followed a short period of questioning related to the identification of the two bodies, then Fox asked, 'When your brother came out of the house with the children and told you that he had seen your wife unconscious, did he say that he had seen anyone else in the house?' Sonny replied negatively. 'And had you any reason to think that there might be?'

'Not at that time, no. Apart from her, all the family were outside with me.'

'When the maids returned, what explanation did they give for their absence?'

'They told us my wife had given them the afternoon off.'

'And did you not think this was strange?'

'No, I was too upset.'

'Mr Feeney, had you anything to gain by disguising the fact that your brother was not dead?'

'Nothing.'

'Did you sincerely believe that the watch you identified did in fact belong to him?'

'I did.'

Fox handed over to Haig. From then it was given to the Prosecution.

Lindley scratched his distorted nose and stood. 'Mr Feeney, before the day of the fire, when was the last time you saw your brother?' After a slight hesitation, Sonny replied that it had been several months. Asked the reason for this, he added that his brother lived in a different house. 'But surely brothers visit one another, do they not?' said Lindley in his silken tone.

'I . . . my brother was out of favour with the family.'

'Because of his Court appearance over the brothel?'

'Yes.'

'Was this the only reason?'

Fox objected on the grounds that this was irrelevant to the case, but was overruled.

Sonny chose the lesser of many evils. 'No. My brother also bought a property that my mother had wanted badly. She told him she never wanted to see him again.'

'And during this animosity between mother and son what position did you take?'

After a pause, Sonny replied, 'I didn't go to see him because that would have upset my parents.'

'Yet you did go to see him on the day of the fire?'

'Yes. I thought it was about time he made it up with our parents.'

Lindley asked several more questions pertaining to the rift. The air in Court was by now stifling, the fans moved ever more feverishly and the Judge was baking under his wig. 'Mr Lindley,' he sighed. 'This questioning does not seem to be leading us anywhere. Could you try not to ramble.'

'I beg Your Lordship's pardon. I was not aware that I was rambling.' Prosecution began a different line of questioning. 'Mr Feeney, I have here a copy of the Last Will and Testament of your brother . . .'

Oh Christ! Sonny fought to retain his calm exterior, whilst his mind imploded. He dared not look at Dick, but felt his eyes – felt *all* eyes – boring into him.

'I see that you were the main beneficiary.'

'That's correct.' *He's going to say it*, panicked Sonny. Any minute now he's going to mention the date on that will. One of them has to have spotted it.

The barrister nodded and put the will down. Sonny felt no relief, deciding it was just stratagem. *Any minute now he's going to seize it and reveal all our lies.* He tried to keep his eyes from straying to the document, as did others: Sutcliffe felt the sweat trickle down the side of his nose but dared not wipe it off for fear of attracting guilt. Behind him, Dickie twisted his thumbs. Thomasin felt that she was going to pass out. The feathers on her hat were wilting in the intense heat.

'Now,' said Lindley, 'as the Court can see, your brother is very much alive. You say you made this discovery last year?' Sonny affirmed. 'Did you then ask yourself the true identity of the man who died in that fire?'

'I have wondered once or twice, yes.'

'You wondered once or twice?' The Prosecution's face showed mild surprise. 'Mr Feeney, I should have thought that this would be of pressing interest to you and indeed to all the members of your family. Did you make no effort at all to find out the identity of the deceased?'

'I'm ashamed to say we were far too grateful that it wasn't my brother.'

'Or was it that you did not need to make investigations because you already knew his identity?'

'I'm sorry, I don't understand.'

'My Lord,' Fox began to rise.

He was silenced by his opponent. 'My Lord, I think my line of questioning is quite clear!'

'Yes, Mr Fox.' Lord Alverstone came down on behalf of the Prosecution. 'There was a man burned to death in that house. If it was not Richard Feeney, it is the duty of this Court to try to establish who it was. Pray continue, Mr Lindley.'

'Since you learned that your brother did not die in that

fire, you have had many months in which to ponder who it might have been. Have you come to any conclusion?'

'No, I'm afraid I have no idea of who it might have been.'

Oh, Son, his brother groaned inwardly, why d'ye always have to look so guilty?

'Then if you are certain you did not know him you must be aware that he was not, at least, a friend of the family?'

Fox attempted to give his client some leeway in which to compose himself, his mouth awry. 'My learned friend might care to unravel that conundrum.' There was a soft ripple of laughter.

The Judge, too, smiled. 'Yes, Mr Lindley, you'll have me thinking I'm going senile.'

'My Lord, it seems very simple to me . . .'

The Judge became stern. 'Are you then perhaps suggesting that I *am* senile, Mr Lindley?'

'I crave Your Lordship's pardon. I will try to put the question more clearly.' Counsel for the Prosecution turned back to Sonny. 'I would like you to look at the Gentlemen of the Jury. Now, can you tell me if you know any of them?' Sonny replied that he did not. 'And how did you ascertain that you did not know them?'

'Just by looking at them,' replied Sonny in bewilderment.

'Precisely! To be able to tell if one knows a person, one has first to see them. We are told that the corpse was burnt beyond recognition, so how can you be absolutely certain that you did not know the man if you had not first seen him alive?'

'Ah, I take your meaning, Mr Lindley.' The Judge nodded.

'Thank you, My Lord,' replied the other insincerely. 'Answer the question please, Mr Feeney.'

'What I meant was . . .' Sonny hestiated. 'When I said that

361

I was certain I didn't know the man I wasn't lying. It's just that . . . I had reason to believe that my wife was having an affair and can only surmise that the man who died was her lover.' Thomasin closed her eyes. Up in the gallery, Josie prayed that they would not dwell too long on this subject.

'And when did you discover your wife's infidelity?'

Sonny licked his lips and glanced at his brother. He would have to risk another lie; he couldn't do that to Dickie, even though Dickie might do it to him were the positions reversed. 'During the summer months.'

'And did you intend to divorce her?' Lindley received a positive answer. 'Yet you had started no proceedings against her.'

'No, but I had made up my mind to sort the matter out.'

'To sort the matter out,' echoed the barrister ponderously. 'Can you tell us exactly what you mean by that?'

'Well . . . to see a solicitor.'

'But of course when your wife was killed in the fire there was no further reason to divorce her. However, it would have looked most suspicious had anyone been aware that the man who died with her was her lover.'

'Objection, My Lord. My client is not on trial for murder.'

'My Lord,' said Lindley in a smooth tone, 'I am not for one moment suggesting he is. I am simply trying to show that in order to avoid a scandal it would have been better for all concerned if the body had been that of Richard Feeney.'

'Objection overruled.'

'Mr Feeney, why did you not mention the possibility of your wife's lover being in the house to the persons who investigated the fire?'

Sonny tried to keep his agitation from the Jury, but inside his stomach quaked. 'I've told you, I was so utterly convinced that my brother had died – why should I raise the sordid details of my wife's affair? What had that to do with Richard? All I could think of was that I'd lost him.'

'So, let us now concentrate on your brother's reappearance. Had you heard nothing at all during those twenty-six years since the fire to indicate that he was still alive?'

'Nothing,' lied Sonny in what he hoped was a firm tone.

'And in what manner did Richard Feeney make his reappearance?'

'I'm not sure what you mean.'

'Did he write to say he was coming? Did he simply walk in . . . ?'

'Oh yes, he wrote. It was a tremendous shock for all of us.'

'To whom was the letter addressed?'

'To me.'

'Do we have the letter as evidence?' asked Lindley.

'I'm afraid I threw it on the fire.'

'How very inconvenient. For any particular reason?'

'I was furious with him for pretending to be dead all these years and then turning up out of the blue. I threw it on the fire out of rage.'

'Did it not strike you as odd that after twenty-six years' exile your brother should suddenly decide to come home? After he had deceived you for so long?'

Sonny could smile now. 'Nothing my brother did could ever surprise me.'

'So you readily admit that your brother was no stranger to deceit?' Sonny's face altered, but Lindley was already onto the next question. 'Why did you tell police officers that Richard Feeney was your cousin?'

'Because . . . I didn't want to get my mother into trouble.'

'So you lied?'

'Yes, but . . .'

'You lied not simply to protect your mother from prosecution, but to hide the truth about your part in the conspiracy.'

363

'No!'

'I put it to you that when Richard Feeney came out of that house with your children he told you of the sight he had seen, of the man in your wife's bedroom, and suggested a plan to fake his own death, thereby saving you all from scandal.'

Sonny looked derisive. 'There wasn't time for any plan! He was only on the pavement a couple of seconds before rushing back into the house. We knew nothing until last year.'

'You are asking this Court to believe that a man would allow his own brother, his own *mother* to think he was dead, would not send so much as a note to let them out of their misery, would continue this abominable fraud for twenty-six years and then blithely return as if nothing had happened?'

'I've told the truth,' insisted Sonny.

'That is for the court to decide.' Lindley sat down.

Haig begged to re-examine. 'Mr Feeney, you say that nothing your brother did could ever surprise you. What did you mean by this?'

Sonny was eager for the chance to make reparation. 'It was just a figure of speech. I simply meant that I wasn't surprised that he wanted to come home to us. We were always very close.'

'I will ask you to reaffirm: before last December, had you any idea, any inkling that your brother might be alive?'

'I had not.'

Haig thanked him and sat down.

The time came for Thomasin to defend herself. Her barrister asked the Judge that she might be spared the walk to the witness box because of her infirmity, but before Lord Alverstone could grant this mercy, Thomasin herself said that she would prefer to stand in the rightful place. Fox was glad of her decision: the sight of this aged widow's painful transfer to the witness box could only inspire pity.

Her journey was accomanied by the whistle of silk, amplified by the surrounding silence. Fox was most solicitous and gave her a bolstering smile before embarking on his questioning, asking her about the fire and where she had lived afterwards, going on to say, 'Mrs Feeney, when did you learn that your son Richard was still alive?'

Thomasin leaned on her walking stick – she had also declined the offer of a chair. 'Just before Christmas of last year.'

'And how did you come to learn?'

'My other son, John, told me. He received a letter out of the blue.'

'And what was your impulse when John broke the news?'

'I fainted.' Thomasin smiled at the Judge but got little reaction.

'So it was a great shock to you.'

'It certainly was! But . . .' Thomasin lowered her eyes, 'it wasn't the only one I got that day.' At Fox's prompting, she explained, 'I believed that my husband had gone for a holiday to Ireland . . . when a friend revealed that he had in fact gone there to die.' She looked up, eyes glistening with tears. They were not faked. 'He was suffering from a terminal illness and he didn't want his family to watch him suffer. He'd always expressed a wish to revisit his homeland. I didn't realise that he intended to remain there until he died.'

Fox allowed her lachrymose interval to take full effect on the Jury, then asked, 'Do you feel ready to continue, Mrs Feeney?'

'Yes, I'm sorry.' Thomasin gave a final sniff into her handkerchief. 'I should be getting over his death by now.'

'Not at all,' replied Fox kindly. 'Such grief can sometimes never be assuaged. One only had to look at our own dear departed Queen after she lost her beloved Prince. Her mourning never ended until the day of her passing. So, Mrs

365

Feeney, if it will not cause you too much distress, will you tell the Court of your first action after you received this terrible news about your husband?'

Prosecution stood. 'My Lord, I fail to see . . .'

'With respect to my learned friend,' said Fox to the Judge, 'I am trying to show the background to this case.'

Lindley gave a soft laugh of ridicule. 'My Lord, the background to this case began, not last Christmas, but twenty-six years ago.'

'My Lord,' argued Fox, 'were I to chop down a hundred year old oak tree in my neighbour's garden I should be pursued for my actions on the day of the destruction, not on the day of its planting.' While both the Judge and the Prosecution tried to interpret this riddle, he added, 'If Your Lordship will bear with me, I shall be coming to the matter of the insurance policy very shortly.'

The Judge was still mulling over the business with the oak tree. 'Oh . . . very well, proceed, Mr Fox.'

'Mrs Feeney, I have to ask you again, what was your first act on receiving the news of your husband's imminent departure from this world?'

'I went to Ireland to bring him back, and to tell him that his son was still alive.'

'How did he meet the news?'

'He was overjoyed. Losing our son had caused him a great deal of torment over the years. He never came to terms with it.'

'Did you ever consider that your son's homecoming would bring about this trial?'

Thomasin raised a sardonic smile. 'I'd have put him straight back on the boat to America if I had!' She relapsed into her languid state. 'No . . . when you receive two shocks like that in the space of five minutes, you don't automatically think of insurance policies.'

'And when was the first time you did think of insurance policies?'

'That was when Mr Rufforth came and I suddenly realised that he'd been the one to meet my claim on Dickie's death – or supposed death.' Fox asked what she had done. 'I didn't know what to do, so . . .' she bit her lip, 'I'm afraid I lied, said he was my nephew. I don't know what possessed me to say it. I suppose the magnitude of it all came crashing in. I was afraid.'

'Afraid that you would be put in prison?'

'Yes, but more than that: afraid that I'd be separated from my son, the son I'd been deprived of for more than half his lifetime. I couldn't bear that.'

'So, it was a foolish action rather than a mischievous one which prompted your deception of Mr Rufforth?'

'Yes. Very foolish, and very shaming. But it was never my intent to deceive anyone for monetary gain.' Thomasin arched her body in discomfort.

'Thank you, Mrs Feeney,' Fox sat down.

When it was Lindley's turn, he lifted his face and stared up into the small window at the centre of the domed roof, appearing to be deep in thought but in fact merely trying to unnerve Thomasin. At last he looked at her. 'Mrs Feeney, if you were indeed innocent of deception why, then, did you wait until you were under arrest before offering to pay the money back?'

'I wanted to – but after that impulsive lie I feared it would make matters worse.'

'As, of course, it did.' Lindley stroked his chin, and delayed the next question, appearing to be reading through his notes until the Judge started to tap impatiently with his pencil. 'When did you make your original claim on the policy which you had taken out on Richard Feeney's life?'

'Let me see,' Thomasin tried to concentrate. 'It would be

a couple of months at least after the fire. As I mentioned, you don't immediately think of money in a tragedy like that.'

'Quite.' Lindley nodded calmly. 'But the claim to which I refer is not the one you made after the fire destroyed your house, but the one made two years earlier in July eighteen seventy-two.'

His question dropped like a sinker into the tranquil exchange. Thomasin's stomach lurched and she stared at him. There was murmuring from the gallery.

'Am I correct, Mrs Feeney? Did you approach the Yorkshire Insurance Company on that date with a view to making a claim?'

Thomasin could feel her family's alarm. She looked at Erin whose fan was moving like a deranged bat. She tried to speak but shock had swelled her tongue. 'There is a record of your application in the Insurance Company's files, Mrs Feeney.'

'I did write to them, yes . . .' She glanced at her barrister's face. It was inscrutable.

'And what reply were you given?'

'But you see . . .' She was told to answer the question. 'I was informed that a claim couldn't be made without presentation of a death certificate – but . . .'

'In effect, without a body?'

'My Lord!' Fox bounced to the floor. He was ordered to sit down.

Lindley pressed on. 'So it is true that even before today's occasion you made false claim . . .'

'Objection, My Lord!'

'Mr Lindley,' warned the Judge. 'May I remind you that the prisoner has yet to be proven guilty.'

Lindley apologised but pressed Thomasin for an answer. 'I thought he might be dead!' she protested.

'But as we can see,' Lindley gestured at Dickie, 'he is not.'

'I . . .' began Thomasin. Lindley cut her off and sat down.

Fox rose. 'Mrs Feeney, may I put to you just two further questions in order to clarify any misunderstanding that my learned friend may have planted in the minds of the jurors: under what circumstances did you make the insurance claim in eighteen seventy-two?'

'That's what I was trying to say: that it wasn't exactly a claim. I just wanted to find out where I stood – I even continued to pay the premium after I'd written to the insurance office. If I'd wished to defraud anybody I'd hardly have done that, would I?' Fox motioned for her to continue. 'You see, Richard left home when he was eighteen. But he didn't tell us he was leaving. We had no idea of what had happened to him. We even reported his disappearance to the police, we were so worried. But they couldn't find him. After he'd been gone for many months I began to fear that he might be dead. One day, it crossed my mind about the policy. I began to wonder what my position was – should I continue to pay it or should I inform them that my son might be dead? It was merely an enquiry, not an attempt to claim. It was they who told me that I couldn't collect on the policy without proof of death. I remember being shocked by the tone of their reply, which implied I was only interested in the money. That's mostly why I continued to pay the premium.'

'As my learned friend has so eloquently repeated, your son was not dead. When did you next see him?'

'In eighteen seventy-four. Though I was greatly relieved to find him alive, I was angry at the way he'd neglected to contact us in all that time. Because of that and because of the argument over property which my son John mentioned earlier, I told Richard I didn't want to see him again – but those words are often spoken in the heat of the moment. Much as my son had annoyed and upset me I was so glad to see him again on the day of that fire . . . I can't tell you how I felt when I thought the roof had collapsed on top of him.' She bowed her head. The Judge told her she could stand down.

Her ordeal over, she was assisted back to the dock. The Judge declared that Court would now break for luncheon and would reconvene at two o'clock prompt.

16

Dickie performed a quick check on his fly buttons before moving to the witness box, the black suit and gleaming collar adding a touch of respectability, badly needed after all the detrimental evidence.

'Now, Mr Feeney,' said Haig, 'I do not propose to dwell on the distant past, but could you tell us briefly why you left home in eighteen seventy-two?'

'It was eighteen seventy-one actually,' corrected Dickie, then answered the question. 'Well, you know how it is with a young man, Mr Haig. I felt life wasn't moving fast enough for me. I wanted to strike out, find my independence.'

'So on that particular occasion there was no rift between you and your family?'

'None at all,' lied Dickie without flinching. 'Though I did feel my parents were too strict – as do many young people.'

'Did you never consider that they might think that some harm had befallen you?'

'I'm ashamed now to say I didn't. The whole episode was based on selfishness. It's only from the experience of maturity that one can look back and see how callous youth can be.'

'How true. Are you a parent yourself, Mr Feeney?'

'I regret not . . . my wife and I have sadly never been able to complete our family. However,' his eyes showed warmth, 'we are in the process of adopting three orphans.' Best call them that, thought Dickie; it sounds better.

371

'Oh, I am sure the Court would wish to offer congratulations,' replied Haig and smiled at the Jury. 'Now, let us go to the months shortly before the fire. We have been told that you were barred from the family home due to an argument over property. Did this exile upset you in any way?'

'It did, very much. By this time I'd begun to grow up a bit, had discovered the true value of a loving family. I missed them an awful lot.' Haig asked if he had ever considered trying to patch things up. 'I considered it many times, but I was afraid they might not want to see me.'

'Mr Feeney, apart from the charge levelled against you, the Prosecution witness Amy Forsdyke has also made certain accusations; one, that you were the proprietor of a house of ill-repute. Would you answer that for us?'

Dickie sighed heavily, and paused long before continuing. 'I had at that time a lodging house. Because one of my chambermaids chose to behave in an immoral manner with a guest, I was held responsible. The police said . . .' He hung his head in shame. 'They accused me of running a bawdy-house – it was a totally unfounded allegation! I was away on business at the time. I'd always kept a respectable establishment, but because of the actions of one slut I was branded a criminal. When the case appeared in the newspapers I knew what it would do to my family . . . but I was too ashamed to go and visit my mother. My whole life was completely ruined by those vile and untrue allegations. I was forced to sell my property, my home . . .'

Haig said that this must have been very distressing for him. 'Now, can you tell us of the events leading up to the fire?'

'On the afternoon of the fire I was in a public house drowning my sorrows when my brother came in.' Dickie gave a wistful little smile. 'I was delighted to see him again. We had a long talk about the family and he told me he was sure my parents would like to see me again too as they often spoke of me. I felt so ashamed that these good people were ready to forgive me for ruining their name – through no fault of my own but nevertheless I was responsible. I felt so humble . . . All the way home I couldn't get it out of my mind how much they loved me an' how much I was looking forward to being among them again . . . then we saw the fire.' He looked stricken and fell mute for as long as Counsel would permit. 'When I heard that the children and my sister-in-law were inside, I saw a way to redeem all my past sins. In truth, I hoped I would die in that fire, so depressed had I become at the state of my life. After I'd rescued the children I went back in, but saw that in her unconscious state there was little hope of getting my sister-in-law down the staircase which was now well alight. The fire seemed to have spread all around me. The route to the front door was suddenly cut off.' He enacted fearfulness. 'I tried to get out of the side door but there was no key in the lock. I panicked, ran down to the cellar which seemed to be the only place not on fire. It was there that I saw my chance to escape: the coal chute.'

'You say that you saw your sister-in-law unconscious. Did you see anyone else there?'

Dickie lowered his eyes, and leaned against the sturdy oak box as if deeply disturbed. 'I saw a man who was also unconscious.'

'And why did you not mention him to anyone when you told them about your sister-in-law?'

Dickie replied in a sombre manner. 'Mr Haig, if you saw a half-naked man in the bedroom of your brother's wife, would you tell him about it?'

The young barrister looked at the Jury and moved his head in sympathy. 'So what occurred after you had escaped from the cellar?'

Dickie spoke with great depth of feeling. 'When I got out, it came to me that once again I'd acted out of selfishness, had left my sister-in-law to die . . . In that knowledge, how could I face my family? So, I ran away down the back garden and climbed the wall, allowing them to think I'd died a hero, hoping that the troubles I'd caused them would at least be over now . . . but instead this coward has once more brought his family into disrepute.' He dropped his pain-filled eyes to the floor.

'I'm sure you have no call to malign yourself, Mr Feeney,' comforted Haig. 'Your rescue of the children could never be construed as cowardice. Now, could I ask you finally: when you made that decision to pretend you were dead, did it not strike you that there might be questions over the insurance?'

Dickie fixed steady blue eyes on the Jury, eyes that erased all the sordid details that had gone before. 'No.'

'Were you aware that your mother held an insurance policy on your life?'

'No, why should I be?'

'Isn't it a simple fact of life that most parents insure their children?'

'Is it?' Wan-faced, Dickie shrugged. 'Well, it never occurred to me.'

'The Jury might find that surprising, Mr Feeney. You must have insurance policies yourself.'

'Why should I? A waste of money if you ask me. Never saw the sense in it.'

Haig raised an eyebrow. 'Not even on your house? Your property? What if you had suffered the same misfortune as your parents and lost everything?'

'I'd say it was my hard luck,' Dickie flashed a sad smile at the Jury. 'Well, when you're young ye don't ever think of things like that happening to you, do you? I guess I just put my trust in my Maker.'

'Thank you, Mr Feeney. Will you remain as you are,

please. My learned friend may have questions he'd like to put to you.'

'I have indeed,' said Lindley and took the floor. At Thomasin's instruction, Fox would not be interrogating her son. 'Mr Feeney, I'm sure the Court is very impressed both by your undeniable heroism in rescuing your nephew and niece and also the consideration you showed your family in not wanting them to think they had a coward in their midst. Nevertheless, there are certain points I would like to clarify. Let us return to your Last Will and Testament . . .'

Dickie's scalp prickled. He could not help the involuntary glance at his solicitor, but maintained his composure.

'I see that it is dated twentieth September, eighteen seventy-four. Only two months before the fire . . .'

Sonny tensed. *He's going to say it.*

'Apart from this coincidence, it seems out of character for a feckless young man – as you have admitted you were – to make his will. Can you tell the Court what led you to the decision to do so?'

'I don't see anything strange in it,' replied Dickie, unperturbed. 'Despite being put out of business I wasn't destitute by any means. I wanted to ensure that if anything happened to me my money was apportioned in the manner I wished it to be. How else could this be done unless I made a will?'

'Quite so. You say, "if anything happened to me" . . . were you expecting it to?'

'Of course not. I was only twenty-one – but accidents happen, don't they?'

'Indeed they do, and that is why I find your attitude rather contradictory. On the one hand you do not see the need to insure your property on the grounds that, "You don't ever think of things like that happening to you", and yet you take the more unusual step of drawing up a will. As the Court has heard, the greater portion of your assets were left to your brother and only a token bequest to your parents, your sister, your nephew and niece. Why was that?'

'In the natural course of events if I hadn't made a will, my parents would have inherited everything – I was unmarried at that time. They were already very prosperous. I love my brother, sir. With my death I could make the generous gesture that I'd omitted to make in life. I was sometimes very uncaring of his feelings.'

Lindley frowned, deeply puzzled. 'Mr Feeney, still I cannot help but feel that you were expecting to die.'

Dickie warned himself to be more careful in his play-acting. 'But we all die,' he pointed out.

'Some more prematurely than others. So . . . what did you do immediately after you had escaped from the fire?'

Now that the questions over the will had seemingly been dealt with, Dickie's stomach uncoiled. 'I emigrated to America.'

'As simply as that? Did you not first go to your home and take a bath, collect your money and belongings?'

'The only stop I made was to ask my fiancée to come with me.' He smiled fondly at his wife in the gallery. 'I took a bath at her house and she lent me some of her father's clothes.'

'Your fiancée who is now your wife? And she was expecting you?'

'Yes, I'd arranged to go and meet her but I was late.'

'And presumably she was ready and waiting with her suitcases.'

'Of course not. She didn't know we were going to America.'

'Oh, I thought when you said you'd arranged to meet her . . .'

'Simply to meet her! I had no inkling this was going to happen.'

'But you told us that you wanted people to believe you were dead.'

'Not her. I couldn't make that sacrifice. I told her what I'd done and she had to decide there and then whether or not to come with me.'

'And she chose to aid your deception.'

'She loved me. Our elopement was a spur of the moment thing. I had to get right away and make my death look convincing and also build myself a new life, but I knew I couldn't do that without her.'

Lindley referred to the will yet again and, still looking at it, asked, 'What was your wife's maiden name?'

'Miller. Primrose Miller.' He hardly dared glance at his wife. But Dusty was too afraid for her husband's safety to carp about the silly name today.

'Primrose Miller . . . I don't see that name written here.' Lindley looked up from the will. 'You have just mentioned your great affection for her yet she was to receive not even the smallest bequest?'

Dickie struggled to escape the web. 'But that will would have been naturally revoked with matrimony and as I wasn't expecting to die between making it and marrying her there seemed no point in including her.'

'On that basis,' said Lindley in tired manner, 'there would seem little point in writing a will at all, would there?' He put the document down. 'Now . . . the visit you paid your fiancée on the night of the fire . . . was that not rather risky? I mean, you must have cut a very conspicuous figure, blackened with smoke. Surely someone could have seen you and when they heard later that you were supposed to have died in a fire . . . well, they would have put two and two together and informed your family that you were in fact alive.'

'I made sure no one saw me when I went to meet her. Anyway, it was dark.'

'When you went to America, did she bring with her any dowry?'

Be careful, Dickie told himself. 'My wife was the owner of a wholesale provision store. She had a very reliable staff who she could trust to run the business in her absence. She brought certain monies with her – enough to set us up in America.'

'Did she not inform her employees of her marriage?'

'No.'

'And after you had landed in America did you receive any money from England?'

'As I said, my wife still had her business at that time . . .'

'But did you personally receive any money?'

'May it please Your Lordship,' Fox intervened here. 'I believe my learned friend is implying that Richard Feeney received money from his mother – the benefits of an insurance fraud. May I save the Court's time by producing Thomasin Feeney's personal bank accounts for a three year period after the fire.' It was fortunate that Thomasin rarely threw anything out, and even documents prior to November seventy-four had not been destroyed, having been stored in a fireproof box. 'This, My Lord,' said Fox, pointing out the figure, 'is the total amount paid out by the Yorkshire Insurance Company in recompense for the destruction of Mrs Feeney's house and for the death of her son. Now, if you look down each column you will see that never during that three year period was there any substantial amount withdrawn, apart from the sum used to purchase a new dwelling house.'

'Er, I beg to differ, Mr Fox.' The Judge tapped his finger. 'There appear to be several large withdrawals for the same amount.'

Fox, who had hoped for this, said mainly for the Jury's benefit, 'Ah yes, I apologise, My Lord. Mrs Feeney is a regular contributor to various charities. Those particular amounts are her donations to the Blue Coats School.'

378

'Most generous,' muttered the Judge, wearing the emotion-less mask he had used throughout most of the proceedings.

'There are receipts to substantiate this, My Lord,' said Fox.

The Judge asked Lindley if he had any more questions. 'I have, my Lord,' said Lindley. 'Mr Feeney, I am not satisfied as to why you did not mention that there was a man in that burning house.'

'I told you – I didn't want to upset my brother.'

Lindley donned a look of contemptuous horror. 'So you allowed a man to die simply because you did not wish to upset your brother?' He ignored Dickie's insistence that it had been impossible to save the man. 'I put it to you that your real cause for concern was not for your brother but for your own wretched skin and the promise of financial gain.'

Dickie remained calm. 'No.'

Lindley sat down abruptly.

Fox rose again. Thomasin leaned forward, ready to stop any unpermitted badgering of her son, but his question was simply intended to remove ambiguity. 'Mr Feeney, you have admitted that you did fake your own death. Was there at any time any discourse between you and John or Thomasin Feeney about financial reward?'

'None. When a man has just rushed into a burning building and rescued two children at the risk of his own life, the last thought on his mind is money.'

When the questioning appeared to have finished, Dickie gripped the edge of the witness box and leaned towards the Jury, eyes beseeching. 'Sirs, through a well-intentioned gesture of a callow youth, a man and a woman stand before you who ought never to be here . . .'

'You must not make speeches,' interposed the Judge.

Dickie turned to him with the utmost politeness. 'It is not in my own favour that I wish to plead, My Lord, but for my mother and my brother. Both are well-known and respected in this city, respected both for their business achievements and their personal ones.' As the Judge opened his mouth to intervene again, he rushed on, 'For twenty-six years they believed me to be dead. If there's anyone to be punished here then let it be me . . .'

'As well you might be,' warned the judge severely.

'. . . not my brother, who's suffered enough from my stupid efforts to spare him the distressing truth about his wife; and not my mother who is innocent of all charges, save the crime of loving an unworthy son.' Finished, he showed reverence to the Judge. 'I'm deeply grateful, My Lord.'

Lord Alverstone tightened his lips. 'You may stand down. There will now be a short adjournment.'

'All rise!'

In the gallery, Belle leaned on the cast-iron railings and tried to ease her spine; these oak pews were not made for comfort. 'Do you think they'll get off?'

'I've no earthly idea,' sighed her mother. 'It could go either way. 'Tis a pity they don't have women jurors, the fancy speech Yankeedoodle put on for them. God, poor Sonny, having to go through all that – and poor Josie.' She clutched her sister-in-law's plump hand.

'I thought Mother coped well,' said Josie.

Francis agreed. 'I'm fairly confident that Sonny and Thomasin will be acquitted.'

'I'm not so sure.' Erin opened her fan and began to waft her cheeks. 'They might believe that Mam would do anything to see the back of him after that brothel business . . . and that Amy! I'm glad she got her come-uppance, the stirrer. God, all this waiting!'

No mention was made of 'Poor Dusty' sandwiched between Belle and Francis. Not one of them bothered to ask what I'm feeling or what Dick must be going through, she thought bitterly. No word of comfort for us. It doesn't matter that our entire lives hinge on this verdict – everyone knows that Dickie doesn't deserve to be a father anyway . . . Erin'll probably be glad if he is convicted. God, I *hate* this family and their stupid squabbles . . .

After the adjournment, came the witnesses to substantiate the defendants' case. First of these was a Mrs Miles, at whose home the Feeneys had stayed directly after the fire. She testified that the family's grief appeared to be genuine and she herself had heard nothing between the accused to indicate that a conspiracy had taken place.

Next, came the family's doctor who told the Court he had been summoned to Mrs Miles' house to administer medical help to Mrs Feeney who was in a very distressed state. He had given her a sedative and had in fact continued to treat her for several weeks after the disaster. In his opinion her actions could not have been faked. Cross-examination failed to shake his stand. The last of the witnesses was Abigail, their old maid, who had arrived two days ago. As yet the Feeneys had not been allowed to relay their gratitude – had not even seen her, as she had been staying in an hotel – but now, Thomasin cast her a warm smile as Abigail picked up the Bible and gave oath.

'Mrs Pfeffer,' said Fox in an admiring voice, 'I believe that you have travelled all the way from Germany to give evidence at this trial?'

'I have, sir. I'd travel to the other side of the earth to put paid to the vile rumours about Mrs Feeney.' She was asked how long she had worked for the latter and answered that it was fifteen years approximately. Fox asked why she had left. 'To get married, sir. We were on holiday – that is, the family and myself – and I met my husband. Mr and Mrs Feeney very kindly allowed me to stay on when they went home. I was sorry to leave them, they were very good to me.'

'Now, Mrs Pfeffer, can you tell the Court what occurred in the domestic quarters on the day of the fire.'

'I'm afraid I can't remember what I did in the morning, but I do recall that the other maid and myself were given the afternoon off by Miss Peggy – that was Mr John Feeney's wife.'

'You're certain that it was she who granted you the time off and no one else?'

'Oh, positive, sir, because there was no one else in the house save the children. We were in the middle of washing the luncheon pots when Miss Peggy came into the kitchen and told us to go out for the afternoon because Mr and Mrs Feeney would be out to tea and wouldn't be needing us. I said we'd better finish the pots first, but she insisted we go there and then. I argued that the mistress might not like us going off and neglecting our duties but she got very cross and practically shoved us out.' Fox enquired when they had returned. 'We were told not to come back before it was time to start cooking dinner – that'd be around six-thirty, so we daren't. When we did get back the house was a-fire.'

'And did you explain to your mistress about your absence?'

'Later we did . . . I felt sort of guilty what with being out when the fire started – I mean, I know it was an accident, but I told the mistress that I was ever so sorry about leaving Miss Peggy on her own with the children; they could be right little monkeys . . . but then she had made us go.' Her voice tailed off.

'Mrs Pfeffer, can you recall if John Feeney was present when you told your mistress about his wife being alone apart from the children?'

Abigail donned a face of woe. 'I recall it very vividly. They were all there together in their grief. Poor Mr John, he was heartbroken.'

'Over his wife?'

'Well, yes, he must've been upset about her. Even if she did cause him a lot of pain it's no way to go, is it? But he was very upset about his brother too. He kept going on about how he couldn't believe he wouldn't see Mr Richard again.'

After a few more enquiries, Fox smiled. 'Thank you, Mrs Pfeffer, for coming all this way. Your evidence has been most useful.'

No brow-beating from Lindley could elicit the slightest hint that Sonny had known his wife had had a man in the house. 'Mr John is a good, kind man,' Abigail told the barrister in no uncertain terms. 'You have no idea what he had to put up with from that wife of his – most men would never have stood it – but he never showed any malice towards her and I won't have you insinuating that he did.'

'Thank you, Mrs Pfeffer,' said the Judge, po-faced. 'Now that you have put our learned friend in his place you may step down.'

'Oh . . . I'm ever so sorry . . .' Abigail looked flustered, but nevertheless cast an impudent smile at her former mistress as she left the witness box. All that remained now was for Counsel to sum up.

Fox had the disadvantage of being first to lay out his case. He stood and appraised the jurors with dark compassionate eyes. 'Gentlemen of the Jury, you have listened to all the evidence for the Prosecution and now you will hear my final word in defence of Thomasin and John Feeney – for which you will not require half so much patience: the facts being very simple I shall therefore be brief. My clients are accused of conspiring to defraud the Yorkshire Insurance Company – that is the basis of this case; you have been sidetracked by various other suppositions, but the only relevant fact among them is the question of conspiracy. So, we have to ask ourselves for what gain Thomasin Feeney – an extremely wealthy woman

– would have sanctioned the deception? There was not the slightest need for her to resort to such drastic methods for a sum of money that would seem insignificant beside the amount which she has already donated to charity.

'Apart from the accusation of financial gain, the Prosecution would have you believe that Thomasin Feeney took part in the conspiracy in order that her son would appear a hero and therefore redress the harm he had done to her public standing, and also to cover up his emigration to America. I ask you, why should she bother to do this? Had she wanted to be rid of him to America could she not have, far more easily, given him a sum of money to persuade him to go? Did she detest him that much? No! On the contrary, despite the hurt his previously boyish behaviour had caused her she did not hate him at all. Throughout the evidence one particular word has cropped up several times – the word love. Despite their petty conflicts, the Feeneys are a very close, loving family – their loyal servant of fifteen years has testified to this. In spite of the hurt that Richard Feeney brought them with his supposed death, they still love him and welcomed him back . . .'

'Did we indeed,' growled Erin. She examined each juror's face as the defence lawyer spent several more minutes emoting his case.

'. . . We have heard from diverse witnesses the magnitude of the family's grief when they thought he had died in that fire. Mrs Feeney's doctor has testified that not only did he have to sedate her on the evening of the fire, but had to continue that treatment for many weeks, so acute was her distress.' Fox lyricised of the magnificent work done for the city by Thomasin in saving historical monuments which might otherwise have been destroyed, her numerous acts of charity. 'The Prosecution has shown not one tittle of evidence to prove that here was a conspiracy between my clients and Richard Feeney.

'Gentlemen of the Jury, I trust that your implicit good sense will triumph over the absurdity of this charge. There can only be one possible verdict, and that is – not guilty.'

Dickie's barrister stood before the Jury and began his case, scarcely moving from that spot during the entire time he spoke. It had not always been so. When first called to the Bar he had displayed many a grand manner, marching up and down, flourishing his hands to compound a point. Only after he had lost several cases had he learned that this style could jeopardize all the reasoned argument that had gone before. 'You want the Jury to listen to what you have to say,' an old hand had instructed him. 'Direct all your energy into your voice. Stand still!'

This was difficult for one who used his hands so much, but Haig wound his thumbs into his stuff gown and set upon his task of convincing the Jury of Dick's innocence, repeating much of the evidence cited by Fox, not only the technical details, but the emotional ones. After orating with gusto for some minutes, he stared at each man in turn, dropped the pitch of his voice and said gently, 'Members of the Jury, I am about to repeat a dirty word used by my learned friend, Mr Fox. I make no apology for it and the more sensitive amongst you may wish to cover their ears. That word is love. Yes! To the Prosecuting Counsel with his talk about money, fraud and adultery the word love does seem to have been treated with contempt. And yet Richard Feeney himself knows what that word means. For the sake of the mother he loves, he has actually admitted under oath that he did fake his death – but that decision was made on the spur of the moment and only then done out of the same love and respect for his family. He was in total ignorance of the insurance policy taken out by his mother on his life, he had never had any dealings with insurance himself. I beg you to remember that, in effect, you are not trying the mature man who stands before you, but a

385

mere youth of twenty-one, afraid and ashamed. All he saw was a way to right the wrongs he had inflicted on his mother. This Court has heard his own valiant defence of her. He did not grasp the opportunity to speak for himself – as one might expect from the immoral ne'er-do-well that some have made him out to be – but pleaded for his mother.

'Once again, I ask you to remember that the prime consideration in this case is that of monetary gain. How, then, could Richard Feeney gain by faking his death when several months earlier he had made out a will that disposed of all his assets? He could not. He could only lose – lose everything save his self-respect. And now, twenty-six years after the self-sacrificial act, he has been put on trial upon the flimsiest of evidence, has risked his life to rescue two small children only to hear himself branded as callous for failing in his attempts to rescue the adulterer of his brother's wife! I ask you this, if Richard Feeney had thought himself to be guilty of any crime would he have come back to England? Would it not be the first act of a guilty man to assume an alias? And once the finger of accusation had been pointed could he not, being now an American citizen, have escaped all this by returning to America at the first intimation of danger, putting this Court to a great deal of inconvenience to have him extradited?'

Haig's dramatic crescendo plunged to little more than a whisper. 'But he did not. He acted responsibly, and in the confidence that he was totally innocent, remained in England to answer all charges. He did this also because he does not wish to be separated from his family. I trust, Members of the Jury, that you will permit mother and son to retrieve these lost, lonely years by finding my client not guilty.' He continued to gaze at the rapt faces for some seconds, before appending in grave murmur, 'Thank you, M'Lord,' and sitting down.

Lindley rose. 'Gentlemen of the Jury, after listening to

my learned friends' most eloquent speeches, you may be forgiven for thinking that we are dealing not with a crime, but an act of love. You have heard Richard Feeney's claim that his faked death was done out of a sense of remorse for the wrongs he had inflicted on his family, and you may like to believe this most touching concept. However, you must not allow any sentimentality to override certain important facts.' He counted these off on his fingers. 'Thomasin Feeney *did* lie to the insurance representative about her son, claiming him to be her nephew. She *continued* to lie when questioned by the police, as did John Feeney. Only when a witness had identified Richard Feeney did both change their declarations.

'John Feeney *was* aware that his wife had a man friend and has admitted that he intended to divorce her. Had he not wished to put himself through the sordid process of divorce then the fire would have provided admirable camouflage. We have heard that the two Feeney brothers were very close. Indeed, Counsel for the Defence says it is preposterous to think that anyone so close could gain from the fire in question. I would dispute this view. Indeed, both brothers stood to benefit from the fictionalization of Richard Feeney's death – John for the reasons I have just stated; Richard, because he had suffered financial and personal damage by the closure of his "lodging house".' The latter was said with great affectation.

'And what of Thomasin Feeney? How might she benefit, you may ask, from a fire which destroyed her home and killed her daughter-in-law? I can think of two ways she might benefit: the first is similar in reason to that of her son John, namely that if it were assumed her elder son had died in that fire then no questions would be raised as to the identity of the second body and therefore a scandal would be avoided; secondly, her son Richard had brought her nothing but pain and embarrassment. If he were to appear to die a hero he would not only redress the balance but his emigration to America would rid her of his constant humiliations – have we not heard that he had been banished from the family home for his actions? The report from the eminent pathologist who testified as to the similarity between Richard Feeney and the dead man adds even more weight to the charge: when Richard saw that man unconscious, saw how similar in build he was to himself, he made no effort to rescue him, but left him there to die, knowing that the body would be assumed to be his.

'What you must decide is, did he share this information with Thomasin and John Feeney, either on that day or shortly afterwards? Is it possible to believe that this man – who professes to love his family so much – would have allowed them to continue to think that he had died in that fire, or would he somehow let them know he was alive? And then there is the Will . . .' He reiterated the inconsistencies of this. 'But the two indisputable facts of this case are that Thomasin Feeney accepted eight hundred pounds to which she was not entitled, and Richard Feeney did not die in that fire. I submit, Members of the Jury, that there can be no other verdict than guilty.' Lindley flicked out his robe and sat down.

Lord Alverstone laced his fingers and leaned forwards. 'Members of the Jury, you have heard all the evidence for and against the accused. What it is now your duty to do is weigh all that evidence carefully and decide whether or not there was a conspiracy to defraud . . .'

Dusty hugged herself nervously, urging him to get on with it. Lindley had done enough to counteract the good impression of the Defence's speeches without this silly old fool adding to that. She looked at each juror's face, trying to guess what lay behind those eyes.

The Judge droned on for a good many minutes, before coming to his close. '. . . Members of the Jury, I will leave you to consider your verdict.'

* * *

The Jury was out for thirty minutes, during which time Erin twittered and twitched until Dusty thought she might throttle her. She herself began to count the plaster marigolds on the frieze that encircled the dome. It was still oppressively close. Her underclothes were sticking to her back. She kept losing count of the marigolds and went back to the beginning – then suddenly the Jury was filing back in and Court reconvened.

The Foreman was asked to stand. 'Have you reached a verdict on which you are all agreed?'

'We have.' All in the gallery tensed and leaned forward.

'On the charge of conspiring to defraud the Yorkshire Insurance Company, how do you find the accused John Patrick Feeney?'

Thomasin swallowed. *Oh please, please* . . .

'Not guilty.'

A great 'Oh!' of relief went up from the gallery and Erin hugged Belle. Thomasin chanced a tremulous smile but still held her breath for the verdict on herself.

'. . . how do you find the accused Thomasin Feeney?'

Thomasin bit her lip.

'Not guilty.'

Once again, there was a brief but enthusiastic surge of relief from the gallery. But there was soon hush.

'. . . how do you find the accused Richard William Feeney?'

To Dickie and his tortured wife there seemed to be a longer pause than with the others . . .

'Not guilty.'

Thomasin was so surprised she could not stop a little exclamation. The gallery erupted, people started to pour from their seats. Dusty threw her arms around Josie, while Erin shook her head. 'Christ, he's got the luck o' the devil that boy.' The Judge banged sharply on his gavel attempting to bring order while before him Thomasin and her two sons

389

hugged and congratulated each other, Thomasin in tears of joy. There was no lessening of high spirits when the Judge declined to award them costs, nor did they even notice his departure from the courtroom, far too euphoric at the verdict.

After kissing and embracing Thomasin, Sonny pumped his brother's hand. Dickie hauled him into a bearhug, face oozing mischief, 'How did I do, Son? Bloody great, wasn't I? They'll have me on the bill at the Theatre Royal next week.' His brother clipped him round the ear and told him not to push his luck. Then, Dickie spotted Rufforth who had come back to the Court to hear the outcome.

'Hey, d'you think Mr Rufforth would be upset if I told him I want to take out an insurance policy?'

'For God's sake, let's get this man out of Court, before he has us hanged!' Sonny shoved his brother forwards.

'We'll stop at the off-licence for a celebratory bottle,' laughed Dickie and leaned over to deliver a hefty pat to Haig's shoulder.

After saluting her own barrister, Thomasin paid homage to the younger man and told him she could not thank him enough for defending her son so ably. Sonny, too, performed strenuous handshakes with both lawyers.

'Don't overdo it,' urged Dickie as they moved in a huddle to the exit. 'It was my performance that got us off.'

His mother gave a sound of exasperation. 'Whatever you do, don't say anything like that in front of Erin.' She was smiling at her daughter who was fighting her way from the gallery, but her tone was stern. 'You might've escaped a prison sentence but your sister's capable of much worse. I want a peaceful house from now on.'

Dickie smiled up at his sister too. 'Don't worry, Mam. I'll buy us a bottle of champagne that'll sweeten her up – oh, damn! I left all me money at home . . .'

'Any excuse,' sighed his brother, but smiled happily.

'No, honest I have! I thought I was going down for a few years, I wasn't going to fetch money for some gaoler to pinch. Can you buy it, Son? I'll pay ye back when . . .'

'Never mind!' Sonny laughed and urged him on to the entrance hall. Here they met up with the rest of the family and surged out through the double doors to the sun-warmed portico where they spent some further time kissing and chattering.

'Now for that holiday!' Sonny curled his arms round his fleshy wife.

There had been little celebration for Thomasin's recent birthday, nor Erin's, nor Belle's, but now there could be.

'Remember your promise, Dickie!' said his overjoyed mother. 'You're here to stay now.'

Dickie fell against an Ionic column and uttered a laughing groan. 'Oh, Dusty . . . can we bear it d'ye think?' Then he lifted her off her feet again and squeezed her. His wife made a grab for her black straw hat which threatened to become dislodged, her face wearing the same joyous expression as the others. Dickie threw back his head and laughed again. 'Christ, the amount o' times he was waving that will around an' never once caught on! The sucker.'

'Mr Feeney.'

All heads turned in expectation of more good wishes. 'Richard William Feeney?' asked the short, dour-faced individual.

Dickie set his wife back on her feet and answered with caution. 'Yes.'

'I'm arresting you for the murders of Victoria Hughes and . . .'

Dickie grabbed his brother and hurled him at the man, the collision knocking both off their feet. With his wife and mother's cries echoing in his ears he sped away.

17

'What're you doing coming in the back way?' Sally shouted to Belle from her position at the sink where she was rinsing a pair of child's knickers. 'You must . . . oh!' A soapy hand left bubbles on the breast of her pinafore as Dickie came around the door. 'Mr Feeney, you did give me a start! I thought it was Belle back from Court.'

'Wasn't sure who'd be here so I snuck in the back!' Dickie, still breathing heavily, closed the door and leaned on it. Hearing his name mentioned, the children had come to crowd around him, Freddie asking, 'Where's me mother? Are we going to America yet?'

Dickie ignored him and, regaining his wind, moved on to the inner room and threw his hat on the table, raking agitated fingers through his hair. Sally followed. 'How did the case go, sir?'

'They found us not guilty.'

Sally beamed and wiped her hands with the towel she carried. 'Oh, I'm so glad! Belle must be relieved – where is she, then?'

'Probably gone for a celebration at Peasholme. I had to leave rather abruptly.'

She frowned. 'Has there been some trouble?'

He answered with a request. 'Look, can I ask ye to do something for me, Sally? If anyone comes knockin' at the door will ye say ye haven't seen me?'

'Oh, Lord . . . just anyone, sir?'

'Anyone, especially the p-o-l-i-c-e.'

Freddie was reciting the letters thoughtfully. 'Is a police-man chasing you?'

Dickie scowled and addressed himself to Sally. 'He's a very sharp lad, isn't he? He'll have to be careful his tongue doesn't slip and cut his throat.' Bending down, he said to Fred sternly, 'You're not to say anything about me bein' here, right? Any of ye. Otherwise I might get put into prison.' Faith started to howl. 'Oh, my big gob – I didn't mean it, honey!' He pulled out his handkerchief. 'Don't you worry now. They'll never catch me. We'll soon be on our way to America, the five of us.' Fred elbowed his sister out of the way to ask if his father knew what a bastion was. The man looked down at him, muttering, 'It's a little boy who asks silly questions when his father's up to his neck in it.'

'You don't know, do you? It's part of a fortification.'

'Oh, thanks Fred, that's just what I needed to hear.' The maid uncovered her mouth to ask if Belle knew he had come here. 'No, but she'd let me hide out here till it's safe to get away.' Dickie lit a cigarette, looking slightly less persecuted now. At that same instant, his relief was snatched away by someone knocking on the door. Sally pushed him at the staircase and he wasted no time in bounding up it. Which was just as well, for the person didn't wait to be admitted. Directly after the door had closed on Dickie, Brian poked his face round another one.

The delighted children pulled him into the room, scolding that he hadn't been for ages. Sally would have been pleased to see him too, at any other moment but this one, saying that if he had come to see Belle she wasn't here. Brian patted the collection of heads as he spoke. 'Is she still at Court?' Sally asked, had he been there? 'No, but I've been following it in the paper. I knew it was the verdict today and . . . well, I was concerned to know the outcome, thought she might be glad of support.'

'Oh, they were found not guilty, Doctor,' Sally smiled.

'That's splendid!' Brian pushed his dispositioned spectacles back up his nose. 'You've been at the Court then?'

'Wha . . . ? Oh no, Belle sent word to say she'd gone to celebrate at Mrs Feeney's house.' He asked, who with. 'The rest o' the family.'

Brian laughed. 'No, I meant who brought the message.'

'Oh! Er, a neighbour of ours saw her outside the Court and she asked him to tell me she'd be late home.'

'Not much point my staying then, is there?' Brian sounded regretful, then smiled down at Frederick who had donned a panama hat that came right over his eyes. 'That's a fine hat, Fred – fits perfectly.'

'It's me dad's,' replied Frederick. 'He isn't here, though.'

Sally felt herself go red and turned away to cover it, but Brian seemed not to interpret the child's statement. 'Very nice. Well, I'd better be on my way.' He didn't appear too eager to leave. 'Has anyone got any coughs or sneezes for me to cure while I'm here? No? All fit and healthy; that's good.' He turned to Sally. 'You might tell Belle I came.'

'I will, sir. She'll be grateful, I know . . . oh, wait a minute, that sounds like her.' The door had slammed – typical of Belle's entrance when something had angered her. 'She must've changed her mind.'

'You'll never guess what's happened!' Belle came clomping along the passage.

The maid, seeking to prevent a storm of indiscretion, shouted hastily, 'The Doctor's here, Belle!'

If Belle had felt any surprise on hearing the announcement, it had disappeared from her face by the time she entered the room. 'Such a long absence, Doctor. Can we gather you've not many patients today?'

394

Brian swallowed his disappointment. 'I'm really pleased the verdict ended happily, Belle.'

If only you knew the half of it, thought Belle, but answered, 'Thank you. You must have been in Court, then. I didn't notice you in the gallery.'

'No, I told him,' said Sally hurriedly. 'Ronnie Maynard passed on your message. You must've changed your mind about going to Peasholme?'

'What?' Belle frowned. Sally gave a quick look at Brian whose eyes were on Belle. She tried to convey the warning by twitching her mouth and gesturing to the hat on Frederick's head. But Belle was slow in grasping the code. 'Freddie, you look a proper juggins!' She laughed and pulled the brim down under his nose. 'Where did that come from?'

'You'll want me to put the kettle on!' Sally's voice was rather shrill.

'I could certainly do with a cup of tea,' sighed Belle. 'But I'll have to have it while I'm catching up with my work.' She wished Brian would go so she could let rip to Sally about her uncle. 'Children, go fetch your books.' In their absence she told him, 'I'm sorry I can't entertain you, Brian, but as you can imagine I haven't been able to do much in the last few days and I really must get on.' It was said merely to get rid of him.

'Belle.' He toyed with the hat which Freddie had cast aside, pressing the dent back into its crown. 'What I really came for was to say I'm sorry.'

'Fair enough,' she replied and donated a tight smile, but was obviously waiting for him to leave. He looked at her blankly. 'I hope you aren't expecting some sort of effusive reunion after it's taken you four months to get around to it,' came her shirty addendum. 'I seem to remember that my apology was given short shrift in your house.'

'I know.' He looked dejected and fingered the rim of the

hat. 'I was just so blessed mad . . .' the hat moved round and round in his hands. 'It always seemed to be me who had to apol . . .' His attention had become focused on the hat. 'Freddie said this belonged to his dad.' His face darkened with suspicion and he stared her in the eye. 'He's here, isn't he?'

Belle regarded him impatiently. 'Who?'

From the kitchen Sally listened with growing trepidation. 'He's here – hiding!' Brian's angry eyes darted around the room. He marched down the passage and into the front parlour. After a stunned delay, Belle marched after him, but was just in time to meet him coming back. 'Who're you looking for, for God's sake!' But he pushed her aside and set his feet at the stairs. 'What the devil . . . come down! What do you think you're doing? This is my house!'

Brian continued to stride up the staircase. Belle picked up her skirts and stomped after him, making further loud objections as he flung open the door of her bedroom . . . and there was Dickie lying on her bed, grinning up at him.

Hearing the cyclone's approach, Dickie had looked for somewhere to hide, but there was no room in the wardrobe. There seemed nothing else for it but to adopt this brazen posture. 'Good day to ye, Doctor! No illness in the house, I hope?'

Brian teetered on the brink of attack, glaring down at him. Belle had reached the top of the stairs. She took two more steps and launched her breathless objection, 'Brian, what do you think . . .' Her eyes were drawn past Brian's angry expression to the grinning one on her pillow. For the moment she was speechless.

'You know, you almost had me convinced.' Brian's scowl was still aimed at Dickie but his words were for Belle. 'I thought your offhandedness was just hurt pride, thought that underneath you really missed me . . . huh! No wonder you hardly had the energy to smile at me when you've been serviced by the likes of him for the last four months.'

'Now just a minute!' Belle stuck a finger under his chin, but he was already charging for the stairs. 'Brian! I didn't even know he was here! I've just got back from Court – oh damn!' Her surgical boot had mismanaged the stairs. A group of goggle-eyed children stood at the foot. 'Get back to your books!' They darted from the line of fire.

Brian gave one last twist of the knife as he opened the front door, 'I should have known what you were when you slept with me!' then slammed it in her face.

After a second of furious indecision, Belle careered towards the kitchen. 'I tried to warn you!' protested Sally. 'I couldn't say it outright, could I? That would've caused more bother.'

Belle uttered a screech of frustration and swung her leg towards the stairs. The sight of Dickie looking down at her forestalled her ascent. 'Get down here, Uncle!' With a rueful laugh, Dickie ran a hand around the inside of his waistband to tuck in his shirt, then trotted down the stairs. 'Do you realise what you're doing?'

His cockiness gave way to atonement. 'I'm sorry about Brian. I'll explain to hi . . .'

'Damn Brian! You're a wanted criminal – I could be arrested for harbouring you! What would happen to those children if I were thrown in gaol?'

'Belle, this was the only safe place I could think of! They would've come straight to Peasholme.'

'Well, you're not staying!'

'Ye wouldn't throw me to the wolves?'

'They won't eat poison.'

'Belle . . .' his eyes and tone reproached her.

'Uncle, you must go!'

'Just let me stay tonight till the heat dies down, then I'll go to Leeds.'

'And implicate Uncle Sonny again!'

'Mm.' Dickie stopped pleading and rubbed his chin. 'You're right, they'll search his place, too. I'll have to think carefully about this . . . but please!' He cupped her angry face. 'Let me stay here tonight, darlin'.'

His hands burnt her cheeks. Despite the endearment she felt threatened by his masculinity and twisted out of his grip. 'All right, damn you!' She caught Sally's look of disapproval as the maid departed to the kitchen. 'But what happens if Brian shouts it all over the place?'

'No, he'll want to keep quiet about it,' said Dickie.

'You're very sure!' She pressed a hand to her brow. 'God . . .'

Dickie held out his hands. 'He doesn't know I'm a wanted criminal, does he?'

'Not yet, but when he does . . .'

'I'll be well away. What happened after I'd left Court?'

'We didn't tarry when that detective set off after you. I'll have to go and tell the family you're here.'

'No!'

'Uncle, they're worried sick!'

Yes, they would be. He thought about his wife. Poor Dusty . . . but if Belle went and told her where he was she'd come straight here and maybe the police would follow. 'Look,' he told Belle, 'just wait till after I'm gone and tell Dusty I'll be in touch.'

'I think we have a few things to discuss; you are charged with murder.'

'Ye want to know if I did it?'

'It would be rather nice to be able to feel safe in one's bed.'

'An' if I tell ye I didn't do it ye'd feel safe, would ye?' he said lightly. 'Talking about beds, where am I goin' to sleep?' She told him, the sofa. 'Belle,' he groaned, 'ye realise this will ruin my reputation. An' Brian'll be so disappointed to find he was wrong. Couldn't ye just . . .' He laughed roguishly, causing her harsh facade to cave in.

'You're a wicked old villain.' She threw a light punch. 'How you can act so casually . . .'

'Oh, please! Wicked and villainous yes, but never old.'

Belle said, 'Pff!' Then, 'Sally! Put the kettle on now. Are you hungry, Uncle?'

'No, I couldn't touch a thing.' His smile grew frayed as he probed under his breastbone. 'I'm not so cool as I look; that little escapade has churned me up good an' proper.'

'You still haven't answered me about the murders.'

He looked grim and sat down. 'My past has taken a long time to catch up with me but it's certainly made up for lost time. Rest easy, Belle, I'm no murderer.'

'Then why did you run if you didn't do it?'

'Because I did. One of them anyway.' He was told not to speak in riddles. 'Just because I killed him doesn't make me a murderer. I never meant to, and I only hit him in self-defence.'

'But surely you could have told the police that?'

'I can't go through all that rigmarole again!' objected Dickie. 'I consider myself very damned lucky to get off that fraud charge.'

'Mother said you had the luck of the devil.'

He gave a bitter laugh and said, 'She would . . . but I may not be so lucky with these charges.'

Belle found a packet of cigarettes and handed him one, using a taper to light both. 'I don't have time to hear your story now, I have to see to the children, but I would like to hear it later. In the meantime, I think it's best if you go back to my bedroom . . .'

He brightened. 'Now there's an invitation!'

'. . . and keep your face away from the window! There's plenty of books up there to occupy you.'

'I'm not much of a reader. Can't I come an' sit in on the kids' lessons?'

'It would be far too distracting, especially for Freddie. He's got very poor concentration at the best of times . . . Besides, I'd prefer it if you kept away from him and the girls as much as possible.' On that ominous note, she left him.

Later, when the children had gone to bed, Dickie sat with Belle on her sofa, both puffing on cigarettes, and he began to tell her what had led up to the arrest. 'Ye know at the trial when I said about the time I ran away from home and everyone thought I was dead?'

'You could make a living on the stage playing corpses.'

'Well, as I said, I was eighteen at the time . . . what I didn't say in Court was that I was in a tight corner, never mind the reason . . .'

'I think I know that already.' Belle glanced at him. 'It would be round about the time that Nick was born.'

He studied her. 'Ye know about all that?'

'"All that", being you and Uncle Sonny's wife? Yes, I know. I was rather afraid it was going to come out at the trial when the Prosecution kept harping on about her being unfaithful.'

'Me too. Your mother told you, I suppose?' When she nodded he sighed. 'There aren't many things I'm ashamed of, Belle, but that's one of them. Sonny worshipped that girl. It doesn't matter that she was a whore, I didn't have to go and prove it but I did . . . anyway, we'll be here all night if I tell you every gruesome detail, but to cut it short, it looked as if I was going to be forced to marry her an' I just had to escape. I was away for three years. During that time I lodged with an old biddy name o' Torie Hughes.' He grinned

400

fondly. 'Me an' her, we got on like a house on fi . . . Christ, I could've picked a better phrase.' He flicked ash at the fire. 'Anyway, one day I'd been to market an' when I came back there were two blokes attacking her. An' d'ye know what I did? I hid myself in the pigsty till they'd gone, listened to them thumping the life out o' her an' never lifted a finger . . . When I came out she was dead. My first thought was: what if somebody thinks I've done it? So instead o' reporting it, like an eejit I buried her and took what money she had, used it to make myself into a rich man.' He fell silent.

'What about the other one – I presume there is just the one?'

He sighed. 'That happened a couple o' years later. I'd come back to York, wanted to show the family just how well I'd done . . . you already know how that turned out. By chance I met up with a woman I'd known a long time ago when I was a lad. She was a prostitute and in a right old state with herself – came to me for help. I was in a hotel room at that time 'cause this detective was after me. Anyway, her pimp comes elbowing his way in an' starts beating her. She cried out to me to protect her. I remembered how I'd stood by an' let those men kill Torie. I had to do something. So, I picked up this heavy bowl and clouted him with it – lots o' times. God, he had a head like an elephant, I thought he'd never go down. Anyway, in the end he did . . . but he cracked his temple on the fender an' killed himself.'

'Gosh, what did you do?'

'Stuffed him in the wardrobe an' ran like buggery. A while later I met up with Sonny. Ye know what happened after that.' He narrowed his eyes. 'This detective fella, I can't recall his name but I know he was from a West Riding force 'cause it was in his district that Torie was killed. Anyway, he'd been tailing me for quite a while . . .' Dickie frowned. 'How in hell did he manage to catch up with me after all these years?'

'He must have wanted you very badly,' said Belle. 'You realise that running away like this is going to make you look even more guilty.'

'Tell me what else I can do.'

'Why don't you try facing up to your problems for once?' When he made a face she asked, 'Have you made up your mind where you're going to run to?'

'It'll have to be Leeds – that detective won't expect me on his own patch – but Nick's place, not Sonny's.' Belle gave her opinion that he would be better off making for the nearest port. 'I can't go back to America yet, I promised Mam. Still, if we get the adoption contracts signed . . .'

'Ho no!' said Belle tartly.

'Ye said if the trial worked out OK we could have them!'

'It's hardly worked out OK.' The children's grandmother had been apprehensive enough about the fraud trial, what would she say to this?

'Come on! Dusty hasn't done anything wrong, there's no call for you to punish her.'

'I don't see it as punishing anybody! No one in their right minds would send the children to such a hazardous life.'

'It wouldn't be hazardous once we got to America.' His niece pointed out that he could still be extradited. 'No, I've got friends in the New York Police, they'd tell me if there was any danger o' that. Come on, Belle.'

'It's not open to discussion, Uncle. All I'm prepared to give you is a fair chance to get away.'

He looked at her sourly. 'Well, I'm not heading for any seaports yet. At least if I lie low at Nick's for a week or two I'll have more chance of escape than you're willing to grant me.'

The door to the kitchen opened. Sally entered, unfastening her apron. 'Right, I'm going up – unless there's anything else you want doing?' Belle thanked her and said there wasn't.

'You'll want some sheets putting on that sofa for your guest, won't you?' She didn't look at the man, but her sternness of tone implied he was not welcome.

'We're sitting on it at the moment,' replied Belle.

'Yes, well, I'll just get you some out and you can put them on when you finish talking. You'll be coming up soon, won't you? It's getting on, you know.'

'Yes, I can tell the time, Sally, thank you. Leave the sheets, we can get them.' Belle was firm. 'You've heard the most of it now, off you go. If he springs any more secrets I'll tell you tomorrow. Goodnight.' She laughed softly as the indignant maid stalked off to bed. 'Don't worry, Uncle, she won't give you away, much as she disapproves. Now to return to the topic – how will you get to Leeds? You can't take your car, it's at Peasholme.'

'I could if somebody brought it for me.'

'Me? I can't drive.'

'I understood you could do just about everything.' It was meant as sarcasm.

'Even if I could, the police would follow me, wouldn't they? Talk sense. That car would stick out like a sore thumb.'

'Well, I'm not walking twenty bloody miles,' vouched Dickie. 'I'll get the train.'

'If you want to take the risk.'

'I've been thinking about this: they won't have the whole blasted police force out looking for me over a crime that's a quarter of a century old, surely?'

'What you've got to decide is which places *will* they be watching?'

'It's almost a certainty they'll be watching Peasholme,' said her uncle.

'So you'll risk the train?'

He thought for a moment or two. 'A cab might be the safer bet.'

'It'll be awfully expensive, and didn't I hear you say you'd left your money at Peasholme?'

'Sod an' dammit! I don't suppose . . . ?'

'Sorry, Uncle Dickie, I'm on a strict budget.'

'Remind me to tell Brian what a lucky escape he's had.'

Her face showed that she did not wish to be reminded of Brian. Silence reigned for a time whilst she pondered on this afternoon's débâcle. Then she sighed. 'Poor Brian . . . I wish I'd kept things on just a friendly basis like we had at the beginning; it's terrible when one partner loves the other more. I suppose you and I are somewhat alike in that position.'

Dickie looked at her as though she were mad and said she could not be more wrong. 'Dusty could never love me more than I lover her. I often think . . .' he laughed in embarrassment, '. . . well, when ye get to my age ye start to feel mortal, especially seeing the old fella like that . . . I dread to think what'd happen to me if Dusty went first.'

Belle saw that his utterance was genuine and shook her head in disbelief. 'How you have the gall to say that . . .'

''Cause I kissed you, ye mean? That was very enjoyable but it doesn't mean I've stopped loving Dusty.' He turned his body around on the sofa and took hold of her hand. 'In fact, now I come to think of it, it was most enjoyable indeed and it's been a long time since it happened. D'ye fancy a bit more?'

Belle stared into his face. There could be no denying the attraction she felt for him. The pit of her stomach felt tight just at the thought. It would be so easy to take him into her bed. Just for tonight. Where was the harm? No one would know . . .

The baby started to cry and Sally's footsteps thudded overhead. The danger was over. Belle looked at the clock. 'Time for bed.'

Dickie raised an expectant grin. 'An' here's me about to say what an ungenerous body you are.'

'There's some sheets in that cupboard; take what you need.' With this abrupt ending she went off to her own bed, thinking that it was going to be a very long night.

Dickie sat there for an hour after she had gone before getting some sheets out and making himself a bed. He should have been tired out with all the running he'd done, but he couldn't get to sleep and proceeded to light one cigarette after another, taking them from Belle's packet. A bed creaked. He thought of Dusty and the children, and thought, and thought . . .

He must have dozed finally, though, for when he opened his eyes the room was bright with sun. Yawning, he craned his stiff neck to squint at the clock. It was only six. He sat up and remained in this position for a while, kneading his aching shoulder muscles. A sniff of his bare armpit brought a grimace. Tossing aside the crumpled sheet, he went to the kitchen and used a dishcloth to wash his body, then splashed some water on his face. Reaching for the towel, he rubbed it briskly over his eyes to aid consciousness. When he removed the towel a small figure was standing watching him.

Dickie groaned. 'A bit early for you to be awake, isn't it?'

'You're awake,' contradicted Frederick.

'Am I? I seem to be havin' some sort o' nightmare, keep seein' this bloody apparition in front of me.' He shoved the boy out of his path and went to get his shirt which he had laid over the back of a chair with the rest of his clothes; he wore only his underpants at the moment.

Fred watched. 'What're them?' Dickie paused in the action of pulling the shirt over his head. 'Them hairy things under your arms.'

'They're bloody paintbrushes, what d'ye think they are?'

405

'What're they for?'

'How the hell do I know? Ask God.'

'I haven't got any under my arms,' said Fred. His adoptive father mumbled something as he brought the shirt down over his naked torso. 'What did you say?'

'I *said*, you'll no doubt grow some if ye live long enough, which is unlikely, the way ye keep sneakin' up on folk.'

'You've got 'em on your legs an' all,' observed Fred as the man reached for his trousers.

With an exasperated laugh, Dickie shook the trousers straight and slipped his legs in, using a hand to ram the tail of the shirt down under his buttocks. After donning his jacket, he visited the outside closet, then took out a comb and with knees bent – for the mirror was set low to accommodate Belle – he ran it through his hair. Fred seemed captivated by the man's handsomeness.

'What's that mark on your head?' It was something the boy had been meaning to ask for a while.

Dickie traced the L-shaped scar on his forehead. 'Somebody knifed me.' Whilst performing his toilet, Dickie had come to a decision on how to get to Leeds. With enough for the train fare he would check the railway station first, then if that proved too dangerous he could set off on foot and maybe hitch a lift on the way. As contingency for this, he took several items of food from Belle's larder, stuffing them into one of her bags.

'Are you getting my breakfast ready?' asked the boy.

'Nope.'

'Well what are you having for yours?'

'Bread an' water,' replied Dickie. 'I'm practising.'

'What can I have, then?'

In answer, Dickie flung a bread roll at him. 'Stick some jam on that. I haven't time to be seeing to you.'

'Where y'off?' Fred did not eat the roll but played with it

like a ball. The man told him it was a secret. 'Can I come?' His father said no. 'Why?'

''Cause the police will lock y'up if they catch ye with me.'

'I'm not bothered,' said Frederick.

'Well, I am – ye don't think I want to be stuck in gaol listening to your daft questions for twenty years, do ye?'

'Why're you mad at me?'

Dickie stopped to look at the woebegone face. 'I'm sorry, son ... I never was very good company first thing on a morning. I'm not mad at ye, but I haven't a lot o' time, that's all.' He continued to pack his requirements into the bag.

'Why do they want to put you in gaol?'

'They think I did something bad.'

'But you didn't, did you?'

'Now, would your father do anything bad? Listen, ye do want me to be your father, don't ye?' At Frederick's eager nod he added, 'Then ye have to help me get away. The thing is, Fred, I need some more money.'

'You can have all mine,' said the boy generously.

'Good lad, go fetch it.' While the boy was gone, Dickie made rapid examination of all the vases and other receptacles on the mantel. The loose silver he turned up amounted to less than a pound. He spun as Fred returned. 'Ah, let's see.' He held out his palm to receive the boy's wordly wealth – threepence. He snorted and offered exaggerated thanks. 'Can ye tell me where your Aunt Belle keeps her money? She was going to lend me some this morning but I have to leave now an' I don't want to wake her.'

'It's in that pot on the mantel,' Fred told him.

'Is there none anywhere else?' When he received a vacant shake of head, he swore under his breath and made ready to leave.

Fred walked with him to the rear exit. 'What time will you be coming back for me?'

'What?' Dickie swung round with an impatient expression. 'Oh ... I'm not sure. It depends if I can escape these policemen.'

'If I come with you I can help you escape.'

'No, 'tis best if you stay here.' Without further argument, Dickie left.

Immediately, Freddie ran to get his trousers, struggled into them and scrambled back downstairs. No one heard the door go. Two more hours passed before Belle discovered that not only had Uncle Dickie vanished, but Freddie had gone too.

'The wretch!' complained Belle to Sally when it was confirmed that the boy was not in the house. 'I hide him at great risk to myself and this is what he does. Well, just let him try to leave the country with that boy. America or no, I'll have him hunted down. In fact, I'm going to the police right now!'

'Ooh, d'you think you should?' queried Sally. 'It'll mean having to explain why you waited till now to report he was here – and Freddie might just be hiding.'

'Of course he's not! It's obvious to an imbecile that Dickie's taken him. He knew I'd never let him have the children legally.' She became thoughtful. 'Still, you're right about the police. I don't want to be caught up in questioning for hours ... but I'm going round to Peasholme straight after lessons to speak to that wife of his! And I want you to stay in the house to guard those girls. I wouldn't put it past him to sneak back for them.'

After eating breakfast, the children had been told to sit quietly with their schoolbooks in the front parlour until Belle came. While she was heading for this room, the doorknocker sounded. She shouted to Sally, 'I'll get it!' then faltered, thinking that perhaps it might be the police. But remembering that this was rent month, she realised who it would be and finally answered it.

'Good morning, Miss Teale!' The landlord, a heavy-jowled, pasty-looking man in a checked suit, doffed his hat.

'Oh, hello, Mr Clark, I'll just get your money.' She started to reverse along the passage.

'Er . . .' He held up a delaying hand. 'I ought to tell you that I've had to raise your rent, Miss Teale.'

Belle set her chin at him. 'Oh yes, and why's that?'

Clark's smile was rather condescending, she thought. 'Well, you've been here now . . . let's see, five or six years, haven't you?' He received a curt nod. 'You wouldn't expect to be paying the same rent as when you first moved in, now would you?'

'I must say, it's short notice,' snapped Belle.

'I was going to broach the subject last month, but you weren't in.'

No, that's right, thought Belle, remembering how she had sent Sally to the door, I was keeping out of your way. 'So how much is the increase?' she demanded.

'Five shillings,' replied Clark evenly.

Her response was incredulous. 'What! A five shilling increase?'

Clark donned a look of mild rebuke. 'If I may say so, the property's much improved to what it was when I first let it to you, Miss Teale.'

Belle performed a gasping laugh at this audacity. 'And who made the improvements, might one ask? This place was virtually ramshackle when I moved in. By rights you ought to be dropping my rent. Through my hard work I've made your property worth twice as much!'

'That's not the point, Miss Teale. I can hardly get twice as much for it while you're in, can I? Besides . . . there's another

409

matter I wanted to discuss.' He shuffled uncomfortably. 'It's about the men you have here.'

Belle's lower jaw fell open. 'I *beg* your pardon?'

'Don't misunderstand!' he hastened to explain. 'I've no wish to pry. What you do is your own business. But if you're taking in lodgers . . .'

'I am not taking in lodgers! If you are referring to the gentleman who admitted you the last time you were here, then that happens to be my uncle.'

'That's fine, fine,' said Clark, nodding casually. 'I've said I don't mind who you have here . . . Is the other gentleman your uncle as well?' She asked, which other gentleman. 'The one who's been seen coming out of here on a morning.'

'How *dare* you! How dare you spy on me!'

'There's no question of spying, Miss Teale, I'm only trying to protect my livelihood. I set your rent at a low price on the premise that this was a charitable organisation, an orphanage, but if you're taking in lodgers . . .'

'Rubbish!' Accompanying Belle's declaration, a tiny remnant of her breakfast shot from her mouth and landed on Clark's lapel, but her embarrassment at this was concealed by the fact that her face was already crimson with anger. 'The rent was so low because it was a hovel! Nobody else would live in it! It's only now when you've been allowed to see the results of all my slaving that you've decided to take advantage of me! Well, you can go sing for it! I'm not paying it – and I am *not* taking in lodgers!'

Clark leaned a pudgy hand on the door jamb. Belle noticed with distaste that his nails were filthy. 'I'm afraid if you won't pay it I'll have to give you a month's notice to quit.'

'You think I'm staying here after being so insulted?' she hurled, eyes darting sporadically between his face and the piece of breakfast on his collar. 'I can assure you, my good man, I don't require a month or even a week. I shall be out of this house by tonight! I wouldn't want to deprive you of the extra five shillings you can extort from some other poor dupe!' He opened his mouth but Belle didn't give him time to speak. 'And please don't have the gall to demand this month's rent! I've always paid a month in advance. We're straight. Good day!' She slammed the door in his face and lurched angrily down the passage, shouting at Sally, 'Did you hear that? Did you hear the insinuations he was making? The maggot-faced pig! Come on, don't stand there! We have to get packing, I've told him we'll be out by tonight.' She herself was already piling books together, snatching pictures from the wall.

'So I gathered.' Sally looked on in alarm. 'That was a bit rash, wasn't it? How're we going to get all this shifted by tonight – and more precisely, where to?'

Belle slammed another book on the pile, then leaned heavily on it. 'Oh, God . . . men. And one wretch of a man in particular! If he hadn't let Clark in . . .' She tutted. 'I couldn't stay here, Sally, after he'd said what he did. He was almost leering!' She mimicked Clark, '"*What you get up to here is your own business*" . . . the filthy, lousy – oh come on! It's no use moaning. I've done it now. We'll have to get packed.' Puffing, she put her hands on her hips and looked around her. There would have to be a strict method if all were to be done by tonight. 'First we have to have a removal van . . .'

'I'll let you do the organising,' said Sally, launching into action. 'I'll make a start on the donkey work. We could do with Cedric here.' The strapping lad, one of Belle's first orphans, worked at Thomasin's factory. 'What d'you want the others to do?'

'They can gather their personal belongings and clothes together and put them in the big trunk.' Belle sighed exasperatedly. 'The *only* trunk. What won't go in there will have to be knotted in sheets – anyway, I'd better get this removal van sorted out first.' She rushed off.

When she returned with the news that a van would be calling this afternoon, the seven children had already been put to work. 'But where're we going?' asked Anna from behind a pile of towels, tablecloths and curtains.

'I've decided we'll go to Peasholme, just until I can get somewhere else of my own,' said Belle, rolling up her sleeves. 'I've arranged to have the furniture stored so there'll just be bodies for Nan to put up.'

'You've been and asked her?' Sally finished unhooking the curtain and stepped down off her perch.

'No time. She won't mind, anyway. Besides, the children'll take her mind off her wretched son.' Belle grabbed a pile of newspapers and started to wrap the ornaments that had been taken off the mantel. 'Where did you put the money out of here?' She held up a jug.

Sally looked at her meaningfully. 'I didn't have to put it anywhere – it had already gone. The other pots were empty too.'

This information didn't take long to sink in. 'The swindling blood-sucking . . . it's just as well I didn't have to pay the rent then! A good job I keep my purse under my pillow, too – though some people are trying to make out that that's the most accessible place of all!'

It had been a mistake to set off so early. Dickie felt very vulnerable as he made his way through the sparsely-populated streets to the railway station. Each corner was approached with caution, lest a policeman be lurking behind it. However, he reached the outer walls of the city without mishap, and proceeded under the stone arch towards his goal.

He was almost past the Cholera graves when he heard something behind him and spun round. There was no one in

412

sight, but he sensed their presence. With growing unease he paid closer heed to the iron fencing that edged the graveyard. The presence manifested itself, attempting to blend with the railings but not quite thin enough to do so. He was almost relieved to see it was Frederick.

'You little . . . I oughta tan your backside – in fact I will!' He grabbed the boy round the waist and upturned him, using one arm to imprison whilst the other administered three hearty smacks. That done, he dropped the child back on his feet. 'I hope you realise this has added kidnapping to the bloody charges now!'

Frederick, bottom stinging, set his mouth in defiance. 'I don't like you any more. I'm not having you as me dad!'

'You're damned right you're not!' Dickie grabbed him again. 'But whether ye like it or not you're gonna have to come with me. I can't leave ye here for somebody to murder – much as I'd like to.'

'Get off!' Frederick tried to wriggle out of the grip, but Dickie held him higher, forcing him to walk on tiptoe. The boy clawed a hand over his shoulder, encountered skin and dug his nails in deep.

'Aagh!' Dickie sucked at his wounded hand. 'You little bastard, I've probably got rabies now.' Temporarily freed, the boy made a run, but Dickie's left hand shot out to collar him again. Still Fred kicked and struggled.

A carriage pulled up and its occupant leaned from the window. 'You there! What're you doing to that boy? Do you need help, young fellow?'

Fred stopped twisting and looked at the man. 'No, he's me dad.'

'Are you?' demanded the man.

'Yes.' Dickie's stance was challenging. 'Was there something you wanted to say?'

The man looked Dickie up and down, harumphed and said,

'Not at all. I was merely worried that the boy was being taken against his will. Good day to you.' He banged testily at the carriage roof ordering his driver to pull away.

'Taken against his will,' muttered Dickie as the pair waited for the carriage to disappear. 'Doesn't think about me being hounded against my will – come here, you!' He made a grab for Fred, but the boy kicked him on the ankle and ran up the road.

'Go on, bugger off then!' shouted Dickie, standing on one leg to rub his ankle. 'Ye're not worth running after.'

Fred stopped and waited for Dickie to catch up. 'I don't like people who hit me.'

'An' I don't like people who kick me!' Dickie walked past him.

Fred tagged on. 'Where we off?'

Dickie's answer was surly and was made without looking down. 'I'm off to my son's. I don't know where you're off.'

Frederick stopped in his tracks. 'I didn't know you had any children.'

At the plaintive tone, Dickie halted too and looked back. 'He's not a child, he's a man . . . anyway, he's not really my son, I was lying.' He stared at Frederick's crestfallen face. 'Have ye ever been on a train before?' The boy shook his head dumbly. 'I suppose ye'd better come with me, then.' He hooked a thumb and carried on marching towards the station. 'Come on, son.'

18

The silly things that come into your mind, thought Thomasin.
It was twenty years since she had sacked George Ackworth for
stealing and yet now that her own trial was over he, and not
Dickie, was the one occupying her head. Had she been too
hard in calling the police? How had his family coped while
he was in gaol? There but for the grace of God . . . 'S'truth,
isn't it quiet?' She pushed herself from the chair and hobbled
over to the window.

It's a wonder the carpet hasn't been worn away, thought
Erin, irritated by her mother's constant action. Back and
forth, back and forth. For pity's sake, Mam, sit down!
Thomasin did . . . but in the space of five minutes she
was at the window again, making Erin dig her nails into
her hand in order to prevent words which she would later
regret. Through the open window came the scent of lavender,
bringing memories of her stillborn child, to whom she had
given birth with the smell of this plant filling her nose. Ever
since, she had hated it. And every summer, as if the memory
were not bad enough, the smell would drift in to haunt her.
Were she to own the house she would pull every last shred
of it up. She rose and hauled down the sash. Even the cloying
heat was better than that smell.

After her criminal of a brother had made his escape they
had hurried home, but had not been allowed to relax before
the police had arrived with a warrant to search the house.

They had also spent some time grilling the family as to where Dickie might have gone. Erin had suspicions that he was at Belle's, but like the others said that she did not know. She glanced at her sister-in-law and wondered what was going through her head.

Dusty was marvelling at the loyalty shown by this family towards their errant son. Like the willow, in times of drought their roots grew deeper to find sustenance. Dick had the shallow footings of a cypress; a strong puff of wind, a crisis, and the forest would lose one of its number. Even their ex-maid showed more solidarity.

Abigail had postponed her return passage to Germany until tomorrow. At Thomasin's insistence she had also moved out of the hotel into Peasholme. It seemed odd sitting here drinking tea with the lady to whom she had once been servant – and they hadn't given her an attic room either. Oh no, she'd been treated like an honoured guest. Wait till she got home and told Gerry!

Thomasin was up and peering again. Sonny shared Erin's frustration. After the fiasco at the Court and the ensuing questions from the police, he had decided to stay the night just in case of any new developments, but now he was itching to be away. 'I think I'll just go and telephone Josie again.' His wife had gone home to tend her family. He rose from his chair. 'See if Dickie's made an appearance at that end.'

'Wait a minute!' Thomasin bent nearer the window. 'There's somebody . . . oh, it's Belle.' She sounded disappointed. The sight of a band of children produced a 'Tut!' as she limped back to her chair. 'What did she have to bring all of them for? Erin, don't let her fetch them in here, I can't do with them just now.'

'You were just complaining how quiet it was.' Purselipped, Erin stood and glanced through the window, then frowned at the large bundles carried by the children. Cicely

416

was in charge of the wickerwork pram with its buckled wheels, trying to steer it with one hand, whilst her other tried to keep hold of yet another bundle wobbling atop the chassis. 'Looks as if she's brought her washing – oh, Holy Virgin they've brought that blessed cat too.' She went into the hall just in time to prevent Cicely from carving a chunk out of the oak panelling with the pram wheels.

Belle hustled her charges inside, asking how the family had fared with the detective. Erin told her that he had gone but the two men who appeared to be street loafers enjoying the sun outside The Black Swan were in fact plainclothes policemen who had been watching the house since yesterday evening. 'They must think we're soft. You can spot them a mile off. Every time one of us goes out, there they are. I wonder they didn't accuse you of trying to smuggle your uncle in in those bundles.'

Belle dropped her burdens to the floor, commanding the children to stand where they were. 'Mother, were I lucky enough to have my uncle in one of these bundles I would cheerfully toss it in the drink. Is Nan in there?'

'No, she's in the front,' said Erin, clutching her brow at the noise that erupted from the pram. 'But wait a minute – Eddie, take the others down to the kitchen and ask Vinnie to give them some lemonade. No, not the baby,' she replied to his joke. When Eddie and the rest had gone, she whispered to Belle, 'I hope you aren't going to inflict them on Nan all day, she isn't coping very well.'

'That's a shame,' said Belle and chewed the inside of her cheek. 'I was going to ask if she'd mind having them for a week.'

Erin started to laugh, then stopped and looked down at the bundles. 'You're serious, aren't ye?'

'I'm afraid so. Can we go in so I don't have to repeat myself?'

Erin said of course and, eager to hear what was amiss, hurried her into the front room. 'Have ye seen the paper? There's a big piece in about the man wanted for murder. As if the insurance fraud wasn't bad enough . . . God, I don't know how this family is ever going to live it down.'

After greeting her grandmother, and nodding to her uncle and aunts, Belle said bluntly, 'I've been evicted – well, not exactly evicted, I refused to pay the five shilling a month rent increase.'

'But why?' cried Erin.

'He was trying to extort me, Mother.'

'No, I mean why has he suddenly decided to increase it after all this time?'

'Ask my dear Uncle Dickie.'

Dusty rose involuntarily. 'You've seen him?'

'He spent the night at my house.' Belle watched her aunt's expression change from worry to mistrust, and ended the speculation. 'When I came down this morning the sofa was empty, my money had gone and Freddie had gone, too.'

'Does he never learn!' Thomasin heaved a sigh and rubbed vigorously at her aching knee.

'Have you any idea where he's gone?' asked Dusty.

'Not for definite, but he mentioned Leeds last night.' Belle sat down.

'I'd better get back right away.' Sonny kissed his mother then fled, calling, 'I'll telephone you when I get there!'

'You haven't said how it comes to be Dickie's fault that you've lost your home,' Dusty said to her niece.

'The landlord believed he was cohabiting with me,' replied Belle. 'Some people have very lurid imaginations.' She turned disdainful eyes away from her aunt and said more evenly to Erin, 'It wasn't until Uncle Dickie let Clark get past the door the other month that he saw what improvements I'd made to the house and decided to cash in on it. I wasn't having that.

Told him what he could do with his house . . . in retrospect it was a bit rash. I was hoping you could put us up, Nan, just till I've found another place. It won't take more than a few weeks.'

'Of course I will, dear,' said Thomasin genuinely. 'You don't think I'd throw you out, do you? You can stay here as long as you need.'

Belle leaned forward with an affectionate gesture. 'Oh thanks, Nan. I really only came to park the children so they're not in the way of the removal men, if you wouldn't mind giving them lunch. I'll have to go back and help Sally. You'll be able to put her up too, won't you?' At her grandmother's nod of assent she looked relieved and actually laughed. 'I hope Mr Clark wasn't hoping to move his new tenants straight in; he'll have some cleaning up to do.' Her face was impish. 'I can't think how it could have happened, but somebody upset two chamberpots – splashed the contents all over the bedroom floor and had it dripping through the downstairs ceiling. Then one of the babies got hold of a red crayon and scribbled on nearly every wall before I caught her. Naughty child! I tried my best to clean it up, naturally, but I had so little time to vacate the premises . . .'

Thomasin joined in the laughter that followed, but soon her eyes had clouded over at the thought of her son somewhere out there; lost to her yet again.

From his room at The Black Swan, Nettleton watched the red-haired man drive away, but made no move to tail him. Besides the fact that he didn't want the York detectives to know he was here, his quarry's wife was still in the house; Feeney wouldn't be going far without her. He had also seen the gang of children roll up and, remembering what had been said in Court, deduced that amongst them would be the three orphans whom Feeney intended to adopt. He would surely be back some time. If not, well, Nettleton had the address of the man who had just left and it would not be difficult to trace other relatives. Feeney would turn up sooner or later.

One irritation was that yesterday's chase had been witnessed by other law officers and Nettleton had been obliged to state the reason for his actions. Being unable to produce his warrant card, he had been forced to tell them that he was now retired. They had warned him to stay out of the case and had taken over. But Nettleton had waited too long to let himself be robbed of the double murderer. He could sit here as long as he pleased, weighing the comings and goings. One of them would lead him to Feeney.

'Dickie isn't here, is he?' were Sonny's first words to his wife on arriving home around a quarter to eleven.

She clasped plump hands and came towards him. 'No – have you seen him? Is he coming?'

'God knows.' He bent to swing Paddy up into his arms and walked across to the window, peering out. 'Apparently he spent the night at Belle's and when she got up this morning she found he'd absconded with her money.'

Josie gasped. 'Isn't he the limit?'

'Not only that,' said Sonny, grim-faced. 'He's taken Fred with him. Belle said he mentioned Leeds so I rushed back here to warn you. There's a police watch on Peasholme; we could be getting one too. Mam's in a hell of a state. I didn't really like to leave her but she was driving me crazy.'

'Knowing him,' pronounced Josie, 'he'll arrive when there's food on the table.'

Sonny shook his head. Kissing his son he put him down. 'No, if he was coming to our house he would have been here by now – he'd set off before Belle got up. I'll bet he's at Nick's, the fool. I'd better whip over there.'

*   *   *

Remarkably, Dick's train journey to Leeds had been uneventful, save for the embarrassing moment when he thought he hadn't enough money for the tickets, and the disapproving look from the ticket clerk for his unshaven appearance. There had been a ninety-minute wait for the train to arrive, for apparently the engine had broken down, but after this things went more smoothly than he could have hoped for. The worst part was the approach to Nick's house which he reached a little after ten, but this too proved to be a needless worry; the gate was unattended by police.

He chose not to ring the bell, but tapped at the door of the drawing room before entering, not wanting to give Win a start in her delicate condition.

'Why, Uncle!' She rose in cumbersome fashion and came to greet him. 'Nick didn't say you were calling.' She was told by Dickie that her husband did not know. 'He'll have a nice surprise when he comes in, then.' This was sheer politeness; Nick would have a fit. She looked at the clock which had just struck the quarter hour. 'Oh! and I'm so pleased about the trial. Dad telephoned Nick at the store yesterday with the good news.'

Dick thanked her warily. 'He didn't mention anything else?'

Win lowered her bulk back into the chair. 'Er . . . no, I don't think so.' She sought his face for further explanation but Dickie leapfrogged the subject, talking for some ten or fifteen minutes about matters irrelevant, before shouting at the boy to stop meddling with ornaments. 'Hope ye don't mind if I brought Freddie to keep me company?'

Win smiled at the boy and said of course she didn't. She had noticed that they were both rather sooty. 'Did you come by car?' Dickie answered that they had travelled by train as the boy hadn't been on one before. 'Well . . . would you care to refresh yourselves?' At Dickie's affirmation, she attempted to rise. 'I'll just ring for the maid, she'll show you up . . .'

'I'll do it.' Dickie motioned for her to sit back and reached for the bell-pull himself.

'Thank you. Did Aunt Dusty not wish to come with you?'

'No, er, she's not feeling so good.'

'Oh, I'm sorry to hear that.' The man's strange behaviour cautioned Win not to probe.

'And how is your own health, Win?' Dickie smiled. ''Tis only from courtesy I ask, I can see from your beautiful complexion that you're thriving.' Win said she was feeling well, but rather uncomfortable. 'Ah well, there'll be joy at the end of it. Er, have ye got today's newspaper, Win?' He looked around.

'I'm sorry, Nick took it to work with him this morning.' Win looked up as the maid came in. 'Ah, just a moment, Jane – Uncle, will you be staying to luncheon?'

'I'd love to if that's not inconvenient.'

'Of course not, we'd love your company.'

'Er, d'ye think Nick'd mind if I borrowed his razor an' stuff? I didn't have time to shave this morning.'

This grew more curious by the second. Win gave a puzzled smile. 'I'm sure he won't. Jane, show Mr Richard up to the master's dressing room, then inform Cook that we have guests – we'll have some coffee too when Mr Richard comes down.'

Dickie was escorted from the room, Fred pattering alongside. The maid smiled down at him and pulled a lolly from her apron pocket; having a sweet tooth herself she always kept a supply here. 'Is it all right if I give the young gentleman this, sir?'

'Listen carefully, Fred. This is probably the only time ye'll be called a gentleman.' Dickie grinned at the maid.

422

'Aye, give it him – it might keep his mouth occupied for a while.' He examined her figure as they strolled up the stairs. 'Jane, is it?'

'Yes, sir.' She handed Fred the lolly which he jammed between his teeth.

'You're anything but plain.'

The maid accepted his flattery without coyness and told him, 'The Master's dressing room is just through here, sir.' She opened the door of a bedroom and led him through to another, smaller room. 'There's the washbasin, and you'll find everything you need.'

Dickie thanked her. 'If I don't find everything I need can I call on you, Jane?'

She looked him up and down and, with a suggestive tilt to her lips, said, 'I'm always willing to help, sir,' then left.

'What d'ye think to that one?' Dickie flung himself on the bed and closed his eyes.

'She's nice,' replied Frederick, cracking off a portion of lolly with his teeth.

'Aye, not bad at all, Fred.' Dickie grinned and without using his hands prised his boots off, letting them clatter over the side of the bed. Fatigued from the early rise and the train journey, he decided to have a nap. This lasted all of five minutes.

'Aw!' Fred's effort had snapped the lolly from its stick and it had fallen to the floor. He looked down on it miserably.

Dickie tutted and opened one eye. 'Ye can't eat it now. Pick it up an' chuck it in this bin here.'

The disappointed child did as he was told, then stood twiddling the naked stick, watching Dickie. Unable to sleep with Fred's eyes boring into him, the man sat up, shucked off his jacket and lit a cigarette which was smoked under the boy's unhappy stare.

When he had finished it he stripped down to his trousers

and went to stand before the mirror. The boy's eyes followed him. Dickie looked at the forlorn expression through the glass. 'I'll buy ye another one later.'

Fred brightened and came to stand at the blue and white wash basin as Dickie filled a shaving mug with hot water and began to lather his cheeks.

'Ye'd better scrape some o' that muck off your face too,' his adoptive father suggested and turned the tap on again.

The boy rolled up his sleeves and dipped his hands into the water, withdrawing them immediately. 'Ow! It's too hot.'

'Needs to be hot for a proper shave.' Dickie was sweeping the borrowed razor around his jaw.

Fred picked up the shaving brush, waited a second for his father to object, then dabbed it experimentally on his cheek. Dickie's eyes smiled amusedly at him through the mirror. Encouraged, Fred worked up a full lather, then exchanged the shaving brush for the lolly stick and, copying Dick's movements, used it to scrape off the foam. His father laughed – then sucked in his breath and swore as blood seeped through the lather. Seizing a flannel, he pressed it to his neck. 'Christ, let's get this blood mopped up quick before your Aunt Erin gets a whiff and comes haring down the Leeds road for my jugular – oy! Put that down.' Fred had sneaked the razor up to his face, but Dickie snatched it away before he had the chance to do any damage. 'Ye'll be slicing your bloody nose off. Gimme a piece o' that tissue paper, there.' He pointed. Fred dripped his way over to the box of toilet tissue and handed it to his father. A piece was torn off and stuck over the nick. 'Come on now, get washed an' let's get some coffee.'

Dickie finished shaving, slapped the flannel around his upper body and towelled himself briskly. Sniffing his own shirt, he removed the collar studs, threw it back on the floor and took one from Nick's wardrobe. With the studs inserted through a clean collar and his jacket in place, he took charge of Fred, slicking his damp hair into place and giving his clothes a brush. Then the two went down.

'Why did you tell me that the man what lives here is your son, and then say he wasn't?' asked Fred. 'Is he or isn't he?'

Dickie laid a hand on top of the boy's head and used it to propel him in the right direction. 'Oh, 'tis a complicated story, Fred. I'll maybe tell it ye some time – only you're not to repeat it to anyone here.'

They had reached the drawing room and went in. Win turned from the window where she had been standing rubbing her back. 'Ah, Uncle! Nick's father's here. He's just gone to put his car into the stable.' She waddled over. 'He seemed inexplicably annoyed when I mentioned that you and Freddie were here.'

'Oh . . .'

Win was watching his reaction closely. 'He said he'd better just go and check outside to see if he'd been followed.'

Dickie looked apologetic. 'I'm sorry I didn't tell ye the main reason for our being here, Win.'

'Well, I hardly thought it was a social visit what with you asking to borrow Nick's razor, but I didn't realise I had a desperado on my hands.' The young woman tried to look severe.

Dickie covered his face. 'Told you everything, did he?'

'After some threatening he deigned to give me the gist of it, yes.'

'I was only trying to spare you, Win.'

'That was Dad's excuse for not telling Nick yesterday.' She glanced at the boy who had been looking from one face to the other. 'Freddie, would you like to go to the kitchen and get some biscuits to keep you going until we eat?' She waited for him to leave before proceeding on the ticklish subject. 'Now, Uncle, would you care to give me the story before Dad gets back?'

Dick barely had time to explain the situation before his irate brother came bursting in. 'What the heck d'you think you're doing getting Nick and Win involved in this!' Sonny flung his checked driving hat on a chair but didn't sit down himself. His face was furious.

'I didn't know where else to go, Son,' replied Dickie lamely.

'You should've come to our house!'

'I thought the police might've been there.'

'I don't suppose it'll be long before they are! They're already on guard at Peasholme.'

'Oh, sod.'

Win looked disapproving. 'Uncle, you're welcome to stay as long as you like but I won't have foul language in my house.'

Coffee arrived but failed to dampen tempers, which were still high when Nick came in at luncheon.

'I didn't know we were expecting luncheon guests.'

'I should expect a few more uninvited guests,' said his father, still fuming. 'Ones in uniform.'

Win frowned at her husband's insouciance. 'You knew, didn't you?'

Nick admitted that his father had told him yesterday. 'We didn't want to worry you.'

'It might have been nice to be prepared,' she objected and asked for the whole story.

'Could we give it you over lunch?' begged Dickie. 'I've only had a bit of bread and cheese this morning.' The food he had taken from Belle had been consumed before nine.

His brother heaved another sound of vexation, but everyone moved into the dining room, Win sending instructions to

426

the kitchen that yet another guest would be requiring lunch and for Frederick to have his meal downstairs.

Nothing of import was said until the soup had been eaten and the main meal served, when Nick took the unusual step of dismissing the maid. 'Now, how long are you going to lodge with us?' he asked his uncle.

Before Dick could answer, Sonny put in, 'I don't think he should stay at all.' He watched his brother stuff his mouth full of roast lamb, peas, potatoes, carrots. 'Apart from anything else you'd be bankrupt after a few days of trying to keep him fed.'

'He might as well stay now he's here,' said Nick, casually slicing his meat. 'Nobody saw him come, did they?'

'That's not the point,' argued Sonny.

Dick had been trying to fathom the deadpan expression; did Nick genuinely not care – after all the efforts by his natural father to provoke him? 'Listen, I can see my being here is gonna cause trouble for everybody,' he pronounced between mouthfuls. 'Soon as I've eaten this me an' Fred'll be on our way.'

'Where to?' demanded his brother and, receiving a shrug, pointed his knife. 'No, well leave the talking to them as talks sense! You had no right to bring your troubles here, especially with Win in her condition.' Contrary to her thoughts, Win said that it was no hardship, and as Uncle had already pointed out, the police would be more likely to visit Roundhay than here. 'I don't doubt they'll be paying you a call sooner or later, Win,' replied her father-in-law. 'I don't know what your parents are going to think of us involving you. I find it highly embarrassing. Anyway,' he turned to Dickie, 'I can't see the point in you coming to Leeds at all – you should be heading back for America.'

'You know why I can't,' said Dickie, munching.

'The children?'

427

'And Mam. I promised her, Son.'

'Why you have to start having a conscience this late in life beats me!' said his brother. 'But if you must, then we have to get this police business sorted out. You can't possibly live like a fugitive indefinitely. A couple of days of being cooped up and you'll be climbing the walls.'

'Ye're not suggesting I give meself up?' When his brother said yes, Dickie laughed. 'No, siree. I've had enough o' courts.'

'You got off once, didn't you? Wouldn't it be better to have it over and done with rather than looking over your shoulder all the time?'

'Over and done with could have a more permanent meaning than the one you have in mind.' Dickie massaged his neck. 'It is murder we're talking about – don't worry, Win, I didn't do it.' He had seen her blench.

'Yes, you haven't told us about that yet,' Sonny reminded him, mopping his lips with a napkin. 'Don't you think you'd better?'

Dickie sighed, wiped his own lips and, as briefly as he could, repeated the story he had given Belle, concluding with, 'And with no witnesses save an old trollop, who'll probably be dead by now I'm kna ... snookered.' Sonny tried to be optimistic, pointing out that there were no witnesses to say he hadn't done it, but there were none to say he had, either. 'I'm not chancing it, Son. Sorry.' Dickie slapped the table with an air of finality. 'But, if ye want me to go I'll go.'

Sonny was exasperated. 'Oh, sit down!'

'If you don't mind,' cut in Win, 'could we continue this over coffee in the drawing room?' She pressed her palms against the dome beneath her ribs and arched in discomfort. Nick asked concernedly if she was all right. 'I will be when I get rid of this lump,' sighed Win.

'My sentiments exactly,' replied Sonny with a look at his brother.

Win laughed and kneaded her aching ribcage. 'Roll on next week.'

'I'm not sure you'll last that long, looking at the size of you,' said Nick.

She censured him, 'You're so indelicate!' and led the way back to the drawing room, where she rang for coffee.

'At least there's one good thing in this,' said Sonny. 'I'll get your portrait finished while you're stuck here. Well, I suppose I'd better go and telephone York to tell them you're still free – and that's another thing: you're in a bad position here with no telephone. None of us can warn you if the police decide to pounce. I'll go after I've finished my coffee. At least Dusty'll be relieved.'

'Relieved?' said Dick. 'She'll kick me inside out.'

'She'll have to fight Belle for the privilege. Not only did you steal Freddie . . .'

'*Steal* him – ye think I want to be lumbered with *him?*'

'Be that as it may, Belle holds you responsible, and not only for that. You stole her money . . .'

'Christ, 'twas only a few bob.'

'. . . but worst of all you've had her evicted!'

'How the devil . . .'

'I didn't stop to find out! But she's there at Peasholme with all her kids and her belongings.' When Dickie groaned and rubbed his face, Sonny added, 'At least we can put one thing right. I'll take Freddie back.'

'I don't want to go back!'

All heads turned. 'Who gave you permission to walk straight in here?' asked Dickie, putting down his cup.

Fred ignored the question and came stamping up to hang on his adoptive father's arm. 'Don't send me back! I want to stay with you.'

'Your Aunt Belle's worried about you, Fred,' explained Sonny.

'You can tell her I'm all right, I'm with me dad.'

'See?' Dickie spread his hands.

'Well . . .' Sonny looked dubious. 'I'd better telephone first and see what Belle says.'

When he returned he was the conveyor of bad news for the boy. 'I'm sorry, but Belle insists I take him back or she'll come over herself. She's livid.'

Dickie turned to the child. 'Well, there y'are, Fred, looks like ye gotta go.'

'Don't let him take me!' pleaded the boy.

Sonny approached with a kind smile. 'It's best if . . .' Fred scrambled onto Dickie's lap, eyes full of panic. Sonny was unaccustomed to playing the role of villain and hated the way Fred was looking at him. 'Oh . . . all right, then.' He retreated to a chair. 'But I don't know what I'm going to say to your Aunt Belle! I'll have to telephone her again.'

'Right, Fred, you can go back downstairs till we send for you.' Dickie was unsuccessful in removing the boy from his lap and had to stand so that Fred slid off. 'Go on!' After much confirmation that he would not be sent back to York, the boy left. 'What're ye going to say to her ladyship, Son?' asked Dickie.

'I think I'm about to save the day,' said Win in a small voice. When the men looked at her she was cradling her abdomen, a fearful smile on her face. 'You were right, Nick, the baby thinks it's waited long enough.' She gave a little laugh at her dumbstruck audience. 'You wanted an excuse for not taking Freddie back, Dad, well you've got one.'

Nick went to her side. 'Come on, I'll help you up to bed.'

She shoved him away. 'Leave me be! I'm not going up yet. It might be hours.'

Nick looked agitated. 'I'd better go over and let your mother and father know.'

'There's bags of time yet, sit down! I've only had three twinges. I'm not having my family hovering round for hours on end waiting for me to produce. I'd feel like a circus act. But I suggest you telephone Belle, Dad, it might take the heat off things. Tell her we're keeping an eye on Freddie and he's perfectly safe.'

Dick tutted at the lack of confidence in his fatherly skills, then asked, 'Did Dusty send any message?'

Sonny shook his head. 'Sorry, Belle monopolized the telephone. I'd better go and call her back. I can speak to Dusty too.' He turned to look at Nick. 'Do you want a lift over to Win's parents?'

'Yes please, and could you take Johnny to your house for the night? He'll be a bit of a nuisance here.' So saying, Nick left with his father.

Dickie looked at the young woman uneasily. What if she should give birth while they were away? 'Er, can I get you anything, Win?'

'No thank you, Uncle.' Win had picked up some knitting. 'It's just a matter of waiting.'

The telephone rang at Peasholme. Dusty, much peeved that Belle had not paid her due consideration before, leapt from her seat and was into the hall before anyone else had the chance. 'Hello!' She pressed the handpiece to her ear and shouted into the box on the wall. 'Sonny, is that you? Look . . . yes, yes!' She couldn't hide her impatience. 'Just put that wretch of mine on, will you! . . . What? Well, where are you telephoning from? . . . and he's still at Nick's? . . . Right, I'm on my way!'

'Dusty, wait! Please . . .' Sonny fought to get his words in: 'I'm not sure that's a good idea, you'll be followed.'

At the silence that ensued, he asked urgently, 'Are you still there?'

'Yes . . . I'm here,' came the dull response. Dusty slumped against the wall.

'Listen, Dick's fine and so is Freddie, that's partly why I'm telephoning. Belle insisted that I bring him home but he refuses to come. Short of violence I can't persuade him to leave Dickie . . . Belle isn't in earshot, is she?'

Dusty did not have to turn; the entire family were gathered in the doorway. 'Yes,' she replied simply.

'Oh . . . well look, can you tell her that we've got a bit of an emergency here. Win's gone into labour and I'm having to do a lot of running around, so I can't see me getting to York with Freddie tonight.'

'I'm sure your mother'll be delighted to hear that.' Dusty turned her head away from the wall to tell the gathering, 'Win's baby's on its way.'

Thomasin and Erin looked highly pleased. Belle was more irritated. 'But what about Freddie?'

'Excuse me a moment, Belle.' Dusty turned back to the telephone. 'Look, Sonny, whatever you do, don't give Dick any money or else he'll skip off again. I want him where I can find him. All right, I'll bring a bag over with some clothes and stuff. Thank you for ringing, Sonny – oh, d'you want to speak to your mother?'

'Yes, I'll have a few words if she's handy.'

Dusty gave the earpiece to her mother-in-law and hovered whilst Thomasin shared a sentence with her son.

'I want a word too,' said Belle.

'Hang on, Sonny, Belle wants a wo . . . oh, sorry.' Thomasin turned to her grand-daughter. 'Too late, the line's broken.'

'He asked me to pass on a message,' said Dusty.

'So what was it?' demanded Belle.

Dusty was cool. 'With Win being about to give birth it's

432

obvious he wants to be around. He said he can't possibly fetch Fred back tonight.'

'Then I'll have to go myself!' Belle swung towards the door.

'For God's sake, anybody would think he was in mortal danger!' shot Dusty, stopping the other's exit. 'Dickie's not going to harm him.'

'Maybe not mortal danger,' snapped Belle. 'But certainly moral!'

Thomasin stepped in. 'Belle, I don't want you going over there upsetting things when Win's having her baby. It'll be a bad enough time for her as it is without having people fighting downstairs. When she's had the baby we'll all go over and see what can be done.'

Dickie had no experience of birth. He had only been fifteen months old when his brother was born. Therefore, he was unprepared for the screams that reverberated around the house.

It had all started fairly smoothly. Win had spent the afternoon in conversation with the men. Towards evening, however, she had decided that the arrival was going to be somewhat quicker than formerly anticipated and had retired to her bed. The midwife had been sent for and had arrived; so too had Win's parents. Her mother was assisting at the birth, while her father sat waiting for the outcome with his son-in-law and Dickie. From necessity, Nick had divulged his lodger's secret – for one thing they could not keep him hidden away and for another there had already been news of the escapade in the local evening paper. His in-laws had been alarmed for their daughter's safety, not to mention their own good name, but Nick had assured them that his uncle had been unjustly labelled and would only be here until he decided the best course of action. Only this, and the fact that he thought highly of his son-in-law, allowed James Cordwell to sit here chatting so leisurely.

It was a warm sunny night and Frederick was out in the garden playing; somehow his presence had been overlooked when plans had been made to distance Johnny from the ordeal. Everyone in here seemed calm – everyone bar Dickie. He got up and began to pace. 'How much longer is it going to be?'

Nick shrugged and took a drag of his cigar. 'Who knows?'

Another scream rent the peace. 'Christ!' Dickie marched over to a cabinet and lifted a decanter. 'D'ye mind?' Nick gave him leave to help himself. 'Can I get anybody else one?' At the nods, Dickie poured three glasses of Scotch and distributed them.

'Not very nice to listen to, is it?' said James Cordwell and looked at the American guest who shook his head, his face pale. 'I still think of her as my little girl. Have you any sons, Richard?'

Dickie glanced at his son but shook his head.

'Like me, only daughters, eh? It was a grand day for me when Win produced young Johnny.'

'I haven't any children at all,' replied Dick.

'Oh, that's a shame,' Cordwell sympathised.

No it isn't, thought Dickie, trying to block his ears to another scream. I'm glad she can't have any. I'd never want Dusty to go through that.

'My uncle's hoping to adopt young Freddie out there,' Nick explained.

Cordwell hoisted his glass. 'Oh well, I wish you every happiness.'

Dickie tossed back his whisky and muttered thanks. The gaps between the agonized wails were becoming shorter. There came yet another. 'Mother o' mercy, what're they doing to the poor girl?'

'Don't worry yourself, Uncle.' Nick sipped his drink in blasé fashion. 'It's quite a normal birth.'

'Normal?! My God . . . I think I'll take a walk round the yard.' Dickie left.

Nick smiled at his father-in-law. 'I thought I was bad enough. You'd think he was the expectant father.'

Even in the two-acre garden Dickie could not escape the sound of Win's birthpangs. Stomach taut, he wandered along the different paths, trying to get as far away as possible from the house. As this cigarette was extinguished another was lighted. He could think only of Dusty screaming that way.

'What's she making all that din for?' Dickie looked around but could see nobody. 'I'm over here.' Frederick waved from his hideout in an untidy corner of the garden. 'I've made a camp.' He crawled out from behind a leaning clump of Golden Rod to join his adoptive father.

Dickie eyed the green bits in the boy's hair and used a hand to brush them out. 'Been spying on me, have ye?'

'What's spying?'

'Watching me when I didn't know you were there, seeing what I did.' He narrowed his eyes against the evening sun and the cigarette smoke, viewing the lanes of delphiniums gone to seed, the petal-strewn earth.

Frederick went back to his original question. 'What's she making all that row for?' Dickie did not respond. The boy's face turned worried. 'I think she's having a tooth pulled. I once heard somebody shout like that and they were having a tooth pulled. It must be a big'n though, she's been shouting for ages . . . he won't come and take mine out, will he?'

'Who?' Dickie seemed confused.

'That dentist fella.'

Dickie looked down at the concerned face and decided to be honest. 'She's not having a tooth out, Fred. She's having a baby.'

435

'Oh.' It was said in wonder. 'But . . . why's she screaming, then? Women like babies, don't they?'

Dickie teased a strand of tobacco from his tongue. 'Aye, but . . . they take a bit o' trouble in getting out.'

'Out o' the bag, you mean?'

'Er . . .' Dickie was about to say yes, when another scream changed his mind. 'No, Fred, out o' the woman's belly.'

'Heck.' This was obviously a great revelation. 'Do they have to cut her open, then?'

'No, it just comes out between her legs, but it takes a lotta work to shove it out an' that's why Win's screaming.'

Frederick picked a ladybird from a leaf and let it run from one grubby finger to another. 'Out of her bum, you mean? Blimey, I wouldn't like a baby coming out o' my bum, would you?'

Dick chuckled. 'I would not . . . but 'tis not exactly her bum, it's just a special place that only women have.'

'Oh . . . well, how does it get there in the first place – the baby, I mean?'

That was predictable. 'The man plants his seed in her special place an' it grows into a baby.'

'But how . . . ?'

Dickie scrabbled for words. 'Look, ye know what your prick is?'

'Yes, I did prick meself with a needle once.'

'No, no! The thing ye keep in your trousers.'

The boy was thoughtful, mentally listing the items in his trouser pocket.

Dickie heaved a sigh. 'Your prick, man – your willie or whatever ye call it.'

'Oh, that!'

'God love us! Yes, that.'

Fred covered a smirk. 'You're rude!'

'It's not rude. It's what ye use to plant babies in women

– but not till you're married, understand? I want no son of mine . . .' Bloody hell, I sound just like my father, thought Dickie. He dropped the cigarette end and mashed it into the crazy paving.

Freddie nodded in pleased manner. 'I never knew that, Dad.' Still thoughtful, he uncrumpled the bag he was holding and dipped into it.

'Well I'm sure glad I can teach ye something. What ye got there?'

'Gums. That nice woman Jane gimme them.'

'Let's see.' Dick snatched the bag.

'Aw, I was saving the black ones till last!' objected Freddie as the sweet disappeared into the man's mouth. 'They're my favourites.'

'Sorry, Fred.' Dick selected another black one. 'I have special dispensation from the Pope to eat all the black 'uns.'

'What's dispensation?'

Dick was quite at home explaining the facts of life, but words were a different matter. 'You're too little to understand.' He purloined the last black gum and handed the bag back.

Fred looked hopefully inside, but was disappointed. However, he had learnt two valuable lessons here: one about babies, the other was not to trust his father. He screwed the bag up. 'She must've had it.'

Dickie stopped chewing. 'What?'

'She must've had the baby, the yelling's stopped.'

Dickie cocked his ear. 'So it has.' He grinned and began to chew again. 'Come on, let's go see what she's had.' Fred was not really interested, but walked back to the house with his father.

'It's another boy,' said James Cordwell cheerfully as they entered. 'Nick's gone up.'

Dickie gave a relieved smile. He was about to suggest a

celebratory drink when Nick returned; he was carrying a bundle.

'Meet James Nicholas, Grandfather.' He placed the bundle in his father-in-law's arms.

James Cordwell beamed down at his namesake who was quite alert. 'Why, thank you for the honour! How's my girl?'

Nick smoothed his blond hair. 'It was a pretty quick exit, I'm afraid. She's just waiting for the doctor to put some stitches in – oh . . . it sounds as though he's started.' The horrible wails had begun again – were even more ghastly to Dickie's ears.

He felt sick, both at the screams and at the fact that the man over there was holding his grandson. It should have been a time of jubilation, but all he could do was watch from the sidelines. Anger flared. 'The bloody butcher! What's he doing to her?'

Cordwell looked up from the wrinkled face of his grandson, amazed that Nick's uncle should be so sensitive. However, at this point Sonny arrived to see how things were progressing.

'Good Lord!' He stared at the new infant. 'That was quick. I only came to see how things were going and report back to your mother. She said she wouldn't bother coming as it'd be ages yet.' He came forward as Cordwell offered him the baby.

Nick explained the noise. 'Win's just having some stitches in.'

'Poor lass.' Sonny cradled the new addition. 'What is it then, boy or girl?'

'A boy,' said Nick. 'James Nicholas.'

His father nodded smilingly. 'He's like you, James; bald as a coot.'

Cordwell laughed, then excused himself to go to the lavatory. Nick wandered over to stand beside his father, both smiling proudly at the newborn.

'I know where babies come from.' Their faces came up to look at Frederick. 'Me dad told me,' said the boy.

'I've warned him not to go abusing his role,' added Dick.

Sonny showed amusement at first, then saw the underlying emotion on his brother's face and understood how he must be feeling. He came over and placed the baby in Dick's arms. 'There you are, cop hold of that.'

Overcome by this act of generosity, Dickie resorted to bluffness. 'God, he's an ugly wee brute.'

His brother laughed and glanced at Nick for reaction, but his son's back was turned.

Dickie poked about among the blankets and examined the baby's hands. 'Christ, look at the length o' these – them's pickpocket's fingers!'

Nick stepped forward. 'I'd better be getting him back upstairs or I'll be in bother.' He scooped the child from Dickie's grasp, leaving the man standing there lamely.

When he returned, Sonny said, 'Well, I'd better go home and tell your mother and telephone your Nan, they'll want to come tomorrow, no doubt.'

'Oh . . . can you possibly put Nan off for a few days?' asked Nick, pulling his earlobe. 'I don't mind, but Win finds her a bit overpowering at times and well, you know what women are like if they think somebody's trying to take over.'

'I know all about it,' said his father. 'I've had it all to face from your mother when the girls were born. Tell Win not to worry, she'll have a few days' leeway before having to face the clan. 'Bye then, I'll see you tomorrow.'

Dick said goodbye, then looked down at the boy who was yawning. 'Looks like this one should be in bed.'

'Ah yes,' said Nick. 'I'll get Jane to take him up.' He pulled the bell-rope. 'I'm sorry I've only got the one bed, Uncle.'

'Ye mean I have to sleep with *him*?' Dickie was aghast.

439

'You might have been lucky enough to furnish your house in one go, but most of us have to do a bit at a time.'

The maid arrived, saying that the doctor was leaving. While her master went off to see the man, Dickie pushed Fred from his seat. 'Come on, Tiny Tim, time for bed.'

Fred, conversant with Dickens' novels, said indignantly, 'Tiny Tim's a cripple.'

'And if you don't go to bed you'll be one too.' Dickie gave him to the care of the maid. He himself remained to chat with the Cordwells and Nick for a while. When Win's parents went home, though, the young man made it clear that he didn't wish to talk any more and Dickie rose. 'Well . . . I suppose I'd better hit the hay.'

'Here, take a lamp.' Nick lifted the fluted globe of a paraffin lamp, lit the wick and handed it over.

Dickie thanked him, then said hesitantly, 'Nick . . . ye won't give me away, will ye?' The young man looked blank. 'To the police. Ye won't tell them where I am?'

With a snort, Nick thrust his hands deep into his pockets. 'And that just about sums up your opinion of me.'

Dickie waved his hand rapidly. 'No, no – I'd understand it if ye felt that way.'

Nick looked tired. 'Some of us have a little more loyalty to our families than others.'

'Sorry . . . but I have caused a lot o' trouble for ye.'

'Would I have said you can stay here if I felt that way?'

'Ye just seem . . . as if it's too much effort to talk to me.'

'It is, but that doesn't mean I'm about to have you arrested. So . . . you can go to sleep and not worry about anything, can't you, Uncle?'

Dickie studied him for a moment, then, holding the lamp before him said goodnight and wound his way up the shadowy staircase.

At the door of his room he turned the lamp down and

crept inside. Undressing, he turned the lamp out altogether and slid into bed beside the boy.

'What time is it?'

Dickie sighed and made himself more comfortable. 'I thought you were asleep! I've been creeping about . . .'

'I stayed awake for you.' When Dickie said how kind this was, Fred asked the time again and was told eleven o'clock. He seemed pleased. 'I have to go to bed at half past seven at home.'

'Well don't think ye'll be stopping up this late every night. 'Tis only because o' the baby.'

There was a thoughtful pause. Then, 'Tell me again how babies get there.'

'If ye've forgotten already I don't give much for your chances o' being a father.' Eyes closed, Dickie gave a briefer version of the facts of life.

After a moment the little voice said, 'You know, I think you must be wrong about the husband putting it there, Dad. You see, our real mam wasn't married, we've never had a father.'

Dickie said that she must have had an admirer, then, but the boy refuted this. 'Ah well, you must've been one o' them miracle babies, Fred.' His bedmate asked for explanation. 'A gift from God – now shut up and get to sleep.'

'Night night, then.'

'Night.'

A pause. 'Dad?'

A heavy sigh. 'What?'

'Will you kiss me?'

'Oh . . . bloody hell!' Dickie turned his head to plant a smacking kiss on the boy's cheek. 'Now go to sleep!'

'Night, night.'

'Night, night!' Dickie gave a violent turn and settled down to sleep . . . then smiled into his pillow as a hand patted his bottom.

19

He wasn't smiling much the next morning when the maid announced that some gentlemen from the police were in the hall. Panic ensued, until Nick took charge, giving Jane instructions and leading his uncle by another door to the dining room. Once this door closed on them, Jane admitted the police, allowing Nick and his uncle to dash out into the hall and up the stairs.

Win was breastfeeding the new baby when her husband and Dickie broke in on her. Fortuitously, the midwife had gone down for her breakfast. 'I'm sorry about this, Win!' Nick lifted the overhanging coverlet for his uncle to crawl underneath the bed. 'If any more strange men barge in on you, just smile and look radiant.'

He dashed off to meet the deputation who informed him they had a warrant to search the house for a wanted man. Coolly, he voiced the opinion that they would find no one but they could search the house if they wished. 'But please show consideration for my wife; she has just given birth to our son and I don't wish her to be upset.'

Having gone through the ground floor rooms the officers duly moved upstairs. Dick lay on the hard linoleum under Win's bed, staring up at the springs, waiting and listening. The door opened. He tensed.

Apologising to Win who had hurriedly covered her breast at their entry, the officers made cursory examination of the room, then left. Dickie breathed again. Win, too, relaxed.

However, when Nick came to say the coast was now clear he informed his uncle that another officer had remained outside in the guise of a roadsweeper. Whether any of them liked it or not Dick was here for a while.

There was little to laugh about, either, when the family came over two days later. A struggle took place as to who would get to him first. Belle was the one to win the honour and by the time her grandmother entered the room, was well and truly into a verbal thrashing. Dusty stood there looking furious, but not as furious as Erin who had only recently been told about Brian catching her brother in Belle's bedroom, so ruining all hopes of a truce.

'Belle, can't it wait!' censured Thomasin. 'At least till we've seen Win – it is her house, you know.'

Belle stopped shouting, but narrowed her eyes at Dickie and told him she hadn't finished with him yet.

He turned penitent eyes to his wife. 'Sorry, Dust . . . have ye brought some things for me?'

She sighed and kissed him, handing over a valise. 'Yes, here's some clothes and your razor and stuff.' Here, Nick muttered thanks; his razor didn't feel the same after his uncle had used it. When Dick asked about finances she told him, 'Sorry, I didn't realise you'd be wanting any . . . I mean you won't be going anywhere with a police guard outside, will you? Here, you can have this loose change to buy cigarettes. Now, where's Freddie?' With sickened features Dickie pocketed the coins and told her the boy was probably in the garden. She said she would go look for him when she came down, but right now she must go and see the new baby. The rest of the family accompanied her, all except Belle who took the opportunity to lay into her uncle again about the boy's kidnap.

443

'Honest, Belle, I never took him,' pleaded Dickie. 'He followed me.'

'And what about my money and my food, did they follow you too?'

'I didn't think you'd mind helping a . . .'

'I *do* mind. I mind being robbed and I mind being called a woman of loose morals by my landlord!'

'Surely that's due to Brian, not me. I only stayed at your house the once. Have ye seen anything of him, by the way?'

'No! And we're talking about you and Freddie.'

'I really can't see what harm it'll do to let him stay here for the time being.'

'Can't you? What happens if the police decide to search again and arrest you? Imagine the impression that would leave on him, especially if you were convicted. I rue the sentimental twaddle that allowed me to even consider you for the adoption, and I detest the idea that it's going to have to be me who dashes their hopes . . . but rather a moment's hurt than a lifetime's.'

'What about my hopes?' demanded her uncle. 'Dusty's hopes.'

Belle was dismissive. 'They're not the same as those of a child. She'll recover after a time, but if Freddie is led on like this it could affect his whole life.'

'And ye think it won't affect Dusty? Christ, Belle, you've seen the way she is with those kids . . . if ye knew what you were doing to her . . . Don't tell her ye've changed your mind, please.' She didn't respond. 'I'd've thought you'd sympathise with her, not having given birth yourself.'

'I'm not sure I understand.'

'Well, isn't that what every woman wants? It must have been a disappointment in your life.'

'God, you men! I'm sorry to disillusion you, Uncle, but

we don't all consider ourselves as brood mares. Personally I can think of nothing more repugnant than carrying another person round inside my body.' She gave a sound of disgust; her uncle had a knack of winnowing people's innermost thoughts. 'Damn! I never even told Brian that. Don't you go repeating it.' She frowned as a piece of paper appeared under the door, and limped over to inspect it. After reading the note her lips tightened and she flung open the door in time to catch Fred pelting up the staircase. 'In here, Frederick – *now*!' With trepidation on his face, the boy came into the room. Belle flourished the letter at him. 'I suppose you are the author of this?' When he didn't answer she upbraided him further. 'Don't you know it's the depth of cowardice to leave a letter of this nature unsigned? And even more cowardly not to own up when confronted. I shall ask you again – did you write it?' Fred nodded, shamefaced. 'Right! Well, it's going to come as a shock to you, Freddie, but I've been called much worse things than bumface. If I say you are going home then you are going home.'

The boy looked hopefully at Dick who looked away. Then he turned back to Belle and said. 'All right, if you say I have to . . . but I hate you.'

Belle opened her mouth to respond, but at that point Thomasin reentered.

'Belle, we could hear you shouting in the bedroom!' she told her grand-daughter. 'Win had the good manners not to mention it but I could see she was upset that you thought chastising your uncle more important than seeing her baby. You'd better go up and show some consideration.'

Belle tutted. 'Right, Frederick, you can come with me. You're not to be trusted.'

Dickie curled his lip in a sneer. 'If you're worried about me kidnapping him, forget it.' He marched out into the garden and lit a cigar.

'I'll keep my eye on him,' Thomasin told Belle who then left. The boy remained standing, head lowered in an attitude of dejection. 'Come and sit by me, Freddie,' said the old woman kindly, holding out her hand. Fred allowed himself to be led to the sofa. 'Your Aunt Belle's only doing it for your own good, you know, love.'

'How can it be for my good when I want to be with me dad?'

'Well . . .' Thomasin looked awkwardly at her son in the garden. 'She just doesn't want you to be hurt.'

Freddie beseeched her. 'But I hurt already. I hurt inside.'

Thomasin gathered up his hand. 'I know . . . but your dad's in a lot of trouble. God forbid, but he might even be put in prison . . . you couldn't be with him then, could you?'

'But I'd go and visit him,' said the boy earnestly.

'It wouldn't be the same as having a father there all the time though, would it?'

'Me mam'd still be there.'

'But that'd just be like living with your Aunt Belle and that was the reason she wanted to find a new home for you in the first place, Freddie, so that you'd have a mother and a father and be a proper family . . . but now things are different.'

'Can't you talk to her?' he begged.

'I don't know that she'd listen to me, Freddie.'

The boy leaned on his knees and looked deeply thoughtful. 'You see, Nan, me dad needs somebody to look after him.' Thomasin smiled at the childish air of wisdom. 'He hasn't got any children, you know. I don't know what he'll do if he can't have me. I mean, you need children to look after you when you get old, don't you?'

Thomasin nodded in concord. 'I'll talk to your Aunt Belle, love, see what I can do. But don't get your hopes up. Now, you sit there while I go and have a word with your dad. Ooh, give us a shove out of this sofa, I'm like an old wreck.' With his help, she managed to rise. 'Don't move one inch or you'll have me shot.' She limped out into the garden and joined Dickie. 'By, that lad of yours he's like a little owd fella.'

Dickie gave a snort. 'Lad of mine? Belle's got other plans for him.'

'He tells me you need looking after.'

'Aye, he could be right.' He turned to his mother. 'How's business?' She said that the adverse publicity of the trial had affected the takings slightly. He commiserated, but said that he had actually meant the situation at Peasholme.

'Oh, it's lovely. I've got a dozen kids running amok, a baby going wah-wah-bloody-wah all night long, a cat ... well, I believe the polite word is defaecating, all over the place – thank God it can't fly – and two coppers watching every time I go to the closet.'

Her son hugged himself and heaved a groan. 'What the hell am I going to do, Mam?'

'Are you a murderer?'

His eyes reproached. 'How can you ask me that?'

'You keep telling me half-stories, I don't know what to believe . . .' Then she patted his arm. 'No, son. You've done some rum things but if I thought you were capable of that, I wouldn't be standing here.' She laughed at herself. 'What am I talking about, of course I would.'

He told her the truth about his past. When he had done, she said, 'Then there's only one thing you can do unless you want to keep running for the rest of your life.'

Dickie shook his head. 'No, I have to get back to America, Mam – yes, I know I promised, but ye wouldn't have me stay here and risk execution would ye?'

'Where's Freddie?'

Dickie and his mother turned at Belle's loud query. Thomasin leaned on her stick and stared into the room. 'He was in there.'

447

'Well, he isn't now!' Belle lurched off, searching the house from top to bottom, but Freddie wasn't in it. 'Freddie!' She cupped her hands and bawled down the garden. 'I know you're out there! You think I'll get fed-up of waiting and go home on my own but I'll wait all night if I have to!'

Her grandmother winced at the noise. 'Belle, do leave off.' She limped inside, where a family conference took place. It was decided that Dickie would stay here for a week – hopefully less if the police grew tired of waiting. Dusty would go back to Peasholme, for the 'roadsweeper' had probably counted them as they went in: if Dickie's wife didn't come out the man would twig he was here.

'I'll have to cancel the holiday,' sighed Sonny. I can't go to Ireland and leave you to cope, Mam.'

'It'll do no good depriving your family of their holiday,' said Thomasin. 'You don't go until the third of August, it could all have died down by then. Josie deserves a rest after what she's been through – you both do.' She turned to Dickie. 'And listen, I'm trusting you not to try sneaking past that policeman on the gate. You stay in the house till we tell you different. Belle, it doesn't look as if that lad is going to come out of hiding and we can't stop much longer. Leave him here, he'll come to no harm.'

Reluctantly, Belle gave way but with bad grace. Still in poor humour she made ready to depart. 'Right, does anybody want to go to the lavatory before we leave?' Realising what she had said, she was forced to relax her cross features. 'Sorry, I'm so used to talking to children.'

'I do want to go as a matter of fact,' laughed her grandmother. 'You lot can wait in the car and give these two a few minutes on their own. Goodbye, love. See you soon.' She kissed Dickie and led the exodus.

After much tearful leave-taking Dusty joined them outside.

Dickie watched the car disappear down the lane. When he looked round Fred was standing there smiling at him.

Before the weekend was over everyone, including Dickie, was realising what a mistake it had been to think he could hide here. Sonny had paid regular visits in order to relieve the pressure on his son – he knew what a bored Dickie could be like – but as his intervention meant Dickie having to pose for the portrait, this hardly eased the monotony. Only Freddie seemed content with the situation.

'It's nice this, isn't it?' he confided while the two of them sat waiting for Nick who was working late at the store. 'Just us two men.'

'I can't think of anywhere I'd rather be,' answered Dick with glum features, wondering what his wife was doing. His mind roved to female company of any sort, in particular the maid, Jane. Mentally, he stripped and fondled her . . .

'I wonder how me cat's getting on.'

Dick was annoyed at having his concentration broken. 'I was just getting to the best part then.' The boy asked what he meant. 'Never mind, just go fetch the bloody cards.'

'Can we have a game of chess instead?'

Dickie said he did not know how to play, to which Fred answered that he would teach him. They positioned themselves, one on either side of Nick's burr-walnut gamestable, but hardly had the pieces been set out than Dickie announced it was too boring and told the boy he preferred cards. He lost every game; not through chivalry, but because his mind dwelled on other things. When he chased Fred off to bed he had decided that he was not going to spend another celibate night.

Alas, the boy did not conform to his plan. 'Bloody hell, are you awake again!' exclaimed Dickie two hours later at the pair of brown eyes that peeked over the bedclothes. Fred said he got lonely on his own. 'Well I'm here now, so just shut your eyes.' Dickie stripped off and climbed into bed. He lay there for twenty minutes or so until he guessed that the boy must be unconscious, then slipped out of bed.

'Where you going, Dad?'

Dick sagged. 'I'm just going to get a drink of water.'

'Will you fetch me one?'

With great deliberation, Dickie strode over to a table, lifted a jug and poured some water in a glass. 'Here, get that down ye then get to sleep.' Fred put the glass to his lips, then handed it back, saying that his father could have one first. 'Freddie, I'm gonna get mad in a minute – just get it down ye!'

Freddie did so, then handed the glass back. Dick replaced it on the table, ripped off his trousers and got back into bed. After another half an hour he felt sure that Fred was asleep and when no voice interrupted his exit this time he heaved a sigh of relief and stepped onto the landing.

The maid's room was in the roof at the top of a short flight of stairs. Her fascination for the handsome man had doubled since she had discovered he was a fugitive and she had made it very plain he would be welcome here. Dickie entered as quietly as he could. She was all warm and sticky from sleep as he groped under the covers and let himself in, stifling her cry with his hand. When he realised who it was, she wrapped her arms round his neck and Dickie ran his hands under the nightgown. The folds of her breasts were damp with perspiration. He massaged her body hungrily, sinking his face into her neck and breasts . . . when from the corner of his eye he saw a small figure standing beside the bed. 'What the f . . . ?' Jane let out a little shriek.

'I was lonely,' announced Fred.

Dick let his head sag to the maid's bosom, whilst she tried frantically to push him off.

'What're you in her bed for? Don't you like sleeping with me?'

Dickie lifted his face again. 'Look, Fred, I'll be back in a minute.'

'No sir, you'll have to go with him!' pleaded Jane. 'The mistress'll hear us talking and I'll get the sack.' When Dickie whispered in her ear that he would take the boy back to bed and see her in a moment, she beseeched him, 'No, sir, better not. It's late and I might oversleep tomorrow.'

With disgruntled face, Dickie got out of bed and grabbed the boy by the neck. Back in their room he growled his anger and told Freddie that if there was a recurrence then he would be sent back to York immediately.

The next night he waited for Freddie to go to sleep, then sneaked along to the maid's room. He was nearly to the door when he saw that someone else had beaten him to it.

Nick almost jumped out of his skin before realising that his uncle had been up to the same purpose. He gave a smile of one caught in the act and made signals to suggest that they both go down for a drink instead. In the drawing room he poured two whiskies, handed one to his uncle and went to sit by the fire. 'Sorry for spoiling it for you, Uncle.'

'Likewise.' Dickie took a seat nearby and sipped his drink. 'Though for the life of me I can't think why ye want to be sniffing round her with a nice little wife like you've got.'

'I could throw that one at you,' retorted Nick. 'In my case, Win's not long given birth if you'd forgotten.'

'Oh aye.' Dick scratched his head. 'I'm a bit ignorant in that area. Must be hard.'

'It was till you disturbed me,' quipped Nick. His uncle said it shouldn't be long before Win was back on form. 'It'll be a while before I am.' Nick looked sheepish. 'I just can't stand the stink of milk, even the thought of it makes me go soft. I was like it all the time she was feeding Johnny.

451

Thank the Lord she could only manage it for a couple of months.'

'So her upstairs, she sees you're all right, does she?'

'Win doesn't allow her to have followers. Someone has to keep her happy – but we could come to some arrangement.'

'Ah, no, I don't want to tread on your toes. I'll stick with Freddie – though I'm not used to having such an intellectual bedfellow. Ye've never heard the likes of him. Tonight he wanted to know what God was doing before He made me.'

'You'd tell him God was making the cockroaches and forgot to wash out the mould, then.'

'Eh, that's nasty. Just 'cause I spoilt your bit of humpy. Go on up, if ye want. I won't rat on ye.'

'No, I've left it a bit late now; she's up at six.' Nick filled his cheeks with whisky and poured another. 'James wouldn't't've been so generous tonight if he'd known what I was up to. He was so flattered that we'd named the baby after him, he's finally agreed to hand over his business to me and retire. His shoe shop is the first round the corner from us in Boar Lane. I've been trying to persuade him for ages to come in with us and let me knock the wall through into Briggate and make it part of the store but I think he thought we'd swamp him. Anyway, this is an even better coup. I'm hoping Nan will be impressed; though I don't hold out much hope.'

'You mean because of me? I don't want your business, son.'

'No, I meant she doesn't seem impressed at anything to do with the business these days. Quite frankly, I think she's going batty. D'you know she's hired a private detective to find some bloke, George Ackworth, who she sacked twenty-odd years ago, because she feels guilty. God knows what she's going to reward him with when she finds him – probably my Chairmanship.' He glanced at Dick. 'Still, I'm glad to hear you've given up your claim to it.'

Dickie sighed. 'I never had any intention of taking it, son. It doesn't interest me at all. I was only keeping you on tenterhooks 'cause ... well, maybe Francis was right about me. Maybe there was a bit o' spite in it. I don't know why. I could hardly expect ye to like me after I abandoned ye. But I'm proud o' what you've done and I'm glad ye've made an honest living – which is more than ye would've done had I married your mother.' He smiled and pointed his cigar. 'Tell ye what, we've both had a rough time of it lately; let's risk a night out tomorrow and celebrate your good news.'

Nick pondered the situation for a moment. 'Who's going to pay?'

'Ah ...'

Nick uttered a genuine laugh. 'All right, my treat.'

When Sonny came round the next evening he was horrified to be told that his son and Dickie were going out as soon as it grew dark. 'Out where?'

'On the town to get us some women,' grinned Dickie. His brother told him he was mad. 'There's no risk. We're going to bring your car right up to the back door and smuggle me out in it – come with us, it'll be great.'

'I can't!' returned Sonny. 'Josie's expecting me back for ten.' His brother said they could call on the way out and tell her. 'Oh yes, and what am I going to say? Shan't be in for a while, I'm just going to look for a bit of stuff. Nick, what were you thinking of, letting him talk you into this?' He sighed and sat down next to them on the sofa, muttering about their stupidity.

It was quiet for a time, then Dickie's body started to shake in silent laughter. He gave a sideways glance at Nick, who laughed too though he didn't really know what at until his uncle pointed to each of them in turn, blurting, 'Nick, Dick and ... Prick.' He shook with amusement.

'I'm trying to keep you out of trouble!' exploded Sonny.

'Look, Son, we're going,' came Dickie's flat answer. 'Come with us if ye like, but don't ask me to stop in this bloody house one night longer without female company.'

'For God's sake can't you even last a week without it?' demanded his brother. 'And you've no money!'

'Nick's paying.'

'I'm ashamed of you,' Sonny told Nick. 'Your aunt specifically told us not to give him any mon . . .'

'Oh, did she?' Dick looked tough. 'Wait till I see her.' He went to the window and peered round the curtain at the detective in mufti who was still busy with his brush. 'That bloody road's so clean you could roll pastry on it. Go sprinkle a few cig ends round, Nick, give the poor bugger summat to sweep.'

On his way back to the sofa he collected the deck of cards and for the next hour proceeded to win himself a few shillings. With each new hand that was dealt, Sonny continued his attempts to talk his brother out of the madcap scheme, to no effect. Came ten o' clock, Nick went upstairs to kiss his wife and tell her he was turning in for the night. 'Check on the lad for me, will ye?' asked Dickie, tucking the cards back into their box. 'And fetch my black shoes from under the bed.'

In the young man's absence, Sonny hissed, 'I could kill you for enticing him into this, Dick.'

'Me enticing *him*?' Dickie sounded amazed. 'Listen . . .' He was about to tell his brother about last night's incident with the maid, but decided not to break Nick's confidence. 'Ah, never mind. Go home to your bed, Son. The less you know the better.'

'I'm not bloody leaving you to get my son into trouble. I'm coming with you.'

Dickie laughed. 'Why, you horny old bugger, you were

coming all along, that's just an excuse to give Josie. Ah thanks, Nick!' The shoes had arrived. Swinging his slippered feet to the carpet, Dick asked if the boy was asleep. Nick told him that all was quiet and handed him the shoes. Dickie shoved his feet into them and tugged at the laces . . . and tugged . . . and tugged. Instead of tightening, they stretched to almost a foot long. Dickie started to laugh. 'The buggeroo, he's swopped my shoelaces for liquorice ones!'

Sonny had to laugh at Freddie's joke while his brother went off to find more laces. But when his son asked him to bring the car round to the back door, hilarity ceased.

'Right, where do we start!' Dick clapped his hands and rubbed them in glee. Spotting a group of not bad-looking girls, he stuck his fingers in his lips and emitted a shrill whistle. As the group approached, Sonny made a last ditch attempt to stop this. They had parked the car elsewhere and walked to this notorious soliciting ground, with Sonny looking over his shoulder at every step of the way.

'Look, you're going to land us in trouble, there's a man with them.'

Dickie ignored him and stepped forward to greet the females, putting his arm around one to show he had made his choice. 'Good evening,' he said congenially to the pimp and raised his hat. 'My colleagues and I are from the Society for Friendless Girls. Is there some wee charitable act we can perform for three of your ladies during the next hour?'

Sonny panicked. 'Eh no, Dick, not for me!' but one of the women was already clamped firmly on his arm. He threw a helpless look at Nick who was similarly encumbered. 'What do we do?'

'Just copy what I do, Son,' grinned Dickie, making the girls laugh.

Sonny was exasperated. 'I didn't mean – look, Dick, I can't be seen with this.'

'Eh, I do have a name, y'know!' objected the prostitute.

'I'm sorry, I didn't mean to offend but I'm a happily married man and so is my son here. We don't have to resort to this.' He saw the lust in Nick's eye and hissed a warning. Nick shrugged.

'Good evening, Mr Feeney, sir.'

Sonny turned to the speaker in horror – it was Kelly, the overseer at his mill. He performed a stumbling greeting and Kelly walked on, but not before his sly grin had made it obvious what he thought. 'Now look what you've done!' he raged at Dickie and finally succeeded in removing himself from the woman's grasp. 'You've humiliated me in front of one of my workers. It'll be all over the mill tomorrow – oh shi ... Dickie, d'you realise he could tell the police your whereabouts?'

'Then threaten to fire him,' suggested Dick casually, and tightened his hold on the girl. 'Now then, my petal, where can we go for our romp?' She led the way with Sonny complaining bitterly behind. Once in the seedy hotel, Dickie leaned on the reception desk. 'Three rooms, if you please, my good man.'

'Count me out!' barked Sonny and disengaged himself from the pack. 'You can meet me back at the car when you've finished betraying your wives!' He marched off, leaving the woman to crab about the loss of custom.

Nick exchanged looks with his uncle, then turned back to the man at the desk. 'Two rooms.'

Dickie looked at the spare woman and held out his hand to her. 'Ah well, Christmas comes but once a year – as Mrs Christmas said.'

The next morning, Sonny alerted his ears for any mention of his brother on the factory floor, but judging by the smirks

456

on his workers' faces, Kelly appeared to have been too busy laughing over catching his employer with the prostitute to notice the fugitive with him. That evening, having suffered a day of acute embarrassment, Sonny lectured Nick about the debauchery of the night before, saying that if he wanted to cheat on Win then that was his private affair but he must not fund any more nights out for Dickie. Nick felt guilty enough about Win already and so agreed without persuasion. However much Dickie cajoled and pleaded he refused to hand over money, saying he could not afford it, leaving Sonny able to embark on holiday a little easier in mind.

With the police still stationed outside the house and no car to get him into town, Dickie took to lying in bed late on a morning, whilst Frederick roamed the house at will. On Bank Holiday Monday he rose at eleven and looked out of the window to see that the police guard had gone. Delighted, he went down to tell the others but was informed rather sullenly by Fred that the family would be out for the day. Dickie tutted and picked up a newspaper which told that with no sightings of the wanted double murderer police were assuming that he had fled the country. 'Hah! So that's why they've taken the watch off.' He put the paper aside and looked business-like. 'Well, I should get in touch with Dusty and make some arrangements, I suppose. Where's Nick gone – did he say?'

'The seaside,' mumbled Fred. 'He said he couldn't take me.'

Dickie looked interested and rubbed his chin for a moment. After a brief sortie to the kitchen he was back, wearing a straw hat. 'Come on, Fred, we're off to Scarborough!'

With little money at his disposal he entertained the idea of rifling through his host's cupboards, but for once conscience prevailed. Besides, he had come up with a better form of transport than the train. Sonny had ferried all his household staff with him to Ireland but he had not taken the car. He

457

had also left his son a spare set of house keys. After pelting down the drive and making sure that they were not under surveillance, the pair went over to Sonny's house, where Dick lifted one of the pictures from a wall, silencing Freddie's accusation of theft with the retort that his brother had told him he could have one. He carried it out to the rickety stable wherein lay the car. Then, with the picture on the back seat they drove to Scarborough.

Dick answered his son's worry that they might be caught, by saying that amongst the Bank Holiday crowds they would be anonymous, and this turned out to be so. Parking the car in town, they took one of the cliff railways down to the seafront and first visited the gentlemen's washroom to remove the grime thrown up by the car wheels. Outside again, the smell of carbolic and urine was whisked away on the breeze, replaced by a more mouthwatering variety. Dick passed the boy a half-crown and told him to go buy them both something to eat. 'I'll just stand in the sun and take the sea air.' He put a cigarette to his lips, found that the emery on his matchbox was ripped and instead struck a match on a shop front. Exhaling a cloud of smoke, he glanced idly at the trippers promenading . . . amongst them a police officer who was heading straight towards him.

Frantic, he looked round for the boy but Fred was still in the shop. There was the urge to run – once free of his pursuer he could always double back for Fred. But the boy would be frightened if he came out and found himself deserted. He made the hardest decision of his life and remained where he was, waiting for the officer to reach him.

The young constable clasped his hands behind his back and aimed a supercilious eye at Dickie. 'Do you know it's an offence to strike a match on a shop front, sir?'

Dickie's lips parted in surprise. 'No . . . no, I was unaware of that, officer. Ye see, the sandpaper on my box was all scuffed . . . Sorry.' He found it hard to keep his face straight.

'There'll be no charge this time, sir – but I suggest you buy a new box of matches.' The constable was about to turn away when Fred, having come out of the shop and read the situation, came crashing into him, wrapping his arms tightly round the officer's legs. 'Run, Dad!'

The constable tottered under the onslaught and Dick put out a steadying arm before wrenching the boy free. 'Freddie, look where you're going! Ye'll be causing an accident. Off ye go to the beach and I'll be along in a minute.' Shoving Fred at the kerb, he said, deeply apologetic, 'I'm dreadfully sorry, Constable! As ye can see I have my hands full with the boy.'

Adjusting his helmet, the officer gave him a sour look and walked away. Dickie headed purposefully across the road.

'I thought he was arresting you!' Fred could not understand the man's wrath.

Dickie glared down at the earnest face, and after a moment's thought, relented. 'Well . . . I suppose it did look that way. Thanks, Fred.' The boy asked what happened and his father laughingly told him. 'Now, where's that food? I'm starving.'

Fred dipped into his pockets and brought out two bags of sherbet. Dickie almost collapsed. 'I meant get something substantial! Christ, I've only a couple o' bob left till I sell the picture . . . Oh, come on, we'll go get a proper meal.'

When they came out of the café it was high tide, forcing the hordes of day trippers onto a strip of dry sand close to the railings. Fred wanted to go and build sandcastles but Dickie said he didn't intend to be crushed to death and instead they strolled along the Foreshore Road where lines of horses and

459

donkeys hung their heads in the sweltering heat, swishing their tails against the attack of flies. Constantly dodging the army of parasols that posed a threat to ear and eye, Dick led his son around the bay to the gribbled walls of the harbour where the stench of sun-baked fish soon drove them back the way they had come and up a cobbled incline to the town. Fred used the man's jacket to haul himself up, whining that Scarborough was all steps and slopes.

'I thought I was supposed to be the old fella,' said Dickie when they reached the top. 'Look at ye, Puffing Billy.'

But the sight of a toyshop on Eastborough had a miraculous cure on Freddie's lungs. Eyes filled with awe, he dragged his father inside. After picking up several items he pounced on a game and asked, 'Will you buy this for my birthday, Dad?' Dickie asked how much it was. 'It's seven and six – look, it's got a real electric buzzer in it.'

'Seven and six? Forget it. I can stick a wasp in a matchbox for nothing and ye've got your buzzer. Besides, ye've been reckoning on having that many birthdays ye must be about fifty-six by now – too old for games.' He took the box off Fred and after putting it back on the shelf, hustled him from the shop.

Outside, he gave a furtive glance to see if the shopkeeper was looking, then picked up a bucket and spade from the selection on display. 'Here, Happy Birthday.'

'You have to pay for them,' the boy instructed. When this was met with impiety, he used Dickie's own words to remind him, 'Do you want to add theft to the bloody charges?'

Grinning, Dickie handed over a shilling. 'Okay, Conscience, go pay for it – but that's the last time you swear at me, ye hear?'

At Fred's request they re-took the cliff lift to the seafront, and spent a good hour in an underground grotto crammed with vulgar amusements. Fred spotted some coconuts on

460

a shooting gallery and saying that he had always wanted one, begged his father to win one for him. When this was accomplished, Dickie said they needed a stone from the beach to smash it open.

'I don't want to *eat* it,' said a horrified Freddie. 'I want it to keep and look at.'

'God, you're the queerest bugger unhung,' sighed his father.

When the tide ebbed the rest of the afternoon was devoted to donkey rides, paddling, stuffing down platefuls of cockles, watching the women bathers, their wet cotton suits adhering to every contour of their bodies, and small girls in great florid hats, pinafores tucked down bloomers. At the end of the day when the tired mokes were led back to their pasture and the sunburnt crowds made their exodus to the station, neither the man nor the boy felt inclined to join them. With one of the last coins left in his pocket, Dickie suggested they take refreshment and made for the nearest public house where he ordered two pints of beer and two meat pies. The landlord indicated the top of the boy's head, the only part showing above the counter. 'How old is he, then?'

'Fifty-six – he's a dwarf.' Dickie led the boy over to a quiet corner where the pies were consumed. Fred only had a sip of his beer and said he didn't like it. 'Get it down ye,' said his father. 'It adds lustre to your cluster.'

'What's a cluster?'

'Never mind, I'll sup it.' Scarborough was like a different town without its crowds. The evening sun shone down on a beach deserted but for a row of bathing machines, a ton of waste paper and a trail of donkey droppings. Dickie looked back on the afternoon with pleasure and felt as young as his companion. Enthused, he told Fred, 'Let's make a camp, spend the evening under the stars. Come on, we'll get the car and go along the coast a few miles, we're easy prey now

461

the crowds have gone.' So hand in hand they walked, skipped and ran to the place where they had left the car and drove some six miles south, until Fred espied a wondrous bay where the sea glimmered sapphire and turquoise in the last rays of the sun.

Pulling the car off the road, they embarked on a somewhat treacherous path down to the bay, deserted of all other beings. Here, between the limpet-encrusted rocks the sand was firm and clean, sweeping round into a wooded headland. Once more, they threw off shoes and stockings, Freddie laughing at his father's chalk-white legs as they answered the call of the sea. The last hour before dark was given to dallying in the gentle swell of the waves, tottering over banks of shingle, exploring rockpools with their bright green weed and strands of bladder-wrack, tiny darting fish that tickled the feet, until the sun sank into the ocean and Fred complained of being cold. Dick picked up his gritty blazer and laid it around the juddering shoulders. With Fred riding piggyback, he clambered up the high bank of red clay to search for a bivouac.

Once over the top of the incline the land dipped. In this tree-lined hollow they made camp. Dickie ordered his son to look for anything that might come in useful to them. Knowing his father's unpredictability, the boy was rather hesitant in showing his find – a coil of wire, some paper and a tin can – but the man seemed pleased enough. Dickie then built a fire, saying that they would have to break into the coconut to stem their hunger. Alarmed, the boy said, 'I'll get you some bread and cheese!' and ran over to a bush, presenting Dickie with a handful of hawthorn leaves. At the man's look of disdain, Fred insisted that he eat them, then sat on his coconut in a manner of protection.

Before retiring, they wandered up to the top of the slope to take a last look at the sea. Their legs swished through the knee high grass, disturbing a squadron of tiny purple moths. Fred blinked tired eyes and stared out over the glittering ocean. 'It'd be nice if we were all together, wouldn't it?'

Dick thought of his wife and the girls. 'It would that.'

'I wonder if God'll help us?'

'Don't ask me about God, I've never understood Her – well, it has to be a woman, doesn't it? A man would never have all those sneaky tricks up his sleeve.'

The boy looked wistful. 'Sometimes, I wish I was somebody else.' He tilted his face up at Dickie. 'Have you ever looked at another person and wondered what it feels like to be them, and sort of made your mind go into their body?'

'No, I sure haven't. It's hard enough being me without taking on some bugger else's worries.' After a period of thought, he asked, 'How would ye like to spend a week here, Fred?'

'I'd like to spend forever here.'

'Ah, well now, there's some places in America like this, ye know,' replied Dick cheerfully.

'But when are we going to get there?'

Dickie was pensive again. 'I don't know, Fred . . . But be sure we will.' He shivered. 'Jeez, I should be tucked up in bed now with a hot maid – water bottle!' He laughed at the intentional slip, then spotted some rabbit droppings. 'Come on, I'll teach ye something ye don't know.' Choosing a place away from the camp, he laid two snares, using the coil of wire that the boy had found. After which, with Fred almost asleep on his feet, they settled down by the fire.

In the morning, Dickie was the first to wake. One of his legs had gone dead. Raising himself onto an elbow, he saw that Frederick was the cause; curled up like an ammonite, his head was pillowed on the man's thigh. Dick stared down at the sleeping face and the happiness of the previous day flooded back. He grinned to himself and, dipping a finger into the cold ashes of the fire, ever so gently drew a moustache on Fred's upper lip. At the finished result the grin bloomed into laughter. His body vibrated, waking the boy. After a moment's confusion, Fred rubbed his eyes, yawned and smiled. His father blurted another laugh, causing Fred to grumble, 'What's funny?'

Dickie took out his cigarette case, flipped it open and showed Fred his reflection in the mirrored interior. Fred scowled, making his father laugh aloud. 'I thought we needed some disguise, Fred! Ah, come on, don't sulk, I'll let ye give me one.' He sat patiently while his son drew a moustache on him. After which there was a boyish enactment of cops and robbers, then Dickie lit another fire and advocated a dip in the sea before breakfast.

The sky and sun were bright but from the temperature of the water it could have been winter. They scampered, blue and shivering, back up the beach. With no towel to dry them, their clothes were difficult to pull on, rasping uncomfortably around their sand-coated limbs. On the way to check the snares Dick remembered that yesterday they had passed a field of cows, and scrambled to the very top of the cliff to find them. Cornering one of the animals, he used the tin can for a pail and managed to syphon enough milk for breakfast. After a quick gulp each, they proceeded to the snares.

'Ooh, you've got one!' Fred jumped up and down excitedly as the terrified rabbit, caught by its middle, waited in mute acceptance of its fate. 'You are a clever dad.' He squatted and watched with interest while his father handed him the can of milk, disentangled the snare and held the rabbit by its ears and hind legs. 'You're not meant to hold it like that, though; you'll hurt it. Can I have it?'

Dickie rubbed his mouth. 'Look, we need some meat, son.'

Fred suddenly grasped the meaning of all this, and asked in a small voice, 'You're not going to kill it, are you?'

'Well, its a bit injured where the wire's cut in . . .' Dickie looked into the horror-stricken face and donned a look of indignation. 'No, of course I'm not gonna kill it! Here, you have it then. Put your can down.'

He handed the struggling creature to Fred who, finding it hard to handle, put it on the ground where it immediately ran away. Fred watched its white rump disappear into the undergrowth. 'Never mind. It's better to let things go free, isn't it, Dad?'

In that one instant, the boy reminded Dickie of his brother as a child. He smiled his affection. 'Tell ye what, Fred, I'll go to the butcher's and get some proper meat. You see if ye can find any mushrooms while I'm gone – but don't go picking any toadies.'

'Er . . . I need some toilet paper.'

'What would I be doing carrying bumf round with me? Ye'll have to use dockleaves.' When they parted company Dickie went to check on the other snare which had been more efficient and strangled the rabbit. Whipping out his pocket-knife, he skinned and gutted it, then cut it up into un-rabbit-like pieces, wiped his bloody hands on the grass and took it back to the camp.

'What's that?' asked Fred suspiciously.

'It's butcher's meat,' Dick impaled the pieces on a stick and laid them over the fire to cook. The mushrooms were cooked in the milk that remained in the can, and the unusual breakfast was pronounced a great success.

'Ye know what I'm going to do today, Fred?' Dickie wiped his greasy mouth on a handkerchief. 'I'm going to send your mam a postcard and ask her to fetch the girls over here for a week.'

'Ooh, that'll be lovely! They'll like our camp, won't they?'

'Ah well, it was fun but I think one night is enough for me, Fred. Your Nan has this house in Scarborough, we'll go back there and see if there's anybody in it. Then I'll have a go at selling that picture.' He got to his feet.

Freddie had been watching a swift skimming low over the grass. As he rose with his father, he asked, 'What's that bird called?'

'No good asking me, I don't know a wren from a turkey. We should have your Uncle Sonny here, he'd tell ye.'

'I know already,' said the boy. 'It's a swift.'

'Then what did ye ask for?'

'I wanted to know if you knew.' He retrieved his coconut from its hiding place.

Dickie made a face. 'Away now, let's sort you out.'

Tidying themselves up as best they could they drove back along the cliff top. It was still fairly early when they arrived, which was lucky as the car ran out of petrol and they had to leave it parked rather conspicuously. The picture under his arm, Dickie kept his eyes open for police whilst proceeding on foot to Thomasin's house. This was on the Esplanade, among a row of tall and elegant white buildings that looked out to sea. Though it was used by employees, its size and placement were not really for their benefit, in fact they were only permitted to use three of the rooms, the rest being restricted to the family's comforts. Fred scaled the flight of steps to the front door and rapped several times. Dickie shushed him and looked round to see if anyone had heard, but there were no cries save those of seagulls. Leaning over to peer down into the basement window, Dick spied a flowerpot on a ledge and guessed, rightly, that it concealed the key.

Once inside he took a nap on one of the beds then later he and Fred had a proper wash and brush-up. With no servant to clean their dusty boots Dickie employed a corner of the bedcovers, and went out to find a buyer for the oil-painting.

The dealer offered him two pounds. Dickie gave a derisive laugh and tapped the painting, telling the man to take another look at the signature. The other peered more closely, then reiterated his offer. Cursing him as stupid, Dickie asked what sort of art expert did not recognise a work by John Feeney when he saw one; the painting was worth at least fifty times that amount. To his acute mortification, the dealer then maliciously informed him that this would be true were the painting a genuine Feeney but unfortunately, the signature was not authentic. This had been done by an amateur. Dick took a closer look and saw that the initial was not *J* but *N*; of all the paintings in his brother's house he had to choose one of Nick's! Refusing the pittance, he tucked the frame under his arm and left. Maybe there was some way he could alter the initial if he got truly desperate for money. Until then, he was damned if he would insult his family's talents by accepting a measly two pounds. With the small amount left in his pocket, he purchased two postcards: one was sent to Nick to explain their absence; the other to Dusty, summoning help.

20

When Nick returned on Monday evening to find the fugitives departed and the keys to his father's house gone with them, he went immediately to check on Sonny's house, then telephoned Peasholme. Naturally, all were concerned, but Nick soothed them by saying that there had been no police visit and the guard had been removed.

Thomasin told him that they no longer had a sentry, either. What she was not aware of was that Nettleton continued to watch the family's comings and goings from his room at The Black Swan. He had also ambushed their postman each morning before he delivered the mail, looking for any clue in the postmarks. Today a different man was on. Nettleton whistled, indicated for him to stay where he was and went down to meet him. This one was less cooperative than the other, saying that he could not hand the mail to anyone but the addressee; however, on receipt of half a crown he allowed Nettleton to shuffle through it. Aside from the letters there was a postcard franked in Scarborough. Nettleton dwelled over it for a second or two before handing the whole lot back and disappearing into the inn.

The postman, Joseph Kettley, went on his way. Before he could post the letters, however, the door was opened and a young woman came out. Joe saw first that she was exceptionally pretty, then that she had some disability. She was surrounded by a bunch of children, some of whom came running up to Joe, who greeted them cheerily.

Belle waited for him and accepted the letters. She thanked him but did not smile. Joe, wanting to stand and look at her, said, 'It's a lovely morning.' Belle continued to flick through the mail and made affirmation without looking up. 'A nice day for an outing. You their governess, then?'

Belle raised cold eyes at the impudence and was about to offer rudeness when she noticed the way he was looking at her, and also that he was quite attractive. 'No, I'm their foster mother.'

'Oh, I beg your pardon, ma'am.' Joe's eyes dropped automatically to her hand, but saw that she wore no ring.

Belle was about to excuse him, when she came across the postcard, flipped it over and saw, *To Dusty and the girls, having a lovely time, wish you were here but you'd need plenty of money and a change of clothes.* Her face darkened. She turned back to the house.

Joe wondered whether to tell her about the man who had intercepted her mail, but while he was still in the process of deciding, she had called to the children and ushered them into the house. He went back down the drive, hoping that she would be there tomorrow.

Belle threw the rest of the letters down and tore into the drawing room brandishing the postcard. 'He's in Scarborough!'

Dusty snatched the postcard and after reading it, declared, 'I'll have to go.'

'You're not taking the girls.' For once, Belle had lacked the courage of her convictions. She knew that the right thing to do was to tell the girls that the adoption could not possibly go ahead . . . but she hadn't. Neither had she told her aunt and Dusty had been too afraid to ask.

'What d'you think we're going to do?' snapped her aunt. 'Catch a fishing boat to America?'

'He must be at my house,' decided Thomasin, pushing herself out of the chair and limping over to a bureau. 'He's got no money to go anywhere else. I hope to God there's none of my employees there.' Searching through her papers she unearthed the private detective's report about George Ackworth the employee whom she'd had imprisoned for theft two decades ago, which had been causing her endless guilt these weeks since her own trial. At least that had been one piece of unanticipated good news. Expecting George to be living either a life of crime or penury, she had been comforted to hear that he had been found in a very respectable district with a well-kept family and a good work record. Obviously some employer had given him more of a chance than she had. Asking herself why, then, she should still feel guilty, she put the report aside to find the book she was looking for, leafed through it, and to her relief found that none of her employees were recuperating at the moment.

Dusty elected to pack straightaway. 'I'll write when I find out what he's up to.' She went to tell the girls she would be going away for a few days, then put some clothes in a bag and got the manservant to drive her to the station in the Daimler.

Nettleton watched her go, rewarded himself with a knowing smile, then went upstairs to pick up his bag.

On arrival in Scarborough, Dusty made several detours before going to the house, just in case she was being followed. Dick and Fred weren't in when she got there. This worried her but she decided to wait. Around noon she heard the door go and the sounds of voices, one of them saying, 'If your mam isn't here we might have to crack that coconut yet, Fred.'

'She is here!' Dusty sprang into the passage, almost causing heart failure. 'And she's ready to crack heads, never mind coconuts – what do you think you're playing at?'

Dickie stalled her outburst by picking her up and swinging her round, his face shining with delight at her being here. After kissing him, she demanded again to hear his explanation.

'Oh, we've had a lovely time, haven't we, Fred?' Dickie toppled into a chair, dragging her with him. 'We thought it'd be even nicer to have us all together – where're the lasses?'

'Belle wouldn't let me bring them,' said his wife. When he swore she added, 'You can hardly blame her, with the whole police force looking for you.'

'Looking for a dangerous desperado, not a family man,' argued Dickie.

She sat up. 'Oh, so that's why you wanted us here, simply to provide good cover.'

'Ye silly wee bitch, ye know that's not true – anyway, didn't ye see the piece in the paper? They think I've skipped the country.' He rubbed his hand up and down her back. 'Well, if ye haven't brought the girls, have ye at least brought some clothes?'

'Yes, and you could do with them by the smell of you both.'

'How very genteel – and the cash?'

'I'm hanging on to that.' She left his lap to prowl the room.

'Dusty, c'mon, I'm bustin' for a ciggy – an' there's nothing in the place to eat. Himself is hanging onto that coconut like it's made o' gold.'

'I want to keep it,' argued Freddie.

'I know! Ye've told me sixteen times but try telling my belly that.'

'Sell the painting, then,' retorted the boy.

'What painting is this?' Dusty looked at her husband who shrank guiltily and tried to bluff his way out. On extracting the truth, her anger was renewed, but she decided not to

471

vent it in front of the boy. Pulling a coin from her bag, she told him, 'Here, Freddie, run and fetch some pies for us, I'll cook something later. Get a packet of cigarettes too.'

'I want to go see the Punch and Judy show.'

'Go find me a big lump o' wood and we'll stage one here,' said Dickie, looking at his wife.

Fred was told he could see the show later, right now they needed something to eat.

'Will you guard my coconut?' He knew better than to trust his father.

Dusty promised she would. When he had gone she turned on Dickie. 'The painting wasn't the only thing you stole, was it? Nick told us that the stable door was open and the car had bolted.'

'How can ye steal from your own brother?' scoffed Dickie.

'I think that's my line, isn't it?'

'I just borrowed it,' said Dickie. His wife asked where it was. 'It ran out of gas so I left it parked a few blocks away. Can't leave it there too long, though. I'll fill it up later.'

'I'll have the keys to Sonny's house if you don't mind,' said Dusty and held out her hand. When told they were on the dresser, she picked them up and put them into her bag, then looked around at the mess he and Fred had created. 'Have you been staying here all the time?'

'No, we camped out at first.' He smiled. 'That took me back a bit.'

'What have you been living on, then?'

'Rabbits, dead dogs, the odd vagrant who happened along – oh and two sherbet suckers. Don't tell Fred about the rabbits. I had to call it "butcher's meat" to get him to eat it.' He noticed her preoccupation. 'What's up, aren't ye pleased to see me?'

'I'm just wondering what I'm doing here and how long we'll have to keep scurrying about, looking over our shoulders.' She put two half-crowns on the sideboard, telling him that was his pocket money, then came to sit on his lap again.

'Nobody followed ye, did they?'

'Do you think I'm stupid?'

'Yes.' Laughing, he ducked his head in expectation of a clout and was not disappointed.

'You'll be pleased to hear that Peasholme is no longer under surveillance,' said Dusty. When he endorsed this, she laid her head on his shoulder and stroked him tenderly. 'I wish the girls were here. I wonder what they're doing.'

The night Dusty left, piercing screams filled the house. When they did not stop, Belle struggled her way out of the bedclothes, into a robe and along the landing. Faith was sitting up in bed, screeching, her blue eyes dilated in panic. Sally was trying frantically to calm her, whilst the rest of the children clustered round the bed in alarm. Belle told them all to go back to their beds, Sally too, then took hold of the child and tried to soothe her. But the rigid little body refused to be comforted. After each piercing shriek, Faith gulped in chestfuls of air. The more tightly Belle clutched the child to her breast and begged to know what had frightened her, the more impliant her body became. There was no alternative but to slap her.

Released from the hysteria, Faith allowed herself to be hugged, but still moaned and cried pathetically. Erin came to see what all the noise was about and told Belle to try and stop it as it was disturbing the entire household. Half an hour passed before Belle could get some sense out of the child who, between sniffs and sobs, told her, 'Mammy's gone!'

'You silly sausage.' Belle smoothed the wet mottled face. 'She's only gone for a couple of days. She'll be coming back.'

'Da-addy's gone too,' hiccuped Faith.

473

Stuck for words, Belle tried to reassure the child with cuddles. But Faith would not let go of the woman's nightgown and the latter had to spend the rest of the night in this bed.

When, the following night, the same thing occurred, Belle saw that despite her own misgivings there was only one solution: in the morning she would take the two girls to Scarborough.

Those sun-baked days in August brought out a side of his wife that Dickie had never seen before. Whilst she had always paid a lot of attention to the children, this seemed especially pronounced now that they were here all the time. His initial delight at Belle's arrival with the girls had evaporated when he had found Faith in his bed that night and every following night, too.

'She's frightened,' Dusty had explained, cuddling the child between them. 'She thinks we're going to leave her. But we're not.' She had added a kiss to the last statement for the child's benefit – in fact, thought Dickie, everything she did was for the children's benefit. When Fred, jealous of his sister's monopoly of their parents' bed, had whined to be taken in too, she had let him. And of course if he came then they couldn't leave Julia out, could they? Dusty seemed to have lost the ability to say no; except to me of course, thought her husband malevolently.

The novelty of fatherhood was wearing thin. He began to feel pushed out, especially as he had not made love to his wife since the girls came. Whilst before when there was just the two of them she had done little things for him, had sat on his knee and talked to him, now she barely found time to give him a word in passing, so wrapped up was she in the children. Was this a foretaste of what life would be like when they finally went home to America? Sometimes, in the middle of the night, he would lie sleepless, thinking about this, would feel resentment at the crush of childish bodies between them. Dusty had always put him first. Now he came fourth in her affections. On top of this he had grown tired of building sandcastles and giving piggyback rides. He wanted to be by himself for a while.

Escaping the crowded bed, he dressed on the landing so as not to wake anyone. Then, after lighting a cigarette, he eased open the outer door and stepped into the night.

The silence was acute, with only the whisper of the sea to interrupt his thoughts. He headed towards the sound, down the steps, past the car that was now parked outside and leaned over the railings looking out across the South Bay at the reflection of harbour lights on the inky water. But the sea couldn't solve his dilemma. Once the cigarette was finished he strolled back to the house and, unable to get back into bed, chose to sleep in another room.

Hardly had he closed his eyes than he woke to sailor-suited children clambering all over him, demanding to know what he was doing in this bed. With a bad-tempered curse, he roared at them to get out and hid his tortured head under a pillow. Within minutes Dusty was there to castigate him for making the girls cry.

'How the hell d'you expect me to react with the little pilgrims jumping all over me?' he yelled at her. 'I can't sleep with my own wife 'cause of the crush, I get out for a bit of relief then I can't bloody get back in again! If this is what family life's about then ye can stuff it!' He replaced the pillow over his head.

Dusty felt like pressing it over his face and suffocating him but, scenting burnt toast, she tore out.

The children were very quiet over breakfast. Dusty tried to brighten things by asking what they wanted to do today.

The girls voiced their simple desire to go on the sands again. Frederick said that it didn't look as if his father was getting up and perhaps he should stay behind to look after him, but Dusty said firmly, 'He's a grown man, love. He can take care of himself for once. We won't let that grumbling old cuss spoil our fun.'

Dickie didn't even know he had been deserted until the door bespoke his wife's return at lunchtime. After a moment or two, he rolled out of bed, sloshed some water on his face and, dressed only in his trousers, padded slothfully downstairs. Four faces turned to look at him as he leaned against the door jamb and asked, 'Had a good time?'

'Yes, thank you.' Dusty got up and fetched a plate of salad for him, then sat down and resumed her meal.

When luncheon was over and his wife was in the kitchen washing the plates, Dickie whispered to the boy to take his sisters down to the beach and he and their mother would meet them later. Fred asked if they might go to the People's Palace instead. 'OK, but we'll all go together later, I want a talk with your mother first. Ye know those verandas where folk sit? Well, stick around that bit of sand so we can easy find ye.' When they had gone, he went into the kitchen. 'I'm sorry about this morning, Dust.'

She did not turn from the sink. 'It's the children you should be saying that to. I've got used to your foul temper on a morning, they haven't.'

The floor was cold, making him shift his bare feet. 'I shouldn't've bawled at them, I know, but having them between us every night, well, it's just not natural. I want them to sleep in their own beds tonight.'

She wrung out the dishcloth and proceeded to wipe the draining board vigorously. 'Oh well, if that's what you want we'll all have to oblige, won't we?'

He stared at her back. 'It doesn't matter to you, then?'

It was difficult to ignore the hurt tone. She closed her eyes, turned, then came to hug him. 'Of course it matters and I've missed having you love me . . . but, Dick, we have to put their feelings first. That's what parenthood's about.'

He pressed her close, kneading his chin into the top of her silver head. 'I'm scared it's gonna be like this all the time, Dust.'

'No, no. Once we get them settled into a normal routine we'll be fine.' She lifted her head and kissed his neck. 'I still love you, you know.'

The kiss stirred latent passion. Dick edged her towards a carpeted floor where they made up for all the times spoilt. Afterwards they remained locked together, talking softly.

Dusty sighed and rubbed his chest. 'What will we do when the holiday ends?'

During his sleepless nights her husband had had plenty of time to think about this. 'I know we can't go back to America yet, 'cause of Belle and the children, but we can hardly have a normal life in York until we know the heat's off. Ye've always wanted to go to Paris – how about spending a couple of months there till we're sure things are okay?'

'It's one long holiday, isn't it?' Dusty pulled a face of indecision.

Dickie started to get up. 'There's no rush. We'll have another week here – providing those kids are taught which bed is theirs. Come on now, don't be lying there with no knickers on, they're waiting for us down on the beach.'

A bracing sea breeze carried them along the Esplanade to a flight of steps and the Spa Bridge, rippling skirts and trousers. By the magnificent Grand Hotel they took the last winding path down to the Foreshore and rounded the corner to see the children dangling on the railings eating toffee apples. Afraid that the in-coming tide would wash them away, Faith had dragged her brother and sister onto safer ground. There was a man leaning on the railings nearby, to whom Julia was chattering away. All four had their backs to Dickie, but the instant he saw that man he stopped in his tracks and gripped his wife's elbow. 'The defective!'

Dusty stopped too. 'You're imagining things. You can't see his face.' Then the man moved his head and she saw that her husband was right.

'The devious bastard,' hissed Dickie. 'He must've been watching Peasholme an' followed you and the girls.' Dusty insisted that no one had pursued her. He gripped her shoulders, talking earnestly. 'Look – can you divert him while I get back up to the house for the car? Then we can meet later.'

'He's seen you,' said his wife.

Nettleton's whippet eye was fixed on the couple who stood across the road, but as yet he made no move to apprehend them. Fred, swinging like an ape from the iron rail, sighted his parents and waved the toffee apple. Dick agonised over what to do. Nettleton made the decision for him. The children watched in horror as their father pelted off along the Foreshore Road with the man in hot pursuit. That Nettleton was handicapped by a twelve-year age difference and had little chance of catching their father, made them no less afraid. Freddie dropped his toffee apple and started to run too, but someone grabbed his arm and held him back. 'I've got to help me dad!' He squirmed to free himself.

'No, Fred!'

Faith had burst into tears. Dusty lifted her up, telling her it was all right, it was just a game. Then, with a struggling Freddie in tow and a toffee apple adhering to the feather in her hat, she hustled them back in the direction of the Spa.

Dickie continued to run with the detective panting behind him. By a stroke of luck the cliff railway was just closing its doors and he managed to squeeze through the gap before it began its climb up to town. Nettleton gasped to a halt at the barrier and, with no hope of catching the lift by the steps that ran alongside, he was forced to watch his quarry doff his hat in a cheery goodbye.

Dickie had arrived back at the house before his family and had started the car in readiness for their departure. Seeing them burst from the lift on the Spa, he used a hand to urge them to hurry and opened the doors. The boy's face lit up, but Dusty held him back. She approached the car but did not climb in. 'Children, go into the house and get your things together.' Dickie said they hadn't got time for that, but his wife said firmly, 'Do as you're told.' She waited for them to scamper up the steps before turning to Dickie. 'And where were you thinking of running to this time?'

'Paris, like I said.' Dickie motioned for her to get into the car.

'We're not coming with you.' As he stared at her in disbelief, she told him why. 'I've always stood up for you, Richard, always done as you wanted, but I'm sick of hiding, sick of running with no end in sight.'

Dickie's mood had changed. 'What you mean is, ye've got the children you've always wanted, ye don't need me any more.'

She did not retaliate, but spoke quietly. 'I believed you wanted them too.'

'That was before I knew what they were going to do to us.' He shook his head and stared at the gooey red syrup of the toffee apple on her blouse. 'They've changed you, Dusty.'

She sighed in exasperation. 'Of course they have! Motherhood isn't just a title, it's a whole way of life, but that doesn't mean I love you any the less.'

'Then come with me, all of yese,' he implored.

'No.' She stood firm. 'I will not subject them again to what they've just witnessed. I'd rather they stayed with Belle.'

'Ah, go on back to York, then!' He flicked his hand dismissively. 'Just gimme some money an' I'll be on my way.' He saw her hesitation. 'Oh, thanks! Leave me with nothing, would ye?'

'It won't get you far.' She handed him some notes.

He snatched it. 'It'll do for now,' then, grim-faced, he climbed into the chugging car and drove away.

Dusty felt tired and sooty as she and the children alighted from the York train later that day. By courtesy of a neighbour, she had telephoned Peasholme to say that she would be coming home. Erin, who had answered the call, had no need to ask the reason; the mere tone of her sister-in-law's voice conveyed bad news. When she told the others, her daughter announced that she would go and meet them at the station. Dusty could see Belle now, limping down the platform towards them. She hoped there was not going to be a scene.

But when the two women came together, Belle merely said hello, took hold of Faith's other hand and with the little girl between them, they walked towards the exit. Julia held onto one of the handles of Dusty's valise. Fred, his coconut jammed in his bucket and his spade held like a sentry's rifle, wandered aimlessly behind.

Belle was conserving her questions until the children were safely in bed, though one only had to look at their faces to see that a calamity had occurred. She tried to picture what this might have been, conjuring visions of Dickie with the police in pursuit. Thus occupied, she had been staring at a man without even realising it. Then consciousness returned and she saw that it was Brian. Under her supposed inspection, he had faltered in his step, but now continued weaving towards her through the milling travellers. Belle passed a swift look at the children; had they seen him? When their expressions remained unmoved, she asked Dusty to walk on with them and she would follow.

Thankfully, in the flow of bodies, the tired children walked straight past Brian without seeing him, her aunt too. As he neared, Belle gave a tight smile and said hello, then turned to the young bespectacled woman on his arm.

Brian raised his hat, looking acutely embarrassed. 'Good afternoon, Miss Teale. Have you been taking a trip?' Belle murmured that she had been meeting her aunt. He noticed that her eyes were on his companion and was forced to introduce her. 'May I present my wife, Margaret.'

The young woman was obviously besotted with her new husband and only removed her hold on him to shake hands with Belle. Margaret had known Brian in his professional capacity for some years. He had tended her invalid widowed mother who had recently died. After devoting years of her life to nursing her parent, she had given up hope of losing her spinsterhood, so when the doctor had blurted out a proposal little more than three weeks ago it had come as a complete surprise.

But not as big a surprise as to Brian himself. He wanted to ask Belle now if her uncle was still in hiding at her house, to tell her that he had entertained the idea of sending the police round but his feelings for her had overcome this. He wanted to say how much it hurt to even think of her. But instead, her undisguised shock caused him to jabber, 'I'm afraid we must dash, we have a train to catch. So nice to see you.' And with this he walked on. The woman gave a parting smile to Belle who heard her ask, 'Is that one of your patients?' She stood there gawping after them until the arrival of an express enveloped her in steam and noise. Tensing against the assault on her ears, she hurried after the others.

Her grandmother was the only person there when they arrived. Belle took the children upstairs to wash, whilst her aunt made the grim report from Scarborough. Thomasin noticed that something had unsettled Belle but was too concerned with the fate of her son to question at the moment. Only after dinner, when Dusty had gone to bed and Erin picked up the evening paper did she learn what it was.

Erin gasped and read out loud: '"*Doctor Brian Dyson and his wife Margaret, who were married last Saturday, left York today to spend their honeymoon in Bloemfontein, South Africa. Dr Dyson explained the unusual venue by saying that he hoped to set up practice there, his main concern being the Boer children of the internment camps, where there is said to be epidemics of measles, dysentery and chickenpox.*"' Erin looked agog at Belle. 'That was awfully quick, wasn't it? I can't believe Brian would be so impulsive, he's such a sensible sort. Well, ye know what it is, don't ye? She's caught him on the rebound – and whose fault is that, might I ask?'

'She's welcome to him,' said her daughter bluntly.

Erin was barely listening. 'She must be a right hussy.'

'Actually she seemed very sweet,' said Belle, her face expressionless. 'I met them this afternoon at the railway station. She seemed totally besotted with Brian – never let go of his arm.'

'What was she like?' asked her mother. 'As plain as a pikestaff, I'll bet. Helped him to get over the misery of breaking up with you then snapped him up before he knew what had hit him!'

'Mother, you don't know her, you've no right to judge.'

'Yet another crime to add to my brother's list,' said Erin bitterly. Her daughter said Dickie could not be held responsible for Brian's marrying someone else. 'Yes he can! If Dickie hadn't stirred up trouble it might be you who was

482

going away on your honeymoon now.' Erin's eyes had moved on to the editorial. 'Still, much as I'd like to see you married I wouldn't want to be reading this about you. They're saying Brian should stay in the country where he trained instead of using his skill to treat our enemies. I have to agree with them. I mean, the Boers aren't likely to pay for their treatment, are they? If he has to practise charity there's more deserving cases over here.'

Tired of her mother's opinions, Belle stood. 'Well, I for one commend him, and her too. They're very brave people. Now, I'm going to see what The Great Unwashed are up to; it's too quiet up there.'

When Belle had left, Thomasin said grimly, 'I knew something had upset her; she was very subdued when she came in.'

'She's only herself to blame,' said Erin. 'He's been after her to marry him for years.'

'Yes well, I'm sure she feels bad enough without you harping on about it, Erin.'

Belle found it hard to sleep that night. Her spine was aching but that wasn't the main cause. She just couldn't stop picturing Brian with his wife in bed. 'Is she one of your patients?' the girl had said. Huh! she would be pretty shocked had she been in Belle's room on certain nights. The thought caused her to grow hotter and she flung the covers off. It had only been three weeks since he was blowing his top about her supposed infidelity and here he was married! He must have been seeing this woman for ages, the hypocrite.

The baby started to cry. With a curse, Belle put on a robe and went to pick him up to save Sally the need. The crying had stopped by the time she arrived. She stood a moment watching her aunt lay the infant against her shoulder and shush him gently, swaying from side to side.

Dusty pressed her cheek to the little head, humming and rocking, unaware of her audience. Belle limped back to bed.

Sonny returned from Ireland to find his car gone and a patch of discoloured wallpaper where once had hung a painting by his son. 'I don't know whether to laugh or cut my wrists,' he said to Dusty when she handed over the painting with an apology. 'He thought I did that.'

Losing track of his prey, Nettleton had re-taken his lodgings at The Black Swan, but when a letter arrived for Mrs R. Feeney with a Paris postmark, he took the first train back to Leeds, drew out some cash, and informed his wife that he was going to the Continent. Had he been allowed access to the letter itself, he would have known precisely where to catch his man, but after letting him view the envelope for half a crown, Kettley had snatched it back.

Dusty read the plea for her to change her mind and come to him, then put it into a drawer. She would not be going; neither would she reply. The children needed her here.

Having not yet found suitable accommodation, Belle was still in residence at Peasholme. Her grandmother was beginning to regret her open invitation. Not only were the upstairs rooms full of children, but Belle seemed to have commandeered most of downstairs too, with piano lessons in one room and maths tuition in another – not to mention all the campaigning that was going on. Many times Thomasin was on the brink of telling her grand-daughter that enough was enough, but then she would remind herself not to be so cantankerous; Belle would be gone soon – *and then you'll miss her, won't you?*

The last weeks of August were difficult ones for all, but especially for Dusty. Nothing she could say would cheer Freddie up, and the girls were growing extremely ill-behaved. Normally it was her policy to coax rather than censure, but her efforts to check the highly-strung Julia were proving rather ineffectual today. After setting the older children their lessons, Belle had gone out campaigning. Erin was at the factory. Only Thomasin was in the house. The baby was grizzling and rubbing its face in discomfort. Dusty was trying her best to soothe him, but he just wouldn't stop crying. 'Julia, dear, sit down and I'll come and read you a story in a moment.' Dusty grew more agitated, patted the infant's back and jiggled him up and down. Julia continued to throw herself about the room, giggling and screaming, dancing, jumping. Her sister started to copy her. The baby grizzled and whined. Dusty felt a surge of panic. She didn't know which child to tend first. 'Stop it now,' she told them harshly. Then louder, 'Stop it!' Faith sat down immediately and jammed a thumb in her mouth, looking up at Dusty with wide eyes, but Julia continued to shriek and dance and laugh. The baby screamed louder. Dusty wanted to throw him across the room. Horrified with herself, she carried him back to the nursery and, putting him in his crib, slammed the door on his noise.

Julia was still hurtling about the room, giggling. Dusty took hold of her by the arms and shook her. 'Stop it, Julia! Stop trying to make me angry! I won't have it!' Arms pinioned, the child flopped about like a puppet, still giggling. Dusty jerked her to her feet and slapped her.

The silliness abated. Julia's mouth turned down and her brown eyes welled tears. Dusty bit her lip, then pulled the child into an embrace.

Later, when everything was peaceful, she made her terrible confession to Thomasin, who was the only one she felt able to confide in. 'I tell myself it's because of the worry over Dick, but it isn't. The truth is I just didn't know what to do. Isn't that ridiculous! Fifty-three years of age, old enough to be a grandmother and I can't control two small girls. I'm beginning to wonder . . . well, am I really fit for motherhood? Perhaps that's why I could never have any of my own. I mean, Nature doesn't often get things wrong, does she?'

'Eh, deary me!' Thomasin grabbed hold of her daughter-in-law's hand. 'Fancy getting in such a state after one little smack. I'm only surprised you've taken so long to get round to it, I could swing for that Julia myself sometimes. And just because you're fifty-three doesn't give you some sort of magical power over other first-time mothers; fifty-three or twenty you still have to learn the job. Is it that you've changed your mind about wanting them? Dusty shook her head emphatically. 'Then that's all that matters.' Thomasin ended with the confident announcement, 'You'll manage, lass.'

A brick came through the window that night. The manservant was sent out to find the culprit but returned empty-handed. Belle surmised that it must be the result of either her suffrage campaign or her position on South Africa. Her mother was furious.

'Yes, that's the trouble, Belle! There could be any number of reasons for that brick being thrown. Ye have to make up your mind just who you're going to help. And another thing! While you're spouting your speeches the children are running riot through your grandmother's house – not to mention the filthy habits of that cat. It isn't fair that she should have to put up with this at her age. Ye said you were only going to be here a week and here you still are over a month later.'

'I'm so sorry for the inconvenience!' spat Belle. 'I'll be out of your hair as soon as I can find a place.'

Overnight, of course, she realised that her mother was quite justified in her condemnation, and decided to look for a house of her own immediately after the morning's lessons. As she came through the hall a delivery of mail fell onto the mat and she stooped to collect it. Lifting the first envelope she saw that the one underneath had been delivered to the wrong address. Joe Kettley was at the end of the driveway when she called him back. He apologised, then nodded at the boarded up window. 'Someone been playing football?'

Belle grimaced and told him the cause. 'So, I'm going to have to find somewhere else to live.'

'There's a house on my route for sale,' said Joe at once. 'Lovely place – I'll take you to see it if you like, it's only just round the corner.'

Belle was about to say that if it were just round the corner she could find it herself, but then changed her mind. 'Wait a moment, I'll just get my cloak. It's a bit cool this morning.' When she saw the house, though, she laughed out loud. 'You must think I'm a millionaire!'

Joe was nonplussed. 'Sorry . . . I just thought you'd need a lot of room with all your kids.'

'Needing and being able to afford are two different things.' She smiled. 'But thanks anyway, it was very thoughtful.' Seeing that the house was empty, she peered into one or two windows, nodding approval, before saying goodbye and returning to breakfast. When she laughingly told her table companions about the house, her grandmother immediately offered her the money. Belle refused point-blank. 'We don't even know how much it is yet – a fortune probably.'

'It doesn't matter,' said Thomasin. 'Anything to get rid of you.'

Belle laughed. 'I'd like to oblige but I'd never be able to repay the loan.'

'I don't expect you too,' replied Thomasin, adding the warning, 'Before you open your mouth it's not charity! Your grandfather left me to dispose of his belongings. You're only getting your due.'

Belle was firm. 'No, thank you. I want no snide comments from Nick.'

487

'Never mind Nick. He's had a good whack out of me over the years while you were playing Miss Independent.'

Belle nodded. 'I'll bet he has. I've never known Nick turn down the offer of money.'

Thomasin regarded the sanctimonious expression. 'Yes, and that's why I like giving Nicholas things. Because I know I'll never have it thrown back in my face.'

Belle frowned.

'Oh, I know you didn't see it that way,' accepted her grandmother. 'But it might not harm you to see it from my point of view for once. Us old'uns like to spoil our grandchildren, Belle, and we wouldn't offer what we couldn't afford. It's not charity for God's sake.'

Belle pondered over the amount of times she must have thrown her grandfather's kindness back in his face, and wished she could reverse this. At last, she nodded and said, 'Thanks, Nan. I accept your kind offer.'

'Thank God for that,' said Thomasin. 'I thought I was going to be stuck with you forever. How long will it take to close the sale?'

'I'll tell them my family are desperate to see the back of me,' replied Belle. 'It's vacant possession so it should only take a matter of days.' She turned to Dusty. 'Could I impose on your good nature again, Aunt, and ask you to help Sally look after the children later? I want to get the key and have a proper look.'

Dusty smiled and said of course, but under that smile there was a tinge of worry. 'Belle, what will happen to Freddie and the girls when you move?'

Belle nibbled her lip, remembering the trauma of the last separation. 'Yes, there's a point.' She leaned on the table. 'Would you consider coming to stay with us? I'd appreciate the help and, thanks to my generous grandmother, there'll be plenty of room.'

It was not really what Dusty had been hoping for, but she told Belle that she would love to.

By early September the house sale was completed. On Thursday, the day before Belle was to move in, her aunt, uncle and cousins were coming from Leeds to see the new house. At eight that morning, Feen was searching frantically through her dressing table drawers for some pins with which to shorten a new petticoat that should have been done several days ago; her mother would be furious if it still showed beneath her skirts. Finding an empty pincushion, she racked her brain over where all the pins could be. Then she remembered the voodoo doll tucked away at the back of the wardrobe. Finding it, she pulled out all the pins and with a quick moulding of her hands reduced the doll to a ball of plasticine and tossed it in the waste bin. By ten the petticoat was a more suitable length. Feen climbed into the carriage and set off with her family to York.

When they arrived they were met with the news that Dusty had been taken ill with stomach pains shortly after breakfast and was lying down upstairs. *Shortly after breakfast!* An immediate sense of foreboding overtook Feen – that would have been the time she removed the pins from the voodoo doll. What was she going to do?

No one else seemed unduly concerned, and all went off to be shown around Belle's new residence. However, when they came back for luncheon, the maid informed them that Mr Richard's wife was still incapacitated and seemed to be getting worse. Erin's visit to her sister-in-law's room terminated abruptly when she saw how bad Dusty was. She rushed downstairs, saying that they must send for the doctor. Whilst someone did this, Belle and Erin went back to sit with the patient.

Dusty's face was almost grey with pain. Her legs were drawn up and she kept rolling from side to side in an effort to seek comfort. Waiting for the doctor to arrive, Belle grew more worried. She had seen someone like this before.

The doctor was concerned, too. After examining Dusty, he pronounced that she must be sent to hospital straight away. Thomasin showed her concern and asked couldn't Dusty be treated here. Several people of her acquaintance had gone into hospital and never come out again. But the doctor was insistent that if it was what he feared then delay could be dangerous. 'There's a lot of tenderness there, but she can't tell me exactly where the pain is,' he murmured to those gathered on the landing. 'I fear it may be appendicitis.'

Appendicitis. It was as Belle had feared. Many years ago she had seen a tiny child with this illness. The child had died. 'We have to send for Uncle Dickie,' she told her mother after Dusty had been taken to hospital groaning and writhing and the evening had seen no change. 'I'm going to send a cablegram.'

Erin agreed and looked around at the gathering – Sonny's family had stayed behind to await news of Dusty. 'I'm off to church now. See you all when I get back.'

'Aunt Erin!' Feen came running into the hall after her and whispered, 'Can I come with you?'

Erin looked most surprised, but said that she could indeed. And Feen went off to pay penance, desperately hoping that her prayers would counter the evil influence of the voo-doo doll.

490

21

On receipt of the urgent message at his hotel – *Wife ill, return immediately* – Dickie did not even bother to pack a bag, but jumped on the first available ferry. Halfway across the Channel, though, he began to wonder if this could be a ploy of Nettleton's to lure him back to earth. This thought gnawed at him for the rest of the journey and when the ferry reached Dover he was in two minds whether to turn round and go straight back to France. But the thought of Dusty was stronger bait.

It was dark when he arrived at Peasholme. 'Where is she?' He burst in upon his mother and sister who were the only ones in the drawing room, Belle having moved and the others gone back to Leeds.

'Dickie!' His mother used her stick to lever herself up and came towards him, smiling. 'Don't worry, she's all right. She's been in hospital but she's right as rain now and she's coming home tomorrow.'

'Hospital!' After kissing his mother, Dickie sat down, rubbing his tired eyes.

Erin told him about the stomach pains. 'The doctor thought it was appendicitis, but when she got to hospital they couldn't find anything wrong with her. The pains went as quickly as they'd come.'

Dickie lost his temper, unleashing all the pent-up worry. 'So I've come hundreds of miles, risked my neck to find that there's nothing bloody wrong with her!'

Thomasin demanded. 'Well, would you rather it *had* been something serious?'

His expression was black. 'I'll bet it was just one of her bloody tricks to get me back here, wasn't it?' His mother asked what on earth he was talking about. 'The message, she sent it herself, didn't she?'

'She was in no fit state to know what day it was,' snapped Thomasin. 'Let alone send cablegrams. Don't be so blasted silly. You want to be thankful she's all right instead of accusing her of trickery.'

Dickie was not to be reassured. 'Ah, you're all in it together! I'm sick of the lot o' yese. First thing tomorrow I'm off back to France.'

'Aren't you even going to wait and see Dusty!'

'No.' His chin jutted out like that of a thwarted child.

'But she knows you're coming,' said his sister. 'While she was poorly Belle told her she'd sent for you.'

'I'll think about it tomorrow. Right now I need some sleep. Can I have a room for the night?'

Thomasin asked Erin to sort one out for him, telling her later, 'It's only because of the worry. He'll calm down in the morning.'

On Saturday morning Dickie had calmed down, but was no less resolute about going back to France. His mother tried to persuade him to wait and see Dusty, but he refused, saying that there was a train to London in an hour and he intended to be on it.

'And what have ye done with Sonny's car?' demanded Erin. 'He's had to fall back on the carriage and pair.'

Her brother told her he had sold it down in London. 'I needed the cash till I could wire home for some – tell Son he can have the Daimler with my compliments.'

'That's very generous considering the blasted thing hardly ever goes.' Erin seized the paper and read in silence for

492

a while, before exclaiming, 'Oh dear ... your President McKinley's been shot.'

Dick was brusque. 'Well, don't try to pin that one on me. I was here all night, remember.' He drained his cup. 'Right, I'll be going.'

Erin crumpled the paper. 'Aren't you even interested to know where the children are?'

'Not really.'

'I'll tell you anyway.' Erin wrote the address on a card and gave it to him. 'Belle's bought a new house. Dusty's going to stay with her and help look after them.'

'I'm sure she'll be happy now that she's got what she always wanted.' Dick tucked the card in his pocket without looking at it and bent to kiss his mother. She asked anxiously when they would see him again. He jammed his hat on, replying that he didn't know. 'So long.'

The drought that had shrivelled September ran into another month. Set between two rivers, York suffered less than its neighbours, but there were small irritations such as the shortage of milk which to Belle with her houseful of children was more like a major catastrophe. Dusty continued to live here, her days very full with organising the children, helping with lessons, marking books. Over the months she had grown used to their idiosyncrasies, had learnt that one did not rule by granting every wish but by standing firm. Belle admired the change in her aunt and said that she was welcome to live here permanently if she so desired. When Dusty had taken this lightly, Belle added, 'I'm perfectly serious. Uncle Dickie isn't likely to be back now, is he?'

'Don't be ridiculous! Of course he'll be back.'

Seated at her davenport marking books, Belle didn't look up. 'But he's been away months without a word.'

'He'll be back,' replied her aunt with certainty.

Belle pitied her. 'Well, as I said, you're welcome to stay for as long as you like. I'm glad of the help.' She put one book aside and rippled the pages of another. 'There'll be a new girl coming tomorrow; a little prostitute. Yes, I know – it's disgusting, isn't it? She's been beaten, too.'

Dusty remarked that the children were fortunate to have someone like Belle who would sacrifice a brilliant academic career in order to devote her life to helping them.

Belle lifted one corner of her mouth, still ticking the pages. 'I'm no saint, Aunt. Believe me, it was small sacrifice. I always hated learning for learning's sake – though I do enjoy passing my knowledge to the children if it can free them from the ghettoes. I don't particularly do it because I like them but because it has to be done.' She paused and leaned on the davenport. 'Sometimes I look at them and I hate them for their suffering – can you understand that?' Dusty nodded. Now that Dick was out of play she had taken the trouble to know Belle more intimately. There were still things about her that she did not care for, but she was now more willing to recognise Belle's strengths.

'There are times when I wish I could turn my back on them, but I can't. The trouble is,' Belle looked despairing, 'there's too much of it going on and I can't help everybody. It makes me feel so *useless* . . . Oh dear, how very maudlin!' She laughed and closed the book she had been marking. 'Come on, we'd better get those fireworks over to Peasholme.' She had intended to have a display here and had invited her mother and Grandmother, but with the cold foggy days of November the latter's rheumatism had flared up again and she had asked Belle if the party could take place at Peasholme where a lot of garden rubbish needed burning.

Sally was given the evening off. Belle, her aunt and the children arrived at Peasholme around seven, bearing boxes of fireworks. When all were gathered, the manservant was instructed to torch the bonfire. Spitting and crackling, it roared to full flame, illuminating joyous faces, sparks dancing up into the black night. His eyes watery from the smoke, Sonny shared the whoops of delight at the squibs and roman candles, but as always on November the fifth he remembered his daughter Rosanna, whose thirtieth birthday it would have been. He looked at his frail little mother, wondering whether now was the right time to tell her about Timothy Rabb – Dickie wasn't likely to do it, was he? Mind made up, he weaved his way through the haze of saltpetre, and amid all that laughter unburdened himself of his father's last message.

Erin had worked her way round to Dusty. 'I nearly called in this morning on my way to church, but I thought better of it.' Dusty said yes, breakfast could be rather chaotic at Belle's. 'I waved to her but she was too busy talking to the postman. He must've been in for a cup of tea, had he?'

Dusty called, 'Julia! Don't get too close to the fire – sorry, Erin, I didn't catch that.'

Erin patted her gloved hands and bounced from foot to foot. 'The postman. I mentioned to Mother that I'd seen him coming out of Belle's. She said he'd probably been in for a cup of tea.'

Dusty nodded, but did not verify this.

Erin shook her head. 'That daughter of mine, no thought for her reputation. Whatever must people think?'

Dusty cried, 'Oh dear, look at Fred! I'll have to go stop him, Erin, excuse me.'

Erin searched the firelit garden for her daughter. Finding her on the other side of the bonfire, she asked Belle to fetch some butter from the kitchen for the potatoes that were roasting in the fire.

Butter in hand, Belle laughed as her trip back up the kitchen stairs coincided with her mother's downwards flight.

'I forgot to ask you to bring some napkins,' said Erin, going to a drawer. 'Hang on, I'll walk back with you.' She pulled out several drawers, searching. 'How are things between you and Aunt Dusty?'

Belle sat down to wait. 'Oh, fine. I was just saying this morning that she's welcome to stay if Uncle Dickie doesn't come back.'

'That was rather tactless, Belle.' Erin opened yet another drawer.

'Mother, she's had no letter from him in months.'

Erin was glad that her daughter had raised the subject herself. 'Speaking of letters, I waved to you this morning but you were too busy with the postman to see me.'

Unable to rest her crooked spine with any comfort, Belle shuffled sideways and leaned her ribs against the chair back, knowing what was to come and wondering how long it would take her mother to get around to it.

'I mentioned it to your Nan. She said you'd probably invited him in for a cup of tea. Do you do that often?'

'Quite often.' Belle tried not to smile.

'I said to Dusty, you should consider your reputation, Belle.'

'How many people have you been discussing me with, Mother?'

'Only those two.'

'And what was the general consensus of opinion?'

'Belle, I'm only trying to guard your respectability. People might think . . . well, you know.'

'They'll think he's been there all night.'

Erin looked uncomfortable. 'Yes.'

'Well, he has,' said Belle. And to her mother's horror announced, 'That's right, Mother – I've got myself a fancy man.'

For some seconds Erin could merely splutter. When she

496

became more coherent, she rasped, 'But who is this man? How long have ye known him?'

'You know already. He's been delivering your mail for the last four months.' Belle recalled the start of their intimacy. There had been no courtship; she had just looked at him one morning, and he had looked at her, she'd asked him in for a cup of tea and had added an invitation to supper, and the next morning he had still been there. He was not as intellectual a partner as Brian – she missed their profound talks – but Joe was not unintelligent and he had a dry sense of humour. She found his company very stimulating.

Erin gasped at the flagrancy. 'I can't believe . . . you've known him for a matter of months and now you . . . Well, wait till your grandmother hears about this! She'll go hairless. Can I at least tell her when the wedding's going to be?'

'What wedding?'

'He refuses to marry you after he's . . . ? Well, I'm going to write to the Postmaster and have him sacked!'

'And of course you'll mention my name.'

'I will not!'

'But you'll have to sign your name, won't you? Otherwise how will the Postmaster know it's not from a crank?'

Erin glared at her. 'Then I'll speak to this . . . whatever his name is . . .'

'Joe.'

'. . . and tell him what I think of him!'

'I'm sure you'll find he's very nice when you do speak to him. I asked him to come tonight but he had other plans.'

'Huh! Probably had some other poor chit to foist his attentions on! That's why he won't marry you, he's got a string of silly girls just like you on his round.'

Belle could quite believe that this was true. Far from being put off, it made her feel relaxed to know that he might have other women and so would make no emotional demands on

497

her. She feigned tiredness. 'Mother, you know my views on marriage.'

'But that was before! I understood that you didn't feel romantically inclined towards Brian but now you've met this man who you obviously care about . . .'

Inwardly, Belle raged at her mother's attitude, but kept her voice even. 'Look, I've told you and I'll tell you again: I will never change my views on marriage. Joe knew that from the beginning. It's not serious between us.'

'Not serious. My God, you could have a child!'

'No.'

Her daughter's surety gave Erin a ray of hope. 'Oh . . . forgive me. I thought when you said . . . It hasn't gone that far, then?'

'Mother, when I said he stays the night I meant that he stays in my bed. When I say I don't want marriage, that doesn't mean I'm not entitled to another kind of relationship, and when I say there'll be no children I mean that I have taken great pains to prevent them.'

'How can you prevent God's will!'

Belle had to laugh. 'Oh, Mother, I'm sorry but you're so unworldly.'

Erin was about to slap her daughter's face. Then she remembered the last time she had done this; they had not spoken for many months afterwards, during which time Belle had nearly died. Erin had sworn she would not be so petty again. But this . . . She stared at the woman in front of her, seeing her for the first time as a woman and not simply as her daughter. 'If I'm unworldly then I'm glad. Huh! And you acting the aggrieved maiden when that landlord accused you of taking in male lodgers! All the values I've ever taught you . . . It's bad enough for a couple not to wait till they're married, but to make yourself cheap like this . . .'

'I'm sorry you think that, and I'm sorry you had to

find out this way, but you must understand that it's my life.'

'No! It's not just your life, Belle. How does this behaviour affect the rest of us? What sort of example are you setting those children? And what must the maid think of your behaviour?'

Belle had been told in no uncertain terms just what Sally thought of it. After an angry row she had given a week's notice, then just before she was due to leave she had retracted it, saying that as Belle had been so good a friend for so many years she would turn a blind eye to her failings – 'But I don't know what my mother would say if she knew I was working for such a woman!'

Erin's angry words continued. 'All the things you said about your uncle ... Why, you're almost as bad as he is! And to brazenly admit that you're meddling with God's gift of life ...' Abruptly, she turned back to the drawer. 'Now where are those blessed napkins. Ah, here they are. Come on, they'll be waiting for their potatoes.'

'Mother, I know you're angry at me, but ...'

'Yes!' Erin spun back, eyes glittering. 'Yes, I am angry – but more than that. I'm ashamed of you, Belle.'

'You'd like Joe if you met him!' called Belle to her mother's retreating back. Then with a heavy sigh, followed.

After a conversation with her own mother, Erin handed a napkin to Dusty. 'Why didn't you tell me about Belle's ... friend?'

'It was none of my business, Erin. I'm sorry, you must be upset.'

'Upset? Hah! I can't believe it even now – an' d'ye know what Mother said when I told her?'

'She threw a fit, I suppose.'

'Oh yes! But not for the reason ye might imagine. D'ye know what she said? – "At least Brian was a *doctor*"!'

499

Dusty turned her face away to hide a smile; Erin was obviously furious.

'I'm sorry my daughter has subjected you to such embarrassment, Dusty. Ye must move back here right away.'

'I'd prefer to stay with the children, Erin.'

'Oh yes, of course.' Erin agreed. 'It might be a good idea if you did. Could you do anything to stop her silly behaviour, Dusty?'

'I'm a guest in Belle's house, Erin. If I interfered I'd soon outstay my welcome.'

Erin nodded in despair. 'Is he actually living there?' Dusty said no, but he visited frequently. 'Huh! I'll wager they're nocturnal visits. What sort of man is he? As if I need to ask.'

'He's very nice – and he does seem fond of her.'

'To think he's been delivering my mail,' said Erin. 'I'd have him sacked if I could do it without dirtying Belle's name. The things I've had to put up with from that girl. My own daughter a scarlet woman – it's worse than being an old maid!'

He had forgotten her birthday. She had waited all day for a card that had not come. Joe must have thought her mad when she asked him to search the depot just in case it had gone astray. She lay there in the freezing cold bed, worrying about Dick. What if the detective had caught up with him? That would be the only reason he had not corresponded with her ... unless he was enjoying himself too much in the boudoir of some French tart. She flung herself onto her side, warming her toes against the stone hot water bottle. Belle had thrown a small party for her. If only Dickie had been there ... She fell asleep.

The next thing she knew, a cold draught circulated round her legs. Someone was rolling into bed beside her. It was still dark. Half-conscious, she assumed it was one of the children and put an arm out to pull the body closer. But it was a man's body. A man whose scent she knew. A man who kissed her and wished her Happy Birthday, before delivering the most personal of birthday gifts.

In the morning, before the rest of the house was awake, they made love again. Lying there afterwards, he told her most of what he had been doing in France, leaving out the parts she would not want to hear. 'Then yesterday, I happened to see the detective, no less. Aye, would ye believe it? So I packed my hanky and whizzed home.'

She lit a lamp to see what time it was. 'Well, thank you, Richard. I had hoped you'd come because of my birthday.'

He said he had, then narrowed his eyes in suspicion. 'Hey, just a minute, little Miss Prim – how come you knew it was me last night?'

'I heard the creak of the stairs and thought, that's the tread of a dirty, lousy, cheating, womaniser.' She matched his distrustful glare. 'What I want to know is, how did *you* know which room I'd be in?'

'I didn't, but any port in a storm.'

She gave him a sharp nudge and told him to get up. He stuck his toe out of bed, announced that it was too cold and snuggled back down. 'Ye want to warn Belle to be careful, leaving her front door unlocked like that – it could've been anybody creeping in.'

'You mean like a double murderer?'

'Hey, now stop that.' He flung the covers off and sank his teeth into her naked bottom. Her screech of laughter brought a small face to the door. On seeing Dick, Julia shouted, 'Me daddy's home!' and the room turned into a public thoroughfare. Dusty pulled the covers up to her chin as Freddie and the girls swarmed over the bed, grabbing their father round his neck.

When the pandemonium had died down, Freddie's mien turned to one of woe. 'Me cat's gone, Dad.'

Dick punched the air. 'Ah, drat the thing – when we get back to America I'll buy ye ten cats.'

'No, you won't.' His wife was firm. 'We may get one cat if you're very good – now clear off, all of you. Go on, out! You can see your father when he comes down to breakfast.'

When they had gone, Dick showed admiration for her change in tactics. 'I can see ye've got them licked into shape while I've been away.'

'Yes, and I'm not having you undo all my good work, so that's the last time you mention buying presents.' Leaving her toilet until later, she dressed hurriedly. The bedroom was literally freezing; there was a pool of ice on the windowsill.

'Ye don't like presents?' He pulled on his trousers. 'Shame. I brought ye something back. I'll have to give it to Belle now.'

'I shall have to acquaint you with a few facts before you go downstairs. I don't want you and your big mouth upsetting things.' She told him about Joe.

He laughed cheekily and reached for his tie. 'The postman's been slipping her a little something with the mail, has he?'

'Don't be vulgar – and I don't recall seeing much mail from you!'

'I did send you a letter.'

'One.'

'That wasn't answered.' He looked around the spartan room for a mirror. Finding a tiny one on the wall, he adjusted his tie and smoothed his hair.

She picked up a brush. 'Why didn't you come to see me when I was in hospital?'

502

He hung his head. 'I was mad. I thought ye'd done it on purpose just to get me back. Are ye okay now?'

'There was nothing wrong with me.' She collected her mass of silver hair and wound it into a knot.

'That's what Mam said – that's why I thought you'd set me up.'

'The pain was genuine enough. I've never known anything so bad. I should imagine it was like having a baby . . . The doctor said it could have had something to do with wanting the children.'

He came to hold her. 'Will she let us take them, d'ye think?'

His wife was optimistic. 'We've been on better terms in your absence.'

'It must be this fancy man keeping her happy,' grinned Dick. 'Come on then, let's go down. She's likely waiting for me with her boot poised.'

When they descended there was another welcome from the children who were now at the table, spooning up porridge, all but the naked babe whom Sally was lowering into an enamel bowl by the fire. He sat there round-eyed, watching the confrontation between Dick and Belle like a fat little Buddha.

Aside from a few sarcastic remarks, Belle was quite warm towards her uncle, taking his innuendos about her bedfellow in good part. Joe was delivering mail at the moment, but Belle told her uncle that he usually called back for breakfast when he was halfway through his round. While Dusty took charge of the baby, the nursemaid went to lay rashers of bacon in the frying pan. In between then and breakfast, Dick gave everyone an account of his time spent in Paris. Only when the children had been sent off to do their chores did he tell his niece about the detective. She asked what he intended to do now.

'After I've eaten I'd better show my face at Peasholme.'

'In broad daylight? Isn't that dangerous?'

'Belle, ye give the police more credit than they're due – they couldn't give a damn about a twenty-six-year-old murder.'

'Then the police guard outside my grandmother's was just an illusion?'

'Ah, they had to show willing – but who d'ye think put the news about that I'd escaped to America? I'd be nothing but a headache to them.'

The cavalier attitude sparked anger in his wife. 'The other detective seems to thrive on headaches!'

'Dusty, he's probably still combing the streets of Paris. Don't give him another thought – they're all as thick as pigshit in the West Riding.' Both women exclaimed their repulsion. 'Sorry, ladies, a slip o' the tongue.' His wife declared that her hand would slip in a moment. 'Sorry, sorry, sorry – ah, breakfast's here!' Dick beamed and reached hungrily for the plate. 'As for my long-term plans, Belle, it's back to America for me.' His wife asked despondently if they would go at once. 'I guess we could risk a week or so longer – but you're not to let Mam persuade us to stay till Christmas. I know I said the detective was thick, but that would be shaving things a bit too close. Besides, I'm ready to be off.' He crammed bacon into his mouth.

Dusty picked up her knife and fork, but did not eat. Her voice was dull. 'Do you realise that this will be the second Christmas we'll have spent on board a liner?' She wanted to broach the paramount subject of the children, but feared that Belle would say no. If she did, then it would have to be a choice between going with her husband, or staying with them. She could not say what that choice would be.

The clock struck eight and Joe returned for breakfast. Belle waited until they had eaten to tell him that her mother knew

504

about their liaison. He flopped back in his chair and said he did not dare take Erin's mail now. Dick told him to relax; he and his wife were going to Peasholme, they would deliver it for him. Gratified, Joe downed his tea and sorted out a pile of letters, then left to resume his job.

Whilst Dick had another cup of tea, his wife went to wash and pack her bags. Disliking her uncle's impish scrutiny, Belle took the breakfast pots away, but when she came back his grin still followed her.

'Uncle, don't you know it's rude to stare?'

'Tut, tut, tut.' He eventually shook his head in sly disgust. 'When the cat's away the mice will do all sorts o' naughty things they shouldn't.'

'If it's your aim to humiliate me . . .'

'Humiliate ye?' Dick put his cup down, wiped his mouth and approached her. He used both hands to lift the abundant hair away from her face and back over her shoulders, speaking in a low croon. 'I'm envious as hell.'

She smiled and moved away, which was lucky for at that point her aunt returned. Dickie said he would wait till he got to Peasholme to have a wash. Pocketing the letters, he asked his wife if they had sufficient finances to see them back to America. She said they had plenty. He then sent the nursemaid for his overcoat and hat.

'Don't forget your luggage,' Belle reminded him.

'I'll pick it up on the way out.'

'I didn't mean the bag in the hall.' Belle went to the door and called to Freddie and his sisters, telling them there would be no lessons today. 'Get your hats, coats and gloves.'

She noted the stupefied looks on her aunt and uncle's faces, and spread her lips. 'I hope you don't mind if I keep their other clothes. I'll need them for the next batch and I'm sure you have more money than I do. The legalities will be finalised before you go back to America.'

Dusty opened her mouth but no words came out. Her vision blurred and her heart thumped.

'Ye mean, ye'll let me have them?' blurted Dickie, mouth widening.

Belle took a step forward and spoke quietly. 'Before you get too complacent, Uncle, I have to tell you that you are the most unprincipled rogue I have ever had the misfortune to meet. At your advanced stage of life it is doubtful that you will ever alter your ways. My decision was based on the superior qualities your wife has shown during your absence . . . and perhaps the fact that the children have made it plain they regard you as their father, warts and all – though it was some task to persuade their grandmother that you are not a dangerous criminal, I can tell you.' She watched her tearful aunt gather the children into her arms and hug them tightly. Dusty was too choked to say thanks, but it was evident in her eyes as she gripped Belle's hand.

Dickie grinned down at his son and daughters. 'Well, let's go see your Nan and give her the good news! Oh, wait a minute, the excitement's got to me, I'll have to go see a man about a dog.' He made for the lavatory.

When he came back his wife was ready to go, the children grouped around her . . . and a baby in her arms. He stared at her, then nipped the bridge of his nose and blinked. 'I must be suffering from double vision. I swear I can see six when there should only be five of us.'

Dusty pulled the baby's woollen bonnet around his cheeks. 'You don't mind, do you?' She held the child acquisitively.

'I don't suppose it'd make any difference if I said yes?' asked Dick.

His wife smiled and said it wouldn't.

'God love us, it's gonna cost me a fortune to ship this lot back to America – you're sure ye wouldn't like to get rid of a few more while ye've got me cornered?' The last part was directed at Belle. She explained that Dusty had become so close to the baby that it would not be fair to part them. With an old-fashioned look, Dick tugged the brim of his hat and herded his wife and children to the street. Belle patted each head affectionately and said she would give the children a proper goodbye before they left. She waved them off and was about to go in, when Dick tripped back to whisper with a grin, 'I'll be back for my goodbye kiss.'

Thomasin was enjoying a chat with Francis and Nick when the door opened a crack and a disembodied voice called, 'Now I don't want you to worry if I look different, Mam. I've just had a bit of plastic surgery in Paris.' With bated breath, she awaited her son's entry. A six-inch long nose jutted round the edge of the door. Thomasin's heart lurched, before she realised it was false.

'You daft clot, you nearly gave me a seizure!' She tried to push herself from the chair as he came in, the nose now on his forehead like a unicorn's horn.

'I was only trying to make ye laugh. I got it in France.' He removed the elastic from his head and put it on Freddie, twanging it playfully.

'I'll give you laugh! What are you doing here?'

'Thanks for the welcome.' He delivered the letters Joe had given him.

She checked her tongue and came to shake him. 'I've been worried out of my mind – as far as I knew you could've been caught.'

He told her that Nettleton was still in Paris. 'So you can rest easy.'

'Until the next scrape!'

'Sorry, I promise I'll be a good lad from now on – well, I'm a father now so I have to be.' Face proud, he indicated the children.

507

'So ye finally got round her then?' Erin had appeared at his elbow.

Dickie looked startled. 'I never felt a thing then.' He reached a hand round his back to grope between his shoulderblades. His sister asked what on earth he was doing. 'I'm just looking for the handle – of the knife.' He stretched his lips.

'Clown,' she muttered.

'Well, that's a bit milder,' exclaimed her brother. 'Does it mean I'm back on the Christmas list?'

His mother had lowered herself back into her seat. 'I don't suppose you'll be here for Christmas, will you? You'll want to be getting away.'

'I'll be with you for Christmas, Mam,' promised Dickie, confounding his wife.

Francis, who had anticipated that Thomasin's son would be eager to escape to America, was incensed to hear his intention of staying on. Whilst she was congratulating Dusty on the adoption, he unbent his stick-like body. 'Thomasin dear, forgive my interruption, but I'm afraid I shall have to leave now. I'm expecting my daughter to call.' After taking farewells, he made for the hall before his anger exploded.

'Let me get the door, Fran!' Dickie ran to open it, but instead of rejoining the family, he tailed the old man into the hall and closed the door. 'I've a favour to ask, Fran. Ye once offered me some money to go back to New York.' Francis stopped and nodded, dislike on his face. 'Well, I've decided to take you up on your offer.'

Francis showed contempt for the impudence. 'What makes you think it still holds?'

Dickie exhaled and looked sad. 'Ah dear, haven't got it, eh?' He clicked his tongue. 'That means we'll be stuck here till that detective turns up on Mam's doorstep then. What with having the kids in tow, well, it's gonna cost me a packet to ship us all back . . .'

'How much are you going to blackmail out of me?'

'A thousand pounds should . . .'

'You think I'm paying that!' Francis kept his voice to an irate whisper.

'It's pay or stay, Fran.' Dickie smiled.

Resigned to the extortion, Francis was opening his cheque-book, when a thought presented itself. 'You mother is expecting you to stay – at least for Christmas.'

'She'll be disappointed, but she'd rather I was safe than spend a long vacation at Tyburn by the Sea. That detective is a lot closer than I've admitted.' He watched the old man rest his chequebook on the hall table and looked over his shoulder. 'Can ye make it out to cash? Thanks, Fran.'

Francis tore off the cheque and handed it to him. 'I'm doing this for your mother.'

'Of course. But I appreciate it – and don't worry, I won't tell her that ye bought me off.'

'You're looking very pleased with yourself,' commented Erin when he returned to the drawing room.

'And why wouldn't I be?' Dickie put an arm around his wife, the other hand on Julia's dark head. 'With a fine family like I have.'

'Eh, your father'd be that glad for you.' Thomasin's joy paled. 'My, you wouldn't think it was almost a year since he died.'

Dickie looked at the carpet. 'Aye . . . this time last year I was on my way to wish you Happy New Year – an' I never did get round to it – Happy New Year! Late or early, take your pick. Well, kiddiwinkles, I'd better go send a cable and warn them to have the house prepared for the grand homecoming.'

Thomasin was pole-axed. 'But . . . you said you were staying.'

He came to sit with her. 'No, Mam, I said we'd be with ye for Christmas and we will – you're coming with us.'

'To America!' Thomasin looked at Erin and Nick. 'I can't do that!' He asked why not. 'On these legs – as me mother used to say?'

'You'll be fine. I'll give ye a good rub down with embrocation every . . .'

'Day!' chorused his wife. 'Oh, do please come, Mother. I'm going to need your help to get the children settled in.'

'But what about the house – and the business? I can't just up and leave.'

'Hey, it's only a holiday, I don't want ye living with us for good – anyway, what're ye talking about?' Her son gestured at Nick. 'Ye've got a man here who's capable of running the show on his own.'

'But I can't leave the rest of the family at Christmas!' She held him in her sights for a long time, trapped by indecision. She had been silly to think that her son could stay here forever with the police files still open. She turned painfully to Erin. 'What will you do if I go?'

'Don't concern yourself with me, I'll spend Christmas with Belle.' And there'll be no games of Postman's Knock while I'm there, thought Erin. 'Will ye be going then?'

Thomasin looked dazed. 'Aye . . . aye, I think I just might.' She laughed at her own daring.

'Great!' Dickie slapped his knee and stood up.

'I want to be back for the Coronation though,' warned his mother. 'I'm not missing the party for anybody.'

Laughing, Dusty turned to Erin. 'I'll have to get the children kitted out with new clothes. Have you time to spare for a shopping spree?' Erin said she would be pleased to help.

Thomasin was studying her grandson and knew what he was waiting for. 'Oh . . . all right, Nick, you've got it.'

He had no need to be told what she meant. His face was

510

crestfallen, though his eyes danced. 'You could have injected a bit more ceremony, Nan.'

'It's a Chair not a ruddy throne. You want ceremony? Come here then.' She made him bow down, and touched her walking stick on either side of his fair head. 'Arise, Sir Persistence. Now, you run along and play shops, do your profit-sharing or whatever – I'm going to start enjoying meself!'

By the morning of Friday, December the thirteenth, the trunks had been packed and sent ahead, the berths booked and Thomasin was looking forward to the voyage. She and her son's family would be travelling to London on the evening train. The ship would sail shortly after midnight.

In the afternoon Sonny, Nick and their families came over to say their goodbyes, braving the fierce snowstorm that had been in effect throughout the day. Belle came too, though minus her charges who had said farewell to Fred and his sisters a few days ago. Thomasin held the fear that they would all be stuck here over the weekend if the snow continued to lay – it was already over a foot deep and, lashed by the wind, it had formed huge drifts around the house, sweeping up the doors and windows. Plus, there were reports of roads being blocked and villages cut off.

Sonny had fetched his brother a parting gift, a painting of their father's birthplace done while he was on holiday. 'There's something to show your American friends. Come back next year and I'll do you a family group – at no charge.'

The time for them to leave ticked closer. Dusty was full of last-minute anxieties, castigating her husband for allowing Fred to play out in the snow. 'Those boots will never be dry by the time we need to leave! The servants have packed his spare ones in the trunk, he's nothing else to wear – and he is *not* going home in wet boots.'

511

'Don't fuss, woman.' Dick called his son to him. 'We'll nip into town and buy him some more. I'm sick of sitting round waiting anyway.'

'In this? We might never see you again. Oh, all right – but don't be long! We've only an hour to go.' And then we're on our way, thought Dusty with exhilaration. We're really taking them home.

Dickie met his mother in the hall. 'I hope you've got those knees well wrapped up, ye hobblin' old goblin. It'll be nippy aboard that ship.'

Thomasin said to the boy, 'Close your eyes, Fred.' With a crafty glint to her eye, she hoisted her skirts above knees that were swaddled in thick layers of flannel. 'How's this for you – lagged legs.'

Laughing, Dick pressed Freddie on to the outer door. Both muffled from head to foot against the blizzard, they forged a way down the thickly-coated driveway. The snow now came over Freddie's knees, making it difficult for him to walk. His father swung him onto his back and strode on. Apart from some Council employees who were trying to keep the roads clear, there were few people mad enough to be out in this weather. They did not encounter another soul until they reached the shops. The silence was quite eerie.

The boots were purchased without difficulty. Dick crudged his way back along Saint Saviourgate – avoiding the dark narrow passage that was a quicker route – when, through the swirling blizzard, the lone figure of a woman materialised. The edge of the pavement was invisible under the snow. Dickie stumbled, almost dislodging his passenger, as he stepped aside for her to pass. But she blocked his path, clasping her shawl tightly round her head. 'Oh, sir, can you help me? I've got water running through the ceiling and I don't know how to stop it. I must have a burst pipe or something.'

'I'm no plumber,' said Dick, narrowing his eyes against

the sting of snowflakes, but still able to see that she was quite comely. 'Can't ye call on a neighbour?'

'Oh . . . I've knocked and knocked but none of 'em answer – oh, please, sir I only live down here.'

Dick pondered whether this could be a trick. No. He looked at her again, then said all right, he would come, when Freddie's hot breath hit the back of his neck. 'Me mam said we haven't got to be long.'

Telling his son that the woman's house was on their way so they wouldn't be long, Dickie tramped after her. When she came to the house he put Freddie on his feet and followed her inside. 'It's in here,' she told him worriedly.

Dick entered the room and frowned. 'Where is it? I can't . . .' Everything went black.

When he regained consciousness he was lying on cold linoleum. He groaned and tried to put a hand to his head, only to find it manacled to the leg of a table. Fred knelt beside him, a puddle of melted snow around his boots. 'Are you all right, Dad?'

'Marvellous.' Dickie screwed up his eyes, then heard Fred speak to someone.

'When me dad gets free he'll knock your head off, won't you, Dad?'

Dick lifted his pounding skull from the lino and saw Nettleton on a balloon-backed chair, tapping a life-preserver against his palm. The woman was nowhere to be seen. 'Oh, Christ . . . I don't suppose anybody's got a match?'

'Aye, the salamander,' mused Nettleton. 'A sneaky little lizard that can live through flame. It's taken a long time, lad.'

Fred threw more insults. 'I'll bet you don't know how to catch rabbits. Me dad can.'

Nettleton gave an interested smile, still tapping the cosh

against his palm. 'A poacher too, eh? That's a more serious offence than murder to some folk.'

Dickie pulled himself up into a sitting position; the gloved hand that he was using as a prop, slipped on the wet floor. He shuffled his buttocks and leaned forward. 'Look, ye've got the wrong man. I didn't kill either of them. I had to hit Bearpark to stop him beating up a woman, but he hit his head as he went down, that's what killed him.' Nettleton was unmoved and asked about the other victim. 'I came home to find two men attacking her – I couldn't help, they had a gun. When they'd gone I buried her.'

'And tried to draw money out of her bank account,' Nettleton reminded him. 'And sold her farm, and concealed her death.'

'All right! I'll plead guilty to all that, but I didn't kill her. I liked the old biddy, for God's sake.'

'Aye, I heard you were fond of women.'

Dickie cursed himself for not following his first instinct about the woman who had brought him here, asking who she was and how much Nettleton had paid her to do it.

'She's a chambermaid at The Black Swan. I got quite friendly with her while I was staying there in the summer, asked her to get in touch if she saw any goings-on at the big house. So when I came back from Paris I just had to renew her acquaintance.' The detective began to experience one of his headaches, the frown lines between his eyes deepening.

'If ye've been there watching me, why didn't ye come and arrest me?' Dickie's back ached from being in this restricted position.

'Because as soon as I came in the front door you'd be out the back, and I didn't want the whole of the York force out again. You're mine.'

'You're so sweet.'

Nettleton came over and kicked him very hard. Freddie

514

cried out and punched the man's thigh, but slipped on the lino. 'Led me a merry dance in Paris, didn't you?'

Wincing, Dick squinted up at his oppressor. 'Ah, but I'll bet you enjoyed it.' He gave a defiant wink. 'Wouldn't ye rather be there than stuck up to your neck in snow?'

'I've got what I want, and I'm taking him in.' The hand holding the cosh made a movement. Dickie, fearing he was about to be struck on the head again, cowered and lifted a protective arm. Nettleton laughed, put the cosh into his pocket and took out the key of the handcuffs.

Dickie panicked. 'Look I'm begging ye, don't spoil it for the boy here.' He gestured at Fred. 'D'ye really want to leave him and his sisters fatherless? Don't ye feel any sorrow for him?'

'Aye, I do feel sorry for the poor little sod – he's had a narrow escape, nearly getting saddled with you for a father.'

'Don't lock me dad up,' pleaded Fred.

'Sorry, son.' Nettleton put the key to the handcuffs. 'He's a bad man.'

Fred was defiant. 'He isn't, are you Dad?'

'No, son, of course I'm not.' Dickie turned to Nettleton. 'Did ye have to say that? Isn't it bad enough you're taking me away from him?' With his appeal to the detective's better nature fallen flat, he pulled the last card from his sleeve. 'Surely I'm not worth that much to ye, not after all these years? Wouldn't five hundred pounds suit ye better?'

Nettleton paused in unlocking the cuffs. Now that he had the man's attention, Dick spoke keenly, 'Five hundred pounds to tear up those files on me.'

'Couldn't do it even if I had a mind; I've retired, can't get access.'

'Retired?' Dickie threw back his head. 'Jesus! Ye must be crazy, tailing me all over the blasted place – what the hell are ye getting out of it, then?'

'The satisfaction of catching up with somebody who thought he'd made a mug of me.'

'And that's about all! Christ, I thought ye must be in line for promotion at the very least the way ye've clung to me. Listen, I could have that money in your pocket within five minutes.' He spread his fingers to ram the point home. 'Forget about the files, I'll pay ye just to let me go. Five hundred. Isn't that better than a pat on the head for catching me? I mean, they're hardly likely to be handing out medals for crimes that are a quarter of a century old – ones that I didn't even commit – and I'll be able to prove that in court.'

Nettleton sneered at the bluff, but remained interested.

'Ye said yourself, the whole point of this was catching me for your own peace of mind. And ye have caught me. You know that and I know that, I surrender to your skill and determination. But, what else do ye get from it? If it's fame you're after I'm hardly a top villain and even if I were, the world forgets very easily – you're not going to be in any history books. Wouldn't it suffice to have the knowledge that ye've won and a pocketful of money on top? Now . . . I've made plans to catch the ship back to America. It leaves just after midnight – I could still go and no one need be any the wiser. Your friends think I'm already back there anyway. Think about it carefully. Five hundred pounds.'

'Double it,' said the other.

Dick was encouraged. 'I can maybe scrape seven-fifty but that's all the ready cash I have.' He still had the money he had leeched from Francis, but hoped he would not have to dispense with all of it.

Nettleton was cagey. 'Where is it?'

'I've got fifty here.' Dick reached into his pocket and thrust some notes at the man. 'The rest is at my mother's house.'

'There's only forty-five here,' said Nettleton.

516

'What's a fiver between old pals – there's seven hundred waiting. Unlock me an' it's yours.'

'The boy can go for it,' decided Nettleton.

'He doesn't know where it is.'

'You've just said it's at your mother's.'

'Yes, but it's in different cases. What if his mother asks what he's doing and doesn't let him come back?' He had a terrible thought then – how long had he been unconscious? Hunting for his watch he was relieved to see he still had time to spare. 'Listen, I've got twenty minutes before I have to leave for the London train. If I don't get back soon they'll come looking for me and then we'll have witnesses to our deal.'

Nettleton looked at the boy. 'We've got witnesses now.'

'He won't tell, will ye, Fred?'

Nettleton wasn't to be duped. 'He goes, you stay with me.'

Dickie sighed and told the boy exactly where to find the money, which was in separate packets. 'For heaven's sake, Fred, don't let anybody catch ye.'

During the wait, he asked Nettleton, 'How do I know I can trust you not to hand me over once ye've got the money?'

''Cause I'm a policeman.' Nettleton sat patiently, never moving his eyes from Dick.

After ten minutes, the detective said, 'He's taking a long time. I hope you've not been silly.'

'He'll be here,' said Dick, but his eyes showed the worry.

Fifteen minutes had gone. In spite of the room being unheated, Dickie began to sweat, imagining different casualties that might have befallen his son.

Nettleton decided that he had been taken for a fool. He stood and pulled the hood of his checked Ulster up over his bowler hat, then strode over to Dickie and unlocked

517

the handcuff from the table leg, clicking it onto his own wrist.

'Let me go and see where he is!' pleaded his captive.

Nettleton gave a wrench on his arm and ordered him from the room. The snow whirled in at them as Nettleton opened the door and shoved Dickie out into the street. Both pulled their necks into the warmth of their coats and slitted their eyes. The much smaller man bullied his prisoner along the street. Flakes settled on their eyelashes, stinging, blinding them. Soon their garments resembled wedding cakes.

There was a cry. Freddie, who had been searching frantically for the right house, caught sight of them. Stumbling and falling, lifting his legs like a high-stepping horse out of the snow, he made his way towards them. Nettleton gestured for them to go back into the house, slamming the door on the blizzard. Back in the room they had just left, he told the boy to put the money on the table and spread it out for him to see. Fred was sobbing. 'I couldn't find you, Dad! All the houses look the same.' His nose ran as copiously as his eyes. He wiped his sleeve across his face, plastering it with snow.

'Never mind, son, don't you fret. Just do as he says, we've got to go.' Dick watched the shivering boy take the money from the inside of his coat and spread it on the table, petrified that Nettleton would want more.

The detective examined the money.

Dick felt like screaming for him to make up his mind. Then Nettleton inserted his key in the handcuff and Dickie was free.

He grabbed hold of Freddie and ran to the door. Nettleton let him go. Along the swirling streets he dashed, carrying Fred under his arm. Under his overcoat the sweat poured from his armpits. It was only a short dash home but with the snowdrifts clamping his ankles his thigh muscles throbbed.

'Richard!' yelped his wife when the pair of them almost

fell into the drawing room, casting snow all over the carpet. 'How long does it take to buy a pair of boots?'

Dickie could almost have laughed – he had left the boots with Nettleton.

'That man . . .' started Freddie, but his father clamped an expedient hand over his mouth.

'No time for that, Fred! Sorry, Dust, we couldn't find the right size. Come on – is the car ready, Son?'

'It is now! I like the way you left us all to shovel a path down the drive. Come on before it's snowed up again. I've checked the road, it's been cleared, so we should get to the station on time.'

They took their leave of everyone save Erin and Sonny who would be coming to the station. Dick kissed Josie and all the girls, including a blushing Vinnie, then shared a fond handshake with his natural son and wished him every luck with the business. Coming to Belle, he locked desiring eyes for as long as he dared, gave her an uncle-like kiss, then amid tears and goodbyes, all hurried to the car.

It wouldn't start. Dickie swore. His wife complained that he was the one who had held them up. If they missed the train she would skin him.

The engine began to roll. Everyone cheered. 'The snow's easing up,' said Sonny. Everyone cheered again. Sonny steered the car out onto the road. It got halfway to the station before its wheels began to spin. The men jumped out to rake away the snow in front of it. Dickie was now running with sweat.

They reached the station without further mishap. The train was already in. Poor Thomasin was half carried along the platform and lifted up into the carriage. The guard was coming towards them, slamming doors. There was little time to say goodbye to Sonny and Erin, but for a few hugs and kisses and promises to write.

Brother and sister stepped back from the edge of the platform. The train blew off steam and jerked forward. Dickie and his family stood at the window waving to his brother and sister, waving, waving, until the train took the bend and they were lost to sight. Then he and Dusty turned to each other, heaved a sigh of relief – his far more pronounced – and sat down.

'I hope my coconut's safe in that trunk,' worried Fred.

Nettleton finished packing the money into his overcoat and was about to leave when he noticed the brown paper parcel that Feeney had dropped. Running his hands over it, he guessed it held footwear, but just in case it might have something more valuable hidden inside he cut the string with a penknife and shook the wrapping free. His fingers searched the inside of the boots. Finding nothing, he checked the size, then discarded them.

On emerging from the house, he was pleased to see it was no longer snowing. The myriad flakes had formed themselves into beautiful patterns all along the street, swept high in mounds that sparkled like sugarloaves 'neath an old gaslamp. Nettleton hurried into town, his laboured breath dampening the wool of his scarf. Stamping his boots, he went into an office and approached the counter. 'I'd like to send a telegram to London.' As Feeney had bidden him, he had thought carefully about this. He just could not stand the thought of that villain getting away scot free. Should Feeney inform on the bribe, he had his story ready. Without the money they could prove nothing and Nettleton would make sure the money was safely hidden. He smiled at the thought of Feeney's face when the police bushwhacked him at King's Cross. It was a pity he could not make the arrest himself, but that would just have been greedy.

'Sorry, sir, we're completely ladysmithed tonight.'

Nettleton stared at the young man behind the counter. 'What?'

'We've no communications with the Capital, sir, the wires are snowed up. All telegrams from the North are being sent to those areas where the line to London is good.'

'How long will it take?' demanded Nettleton.

'I regret to say it'll take about four or five hours at the least, sir.'

Nettleton did a short sum, knowing the answer, but wanting to torture himself: it was four hours to midnight, the ship sailed just after. He could of course send a cable to America and have the police waiting when Feeney disembarked . . .

No, Feeney wasn't worth the effort. With a little snort of amused resignation, he turned on his heel and went out into the Arctic night.

Thomasin jumped as a hoot from the ship pierced the darkness. 'Godfrey Norris! I'll be dead before I ever get there at this rate.'

Dickie flicked a cigarette end at the water below. 'Talking of which . . . ye know I'm never one to pry, but in that will ye made, did ye by chance leave me any shares in the company?'

His mother flexed her gloved fingers on the ship's rail and looked up at the black sky. 'I realise everybody thinks I'm daft, but I'm not that bloody daft.'

He sighed his disappointment. 'Ah dear . . . there's not much point me tipping you over the rail then?'

'Oh, don't worry, it'd be worth your while if you're that way inclined: I just thought you'd prefer your portion in hard cash.'

'Right, over she goes then!' Dickie pretended to pick her up, then laughed and tried to coax her away from the rail to go somewhere warmer – the others were undercover

– but she refused. 'If it sinks I want to be near them lifeboats.'

Eventually, though, cold forced her to do as he asked. She linked his arm as they made their way slowly along the deck towards the light and sound of people enjoying themselves. 'I feel very daring, you know. Eh, I don't know what your dad would have to say to me gadding off and deserting the business!'

'I do,' said Dickie. 'He'd say, "Jazers, Mary an' Joseph, what the bloody hell's our Dickie got you into this time?"'

'Aye, you're right.' A tear to her eye, his mother laughed with him.

And both of them felt Patrick smile too.